Praise for beloved romance author Betty Neels

"Neels is especially good at painting her scenes with choice words, and this adds to the charm of the story."
—*USATODAY.com's Happy Ever After* blog on *Tulips for Augusta*

"Betty Neels surpasses herself with an excellent story line, a hearty conflict and pleasing characters."
—*RT Book Reviews* on *The Right Kind of Girl*

"Once again Betty Neels delights readers with a sweet tale in which love conquers all."
—*RT Book Reviews* on *Fate Takes a Hand*

"One of the first Harlequin authors I remember reading. I was completely enthralled by the exotic locales… Her books will always be some of my favorites to re-read."
—*Goodreads* on *A Valentine for Daisy*

"I just love Betty Neels!… If you like a good old-fashioned romance…you can't go wrong with this author."
—*Goodreads* on *Caroline's Waterloo*

Romance readers around the world were sad to note the passing of **Betty Neels** in June 2001. Her career spanned thirty years, and she continued to write into her ninetieth year. To her millions of fans, Betty epitomized the romance writer, and yet she began writing almost by accident. She had retired from nursing, but her inquiring mind still sought stimulation. Her new career was born when she heard a lady in her local library bemoaning the lack of good romance novels. Betty's first book, *Sister Peters in Amsterdam*, was published in 1969, and she eventually completed 134 books. Her novels offer a reassuring warmth that was very much a part of her own personality. She was a wonderful writer, and she is greatly missed. Her spirit and genuine talent live on in all her stories.

BETTY NEELS

Winter of Change
& A Matter of Chance

HHARLEQUIN® SPECIAL RELEASE

ISBN-13: 978-1-335-04508-9

Winter of Change & A Matter of Chance

Copyright © 2018 by Harlequin Books S.A.

The publisher acknowledges the copyright holder
of the individual works as follows:

Winter of Change
Copyright © 1973 by Betty Neels

A Matter of Chance
Copyright © 1977 by Betty Neels

Recycling programs
for this product may
not exist in your area.

Printed in U.S.A.

www.Harlequin.com

CONTENTS

WINTER OF CHANGE

Chapter 1

Sister Thompson made her slow impressive way
down Women's Surgical, bidding her patients a ma-
jestic good morning as she went, her sharp eyes behind
their glasses noticing every small defect in the perfection she demanded on her ward—and that applied
not only to the nursing and care of the ladies lying on
either side of her, but also to the exact position of the
water jugs on the lockers, the correct disposal of dressing gowns, the perfection of the bedspreads and the
symmetry of the pillows. The nurses who worked for
her held her in hearty dislike, and when posted to her
ward quickly learned the habit of melting away out of
her sight whenever their duties permitted. Something
which Mary Jane Pettigrew, her recently appointed
staff nurse, was, at that particular time, quite unable to
do. She watched her superior's slow, inevitable prog-

ress with a wary eye as she changed the dressing on
Miss Blake's septic finger; she had no hope of getting
it done before Sister Thompson arrived, for Miss Blake
was old and shaky and couldn't keep her hand still for
more than ten seconds at a time. Mary Jane, watching
Nurse Wells and Nurse Simpson disappear, one into
the sluice room, the other into the bathrooms at the
end of the ward, wondered how long it would be before
they were discovered—in the meantime, perhaps she
could sweeten Sister Thompson's temper.

She fastened the dressing neatly and wished her
superior a cheerful good morning which that good
lady didn't bother to answer, instead she said in an arbitrary manner: 'Staff Nurse Pettigrew, you've been
on this ward for two weeks and not only do you fail
to maintain discipline amongst the nurses; you seem
quite incapable of keeping the ward tidy. There are
three pillows—and Miss Trump's top blanket, also
Mrs Pratt's water jug is in the wrong place…'

Mary Jane tucked her scissors away in her pocket
and picked up the dressing tray. She said with calm,
'Mrs Pratt can't reach it unless we put it on that side
of her locker, Sister, and Miss Trump was cold, so I
unfolded her blanket. May the nurses go to coffee?'

Sister Thompson cast her a look of dislike. 'Yes—
and see that they're back before Mr Cripps' round.'
She turned on her heel and went back up the ward and
into her office, to appear five minutes later with the
information that Mary Jane was to present herself to
the Chief Nursing Officer at once, 'and,' added Sister Thompson, 'I suggest that you take your coffee

break at the same time, otherwise you will be late for the round.'

Which meant that unless the interview was to be a split-second, monosyllabic affair, there would be no coffee. Mary Jane skimmed down the ward, making a beeline for the staff cloakroom. Whatever Sister Thompson might say, she was going to take a few minutes off in order to tidy her person. The room was small, nothing more than a glorified cupboard, and in order to see her face in the small mirror she was forced to rise on to her toes, for she was a small girl, only a little over five feet, with delicate bones and a tiny waist. She took one look at her reflection now, uttered a sigh and whipped off her cap so that she might smooth her honey-brown hair, fine and straight and worn in an old-fashioned bun on the top of her head. The face which looked back at her was pleasant but by no means pretty; only her eyes, soft and dark, were fine under their thin silky arched brows, but her nose was too short above a wide mouth and although her teeth were excellent they tended to be what she herself described as rabbity. She rearranged her cap to her satisfaction, pinned her apron tidily and started on her journey to the office.

Her way took her through a maze of corridors, dark passages and a variety of staircases, for Pope's Hospital was old, its ancient beginnings circumvented by more modern additions, necessitating a conglomeration of connecting passages. But Mary Jane, her thoughts busy, trod them unhesitatingly, having lived with them for more than three years. She had no idea why she was wanted, but while she was in the office it might be a good idea to mention that she wasn't happy on Women's Surgical. She had been aware, when she took the post, that it would be no bed of roses; Sister Thompson was notorious for her ill-temper and per-nickety ways, but Mary Jane, recently State Regis-tered, had felt capable of moving mountains… She would, she decided as she sped down a stone-flagged passage with no apparent ending, give in her notice at the end of the month and in the meantime start looking for another job. The thought of leaving Pope's was vaguely worrying, as she had come to regard it as her home, for indeed she had no home in the ac-cepted sense. She had been an orphan from an early age, brought up, if one could call it that, by her grand-father, a retired Army colonel, who lived in a secluded house near Keswick and seldom left it. She had spent her holidays there all the while she was at the expen-sive boarding school to which he had sent her, and she had sensed his relief when she had told him, on leaving that admirable institution, that she wished to go to London and train to be a nurse, and in the three years or more in which she had been at Pope's she had gone to see him only once each year, not wishing to upset his way of living, knowing that even during the month of her visit he found her youthful company a little tiresome.

Not that he didn't love her in his own reserved, el-derly fashion, just as she loved him, and would have loved him even more had he encouraged her to do so. As it was she accepted their relationship with good sense because she was a sensible girl, aware too that she would probably miss a good deal of the fun of life because she would need to work for the rest of it; even at the youthful age of twenty-two she had discovered that men, for the most part, liked good looks and failing that, a girl with a sound financial background, and she had neither, for although her grandfather lived comfortably enough, she had formed the opinion over the years that his possessions would go to some distant cousin she had never seen, who lived in Canada. True, old Colonel Pettigrew had educated her, and very well too, provided her with the right clothes and given her handsome presents at Christmas and on her birthday, but once she had started her training as a nurse, he had never once offered to help her financially—not that she needed it, for she had the good sense to keep within her salary and although she liked expensive clothes she bought them only when she saved enough to buy them. Her one extravagance was her little car, a present from her grandfather on her twenty-first birthday; it was a Mini and she loved it, and despite her fragile appearance, she drove it well.

The office door was firmly closed when she reached it and when she knocked she was bidden to enter at once the outer room, guarded by two office Sisters, immersed in paper work, one of whom paused long enough to wave Mary Jane to a chair before burying herself in the litter of papers on her desk. Mary Jane perched on the edge of a stool, watching her two companions, feeling sorry for them; they must have started out with a desire to nurse the sick, and look where they were now—stuck behind desks all day, separated from the patients by piles of statistics and forms, something she would avoid at all costs, she told herself, and was interrupted in her thoughts by the buzzer sounding its summons.

The Chief Nursing Officer was quite young, barely forty, with a twinkling pair of eyes, a nice-looking face and beautifully arranged hair under her muslin cap. She smiled at Mary Jane as she went in.

'Sit down, Staff Nurse,' she invited. 'There's something I have to tell you.'

'Oh lord, the sack!' thought Mary Jane. 'Old Thompson's been complaining…' She was deep in speculation as to what she had done wrong when she was recalled to her surroundings by her companion's pleasant voice.

'It concerns your grandfather, Nurse Pettigrew. His housekeeper telephoned a short time ago. He isn't very well and has asked for you to go to his home in order to look after him. Naturally you will wish to do so, although I've been asked to stress the fact that there's no'—she paused—'no cause for alarm, at least for the moment. I believe your grandfather is an old man?'

Mary Jane nodded. 'Eighty-two,' she said in her rather soft voice, 'but he's very tough. May I go at once, please?'

'As soon as you wish. I'll telephone Sister Thompson so that there's no need for you to go back to the ward. Perhaps when you get to your grandfather's, you'll let me know how things are.'

She was dismissed. She made her way rapidly to the Nurses' Home, thankful that she wouldn't have to face Sister Thompson, her mind already busy with the details of her journey. It was full autumn, it would be cold in Cumbria, so she would take warm clothes but as few as possible—she could pack a case in a few minutes. She was busy doing that when her bedroom door was flung open and her dearest friend, Janet Moore, came in. 'There's a rumour,' she began, 'someone overheard that you'd been sent to the Office.' Her eyes lighted on the little pile of clothes on the bed. 'Mary Jane, you've never been…no, of course not, you've never done anything really wicked in your life. What's up?'

Mary Jane told her as she squeezed the last sweater into her case, shut the lid and started to tear off her uniform. She was in slacks and a heavy woolly by the time she had finished, and without bothering to do more than smooth her hair, tied a bright scarf over it, pushed impatient feet into sensible shoes, caught up her handbag and the case and made for the door, begging her friend to see to her laundry for her as she went. 'See you,' she said briefly, and Janet called after her:

'You're not going now—this very minute? It's miles away—it'll be dark…'

'It's ten o'clock,' Mary Jane informed her as she made off down the corridor, 'and it's two hundred and ninety miles—besides, I know the way.'

It seemed to take a long time to get out of London, but once she was clear of the suburbs and had got on to the A1, she put a small, determined foot down on the accelerator, keeping the little car going at a steady fifty-five, and when the opportunity occurred, going a good deal faster than that.

Just south of Newark she stopped for coffee and a sandwich and then again when she turned off the A1 at Leeming to cross the Yorkshire fells to Kendal. The road was a lonely one, but she knew it well, and although the short autumn afternoon was already dimming around her, she welcomed its solitude after the rush and bustle of London. At Kendal she stopped briefly before taking the road which ran through Ambleside and on to Keswick. The day was closing in on her now, the mountains around blotting out the last of a watery sun, but she hardly noticed them. At any other time she would have stopped to admire the view, but now she scarcely noticed them, for her thoughts were wholly of her grandfather. The last few miles of the long journey seemed endless, and she heaved a sigh of relief as she wove the car through Keswick's narrow streets and out again on to the road climbing to Cockermouth. Keswick was quickly left behind; she was back in open country again and once she had gone through Thronthwaite she slowed the car. She was almost there, for now the road ran alongside the lake with the mountains crowding down to it on one side, tree-covered and dark, shutting out the last of the light, and there was only an odd cottage or two now and scattered along the faint gleam of the water, larger houses, well away from each other. The road curved away from the lake and then returned and there, between it and the water, was her grandfather's house.

It stood on a spit of land running out into the lake, its garden merging into the grass alongside the quiet water. It was of a comfortable size, built of grey stone and in a style much favoured at the beginning of the nineteenth century, its arched windows fitted with leaded panes, its wrought-iron work a little too elaborate and a turret or two ornamenting its many-gabled roof. All the same it presented a pleasing enough picture to Mary Jane as she turned the car carefully into the short drive and stopped outside the front porch. Its door stood open and the woman standing there came to meet her with obvious relief.

'Mrs Body, how lovely to see you! I came as quickly as I could—how's Grandfather?'

Mrs Body was pleasant and middle-aged and housekeeper to the old Colonel for the last twenty years or more. She took Mary Jane's hand and said kindly, 'There, Miss Mary Jane, if it isn't good to see you, I must say. Your grandfather's not too bad—a heart attack, as you know, but the doctor's coming this evening and he'll tell you all about it. But now come in and have tea, for you'll be famished, I'll be bound.'

She led the way indoors as she spoke, into the dim, roomy hall. 'You go up and see the Colonel, he's that anxious for you to get here—and I'll get the tea on the table.'

Mary Jane nodded and smiled and ran swiftly up the uncarpeted staircase, past the portraits of her ancestors and on to the landing, to tap on a door in its centre. The room she was bidden to enter was large and rather over-full of ponderous furniture, but cheerful enough by reason of the bright fire burning in the grate and the lamps on either side of the bed.

The Colonel lay propped up with pillows, an old man with a rugged face which, to Mary Jane's discerning eye, had become very thin. He said now in a thin thread of a voice, 'Hullo, child—how long did it take you this time?' and she smiled as she bent to kiss him; ever since he had given her the car, he had made the same joke about the time it took her to drive up from London. She told him now, her head a little on one side as she studied him. She loved him very much and he was an ill old man, but none of her thoughts showed on her calm, unremarkable features. She sat down close to the bed and talked for a little while in her pretty voice, then got up to go to her tea, telling him that she would be back later.

'Yes, my dear, do that. I daresay Morris will be here by then, he knows all about me.' He added wistfully, 'You'll stay, Mary Jane?'

She retraced her steps to his bed. 'Of course, Grandfather. I've no intention of going back until you're well again—I've got unlimited leave from Pope's,' she grinned engagingly at him, 'and you know how much I love being here in the autumn.'

Tea was a substantial meal; a huge plate of bacon and eggs, scones, home-made bread and a large cake, as well as a variety of jams and a dish of cream. Mary Jane, who was hungry, did justice to everything on the table while Mrs Body, convinced that she had been half starved in hospital, hovered round, urging her to make a good meal.

She did her best, asking questions while she ate, but Mrs Body's answers were vague, so it was with thankfulness that she went to meet the doctor when he rang the bell. She had known him since she was a little girl and held him in great affection, as he did her. He gave her an affectionate kiss now, saying, 'I knew you would come at once, my dear. You know your grandfather's very ill?'

They walked back to the sitting room and sat down. 'Yes,' said Mary Jane. 'I'll nurse him, of course.'

'Yes, child, I know you will, but that won't be for long. He'll rally for a few days, perhaps longer, but he's not going to recover. He was most anxious that you should come.'

'I'll stay as long as I can do anything to help, Uncle Bob—who's been looking after him?'

'Mrs Body and the district nurse, but he wanted you—there's something he wishes to talk to you about. I suggest you let him do that tomorrow morning when he's well rested.' He smiled at her. 'How's hospital?'

She told him briefly about Sister Thompson. 'It's not turning out quite as I expected, perhaps I'm not cut out to make a nurse...'

He patted her shoulder. 'Nonsense, there's nothing wrong with you, Mary Jane. I should start looking for another job and leave as soon as you can—at least...' He paused and she waited for him to finish, but he only sat there looking thoughtful and presently said: 'Well, I'll go and take a look—you'll be around when I come downstairs?'

He went away, and Mary Jane went along to the kitchen and spent some time helping Mrs Body and catching up on the local news until Doctor Morris reappeared. In the hall he said briefly: 'He's fighting a losing battle, I'm afraid,' then went on to give her his instructions, 'and I'll be in some time tomorrow morning,' he concluded.

There was a dressing room next to the Colonel's room. Mary Jane, who usually slept in one of the little rooms, moved her things into it, had a brief chat with her grandfather, settled him for the night and went down to the kitchen where the faithful Mrs Body was waiting with cocoa. They sat at the table, drinking it, with Major, the Colonel's middle-aged dog, sitting at their feet, and discussed the small problems confronting them. Mary Jane finished her cocoa and put down her cup. 'Well, now I'm here,' she said in her sensible way, 'you must have some time to yourself—these last few days must have been very tiring for you. If I'd known, I'd have come sooner.'

Mrs Body shook her head. 'Your grandfather wouldn't hear of it, not at first, but when Doctor Morris told him—he couldn't get you here fast enough,' she concluded, and sighed. 'All the same, I'll admit I'll be glad of an hour or so to myself. Lily comes up each morning as she always does, she's a good girl, and now you're here, I could get away for a bit.'

Mary Jane agreed. 'Supposing you take the Mini for a couple of hours each day? You could go to Keswick or Cockermouth if you want to do some shopping. I'll be quite all right here—I can go for a walk when you get back.'

The housekeeper gave her a grateful smile. 'That's kind of you, Miss Mary Jane, I'd like that. I want my hair done and one thing and another—you don't mind me using the Mini?'

'Heavens, no. Now I think I'll go to bed, it's been a long day. Will you be all right? I'll be in the dressing room and I've fixed Grandfather's bell and I shall leave the door open—besides, he's had a sedative. You will sleep? Or shall I bring you something?'

'Bless you, child, I've never taken any of those

nasty pills yet, and don't intend to. I'll sleep like a baby.'

It was a bright, clear morning when Mary Jane woke the next morning and her grandfather was still sleeping; he had wakened once in the small hours and she had gone and sat with him for an hour until he dozed off again; now he would probably sleep for another hour or more. She put on slacks and a sweater, tied her hair back and went downstairs. Mrs Body was already up, so they drank their early morning tea together and then Mary Jane took Major into the garden and across the grass to the lake's edge. The water was calm and as smooth as silk, the mountains reflected in it so that it took on their colour, grey and green. Across the lake Skiddaw loomed above the other peaks, the sun lending it a bronze covering for its granite slopes.

Mary Jane looked about her with pleasure as she threw sticks for Major, a pleasure tinged with sadness because the Colonel was ill, and although he was an old man, and didn't, she suspected, mind dying, she would miss him very much. He had been all the family she had known; now she would be alone, save for the cousin in Canada. She had never met him and her grandfather seldom mentioned him. She supposed that after her grandfather died, this cousin would inherit the house and whatever went with it. She knew nothing of the Colonel's affairs; he had encouraged her to earn her own living when she had left school and she had always imagined that he had done so because he couldn't afford to keep her idle at home, for although the house was a comfortable one and well furnished and there was no evidence of poverty, common sense told her that the old man and his housekeeper could live economically enough, whereas if she lived with them, she would need clothes and pocket money and holidays… She went back into the house, and after a reassuring peep at the Colonel, went to eat her breakfast.

Mrs Body left soon after Lily arrived and Mary Jane went upstairs to make her grandfather comfortable for the day. He seemed better, even demanding his razor so that he might shave himself, a request which she refused in no uncertain manner. Indeed, she fetched the old-fashioned cut-throat razor which he always used, and wielded it herself without a qualm, an action which caused him to ask her somewhat testily exactly what kind of work she did in hospital. There seemed no point in going too deeply into this; she fetched the post, opened his letters for him, and when he had read them, offered to read *The Times* to him. Perhaps it was her gentle voice, perhaps it was the splendid sports news, one or other of them sent him off into a sound sleep. She put the bell by his hand and went downstairs. It was barely eleven o'clock, Mrs Body wouldn't be back until the afternoon, Lily was bustling around the sitting room—Mary Jane went into the garden, round to the front of the house where she would be able to hear her grandfather's bell; there was a lot of weeding which needed doing in the rose beds which bordered the drive.

She had been hard at it for fifteen minutes or so when she became aware that a car had stopped before the gate, and when she looked round she saw that it was a very splendid car—a Rolls-Royce Corniche convertible, the sober grey of its coachwork gleaming against the green of the firs bordering the road behind it. Its driver allowed the engine to idle silently while he looked at Mary Jane, who, quite unable to recognise the car or its occupant, advanced to the gate, tossing back her mousey hair as she did so. 'Are you lost?' she wanted to know. 'Cockermouth is only…'

'Thank you, but no, I am not lost,' said the man. 'This is Colonel Pettigrew's house.' It was, she realised, a statement, not an enquiry.

She planted her fork in between the roses, dusted off her grubby hands and advanced a few steps. 'Yes, it is.' She eyed him carefully; she had never seen him before and indeed, she wouldn't have forgotten him easily if she had, for he was a handsome man, not so very young any more, but the grey hair at his temple served to emphasise the intense blackness of the rest, and his eyes were as dark as his hair, under thick straight brows. His nose was a commanding one and his mouth was firm above an angular jaw. Oh, most definitely a face to remember.

'I've come to see Colonel Pettigrew.' He didn't smile as he spoke, but looked her up and down in a casual uninterested fashion.

She ignored the look. 'Well, I'm not sure that you should,' she offered calmly. 'He's ill, and at the moment he's asleep. Doctor Morris will be here presently, and I think he should be asked first, but if you like to come in and wait—you'll have to be quiet.'

The eyebrows rose. 'My dear good young woman, you talk as though I were a pop group or a party of schoolchildren! I'm not noisy by nature and I don't take kindly to being told what I may and may not do.'

'Oh, pooh,' said Mary Jane, a little out of patience, 'don't be so touchy! Come in, do.' She added, 'Quietly.'

The car whispered past her and came to a silent halt at the door, and the man got out. There was a great deal of him; more than six foot, she guessed, and largely built too. She wondered who he was, and was on the point of asking when she heard the bell from her grandfather's room. 'There,' she shot at her companion, a little unfairly, 'you've woken him up,' and flew upstairs.

The Colonel looked refreshed after his nap. He said at once, 'I heard a car and voices. I'm expecting some-one, but there's hardly been time…'

Mary Jane shook up a pillow and slipped it behind his head. 'It's a man,' she explained unhurriedly. 'He's got beetling eyebrows and he's got rather a super Rolls. He says he wants to see you, but I told him he couldn't until Uncle Bob comes.'

A faint smile lighted up her grandfather's face. 'Did you, now? And did he mind?'

'I didn't ask him.'

Her grandfather chuckled. 'Well, my dear, if it won't undermine your authority too much, I should like to see him—now. We have important business. Morris knows he's coming and I don't suppose he'll object. Tell him to come up.'

'All right, Grandfather, if you say so.'

She found the stranger in the sitting room, sitting in one of the comfortable old-fashioned chairs. He got to his feet as she went in and before she could speak, said: 'All right, I know my way,' and was gone, taking the stairs two at a time. She followed him into the hall just in time to hear the Colonel's door shut quietly on the old man's pleased voice. After a moment she went slowly into the garden again.

She was still there when Doctor Morris arrived, parked his elderly Rover beside the Rolls, greeted her cheerfully and added in a tone of satisfaction, 'Ah, good, so he's arrived—with your grandfather, I suppose?'

Mary Jane pulled a weed with deliberation. 'Yes, he is—and very high-handed, whoever he is, too. I asked him to wait until you came, but Grandfather heard us talking and wanted to see him at once—he said it was business. He seems better this morning, so I hope you don't mind?'

The doctor shook his head. 'No, I'm pleased. You're both here now—your grandfather was worrying. I'll go up now.'

He left her standing there. She stared after him; he hadn't told her who the stranger was, but he obviously knew him. She went indoors, tidied herself and went along to get a tray of coffee ready, to find that Lily had already done so. 'And lunch, miss—I suppose the gentleman will be staying like last time. I'd better do some extra potatoes, hadn't I?'

Mary Jane agreed, desiring at the same time to question Lily about the probable guest, but if her grandfather had wanted to tell her, he could have done so, so too could Uncle Bob. If they wanted to have their little secrets, she told herself a trifle huffily, she for one didn't care. Probably the visitor was a junior partner to her grandfather's solicitor, but surely he wouldn't be able to afford a Rolls-Royce? She went outside again and had a good look at the car—it had a foreign number plate and it came from Holland, a clue which she immediately seized upon; the man was someone from her grandfather's oldest friend, Jonkheer van der Blocq, an elderly gentleman whom she had never met but about whom she knew quite a bit, for her grandfather had often mentioned him. Relieved that she had solved the mystery, she went back indoors in time to meet the doctor coming downstairs.

'There you are,' he remarked for all the world as though he had spent the last hour looking for her. 'Your grandfather wants you upstairs.' He eyed her thoughtfully. 'He's better, but you know what I mean by that, don't you? For the time being. Now run up, like a good girl. I'll be in the sitting room.'

She started up the stairs, remembering to call over her shoulder:

'There's coffee ready for you—would you ask Lily?' and sped on to tap on the Colonel's door and be bidden to enter.

The stranger was standing with his back to the window, his hands in his pockets, and the look he cast her was disconcerting in its speculation; there was faint amusement too and something else which she couldn't place. Mary Jane turned her attention to her elderly relative.

'Yes, Grandfather?' she asked, going up to the bed.

He eyed her lovingly and with some amusement on his tired old face.

'You're not a pretty girl,' he observed, and waited for her to answer.

'No, I know that as well as you—you didn't want me up here just to remind me, did you?' She grinned engagingly. 'I take after you,' she told him.

He smiled faintly. 'Come here, Fabian,' he commanded the man by the window.

And when he had stationed himself by the bed: 'Mary Jane, this is Fabian van der Blocq, the nephew of my old friend. He is to be your guardian after my death.'

Her eyes widened. 'My guardian? But I don't need a guardian, Grandfather! I'm twenty-two and I've never met Mr—Mr van der Blocq in my life before, and—and…'

'You're not sure if you like me?' His voice was bland, the smile he gave her mocking.

'Since you put the words into my mouth, I'm not sure that I do,' Mary Jane said composedly. 'And what do you have to be the guardian of?'

'This house will be yours, my dear,' explained her grandfather, 'and a considerable sum of money. You will be by no means penniless and there must be someone whom I can trust to keep an eye on you and manage your business affairs.'

'But I—' She paused and glanced across the bed to the elegant figure opposite her. 'Oh, you're a lawyer,' she declared. 'I wondered if you might be.'

Mr van der Blocq corrected her, still bland. 'You wondered wrongly. I'm a surgeon.'

She was bewildered. 'Are you? Then why…?' She

went on vigorously, 'Anyway, Grandfather isn't going to die.'

The old gentleman in the bed made a derisive sound and Mr van der Blocq curled his lip. 'I am surprised that you, a nurse, should talk in such a fashion—you surely don't think that the Colonel wishes us to smother the truth in a froth of sickly sentiment?'

Mary Jane drew her delicate pale eyebrows together. 'You're horrible!' she told him in her gentle voice. It shook a little with the intensity of her feelings and she gave him the briefest of glances before turning back to her grandfather, whom she discovered to be laughing weakly.

'Don't you mind,' she demanded, 'the way this—this Mr van der Blocq talks?'

Her grandfather stopped laughing. 'Not in the least, my dear, and I daresay that when you know him better you won't mind either.'

She tossed her untidy head. 'That's highly unlikely. And now you're tired, Grandfather—you're going to have another nap before lunch.'

To her surprise he agreed quite meekly. 'But I want you back in the afternoon, Mary Jane—and Fabian.'

She agreed, ignoring the man staring at her while she rearranged blankets, shook up pillows and made her grandfather comfortable. This done to her satisfaction, she made for the door. Mr van der Blocq, beating her to it by a short head, opened it with an ironic little nod of his handsome head, and without looking at him she went through it and down the stairs to where Doctor Morris was waiting.

They drank their coffee in an atmosphere which

was a little tense, and when the doctor got up to go, Mary Jane got up too, saying, 'I'll see you to your car, Uncle Bob,' and although he protested, did so. Out of their companion's hearing, however, she stopped.

'Look,' she said urgently, 'I don't understand— why is he to be my guardian? He doesn't even live in England, does he? And I don't know him—besides, guardians are old…'

The doctor's eyes twinkled. 'At a rough guess I should say he was nudging forty.'

'Yes? But he doesn't look…' She didn't finish the sentence. 'Well, it all seems very silly to me, and Grandfather…' She lifted her eyes to her companion. 'He's really not going to get any better? Not even if we do everything we possibly can?'

'No, my dear, and it will be quite soon now. I'll be back this evening. You know where to find me if you want me.'

She went back slowly to the sitting room and Mr Van der Blocq, lounging by the window, turned round to say: 'I don't suppose you got much help from Doctor Morris, did you?' He went on conversationally, 'If it is of any comfort to you, I dislike the idea of being your guardian just as much—probably more—than you dislike being my ward.'

Mary Jane sat down and poured more coffee for them both. 'Then don't. I mean, don't be my guardian, there's no need.'

'You heard your grandfather. You will be the owner of this house and sufficient money to make you an attractive target for any man who wants them.' He came across the room and sat down opposite her. 'I shall find

my duties irksome, I dare say, but you can depend upon
me not to shirk them.' He sat back comfortably. 'Do
you mind if I smoke my pipe?'

She shook her head, and suddenly mindful of her
duties as a hostess, asked, 'Where are you staying?
Or are you perhaps only here for an hour or two?' She
added hastily, 'You'll stay to lunch?'

A muscle twitched at the corner of his mouth.
'Thank you, I will—and I'm not staying anywhere,'
his dark eyes twinkled. 'I believe the Colonel expected
that I would stay here, but if it's too much trouble I can
easily go to a hotel.'

'Oh no, not if Grandfather invited you. I'll go and
see about lunch and get a room ready.' She got to her
feet. 'There's sherry on the sofa table, please help yourself.'

Lily, she discovered when she got to the kitchen,
had surpassed herself with Duchesse potatoes to eke
out the cold chicken and salad, and there was a soup to
start with; Mary Jane, feverishly opening tins to make
a fruit salad, hoped that their guest wouldn't stay too
long; she found him oddly disquieting and she wasn't
even sure if she liked him, not that that would matter overmuch, for she supposed that she would see
very little of him. She wasn't sure what the duties of a
guardian were, but if he lived in Holland he was hardly
likely to take them too seriously.

Ten minutes later, making up the bed in one of the
guest rooms, she began to wonder for how long she
was to have a guardian—surely not for the rest of her
life? The idea of Mr van der Blocq poking his arrogant

nose into her affairs, even from a distance, caused her to shudder strongly. She went downstairs, determined to find out all she could as soon as possible.

Chapter 2

Her intention met with no success however. At lunch, her questions, put, she imagined, with suitable subtlety, were parried with a faint amusement which annoyed her very much, and when in desperation she tried the direct approach and asked him if, in the event of his becoming her guardian, it was to last a lifetime, he laughed and said with an infuriating calm:

'Now, why couldn't you have asked that in the first place? I have no intention of telling you, however. I imagine that your grandfather will explain everything to you presently.'

Mary Jane looked down her unassuming little nose. 'How long are you staying?' she asked with the icy politeness of an unwilling hostess. A question which met with an instant crack of laughter on the part of her companion. 'That depends entirely upon your grand-father's wishes, and—er—circumstances.'

She eyed him levelly across the table. 'You don't care tuppence, do you?' she declared fiercely. 'If Grandfather dies…'

She was unprepared for the way in which his face changed, and the quietness of his voice. 'Not if, when. And why pretend? Your grandfather knows that he is dying. He told me this morning that his one dread as he got older was that he would be stricken with some lingering complaint which would compel him to lie for months, dependent on other people. We should be glad that he is getting his wish, as he is.' His eyes swept over her. 'Go and do your face up, and look cheerful, he expects us in a short while, and don't waste time arguing that he must have another nap; I happen to know that he won't be happy until he has had the talk he has planned.'

Mary Jane got to her feet. 'You've no right to talk to me like this,' she said crossly, 'and I have every in-tention of tidying myself.'

She walked out of the room, and presently, having re-done her face and brushed her hair until it shone, she put it up as severely as possible, under the im-pression that it made her look a good deal older, and went back downstairs, having first peeped in on the Colonel, to find him dozing. So she cleared away the lunch dishes and was very surprised when Mr van der Blocq carried them out to the kitchen, and because Lily had gone home, washed up, looking quite incon-gruous standing at the sink in his beautifully cut suit.

The Colonel was awake when they went upstairs;

Mary Jane sat him up in his bed, arranging him comfortably with deft hands and no fuss while Mr van der Blocq looked on, his hands in his pockets, whistling softly under his breath.

'And now,' said the Colonel with some of his old authority, 'you will both listen to me, but first I must thank you, Fabian, for coming at once without asking a lot of silly questions—it must have caused you some inconvenience, though I suppose you are now of sufficient consequence in your profession to be able to do very much as you wish. Still, the journey is a considerable one—did you stop at all?'

His visitor smiled faintly. 'Once or twice, but I enjoy long journeys and the roads are quiet at night.'

Mary Jane cast him a surprised look. 'You've been travelling all night?' she wanted to know. 'You haven't slept?'

He gave her an impatient glance, his 'no' was nonchalant as he turned back to the old man in the bed. 'Enough that I'm here, I'm sure that Doctor Morris wouldn't wish us to waste your strength in idle chatter.' A remark which sent the colour flaming into Mary Jane's cheeks, for it had been so obviously directed against herself.

Her grandfather closed his eyes for a moment. 'You're quite right. Mary Jane, listen to me—this house and land will be yours when I die, and there is also a considerable amount of money which you will inherit—that surprises you, doesn't it? Well, my girl, your mother and father wouldn't have thanked me if I had reared a feather-brained useless creature, depending upon me for every penny. As it is, you've done very well for yourself, and as far as I'm concerned you can go on with your nursing if you've set your mind on it, though I would rather that you lived here and made it home,' he paused, a little short of breath, 'You're not a very worldly young woman, my dear, and I've decided that you should have a guardian to give you help if you should need it and see to your affairs, and cast an eye over any man who should want to marry you—you will not, in fact, be able to marry without Fabian's consent.' He paused again to look at her. 'You don't like that, do you? But there it is—until you're thirty.'

Mary Jane swallowed the feelings which could easily have choked her. She said, keeping her voice calm and avoiding Mr van der Blocq's eye, 'And your cousin in Canada, Grandfather? I always thought that he was—that he would come and live—I didn't know about the money.'

Her grandparent received this muddled speech with a frown and said with some asperity, 'Dead. His son's dead too, I believe—there was a grandson, I believe, but no one bothered to let me know. Besides, you love the place, don't you, Mary Jane?'

She swallowed the lump in her throat. If he was going to be coolly practical about his death, she would try her best to be the same.

'Yes, Grandfather, you know I do, but I don't need the money—I've my salary...'

'Have you any idea what a house like this costs in upkeep? Mrs Body, Lily, the rates, the lot—besides, you deserve to have some spending money after these last three years living on the pittance you earn.'

He closed his eyes and then opened them again, remembering something.

'You witness what I've said, Fabian? You understand your part in the business, eh? And you're still willing? I would have asked your uncle, but that's not possible any more, is it?'

Mr van der Blocq agreed tranquilly that he was perfectly willing and that no, it was not possible for his uncle to fulfil the duties of a guardian. 'And,' he concluded, and his voice now held a ring of authority and firmness, 'if you have said all you wished to say, may I suggest that you have a rest? We shall remain within call. Rest assured that your wishes shall be carried out when the time comes.'

Mary Jane, without quite knowing how, found herself propelled gently from the room, but halfway down the stairs she paused. 'It's so unnecessary!' she cried. 'Surely I can run this house and look after my own money—and it's miles for you to come,' she gulped. 'And talking about it like this, it's beastly…'

He ignored that, merely saying coolly, 'I hardly think you need to worry about my too frequent visits.' He smiled a small, mocking smile and she felt vaguely insulted so that she flushed and ran on down the stairs and into the kitchen, where she found Mrs Body, unpacking her shopping. She looked up as Mary Jane rushed in and said: 'Hullo, Miss Mary Jane, what's upset you? The Colonel isn't…?'

'He's about the same. It's that man—Mr van der Blocq—we don't seem to get on very well.' She stood in front of the housekeeper, looking rather unhappily into her motherly face. 'Do you know him?'

'Lor', yes, my dear—he's been here twice in the last few months, and a year or two ago he came with that friend of your grandfather's, the nice old gentleman who lives in Holland—he's ill too, so I hear.'

Mary Jane waved this information on one side. 'He's staying,' she said. 'I don't know for how long. I made up a bed in the other turret room. Ought we to do something about dinner?'

'Don't you worry about that, Miss Mary Jane—the Colonel told me that he'd be coming, so I've a nice meal planned. If you'll just set the table later on—but time enough for that. Supposing you go for a little walk just down to the lake and back. You'll hear me call easily enough and a breath of air will do you good before tea.'

Mary Jane made for the door and flung it open. She had a great deal to think about; it was a pity she had no one to confide in; she hadn't got used to the fact that her grandfather was dying, nor his matter-of-fact attitude towards that fact, and the strain of matching his manner with her own was being a little too much for her. She wandered down the garden, resolutely making herself think about the house and the future. She didn't care about the money, just as long as there was enough to keep everything going as her grandfather would wish it to be. She stopped to lean over a low stone wall, built long ago for some purpose or other but now in disuse. The Colonel, a keen gardener, had planted it with a variety of rock plants, but it had no colour now. She leaned her elbows on its uneven surface and gazed out to the lake and Skiddaw beyond, not seeing them very clearly for the tears which blurred

her eyes. It was silly to cry; her grandfather disliked
crying women, he had told her so on various occasions.
She brushed her hand across her face and noted in a
detached way that the mountains had a sprinkling of
snow on their tops while the rest of them looked grey
and misty and sad. She wished, like a child, that time
might be turned back, that somehow or other today
could have been avoided. Despite herself, her eyes
filled with tears again; she wasn't a crying girl, but
just for once she made no attempt to stop them.

Major had followed her out of the house, and sat
close to her now, pressed against her knee, and when
he gave a whispered bark she wiped her eyes hastily and turned round. Mr van der Blocq was close by,
just standing there, looking away from her, across the
lake. He spoke casually. 'You have had rather a shock,
haven't you? You must be a little bewildered. May I
venture to offer you a modicum of advice?' He went
on without giving her a chance to speak. 'Don't worry
about the future for the moment. It's not a bad idea, in
circumstances such as these, to live from one day to
the next and make the best of each one.'

He was standing beside her now, still not looking
at her tear-stained face, and when she didn't reply she
went on, still casually:

'Major hasn't had a walk, has he? Supposing we
give him a run for a short while?'

Mary Jane, forgetful of the deplorable condition
of her face, looked up at him. 'I don't like to go too
far away...'

'Nor do I, but Mrs Body has promised to shout if
she needs us—she's sitting with your grandfather now,

and I imagine we could run fast enough if we needed to.' He smiled at her and just for a moment she felt warmed and comforted.

'All right,' she agreed reluctantly, 'if you say so,' and started off along the edge of the lake, Major at her heels, not bothering to see if Mr van der Blocq was following her.

They walked into the wind, not speaking much and then only about commonplace things, and as they turned to go back again Mary Jane had to admit to herself that she felt better—not, she hastened to remind herself, because of her companion but probably because she had needed the exercise and fresh air. She went straight to her grandfather's room when they got back to the house, but he was still sleeping, so obedient to Mrs Body's advice she went to the sitting room and had tea with her visitor. They spoke almost as seldom as they had done during their walk; indeed, she formed the opinion that her companion found her boring and hardly worthy of his attention, for although his manners were not to be faulted she had the strongest feeling that they were merely the outcome of courtesy; in other circumstances he would probably ignore her altogether. She sighed without knowing it and got up to feed Major.

When she got back to the sitting room, Mr van der Blocq got to his feet and with the excuse that he had telephone calls to make and letters to write, went away to the Colonel's study, which, he was careful to explain, his host had put at his disposal, leaving Mary Jane to wander out to the kitchen to help Mrs Body and presently to lay the table in the roomy, old-fashioned dining room before going up to peep once more at her sleeping grandfather before changing from her slacks and sweater into a grey wool dress she had fortuitously packed, aware as she did so of the murmur of voices from the Colonel's room.

She frowned at her reflection as she smoothed her hair into its neat bun and did her face. If Mr van der Blocq had wakened her grandfather in order to pester him with more papers, then she would have something to say to him! He came out of the adjoining room as she left her own, giving her a wordless nod and standing aside for her to go down the stairs. She waited until they were both in the hall before she said: 'I think you must be tiring Grandfather very much. I don't think he should be disturbed any more today—there's surely no need.'

He paused on his way to the study. 'My dear good girl, may I remind you that I am a qualified physician as well as a surgeon, and as such am aware of your grandfather's condition—better, I must remind you, than you yourself.' He looked down his long nose at her. 'Be good enough not to interfere.'

Mary Jane's bosom heaved, her nice eyes sparkled with temper. 'Well, really it's not your business...'

He interrupted her. 'Oh, but it is, unfortunately. I am here at your grandfather's request to attend to his affairs—at his urgent request, I should remind you, before he should die, and here you are telling me what to do and what not to do. You're a tiresome girl.'

With which parting shot, uttered in his perfect, faintly accented English, he went into the study, closing the door very gently behind him.

Mary Jane, a gentle-natured girl for the most part, flounced into the sitting room, and quite beside herself with temper, poured herself a generous measure of whisky. It was a drink she detested, but now it represented an act of defiance, she tossed off a second glass too. It was unfortunate that Mr van der Blocq chose to return after five minutes, by which time the whisky's effects upon her hungry inside were at their highest; by then her head was feeling decidedly strange and her feet, when she walked to a chair, didn't quite touch the floor. It was unfortunate too that he saw this the moment he entered the room and observed coldly, 'Good God, woman, can't I turn my back for one minute without you reaching for the whisky bottle—you reek of it!' An exaggeration so gross that she instantly suspected that he had been spying upon her.

She said carefully in a resentful voice, 'You're enough to drive anyone to drink,' the whisky urging her to add, 'Are you married? If you are, I'm very sorry for your wife.'

He took her glass from her and set it down and poured himself a drink. 'No, I'm not married,' he said blandly, 'so you may spare your sympathy.' He sat down opposite her, crossed his long legs and asked, 'What did you do before you took up nursing? Were you ever here, living permanently?'

She cleared her fuzzy mind. 'No, I went to a boarding school, although I came here for the holidays, and then when I left school—when I was eighteen—I asked Grandfather if I might take up nursing and I went to Pope's. I've only been home once a year since then.'

'No boy-friends?' She hesitated and he added, 'I

shall be your guardian, you know, I have to know a little about you.'

'Well, no.' Her head was clearer now. 'I never had much chance to meet any—only medical students, you know, and the housemen, and of course they always went for the pretty girls.' She spoke without self-pity and he offered no sympathy, nor did he utter some empty phrase about mythical good looks she knew she hadn't got, anyway. He said merely, 'Well, of course—I did myself, but one doesn't always marry them, you know.'

She agreed, adding in a matter-of-fact voice, 'Oh, I know that, I imagine young doctors usually marry where there's some money—unless they're brilliant with an assured future, and you can't blame them—how else are they to get on?'

'A sensible opinion with which I will not argue,' he assured her, his tone so dry that her slightly flushed face went slowly scarlet. It was fortunate that Mrs Body created a diversion at that moment by telling them that dinner would be ready in fifteen minutes and would Mary Jane like to take a quick peep at the Colonel first?

She was up in his room, pottering around because she sensed that he wanted company for a few minutes. When Doctor Morris arrived she waited while he examined his patient, adjusted his treatment, asked if he was through with his business, nodded his satisfaction at the answer and wished him a good night. Downstairs again, he accepted the drink offered him, muttered something to Mr van der Blocq and turned to Mary Jane.

'Your grandfather's happy; he's put his affairs in order, it's just a question of keeping him content and comfortable. You'll do that, I know, Mary Jane.' He stood up. 'I must be off, I've a couple more visits. Fabian, come to the car with me, will you?'

They talked very little over their meal and anything which they said had very little to do with the Colonel or what he had told them that day—indeed, Mr van der Blocq kept the conversation very much in his own hands, seeming not to notice her long silences and monosyllabic replies. She went to bed early, leaving him sitting by the fire, looking quite at home, with Major at his feet and still more papers on the table before him.

Once ready for bed, she went through to her grandfather's room, to find him awake, so she pulled up a chair to the dim lamp and made herself comfortable, declaring that she wasn't sleepy either. After a while he dozed off and so did she, to waken much later to find Mr van der Blocq standing looking down at her. She wasn't sure of the expression on his face, but whatever it was it changed to faint annoyance as she got silently to her feet. He said briefly, 'Go to bed,' and sat down in the chair she had vacated.

She was awakened by his hand on her shoulder. She sat up at once with an urgent whispered 'Grandfather?' and when he nodded and handed her dressing gown from a chair, she jumped out of bed, thrust her arms into its sleeves anyhow and was half way to the door in her bare feet when he reminded her, 'Your slippers—it's cold.' Before she quite reached the door he caught her by the arm. 'Your grandfather wants to say something to you—don't try and stop him; he's quite conscious and as comfortable as he can be. I've sent for Morris.'

The Colonel was wide awake and she went straight to the bed and took his hand with a steady smile. He squeezed her fingers weakly.

'Plenty of guts—like me,' he whispered with satisfaction. 'Can't abide moaning women. Something I want you to do. Always wanted you to meet my friend—Fabian's uncle—he's ill too. Go and look after him—bad-tempered fellow, can't find a nurse who'll stay. Promised Fabian you'd go.' He looked at her. 'Promise?'

She said instantly, 'Yes, Grandfather, I promise. I'll look after him.'

'Won't be for long—Fabian will see to everything.'

She glanced across at the man standing on the other side of the bed, looking, despite pyjamas and dressing gown, as impassive and withdrawn as he always did. She wondered, very briefly, if he had any feelings at all; if so, they were buried deep. He returned her look with one of his own, unsmiling and thoughtful, and then went to the door. 'That's Morris's car—I'll let him in and wake Mrs Body.'

The Colonel died a couple of hours later, in his sleep, a satisfied little smile on his old face so that Mary Jane felt that to cry would be almost an insult—besides, had he not told her that she had guts? She did all the things she had to do with a white set face, drank the tea Mrs Body gave her, then had a bath and dressed to join Mr van der Blocq at the breakfast table, where she ate nothing at all but talked brightly about the weather. Afterwards, thinking about it, she had to admit that he had been a veritable tower of strength, organising a tearful Mrs Body and a still more tearful Lily, arranging everything without fuss and a minimum of discussion, telephoning the newspapers, old friends, the rector...

She came downstairs from making the beds just as he came out of the study and Mrs Body was coming from the kitchen with the coffee tray. He poured her a cup, told her to drink it in a no-nonsense voice, and when she had, marched her off for a walk, Major at their heels. It was a fine morning but cold, and Mary Jane, in her sweater and slacks and an old jacket snatched from the back porch, was aware that she looked plainer than even she thought possible—not that she cared. She walked unwillingly beside her companion, not speaking, but presently the soft air and the quiet peace of the countryside soothed her; she even began to feel grateful to him for arranging her day and making it as easy as he could for her. She felt impelled to tell him this, to be told in a brisk impersonal way that as her guardian it was his moral obligation to do so.

He went on: 'We need to talk; there is a good deal to be arranged. You will have to leave Pope's—you realised that already, I imagine. I think it may be best if I wrote to your Matron or whatever she is called nowadays, and explain your circumstances. Your grandfather's solicitor will come here to see you—and me, but there should be no difficulties there, as everything was left in good order. I think it may be best if you return to Holland with me on the day after the funeral;

there's no point in glooming around the house on your own, and I can assure you that my uncle needs a nurse as soon as possible—his condition is rapidly worsening and extremely difficult.' He paused to throw a stone for Major. 'He was a good and clever man, and I am fond of him.'

Mary Jane stood still and looked at him. 'You've thought of everything,' she stated, and missed the gleam in his eyes. 'I only hope I'll be able to manage him and that he'll like me, because I promised Grandfather…'

Her voice petered out and although she gulped and sniffed she was quite unable to stop bursting into tears. She was hardly aware of Mr van der Blocq whisking her into his arms, only of the nice solid feel of his shoulder and his silent sympathy. Presently she raised a ruined face to his. 'So sorry,' she said politely. 'I don't cry as a general rule—I daresay I'm tired.'

'I daresay you are. We'll walk back now, and after lunch, which you will eat, you shall lie on the sofa in the study and have a nap while I finish off a few odd jobs.'

He let her go and strolled down to the water's edge while she wiped her eyes and blew her nose and re-tied her hair, and when they started back, he took her arm, talking, deliberately, of the Colonel.

Under his eye she ate her lunch, and still under it, tucked herself up in front of the study fire and fell instantly asleep. She awoke to the clatter of the tea tray as Mrs Body set it on the table beside the sofa and a moment later Doctor Morris came in.

The two men began at once to talk, and gradually,

as she poured the tea and passed the cake, Mary Jane joined in. Before the doctor got up to go she realised with surprise that she had laughed several times. The surprise must have shown on her face, for Mr van der Blocq said with uncanny insight: 'That's better—your grandfather liked you to laugh, didn't he? Now, if you feel up to it, tell me how you stand at Pope's. A month's notice is normal, I suppose—have you any holidays due? Any commitments in London?'

'I've a week's holiday before Christmas, that's all, and I'm supposed to give a month's notice. There's nothing to keep me in London, but all my clothes and things are at Pope's.'

'We will pick them up as we go. What is the name of your matron?'

'Miss Shepherd—she's called the Principal Nursing Officer now.'

'Presumably in the name of progress, but what a pity. I shall telephone her now.' Which he did, with a masterly mixture of authority and charm. Mary Jane listened with interest to his exact explanations, which he delivered unembellished by sentiment and without any effort to enlist sympathy. It didn't surprise her in the least that within five minutes he had secured her resignation as from that moment.

When he had replaced the receiver, she remarked admiringly, 'My goodness, however did you manage it? I thought I would have to go back.'

'Manage what?' he asked coolly. 'I made a reasonable request and received a reasonable reply to it—I fail to see anything extraordinary in that.'

He returned to his writing, leaving her feeling

snubbed, so that her manner towards him, which had begun to warm a little, cooled. It made her feel cold too, as though he had shut a door that had been ajar and left her outside. She went to the kitchen presently on some excuse or other, and sat talking to Mrs Body, who was glad of the company anyway.

'You've not had time to make any plans, Miss Mary Jane?' she hazarded.

'No, Mrs Body. You know that Grandfather left me this house, don't you? You will go on living here, won't you? I don't think I could bear it if you and Lily went away.'

The housekeeper gave her a warm smile. 'Bless you, my dear, of course we'll stay—it would break my heart to go after all these years, and Lily wouldn't go, I'm sure. But didn't I hear Doctor van der Blocq say that you would be going back to Holland with him?'

Mary Jane explained. 'It won't be for long, I imagine—if you wouldn't mind being here—do you suppose Lily would come and live in so that you've got company? I'm not sure about the money yet, but I'm sure there'll be enough to pay her. Shall I ask her?'

'A good idea, Miss Mary Jane. Supposing I mention it to her first, once everything's seen to? I must say the doctor gets things done—everything's going as smooth as silk and he thinks of everything. That reminds me, he told me to move your things back to your old room.'

Mary Jane looked surprised. 'Oh, did he? How thoughtful of him,' and then because she was young and healthy even though she was sad: 'What's for dinner— I'm hungry.'

Mrs Body beamed. 'A nice bit of beef. For a foreign gentleman the doctor isn't finicky about his food, is he? And I always say there's nothing to beat a nice roast. There's baked apples and cream for afters.'

'I'll lay the table,' Mary Jane volunteered, and kept herself busy with that until Mr van der Blocq came out of the study, when she offered him a drink, prudently declining one herself before going upstairs to put on the grey dress once more. The sight of her face, puffy with tears and tense with her stored-up feelings, did little to reassure her, and when she joined Mr van der Blocq in the sitting room, the brief careless glance he accorded her deflated what little ego she had left. Sitting at table, watching him carving the beef with a nicety which augured well for his skill at his profession, she found herself wishing that he didn't regard her with such indifference—not, she told herself sensibly, that his opinion of her mattered one jot. He wasn't at all the sort of man she… He interrupted her thoughts.

'It seems to me a good idea if you were to call me Fabian. I do not like being addressed as Mr van der Blocq—inaccurately, as it happens. Even Mrs Body manages to address me, erroneously, as Doctor dear.' He smiled faintly as he looked at her, his eyebrows raised.

She studied his face. 'Well, if you want me to,' her voice was unenthusiastic, 'only I don't know you very well, and you're…'

'A great deal older than you? Indeed I am.'

It annoyed her that he didn't tell her how much older, but she went on, 'I was going to say that I find it a little difficult, because Grandfather told me that you were an important surgeon and I wouldn't dream of calling a consultant at Pope's by his first name.'

The preposterous idea made her smile, but he remained unamused, only saying in a bored fashion. 'Well, you are no longer a nurse at Pope's—you are Miss Pettigrew with a pleasant little property of your own and sufficient income with which to live in comfort.'

She served him a baked apple and passed the cream. 'What's a sufficient income?' she wanted to know.

He waved a careless, well kept hand, before telling her.

She had been on the point of sampling her own apple, but now she laid down her spoon and said sharply, 'That's nonsense—that's a fortune!'

'Not in these days, it will be barely enough. There's your capital, of course, but I shall be in charge of that.' His tone implied that he was discussing something not worthy of his full attention, and this nettled her.

'You talk as though it were chicken feed!'

'That was not my intention. I'm sure you are a competent young woman and well able to enjoy life on such a sum. The solicitor will inform you as to the exact money.'

'Then why do I have to have you for a guardian?'

He put down his fork and said patiently, 'You heard your grandfather—I shall attend to any business to do with investments and so forth and have complete control of your capital. I shall of course see that your income is paid into your bank until you assume full control over your affairs when you are thirty. It will also be necessary for me to give my consent to your marriage should you wish to marry.'

She was bereft of words. 'Your consent—if I should choose.' She almost choked. 'It's not true!'

'I am not in the habit of lying. It is perfectly true, set down in black and white by your grandfather, and I intend to carry out his wishes to the letter.'

'You mean that if anyone wants to marry me he'll have to ask you?'

He nodded his handsome head.

'But that's absurd! I never heard such nonsense… how could you possibly know—have any idea…?'

His voice had been cool, now it was downright cold. 'My dear good girl, let me assure you that I find my duties just as irksome as you find them unnecessary.'

This shook her. 'Oh, will you? I suppose they'll take up some of your time. I'll try not to bother you, then—I daresay there'll be no need for us to see much of each other.'

His lips twitched. 'Probably not, although I'm afraid that while you are at my uncle's house you will see me from time to time—he's too old to manage his own affairs, and my cousin, who lives with him, isn't allowed to do more than run the house.'

They were in the sitting room drinking their coffee when she ventured: 'Will you tell me a little about your uncle? I don't know where he lives or anything about him, and since I am to stay there…'

Mr van der Blocq frowned. 'Why should I object?' he wanted to know testily. 'But I must be brief; I'm expecting one or two telephone calls presently. He lives in Friesland, a small village called Midwoude. It is in fact on the border between Friesland and Groningen. The country is charming and there is a lake close by. The city of Groningen is only a few miles away; Leeuwarden is less than an hour by car. You may find it a little lonely, but I think not, for you are happy here, aren't you? My uncle, I have already told you, is difficult, but my cousin Emma will be only too glad to make a friend of you.'

'And you—you live somewhere else?'

'I live and work in Groningen.' He spoke pleasantly and with the quite obvious intention of saying nothing more. She had to be content with that, and shortly after that, when he went to answer his telephone call, Mary Jane went into the kitchen, helped Mrs Body around the place, laid the table for breakfast and went up to bed.

Now if I were a gorgeous creature with golden hair and long eyelashes, she mused as she wandered up the staircase, we might be spending the evening together— probably he had some flaxen-haired beauty waiting for him in Groningen. For lack of anything better to do and to keep her thoughts in a cheerful channel, she concocted a tale about Mr van der Blocq in which the blonde played a leading part, and he for once smiled frequently and never once addressed the creature as 'my dear good girl'.

The next few days passed quickly; there was a good deal to attend to and Major had to be taken for his walk, and time had to be spent with the Colonel's friends who called in unexpected numbers. The lawyer came too and spent long hours in the study with her guardian, although he had very little to say to her.

It wasn't until after the funeral, when the last of the neighbours and friends had gone, that old Mr North asked her to join him in the study and bring Mrs Body and Lily with her. Mary Jane half listened while he read the legacies which had been left to them both, it wasn't until they had gone and she was sitting by the fire with Fabian at the other end of the room that Mr North gave her the details of her own inheritance. The money seemed a vast sum to her; she had had no idea that her grandfather had had so much, even the income she was to receive seemed a lot of money. Mr North rambled on rather, talking about stocks and shares and securities and ended by saying:

'But you won't need to worry your head about this, Mary Jane, Mr van der Blocq will see to everything for you. I understand that you will be travelling to Holland tomorrow. That will make a nice change and you will return here ready to take your place in local society. I take it that Mrs Body will remain?'

She told him that yes, she would, and moreover Lily had agreed to live in as well, so that the problem of having someone to look after the house and Major was solved.

'You have no idea how long you will be away?' asked Mr North.

'None,' she glanced at Fabian, who took no notice at all, 'but I'm sure that Mrs Body will look after everything beautifully.'

The old gentleman nodded. 'And you? You will be sorry to leave your work at the hospital, I expect.'

She remembered Sister Thompson. 'Yes, though

I was thinking of changing to another hospital.' She smiled at him. 'Now I shan't need to.'

He went shortly afterwards and she spent the rest of the day packing what clothes she had with her and making final arrangements with Mrs Body before taking Major for a walk by the lake. It was a clear evening with the moon shining. Mary Jane shivered a little despite her coat, not so much with cold as the knowledge that she would miss the peace and quiet even though she had it to come back to.

She went indoors presently and into the study to wish Fabian good night. He stood by her grandfather's desk while she made a few remarks about their journey and then said a little shyly, 'You've been very kind and—and efficient. I don't know what we should have done without your help. I'm very grateful.'

He rustled the papers in his hand and thanked her stiffly, and she went to her room, wondering if he would ever unbend, or was he going to remain coldly polite and a little scornful of her for the rest of their relationship? Eight years, she told herself as she got into bed, seemed a long time. She would be thirty and quite old, and Fabian would be…she started to guess and fell asleep, still guessing.

Chapter 3

Mary Jane had never travelled in a Rolls-Royce—she found it quite an experience. Fabian was a good driver and although he spoke seldom he was quite relaxed, she sat silently beside him, thinking about the last two weeks—such a lot had happened and there had been so much to plan and arrange; she hoped she had forgotten nothing—not that it would matter very much, for her companion would not have overlooked the smallest detail. He had told her very little about the journey, beyond asking her to be ready to start at eight o'clock in the morning.

They were on the motorway now, doing a steady seventy, and would be in London by early afternoon, giving her ample time in which to pack her things at the hospital before they left for the midnight ferry.

'Anything you haven't time to see to you can leave,'

he had told her, 'and arrange to send on the things you don't want—Mrs Body can sort them out later. You can buy all you need when we get to Holland.'

'Oh no, I can't, I've only a few pounds.'

'I will advance you any reasonable sum—do you need any money now?'

'No, thank you, but what about my fare?'

'Mr North and I will take care of such details.'

They had settled into silence after that. Mary Jane stared through the window as the Rolls crept up behind each car in turn and passed it. Presently she closed her eyes against the boredom of the road, the better to think. But her thoughts were muddled and hazy; she hadn't slept very well the night before, and fought a desire to doze off, induced by the extreme comfort of the car, and had just succeeded in reducing her mind to tolerable clarity when her efforts were shattered by her companion's laconic, 'We'll stop for coffee.'

She glanced at her watch; they had been on the road for just two hours and Stafford wasn't far away. 'That would be nice,' she agreed pleasantly, and was a little surprised when he left the motorway, taking the car unhurriedly down side roads which led at last to a small village.

'Stableford,' read Mary Jane from the signpost. 'Why do we come here?'

'To get away from the motorway for half an hour. There's a place called The Cocks—ah, there it is.' He pulled up as he spoke.

The coffee was excellent and hot, and Mary Jane ate a bun because breakfast seemed a long time ago, indeed, a meal in another life.

'What time shall we get to London?' she wanted to know.

'A couple of hours, I suppose. We will have a late lunch before I take you to Pope's. I'll call for you there at seven o'clock.'

'The boat doesn't go until midnight, does it?'

'We shall dine on the way.'

'Oh.' She felt somehow deflated; if he had said something nice about dining together, or even asked her—obviously he was performing a courteous duty with due regard to her comfort and absolutely no pleasure on his part. She followed him meekly out to the car and for the remainder of the journey only spoke when she was spoken to and that not very often. Only when they were driving through London's northern suburbs did he remark: 'We'll go to Carrier's, it's an easy run to Pope's from there.'

The restaurant was down a passage, double-fronted and modern, and Mary Jane, by now famished, chose fillet of beef in shirtsleeves, because it sounded quaint and filling at the same time. She was given a dry sherry to drink before they ate; she would have preferred a sweet one, but somehow Fabian looked the kind of man who would wish to order the drinks himself and she felt certain that he knew a great deal more about them than she ever would; she might be a splendid nurse, a tolerable cook and handy in the garden, but the more sophisticated talents had so far eluded her. It surprised her when he suggested, after she had disposed of the beef in its shirtsleeves and he had eaten his carpet bag steak, that she might like to sample Robert's Chocolate Fancy.

'Women like sweet things,' he told her tolerantly, and asked for the cheese board for himself.

Pope's looked greyer, more old-fashioned and more hedged in by the towering blocks of flats around it than ever before. 'You'll have to see the Matron—you had better do that first,' said Fabian as he helped her out of the car. 'Do you want me to come with you?'

She declined politely and with secret regret; it would have been a pleasure to have walked through the hospital with Fabian beside her; she could just imagine the curious and envious glances that would have been cast at her.

He nodded. 'Good. I've one or two things to do. I'll be here at seven exactly.'

There was a great deal for her to do too. After the interview with Miss Shepherd, which was unexpectedly pleasant, there was a brief visit to Women's Surgical, where Sister Thompson wasn't pleasant at all, and then a long session of packing in her room. It was amazing what she had collected over the years! After due thought she packed a trunk with everything she judged might be unsuitable in a Dutch winter, which left her with some thick tweeds in a pleasing shade of brown, a variety of sweaters, a couple of jersey dresses and a rather nice evening dress she couldn't resist taking, although she saw no chance of wearing it. It was pale blue and green organza with long tight sleeves and a pie-frill collar, and it suited her admirably.

When she had finished packing she went along to the sitting room, where most of her friends were having tea, and found so much to talk about that she had to hurry to complete the tiresome chores of handing in her uniform to the linen room and waiting while it was checked, and then running all over the home to hand in the key of her room, both tasks requiring patience while the appropriate persons were found, the right forms filled in and signed and the farewells made, but she was at the hospital entrance by seven o'clock, wearing the brown tweeds and a felt hat which did nothing for her at all. All the same, she looked nice; her handbag and gloves and shoes were good and the tweed suit and coat suited her small slender person.

She reached the door just as Fabian drew up and got out of the car. He gave her a laconic 'Hullo', put her case in the boot and enquired about the rest of the luggage.

'It's in my trunk—one of my friends will send it on to Mrs Body.'

'Good. And Miss Shepherd—any difficulties?'

'No, thank you. None.'

'Get in, then.'

She didn't much like being ordered about, she was on the point of saying so when those of her closer friends who were off duty or who had been able to escape from their wards for a few minutes arrived in a chattering bunch to see her off. They embraced her in turn and with some warmth, at the same time taking a good look at Mr van der Blocq, who bore their scrutiny with a faint smile and complete equanimity, even when Penny Martin, the prettiest and giddiest of the lot of them, darted forward and caught him by the arm.

'Take care of Mary Jane,' she begged him with the faint lisp which most of the housemen found irresistible, 'and if you want another nurse at any time, I'd love to come.'

He smiled down at her, and Mary Jane, glimpsing the charm of it, felt quite shaken by some feeling she had no time to consider. He had never smiled at her like that; he must dislike her very much. The supposition caused her to be very quiet as they drove away from the cheerful little group on the steps, in fact, she didn't speak at all until they had crossed the river, gone through Southwark and joined the A2.

'You'll miss your friends,' commented her companion, slowing down for the traffic lights, 'and hospital life.' The car swept ahead again. 'There's no reason why you shouldn't go back to work there later on—you could spend your holidays in Cumbria.'

'Oh, I wouldn't do that,' declared Mary Jane, startled out of her silence. 'I shall like living in Grandfather's house and I shall find plenty to do. I shall miss Pope's, of course, but not the ward I was on.'

He shot her a brief, amused glance. 'Oh? Tell me about it.'

She did, rather haltingly at first, but he seemed interested and she found herself saying more than she intended.

'There is certainly no point in you going back to Women's Surgical,' he agreed. 'It sounds a joyless place, and your Sister Thompson needs to go on the retirement list.'

'But she's quite young, only forty.'

'You think that forty is quite young?'

'Heavens, yes.' She broke off as he turned the car

down a side road. 'Where are we going? I thought this led to the M2.'

'There's a good place at Hollingbourne, and we have plenty of time.'

The restaurant was pleasantly quiet and the food exceptional. Mary Jane was beginning to think that Fabian wouldn't go anywhere unless the food and the service were near perfection. She remembered the simple meals she and Mrs Body had cooked and wondered, as she ate her Kentish roast duckling, if he had enjoyed them. Probably not.

They kept up a desultory conversation as they ate—the kind of conversation, she told herself hopelessly, that one sustained with fellow patients in a dentist's waiting room. Before she could stop the words, they popped out of her mouth. 'What a pity we don't get on.'

If she had hoped to take him by surprise, she had failed. His expression didn't change as he answered in the pleasantest of voices.

'Yes, it is. Probably as we get to know each other better, our—er—incompatibility will lessen.' He smiled briefly and changed the subject abruptly. 'Tell me, do you ride? If so, there is a good stables near my uncle's house—they could let you have a mount.'

'Oh, could they? I should like that. I'm not awfully good, but I enjoy it.'

'In that case you had better not go out alone.'

Which remark compelled her to say, 'Oh, I can ride well enough, you needn't worry about that—it's just that I'm not a first-class horsewoman.'

They sipped coffee in silence until she said defiantly, 'I shall buy a horse when I get back home,' and waited to see what he would say. She was disappointed when he replied blandly, 'Why not? Shall we go?'

They were at Dover with time to spare. They left the car in the small queue and had coffee in the restaurant and Fabian bought her an armful of magazines. Once on board he suggested that she should go to her cabin. 'We berth very early,' he warned her, 'half past four or thereabouts. We'll stop for breakfast on the way to Friesland.'

His advice was sound. Mary Jane slept for a few hours, and fortified by tea, joined him on deck as the boat docked, and then followed him down to the car deck. There was no delay at all as they landed; they were away in a few minutes, tearing down the cobbled street towards the Dutch border.

The Rolls bored through the motorway from Antwerp towards the frontier and Breda, going through the town without stopping. It was quiet and dark, although a slow dawn was beginning to lighten the sky; by the time they reached Utrecht there was a dim, chilly daylight struggling through the clouds. Mary Jane shivered in the warm car and Fabian spoke after miles of silence. 'We'll stop here and have breakfast.'

It seemed a little early for there to be anywhere open, but he stopped the car outside Smits Hotel, said, 'Stay where you are,' and went inside to return very quickly and invite her inside, where she was welcomed by the hall porter with a courtesy she would have found pleasant in broad daylight, let alone at that early hour of the morning, but Fabian seemed to take it all very much for granted, as he did the breakfast which was presently set before them. They ate at leisure, lingering

over a final cup of coffee while he explained the route
they were to follow. 'Less than a hundred miles,' he
told her. 'We shall be at my uncle's house for coffee.'

And they were, after a drive during which Mary
Jane, after several efforts at polite conversation, had
become progressively more and more silent, staring
out at the flat, frost-covered fields on either side of the
road, observing with interest the cows in their coats,
the large churches and the small villages so unlike her
own home, and wishing with all her heart that she was
back there—she even wished she was back at Pope's,
coping with Sister Thompson's petty tyranny, but when
her companion said, 'Only a few more miles now,' she
pulled herself together; self-pity got one nowhere, and
if Grandfather could know what she was thinking now
he would be heartily ashamed of her show—even to
herself—of weakness.

She sat up straight, rammed the unbecoming hat
firmly upon her head and said, 'I'm glad, and I'm sure
you must be too—travelling with someone you dislike
can be very tiresome.'

Mr van der Blocq allowed a short sharp exclama-
tion to leave his lips. 'Does that remark refer to myself
or to you?' he queried silkily.

'Both of us.' She spoke without heat and lapsed into
silence, a silence she would have liked to break as he
took the car gently through a very small village—
cluster of one-storied cottages, a shop and an over-
sized church—and turned off the road through massive iron gates and a tree-lined drive, and pulled up
before his uncle's house. She would have liked to ex-
claim over it, for it was worthy of comment; built of

rose brick with a steep slate roof and an iron balcony above its massive front door. It had two stories, their windows exactly matching, and all with shutters. It reminded her of some fairy tale, standing there silent, within the semicircle of sheltering trees, most of them bare now. She was impressed and longed to say so.

Fabian got out, came round to help her out too and walked beside her up the shallow steps to the opening door. A white-haired man stood there, neatly dressed in a dark suit and looking so pleased to see them that she deduced, quite rightly, that this wasn't Jonkheer van der Blocq. Fabian quickly put her right, explaining as he shook the old man's hand, 'This is Jaap, he has been in the family for forty years—he sees to everything and will be of great help to you.'

Mary Jane put out a hand and had it gently wrung while Jaap made her welcome—presumably—in his own language. She nodded and smiled and followed him into a handsome lobby and through its inner glass doors to the hall, an imposing place, its walls hung with dark, gilt-framed portraits, vicious-looking weapons and a variety of coats of arms. It needed flowers, she decided as she glanced about her, something vivid to offset the noble plastered ceiling and marble floor with its dim Persian rugs. She was arranging them in her mind's eye when Fabian said: 'The sitting room, I suppose—the first door on the left.'

She followed Jaap through a double door into a room whose proportions rivalled those of the hall— the ceiling was high, the walls, painted white and ornamented at their corners with a good deal of carved fruit and flowers, carried a further selection of paintings. The furniture was massive and she had the feeling that excepting for the easy chairs flanking the large open fire, and the Chesterfield drawn up before it, the seating accommodation would be uncomfortable—an opinion which Fabian probably shared, for he advised her to take a chair by the fire, taking her coat and tossing it to Jaap.

'My cousin will be here in a moment,' he told her, and went to look out of the windows, while Mary Jane, left to herself, rearranged the furniture in her mind, set a few floral arrangements on the various tables and regarded with awe a large cabinet on the opposite wall; it was inlaid, with a good deal of strapwork, and she considered it hideous.

'German?' she asked herself aloud.

'You're right,' agreed Fabian from the window. 'The Thirty Years' War or thereabouts, I believe, and frankly appalling.'

She turned to look at him. 'Now isn't that nice, we actually agree about something!' She added hastily, 'I don't mean to be rude—I have no business to pass an opinion...'

He shrugged his wide shoulders. 'I'm flattered that we should share even an opinion.'

'Now that's a...' She was saved from finishing the forceful remark she was about to make by the entry of a lady into the room. The cousin, without doubt—fortyish, tall and thin and good-looking, her face marred by the anxious frown between her brows and the look of harassment she wore. Indeed, she appeared to be so hunted that Mary Jane expected to see her followed by Fabian's uncle in one of his more difficult moods. But no one else appeared; the lady trod across the room to Fabian, crying his name in a melodramatic fashion, and flung her arms around him. He received her embrace with a good-humoured tolerance, patted her on the shoulder and said in English: 'Now, Emma, you can stop behaving like a wet hen. Here is Mary Jane come to nurse Oom Georgius.'

He turned round and went to Mary Jane's side. 'This is my cousin Emma van der Blocq—I'm sure you will be good friends, and I know she is delighted to have you here to lighten her burden.'

'Indeed yes,' his cousin joined in, shaking Mary Jane's hand in an agitated way. 'I'm quite worn out, for my father thinks I am a very poor nurse and I daresay I am—I'm sure you will be able to manage him far better than I.' She sighed deeply. 'The nurses never stay.'

It sounded as though the old gentleman was going to be a handful, Mary Jane thought gloomily, but she had promised her grandfather, and in a way she was glad, because she would be too occupied to brood over his death. She said in her pleasant voice, 'I'll do my best. Perhaps when you have the time, you will tell me what you would like me to do.'

Cousin Emma became more agitated than ever. 'Oh yes, of course, but first you shall see your room and we will have lunch.' She looked at Fabian. 'You will go and see Father?'

He nodded and followed them out of the room and up the elegant staircase at one side of the hall, but on the landing they parted, he going to the front of the house while Mary Jane and her hostess entered a room at the head of the stairs. It was a large room, but not, she was relieved to see, nearly as large as the sitting room. It was furnished with a quantity of heavy Mid-Victorian furniture, all very ornate, carved and inlaid. The bed was a ponderous affair too, but the curtains and coverlet were pretty and the carpet was richly thick under her feet.

Here she was left alone to tidy herself before going downstairs again, something she was about to do when she was halted by a thunderous voice from behind a pair of handsome doors across the landing, bellowing something in Dutch, and a moment later Fabian appeared, to lean over the balustrade as she went down the stairs and ask if she would be good enough to visit his uncle.

The room they entered was vast, with a fourposter bed dwarfed against one wall and a great many chests and tallboys and massive cupboards. In the centre of this splendour sat Jonkheer van der Blocq, facing a roaring fire. And a handsome old man he was too, with white hair, a little thin on top, and Fabian's features. He didn't wait for his nephew to speak but began at once in a stentorian voice.

'Hah—so my good old friend died, and you are the Mary Jane he wrote so much of.' He produced a pair of spectacles and planted them upon his nose and stared at her. 'A dab of a girl, too. He promised me that if I should outlive him, he would send you to me. Nurses,' he went on in a triumphant voice, 'don't stay. Do you suppose you will?'

Mary Jane walked up to his chair, not in the least put out. 'I don't see why not,' she said in a reasonable voice, 'and anyway, I promised Grandfather I would.

I'm not easily upset, you know.' She gave him a kind smile and he croaked with laughter. 'We'll see about that! At any rate you will be a change from that fool daughter of mine, always fussing around.'

'I daresay she wants to help you, but some people—and you, I suspect, aren't easy to do things for; they find fault all the time.'

He sat back against his cushions and she thought that he might explode; instead he burst out laughing. 'Dammit, if you're not like your grandfather!' he declared. 'No looks but plenty of spirit. I shall come down to lunch.' He turned to Fabian. 'And you, what do you think of her, eh?'

'I have no doubt that Mary Jane is an excellent nurse.'

'That wasn't what I meant. However, you may give me an arm and we'll go down. I rather fancy a glass of *Genever* before we lunch.'

'You'll not get it,' observed his nephew good-humouredly. 'A glass of white wine is all that Trouw allows you, and that's what you will have.'

The old man, far from being annoyed at this arbitrary remark, chuckled, and the three of them went down to the dining room in the friendliest possible way. The old gentleman's good humour lasted throughout the meal, and when Fabian got up to go, saying that he had an appointment that afternoon in Groningen, begged him to come again as soon as he could. 'Though I daresay you have a good deal of work to catch up on. How long have you been away?'

And when Fabian told him he continued: 'It will

take you a week or two to work everything off, I daresay. Well, come when you can, Fabian.'

His thunderous voice sounded wistful and Mary Jane guessed that he was fond of his nephew, though probably nothing on earth would make him admit to it. Bidden by her host to see Fabian into his car, she walked a little self-consciously to the door and stood in the lobby while he spoke to Jaap, but presently he turned to her and said:

'Doctor Trouw will be here this evening, I believe. He speaks English and will explain all there is to know about my uncle. I hope it has been made clear to you that you are a guest here as well as a nurse, although you will doubtless find yourself called upon frequently enough if my uncle becomes particularly difficult.'

She raised surprised eyes to his. 'A guest? But I understood Grandfather to say that I was to take care of your uncle, I know he's not in bed, but he needs someone, and he's a lot more ill than he allows, isn't he? And he said himself that nurses don't stay. Does he really dislike your cousin looking after him?'

He gave a short laugh. 'I assure you that he does, nor does she like looking after him. Do as you think fit, but I for one shall not hold you to your promise, for you had no idea what it might entail when you gave it, and nor, I believe, did your grandfather. Uncle Georgius is going to get worse very soon now, and he will be what you so aptly describe in your language as a handful.'

'Look,' said Mary Jane patiently, 'you came over to Grandfather when he sent for you and it must have been inconvenient, but I don't think you would have refused, would you? Well, neither shall I.'

She gave him a determined little nod and the corner of his mouth twitched a little. 'Very well,' he said blandly, and turned to go.

'Just a minute,' she was self-conscious again, 'I want to thank you for making my journey so comfortable and for doing so much for us.' She looked at him earnestly. 'You didn't know any of us well, you could so easily have refused—you had every right. I—I heard what your uncle said about your backlog of patients.'

'Like you, I keep my word,' he told her. 'Goodbye.'

She watched the Rolls slip away between the trees and told herself that she was well rid of such a cold, disagreeable man, and the feeling which she ascribed to relief at his going was so strong that she very nearly burst into tears.

Mary Jane slipped into the life of the big, silent house quite easily. She was an adaptable girl and her training had made her more so. In only a few days she had taken over all the tiresome chores which Emma van der Blocq disliked so much; the persuading of the old gentleman to rise in the morning when he flatly refused, the coaxing of him to go to bed at a reasonable hour—more, the battle of wills which was fought daily over the vexed question as to whether his pills were to be taken or not. But at least he slept well once he was in his bed and she had turned out the lights save for one small lamp, turned his radio to a thread of sound, arranged the variety of odds and ends he insisted upon having on his bedside table and wished him a cheerful goodnight, however grumpy he was. She was free then, but too tired to do anything other than write an odd letter or so or leaf through a magazine. She was free during the day too, as she was frequently told, both by Jonkheer van der Blocq and his daughter, but somehow it was difficult to get away, for if the old gentleman didn't want her, Emma van der Blocq did, even if only for a gossip. It wasn't until several days after her arrival that Mary Jane, during the course of one of these chats, asked her hostess why Jaap always referred to her as Freule—a question which kept Emma van der Blocq happy for an entire afternoon, explaining the intricacies of the Dutch nobility. She added a wealth of information regarding their titles, their houses and lands to a fascinated Mary Jane, who at the end of this dissertation, asked, 'So what do I call Fabian? He's a surgeon—is he Mister or Doctor?'

Cousin Emma looked slightly taken aback. 'But of course you have not fully understood. He is also Jonkheer, he is also a professor of surgery, you comprehend? Therefore he is addressed as Professor Jonkheer van der Blocq.'

'My goodness,' observed Mary Jane, 'what a mouthful!' Now she knew why he had looked so amused when she had addressed him as Mister. It had been nice of him not to say anything, though it surprised her that he hadn't taken the opportunity of discomfiting her. Her companion went on earnestly, 'I am old-fashioned enough to set great store upon these things, but I believe that the young people do not. Fabian may not be young any more, but he does not care in the least about his position, he…' She was interrupted by the entry of Corrie, the maid, begging her to ask Miss to go at once to the master of the house, and as Mary Jane got obediently to her feet, she said: 'What a blessing you are to us all. You do not know the relief I feel at not having to answer every call from Papa's room.'

And Mary Jane, skipping up the stairs for the tenth time that day, could well believe her. She was a little puzzled that nobody had offered to relieve her of her duties from time to time—it would be all right for a week or so, but she began to feel the need for a little relaxation and exercise and for some other distraction other than card games and Cousin Emma's rather theatrical conversation.

It was the next afternoon, when after a fruitless effort on her part to escape for a walk, she was playing cards with her patient, that he wanted to know what she thought of Fabian.

'I don't know him well enough to form an opinion,' she told him in a matter-of-fact way. 'He saw to every thing very nicely—we couldn't have managed without him, and Grandfather liked him.' She paused and searched her memory. 'Everyone liked him,' she said in surprise.

'But not you?'

Until that moment she hadn't realised that she had never analysed her feelings towards Fabian. 'I've not thought about it.'

The old gentleman persisted, 'Perhaps he doesn't like you?'

She shuffled the cards and dealt them. 'Probably not. One gets on better with some people than others.'

'You're not much to look at.'

'No—it's your turn.'

He slammed down a card. 'Men fall for a pretty face.'

'So I should imagine.' She smiled at him across the card table and he glowered back.

Presently he went on, 'A pretty face isn't everything. You're delightful company, Mary Jane; it was good of your grandfather to let me share you. You don't mind staying a little while?'

She shook her head. 'Not in the least. I'll stay as long as you want me to.'

He snorted. 'Don't let us wrap up our words. You know as well as I do that I shall probably be dead in a week or so. You're not bored?'

It was difficult to answer that, because she was, just a little. She longed to get away for an hour or so each day; she had known that she would spend some time with Jonkheer van der Blocq each day, but even private nurses were entitled to their free periods, and she wasn't a private nurse—Fabian had told her that. He had spoken of trips to Groningen and getting a mount from the nearby stables; so far she had had no time for either, indeed she had no idea where the stables were, and when, on the previous day, she had mentioned going for a walk to Freule van der Blocq, that good lady had reacted quite violently to the suggestion; it seemed that the idea of being left with her father was more than she could bear, so Mary Jane had said no more about it. When Doctor Trouw paid his next visit, she would have a little talk with him and see what could be done.

She had hoped that Fabian would have come, even

for half an hour to see how she was managing, but
although the telephone rang frequently, she had no
means of knowing if any of the calls were from him;
it was really rather mean of him, and she decided that
she liked him even less than she had supposed, and
told herself forcefully that she didn't care if she never
saw him again.

He came the very next morning, while Mary Jane,
after a protracted argument between her host and his
daughter, was in church. Emma went to church each
Sunday, driven by Jaap in the Mercedes Benz which
was housed, along with a Mini, in the garage at the
back of the house, and she had seen no reason why
Mary Jane shouldn't accompany her. 'Jaap will be
here,' she had pointed out to her enraged parent, 'he
can help you dress and we shall be back very shortly.'

Her father pointed out testily that if Jaap drove them
to church, there would be no one to dress him, and
he certainly wasn't going to wait while Jaap drove
around the countryside just because she wanted to go
to church.

Mary Jane, feeling a little like a bone between two
dogs, felt her patience wearing thin round the edges.
'Look,' she offered when she could make herself heard,
'can't I drive the Mini? It's no distance, and that would
leave Jaap free.'

So they had gone to church and on the return journey when she turned the little car carefully into the
drive once more, it was to find a silver-grey pre-war
Jaguar SS 100 parked before the door. She got out and
went to inspect it with a good deal of interest; it wasn't
an original but a modern version of it, she discovered

as she prowled around its chassis, wondering to whom it belonged, and when Cousin Emma cried happily: 'Oh, good, Fabian's here—this is his car,' Mary Jane, her inquisitive person bent double over the dashboard, remarked:

'I don't believe it.'

'Why not?' It was Fabian who spoke and startled her so much that she turned round in a kind of jump, and when she didn't speak, he repeated impatiently, 'Why not?'

'Well,' she said slowly, 'it's unexpected—I hardly thought that you…'

'I'm too old for it?' His voice was suave.

'What nonsense, of course not, it's just that…' She gave up, staring at him silently. After a moment he laughed and turned to his cousin.

'Well, Emma, how are you? I've been with Oom Georgius. He seems in fine shape, considering all things, though a little annoyed because Mary Jane wasn't at home.'

He looked at Mary Jane as he spoke, and she, aware of his faintly accusing tone, went red, just as though, she thought crossly, she were in the habit of tearing off for hours at a time, whereas the morning's outing, if it could be called that, had been the first since she had arrived. She turned on her heel and walked into the house as Cousin Emma burst into voluble speech.

She was in Jonkheer van de Blocq's room fighting her usual battle over his pills when Fabian came in. He sat down by the fire without speaking, watching her while, with cunning and guile, she persuaded the old man to swallow them down. He still said nothing as she prepared to leave them, only walking to the door to open it for her. She barely glanced at him as she passed through.

They all lunched together in the dining room, and Jonkheer van der Blocq, a little excited at Fabian's visit, talked a great deal, repeating himself frequently and forgetting his words and showing little flashes of splendid rage when he did. The meal took some time and when it was at last finished he was tired, so that for once, when Mary Jane suggested that he might like to lie down for half an hour, he agreed meekly. She accompanied him upstairs again, tucked him up on the chaise-longue in his room, thoughtfully provided him with a book, his spectacles, the bell and the tin of fruit drops he liked to suck, bade him be a good boy in a motherly voice, and went downstairs.

She was crossing the hall when she heard Fabian's voice, usually so quiet and measured in its tones, raised in anger and as she reached the door she could hear Cousin Emma doing what she described to herself as a real Sarah Bernhardt. Her hand on the heavy brass knob, she wondered if she should go in, and had her mind made up for her by a particularly loud squawk. At any moment, she thought to herself vexedly, she would have strong hysterics to deal with, thanks to Fabian. She flung open the door to find Freule van der Blocq standing in a tragic pose in the middle of the room, and Fabian lounging against one of the Corinthian pillars which supported the vast fireplace. He spoke sharply.

'There you are! Perhaps you can answer my questions without weeping and wailing. Have you been out at all since you arrived here?'

'Oh yes—to church.'

'Don't infuriate me, I beg of you, you know very well what I mean. Have you had time to yourself each day, to go out, to ride, to visit Groningen?'

'Well I…'

'Yes or no?' he ground out.

'You see…'

'I see nothing, largely owing to your inability to answer my questions.' He frowned at her. 'There seems to be some gross misunderstanding; you are here as a guest, to give some time and company to Uncle Georgius at your grandfather's request. That does not mean that you have to spend each day cooped up in the house at everyone's beck and call.'

'Don't exaggerate,' Mary Jane told him calmly, 'just because you're annoyed. It's your fault anyway. You should have explained exactly what I was supposed to do—you didn't tell me much, did you, and I dare say you didn't tell Freule van der Blocq anything either. I refuse to be blamed, and I won't allow you to blame her either.'

He gave her a hard stare. 'Oh? Am I supposed to apologise to you, then?' his voice was silky and very quiet.

'No, I don't suppose any such thing, because I can't imagine you apologising to anyone, though you could at least say you're sorry to your cousin. It's unkind of you to make her cry.'

His eyes had become black, he was still staring at her, rather as though he had never seen her before, she thought uneasily. She shook off the feeling and prompted him, 'Well, go on—or perhaps you would rather not do with me here.'

She whisked out of the room before he could reply and crossed the hall to the long drawing room, a very much gilded apartment, with a wealth of grand furniture and huge display cabinets full of silver and porcelain. Not at all to her taste; she hurried over the vast carpeted floor and into the verandah room beyond where there was a piano. With the doors shut she was sure no one could hear her playing, and really, she had to do something to take her mind off things. It was a beautiful instrument. She sat down on the stool before it and tried a scale with the soft pedal down and then went on to a rambling mixture of tunes, just as they came into her head. She played tolerably well, disregarding wrong notes and forgetting about the soft pedal but putting in a good deal of feeling. Halfway through a half remembered bit of *Eine Kleine Nachtmusik*, Fabian stalked in, taking her by surprise because he entered by the garden door behind her. She stopped at once, folded her hands tidily in her lap and waited to hear what he had to say.

'You are the most infuriating girl!' he began in a pleasantly conversational tone. 'I have apologised to my cousin; if I apologise to you will you be kind enough to listen to what I have to say?'

'Of course—though why...'

'Just listen. I apologise for a start, and now to other matter. It seems that Cousin Emma was so glad to have someone in the house who could handle my uncle that she took advantage of that fact. Unintentionally, I should add. In future you are to take what time you wish for yourself. I know that I can depend upon you to do what you can for Uncle Georgius if and when he becomes worse—I imagine Trouw will give you good warning of that, if it is possible. You are free to go where you wish, is that understood? Have you any money?'

'Not much.'

'I will arrange for you to have sufficient for your needs. I will also see Uncle Georgius and explain to him.'

Mary Jane got up and closed the piano. 'You won't upset him? He's such a dear, I like him.'

He gave her a considering look. 'So do I. If you care to do so, I will drive you over to the riding stables in half an hour and arrange for you to hire a mount.'

'I should like that—are we going in that Jag?'

Fabian looked surprised. 'Of course.' He opened the door and they went through together. 'You play well.'

'Thank you—I hope no one minds.'

'No one will mind.' They were in the hall again, where he left her to go to his uncle's room, and she went into the sitting room where his cousin greeted her in a melodramatic manner and a fresh flood of tears. She was still eulogising Fabian, Mary Jane and then Fabian again when the object of her praise walked in, bidding Mary Jane to fetch her coat and go with him—something she was glad to do, for much as she liked Cousin Emma, a little of her went a long way, especially when she was upset.

It was cold in the car, but she had tied her head in a scarf and Fabian had tucked a rug around her. She sat, exhilarated by the fresh air and their progress through the narrow country roads. The stables were a mile or so away; the journey seemed too short; for once Fabian was being pleasant—she allowed him to choose a quiet mare for her use with the secret resolve to pick out something a little more lively once he was safely back in Groningen—there was no use in annoying him over such a small matter, especially as he seemed disposed to be friendly, indeed he seemed in such a good frame of mind that she was emboldened to ask him how his work was going and whether he was still busy.

'Yes, just at the moment, but I shall be able to come over from time to time—in any case, there will be some papers for you to sign in a few days—some stocks I am transferring.' She looked a little blank and he went on smoothly, 'It seems to me to be somewhat of a paradox that you should trust me without question to attend to your affairs while at the same time you dislike me.'

She bit her lip and wished he wouldn't say things she couldn't answer. After a little thought, she said carefully, 'Well, I haven't much choice, have I?' and was annoyed when he laughed.

He went away after tea and she spent most of the evening trying to convince Jonkheer van der Blocq that just because she wanted to go out sometimes it didn't mean that she didn't like his company. She played three games of Racing Demon with him to prove her point.

The best time to go riding was in the morning. Mary Jane had an early breakfast and took the Mini over to the stables and rode for an hour. By the time she got back to the house, her host was awake and clamouring for her and his daughter was wanting her company. It worked very well, for they hardly noticed her absence, and she, refreshed by her morning exercise, felt prepared to be at their disposal for the rest of the day. And Fabian had telephoned each day too, to make sure that she was doing as he had asked, and she had answered truthfully enough that she was riding each day. Time enough to go to Groningen—at present the old gentleman needed her company, so did his daughter. She had no great opinion of herself, but she could see that the two of them rubbed each other up the wrong way, and a third party was necessary for peaceful living.

It was on her third morning's ride that she decided to ask for another horse; the mare was a nice beast, but a little slow. Without actually telling any fibs she managed to imply that Fabian had told her that she might make another choice if she wasn't quite pleased with the mare, and chose a bay, a spirited animal with a rolling eye and a little too big for her. But he went well and now that she had got the lie of the country she knew just where to take him—along the shore of the Leekstermeer, where there were trees and a good deal of undergrowth on either side of the unmade road. It was a dull morning, with the threat of rain—she had put on two sweaters and plaited her hair so that it would be out of the way, not caring at all if she should get wet. She reached the road to the lake and began to pick a way along the path she saw running beside it, looking about her as she did so. It was pretty there—not a patch on her own lake at home, but still charming and peaceful, even though the trees were bare of

leaves and the grass was rough. She and the bay am-
bled along, for there was time enough; she could canter back along the road presently, there would be no
traffic to speak of and there was an ample grass verge
if he should get restive.

They were on the point of turning to go back when
she became aware of horse's hooves behind her and
when she turned to look it was to see Fabian astride
a great roan, coming towards her at a canter. He rode
well, she noted. He also looked very angry, she noted
that too, and pulled in the bay with a resigned sigh.

His 'good morning' was icy, so she merely nodded
in reply and waited silently for him to speak.

'I picked out a good little mare for you. Why aren't
you riding her?' Mary Jane considered him thoughtfully. 'Well, I'm capable of choosing a mount, for one
thing. I'm sick to death of you treating me as though I
were a half-witted old maid you can barely bring yourself to be civil to!' She drew a swelling breath. 'And
another thing, you may be my guardian, but you don't
own me. I've a mind of my own.'

'And a temper, I see,' he observed dampingly. 'You
forget that I had no notion of how you rode. If I had allowed you to choose for yourself and you could barely
sit the beast and had taken a tumble, I should have done
less than my duty to you as your guardian.'

'Oh, pooh!' she tossed her head and the pigtail
swung over her shoulder.

'You look about ten years old,' he said unexpectedly, and smiled at her, 'Shall we cry a temporary
truce? I came out to see you; I have those papers ready

for you to sign and I wondered if you would like to come to Groningen for an hour or so.'

She eyed him with surprise. 'You mean you actually want me to go with you to Groningen?'

His voice was tinged with impatience. 'Yes. You see I'm being civil. We might even manage not to quarrel for a couple of hours.' He spoke without smiling now, his face turned away.

'Oh, very well,' she told him, knowing that her voice sounded ungracious, 'then I'd better go back.'

They rode back in silence. Only when they reached the stables did Fabian tell her quietly, 'I was mistaken, Mary Jane. You ride well.'

Chapter 4

Fabian had come in the Jaguar, so that Mary Jane, with an eye to the weather, tied a silk scarf over her head in place of the unbecoming hat, wishing she had had the sense to bring her sheepskin jacket with her. It was barely November but already cold, and an open car, although great fun, needed suitable clothes, but once they were on their way, she didn't feel cold at all; she glowed with excitement and pleasure. An outing would be delightful, especially if they could remain friends for an hour.

Her patient, in a mellow mood, had agreed to his daughter keeping him company for a short time, only begging Mary Jane to return at the earliest possible moment. His daughter had been rather more urgent in her request not to be left for longer than was absolutely necessary with her irascible parent; she had also given Mary Jane a shopping list of things which she declared she urgently needed. It was a miscellany of knitting wool, embroidery silks, Gentlemen's Relish, chocolate biscuits and a particular brand of bottled peach which could only be obtained at a certain shop in the city. Mary Jane accepted it obligingly, to have it taken from her at once by Fabian, who put it in his pocket with a brisk 'I'll see to these,' and an injunction to hurry herself up. So here she was, sitting snugly beside Fabian, who was making short work of the few miles to Groningen.

She found the city very fine, with its two big squares and its old buildings. Fabian, going slowly through the traffic, pointed out the imposing, towering spire of St Martin's church before he turned off the main street and into a tree-lined one, bisected by a canal. The houses here were patrician, flat-faced and massive, each of them with its great front door reached by a double flight of steps. The sound of the traffic came faintly down its length so that it was easy to hear the rustle of the wind in the trees' bare branches.

'This is beautiful,' declared Mary Jane with satisfaction.

Fabian stopped before one of the houses. 'Yes, I think so too. I'm glad you like it.'

'Is this the lawyer's house?' she asked him.

'No, it's mine. We'll go inside and get those papers dealt with.'

She hadn't thought much about where he lived and when she had, it had been a vague picture of some smallish town house. This mansion took her by surprise, and she was still more surprised when they went inside. The hall was long and narrow and panelled waist high, with rich red carpeting on its floor to cover the black and white of its marble. The wall chandeliers were exquisite and there were flowers on the wall table. She wanted to take a more leisurely look, but an elderly woman appeared from the back of the house, was introduced as Mevrouw Hol and swept her away to an elegantly appointed cloakroom, where she tidied her hair, did things to her face and left her outdoor things before being led to a room close by where Fabian was waiting for her.

She took it to be a study, as it was lined with bookshelves and its main furniture was a massive desk and an equally massive chair, but the chairs by the fire were of a comfortably normal size. Mary Jane took the one offered her and sighed with content; the room was warm and light and airy and quite, quite different from the over-furnished house in which Fabian's uncle lived.

He sat down at the desk now, saying: 'You won't mind having coffee here? We can see to these papers at the same time, they'll not take long.'

She drank her coffee and then, under his direction, signed the papers, each one of which he carefully explained to her before asking her to do so. When she had finished she said with faint apology, 'I'm sorry you've had all this extra work, but I suppose once it's seen to, you won't need to bother, any more.'

'On the contrary.' He didn't smile as he spoke and she felt chilled. 'If you have finished your coffee perhaps you would like to come with me and get Emma's shopping—and by the way, I believe that I promised

you some money for your own use.' He opened a
drawer in the desk and handed her a little bundle of
notes. 'There are a thousand gulden there. If you need
more, please ask me.'

She looked at him round-eyed. 'Whatever should I
want with all that money?'

He smiled faintly. 'I imagine that you will find
things to buy with it.'

She became thoughtful. 'Well, yes—there are one
or two things…'

He went back to his desk and silently handed her
a pad and pencil. A few minutes later she looked up.
'You know,' she informed him in surprise, 'I've made
quite a list.'

'I thought maybe you would. Would a store suit you
or do you want a boutique?'

She shot him a suspicious glance which he coun-
tered with a grave detachment. How did he know about
boutiques? she wondered, and assured him that a large
store would be much easier. 'I'll be as quick as I can,
she assured him.

'No need—I told Cousin Emma that we shouldn't
be back until after tea. We'll lunch out and you will
have hours of time.'

Mary Jane had forgotten how pleasant it was to go
shopping with plenty of money to spend. By the time
Fabian had worked his way through the list Emma had
given them, it was burning a hole in her purse, and
when Fabian left her outside a large store, assuring her
that most of the assistants spoke English and she had
nothing to worry about and that he would be waiting
for her in an hour's time, she could hardly wait to start

on a tour of inspection. Fabian had been right, there was no difficulty in making herself understood; everyone seemed to speak English. She bought everything which she had written on her list and a good deal besides, and when, strolling through the hat department, she saw a velvet beret which would go very well with her coat, she bought that too and, a little drunk with the success of her shopping, put it on.

She was only ten minutes late at the store entrance and when she would have apologised to Fabian for keeping him waiting he said to surprise her, 'Late? Are you? I never expected you back within the hour and a half—we agreed upon an hour, if you remember. We'll have lunch and if you have anything else to buy you can get it later.'

They lunched at the Hotel Baulig, and as they were both hungry they started the meal with *erwtensoep*— a thick pea soup enriched with morsels of bacon and ham and sausage, went on to a dish of salmon with asparagus tips and quenelles of sole, and having finished this delicacy, agreed upon fresh fruit salad to round off their lunch. They sat a considerable time over their coffee, for rather to Mary Jane's surprise, they found plenty to talk about, and although she thought Fabian rather reserved in his manner, at least he was agreeable.

They did a little more shopping after they left the hotel, for it seemed sense to her to buy one or two presents while she had the opportunity. It was when she had declared herself satisfied with her purchases that Fabian remarked, 'But you have bought nothing for yourself.'

'Yes, I have, lots of things—and a hat.' She waited for him to notice the beret and was deeply mortified when he said: 'Oh, did you? Why don't you wear it, then?' He glanced at their parcels. 'It must be a very small one, there's nothing here which looks like a hat bag.'

She boiled, but silently. She wasn't sure if he was teasing her or if he took so little notice of her that he hadn't even noticed what she was wearing. Neither of these ideas were very complimentary to herself. She answered with a sweetness which any of her closer friends would have suspected, 'I know where it is. I think I've finished, thank you. I expect you would like to be getting back to Midwoude.'

He gave her a searching look. 'Why?'

'Well, you've done your good deed for today, haven't you?' Her voice was light despite his look.

'Indeed yes, and it's made me thirsty. Shall we have tea somewhere?'

She kept her voice light. 'No, thank you. I think I should like to go back now. I'm most grateful to you...'

His tone was curt. 'Spare the thanks,' he begged her coldly, and thereafter sustained an ultra-polite conversation during their short journey back to Midwoude where he handed her and her packages over to Jaap, wished her a distant good evening, got back into his car and drove away, a great deal too fast.

Emma van der Blocq, pouring a late tea in the small room at the back of the house where the two of them sometimes sat, professed surprise as Mary Jane joined her. 'I didn't expect you back until much later,' she declared happily, 'but surely Fabian could have stayed for tea—even for dinner?' She interrupted herself. 'No, perhaps not for dinner—he goes out a good deal, you know. Where did you have lunch, Mary Jane?'

She remembered the name of the hotel and felt rather pleased with herself about it, and Cousin Emma nodded, her interest aroused.

'A very nice place. Of course he really prefers the Hotel at Warffrum—Borg de Breedenburg—but that is for his more romantic outings.' She smiled at Mary Jane. 'He has girl-friends, as you can imagine—I wonder why he didn't take you there?'

'I imagine,' said Mary Jane in a dry little voice, 'that I don't qualify for a romantic background.'

'No, perhaps not,' agreed her companion with disconcerting directness. 'Fabian only takes out very pretty girls, you know—and always beautifully dressed, as you can imagine.' She smiled again, quite oblivious of any feelings Mary Jane might possess. 'He's a most observant man.'

'You surprise me,' said Mary Jane waspishly, thinking of the lovely velvet beret he hadn't even noticed. 'And now I'll just go up and see how Jonkheer van der Blocq is. Did he have a quiet day?'

Her companion's face crumpled ominously. 'Oh, my dear, however did I manage before you came? He was so cross, and he refused to take his pills. Doctor Trouw will be here presently and he will be so annoyed.' She sounded so upset that Mary Jane paused on her way to the door.

'He's far too nice to get cross with you,' she assured her, 'and he knows that it isn't always easy...'

Emma's face broke into a simper. 'Oh yes, he is

so good… I've known him for years, you know, long before he married. His wife died last year. She was a quiet little thing—no looks at all. You remind me of her.'

To which remark Mary Jane could think of no answer at all. She escaped through the door and spent the rest of the evening with the old gentleman, who seemed delighted to see her again and to her great relief made no remarks at all about her face or her lack of looks.

It turned a great deal colder the next day, but Mary Jane went riding just the same, bundled in several sweaters against the wind, and returning to the house with glowing cheeks and a sparkle in her eyes. Of Fabian there was no sign, but that didn't surprise her— why should he come anyway? He had only visited the house because he needed some papers signed—it certainly wasn't for her company. Let him use his leisure escorting the beauties of Groningen to romantic dinners, she thought, her lip curling, and then her mood changed and she fell to thinking how very satisfactory it would be if she could be escorted to this hotel Emma had been so enthusiastic about, wearing the organza dress. She sighed and prodded her mount to quicken his pace. Chance was a fine thing, she told him, as they turned for home.

She had her chance the very next day, as it turned out, for when Doctor Trouw called he brought his son with him. A pleasant young man in his twenties, he had recently qualified and was about to join his father's practice. Over coffee he remarked, 'You are stranger here, I don't suppose you go out very much. I should like to take you out to dinner one evening.'

Mary Jane accepted with alacrity, and when, to her delight, he suggested that he should take her to Hotel Borg de Breedenborg on the following evening, she agreed with flattering speed.

She spent the intervening time imagining herself sweeping into the restaurant while Fabian, already there with some girl, would be bowled over by the sight of her in the organza, prettied up for the evening. The urge to shake him out of his cool, casual attitude towards herself was growing very strong, it caused her to take twice as long as usual in her preparations for the evening, which were so effective that when she went along to see her patient before they left, he was constrained to remark upon her changed appearance, as indeed was Cousin Emma, who rather tactlessly remarked that she hardly recognised Mary Jane in her finery.

Willem was rather nice and she was determined to have a pleasant evening. As they drove to the hotel she set herself to draw him out with a few well-chosen questions about his work. It wasn't until they reached the hotel that she was struck by the thought that her chance of seeing Fabian was small indeed. Even if he had a host of girl-friends, he surely didn't dine there every evening. He had his work—presumably that kept him busy, and surely he must spend some of his evenings at home, catching up on his reading, writing, even operating when it was necessary. She left her coat, patted the hair which had taken so long to put up and determinedly dismissed him from her head as she rejoined Willem.

The restaurant was full and she realized with something of a shock that it was already Saturday again—a whole week since she had seen Fabian. She sat down opposite her companion, gave him a brilliant smile and glanced around her. Fabian was sitting quite near their table, and the girl he was with was just as lovely as she had imagined she would be. Mary Jane turned the brilliance of her smile into a polite, tight-lipped one as she caught his eye and turned her attention to Willem, who, once they had ordered, launched into an earnest description of his days, hour by hour, almost minute by minute. She strove to keep an interested expression on her face, and when it was possible, laughed gaily, so that Fabian, whom she hadn't looked at again, would see how much she was enjoying herself. It was a pity that Fabian and his companion should go while they themselves were only half way through dinner. He paused as they passed the table, his hand on the girl's arm. He said austerely, 'I'm glad to see that you are enjoying yourself, Mary Jane,' nodded briefly to Willem and went on his way. Mary Jane watched him smile down at the girl as they went through the door and then wondered briefly where they were going, and then concentrated on Willem, who had started to tell her at great length about a girl he had met at his hospital. She obviously occupied his thoughts to a large extent; by the time he had finished, Mary Jane even knew the size of her shoes.

They went back to the house at a reasonable hour because, as Willem reminded her, his father, who was

dining with Cousin Emma and keeping an eye on her
father at the same time, needed a good night's sleep.
He took his farewell of her half an hour later with the
hope that they might spend another evening together
before she returned to England, and Mary Jane, thanking him nicely, wondered how she could possibly have
been interested in him, even for such a short time; he
was so very worthy, and looking back on their evening
she could remember no conversation at all on her part,
merely a succession of 'really's' and 'fancy that's' and
'you don't say so's'. When he and his father had gone
she gave Cousin Emma a potted version of her evening because she could see that the lady had no intention of allowing her to go to bed until she had done so,
and then she went to Jonkheer van der Blocq's room to
see if he had settled for the night. Somehow or other,
he had contrived not to take his sleeping tablet, which
necessitated her arguing gently with him for the best
part of ten minutes, but when he had finally consented
to do as she asked and she had turned his pillows and
settled him nicely, he enquired after her evening, observing in no uncertain manner that he found Willem
a dull fellow, which naturally had the effect of her replying that he had been a very interesting companion,
that the dinner had been delicious, and that he had
asked her out again.

'What did you talk about?' growled the old man.

'Oh, his work, naturally. And a girl he met while
he was in hospital—he's very taken with her. He—
talked a lot about her.'

Jonkheer van der Blocq laughed until he had no
breath. Mary Jane gave him a drink, told him se-

verely that there was nothing to laugh about, wished him good night and presently went to bed herself. She hadn't mentioned to anyone that Fabian had been at the hotel too, and she didn't think she would.

He came the next morning while they were in church, and this time it was the Rolls parked outside the door when they returned. As they went in he came downstairs, wished them a pleasant good morning, agreed that a cup of coffee would be welcome and when Emma had disappeared kitchenwards to find someone to make it, turned to Mary Jane and invited her to enter the sitting room.

'I'll take my things upstairs first,' she told him coldly, and was frustrated by his instant offer to take her coat, which he tossed on to a chair.

'It can stay there for a moment,' he told her rather impatiently. 'I see you are wearing the new hat. It's pretty—so you found it.'

She gave him a frosty look and said witheringly, 'It wasn't difficult, it was on my head.'

The dark wings of his brows soared. 'Oh dear—I can see that I must apologise, my dear girl, and I do. I could make a flowery speech, but you would make mincemeat of it, so I'll just say that I'm sorry.'

She walked away from him into the sitting room, where she sat down, telling herself indignantly that she didn't care if he followed her or not. He took the chair opposite hers and stretched his long legs and studied her carefully.

'You wouldn't believe me if I say how charming you looked yesterday evening?' he asked mildly.

'No.' She added nastily, 'You haven't a clue as to what I was wearing.'

His smile mocked her. 'Sea green, or would you call it sea blue, something thin and silky. It had long sleeves with frills over your wrists and a frill under your chin and a row of buttons down the back of the bodice.'

She was astounded, but she managed to say with a tinge of sarcasm:

'A photographic eye, I see,' and then because her female curiosity had got the better of her good sense. 'The girl you were with was lovely.'

He picked a tiny thread from a well-tailored sleeve. 'Delightfully so. She wears a different wig every day of the week and the longest false eyelashes I have ever seen.'

Mary Jane turned a chuckle into a cough. 'And why not? It's the fashion. Besides, she would look gorgeous in anything she chose to put on.'

He agreed placidly. 'And you found William Trouw entertaining?' he asked suavely.

'We had a very pleasant evening,' she told him guardedly.

'A worthy young man,' went on her companion ruminatively. 'He would make a good husband—do you fancy him?'

She choked. 'Well, of all the things to say! I've been out with him once, and here you are, talking as though...'

He went on just as though she had never interrupted him. 'He has a good practice with his father, so he wouldn't be after your money, and I imagine he has all the attributes of a good husband—good-natured, no interest in drinking or betting, or girls, for that matter—a calm disposition, he…'

She ground her teeth. 'Be quiet! You may be my guardian, but you shan't talk like that. I'll marry whom I please and when I want to, and until then you can mind your own business!'

'From which outburst I conclude that Willem hasn't won your heart?'

She wanted to laugh, but she choked it back. 'No, he hasn't. As a matter of fact he spent quite a long time telling me about a girl he knew in hospital. I think he intends to marry her.'

'Ah, I wondered what it was that you found so interesting, though surely it was unkind of you to laugh so much during the recital?'

'I didn't…' she began, and stopped, because of course she had, so that Fabian should think she was having a lovely time. 'I enjoyed myself very much,' she muttered peevishly, and was glad to see Cousin Emma and Jaap with the coffee tray, coming into the room.

Fabian stayed for lunch, and his uncle insisted upon coming down to join them, contributing to the conversation with such gusto that Mary Jane feared for his blood pressure. But at least he was so tired after his meal that she had no difficulty in persuading him to take his customary nap, and when she had tucked him up and come downstairs again it was to find that Emma had allowed herself to be driven over to Doctor Trouw's house for tea. Which left her and Fabian. He was waiting for her in the hall and he sounded impatient.

'Shall we have a walk before tea?'

Mary Jane paused at the bottom of the staircase. 'Thank you, no. I have letters to write.'

'Which you can write at any time.' He came towards her. 'It's not often I'm here.'

'Oh—should I mind?'

'Don't be an impudent girl, and don't imagine it is because I want your company,' he added quite violently. 'I had a letter from Mr North asking me to explain certain aspects of your inheritance to you, so I might just as well do it and take some exercise at the same time.'

'Charming!' observed Mary Jane, her eyes snapping with temper, 'and so good of you to fit me in with one of your more healthy activities.'

'And what,' he asked awfully, 'exactly do you mean by that remark?'

'Just exactly what I say. I'll come for half an hour— in that time you should be able to tell me whatever I'm supposed to know.'

She crossed the hall and picked up her coat, caught up her gloves and went to the pillow cupboard, rummaged around in its depths until she found a scarf which she tied carelessly over her hair. 'Ready,' she said with a distinct snap.

They walked away from the village, into the teeth of a mean wind, while Fabian talked about stocks and shares and gilt-edged securities and capital gains tax to all of which she lent only half an ear. As far as she could see she would have a perfectly adequate income whatever he and Mr North decided to do with her money. As long as she had sufficient to run the house and pay for Mrs Body and Lily and have some over to run the car and buy clothes… She stopped suddenly and told him so.

'You are not only a tiresome girl, you are also a very ungrateful one,' Fabian informed her bitterly.

'I'm sorry—about being ungrateful, I mean, but I can't remember being tiresome—was it on any particular occasion?'

He sounded quite weary. 'You are tiresome all the time,' he told her, which surprised her so much that she walked in silence until he observed that since she wished to return to Midwoude within half an hour, they had better go back. They didn't speak at all, and in the hall they parted. When Mary Jane came downstairs ten minutes later, it was to find that he had gone. She told herself with a little surge of rage that it was a good thing too, for when they were together they did nothing but disagree. She wandered across to the sitting room, telling herself again, this time out loud, that she was delighted, and added the hope that she wouldn't see him for simply ages.

But it wasn't simply ages, it was the following Wednesday, or rather three o'clock on Thursday morning. Jonkheer van der Blocq had had, for him, a very good day. They had played their usual game of cards, and she had helped him to bed, just a little worried because his colour was bad. But Doctor Trouw had called that afternoon, and although the old gentleman was failing rapidly now, he had seen no cause for immediate alarm. Mary Jane went to bed early, first taking another look at her patient. He was asleep, and there was nothing to justify her unease.

The peal of the bell wakened her. She bundled on her dressing gown, and not waiting to put her feet in slippers, ran across the dim landing. The old man was lying very much as she had left him, but now his colour was livid, although he said with his usual irascibility, 'I feel most peculiar—I want Fabian here at once.'

She murmured soothingly while she took a frighteningly weak pulse and studied his tired old face before she went to the telephone. It was quite wrong to ring up in front of the patient, but she didn't dare leave him. She rang Doctor Trouw first, with a suitably guarded request for him to come, and then dialled Fabian's number. His voice, calm and clear over the line, gave her the instant feeling that she didn't need to worry about anything because he was there—she forgot that they weren't on speaking terms, that he was arrogant and treated her like a tiresome child. She said simply, 'Oh, Fabian—will you come at once? Your uncle'—she paused, aware that the bed's occupant was listening—'would like to speak to you,' she finished.

'He's listening?'

'Yes.'

'I'll be with you in fifteen minutes. Get Trouw.'

'I have.'

'Good girl! Get Jaap up and tell him to open the gates and the door. Get Emma up too—no, wait—tell Jaap to do that. You stay with my uncle.'

She said, 'Yes, Fabian,' and put down the receiver. 'Fabian's on his way,' she told Jonkheer van der Blocq in a calm, reassuring voice. 'I'm to wake Jaap so that he can open the gates. Stay just as you are—I'll only be a few moments.'

Doctor Trouw came a few minutes later, and in response to the old gentleman's demand to be given something to keep him going, gave him an injection, told him to save his breath in the understanding voice of an old friend and went to Emma's room, where she could be heard crying very loudly.

Mary Jane pulled up a chair to the bedside, tucked her cold feet under her and took Jonkheer van der Blocq's hand in hers. 'Fabian won't be long,' she told him again, because she sensed that was what he wanted above anything else. She certainly was justified, because a moment later she heard the soft, powerful murmur of the Rolls' engine and the faint crunch of its tyres as Fabian stopped outside the front door.

He entered the room without haste, wearing a thick sweater and slacks and looking very wide awake. He said: 'Hullo, Uncle Georgius,' and nodded to Mary Jane, his dark, bright gaze taking in the dressing-gown, the plaited hair and her bare feet. He said kindly, 'What a girl you are for forgetting your slippers! Go and put them on, it's cold, and tell Trouw I'm here, will you. I don't suppose he heard me come, with the row Emma's making.'

His uncle made a weak, explosive sound. 'Silly woman,' he said, in a voice suddenly small, 'always crying—you'll keep an eye on her, Fabian?'

'Of course.' He lapsed into Dutch as Mary Jane reached the door.

Emma was in no state to be left alone; Mary Jane stayed with her as Doctor Trouw hurried across the landing, and was still with her when he came back to tell them that his patient was dead. It wasn't until

poor Emma had had something to send her to sleep,
and Mary Jane had tucked her up in bed, that she felt
free to leave her.

The old house was very quiet; there was a murmur of voices coming from the kitchen, and still more
voices behind the closed door of the small sitting
room. She stood in the hall, wondering if she should
go back to bed, a little uncertain as to what Doctor
Trouw might expect of her. It was chilly in the hall and
the tick-tock of the over-elaborate French grandfather
dripped into the stillness with an oily sloth which she
found intensely irritating. A cup of tea would have
been nice, she thought despondently, and turned to
go back upstairs just as the sitting room door opened
and Fabian said: 'Ah, there you are. Come in—Jaap's
bringing tea.' He glanced at her pale face. 'You look
as though you need it. Cousin Emma's asleep?'

She nodded, then sat down in a chair by the still
burning fire and drank her tea, listening to the two
men talking and saying very little herself. When she
had finished she got to her feet. 'Is there anything you
would like me to do?' she asked.

Doctor Trouw shook his head. 'The district nurse
will be here very shortly. Go to bed, Mary Jane, and
get some sleep. I am most grateful to you for all you
have done and I will ask you to do something else.
Would you look after Emma for a few days? She has
a very sensitive nature and I am afraid this will be too
much for her—I will leave something for her, if you
will give it when she wakes, and be round about lunch
time to see how she is.'

She nodded, thinking that Cousin Emma would be

even more difficult than her father, and went to the door which Fabian had opened for her. He followed her into the hall, shutting the door behind him, and she turned round tiredly to see what he wanted.

His voice was quiet. 'I know what you are thinking. We have imposed upon you and we have no right but I too would be grateful if you would stay just for little while and help Emma—she likes you and she needs you.'

She said shortly, 'Oh, that's all right. Of course I'll stay.

He came nearer. 'You have had a lot to bear in the last few weeks, Mary Jane. Once I called you a tiresome girl. I apologise.' He bent and kissed her cheek with a gentleness which disturbed her more than any of the harsh words he had uttered in the past. She went upstairs, not answering his good night.

The next few days were a peculiar medley of intense activity, doing all the things Cousin Emma insisted should be done; receiving visitors, whose hushed voices and platitudes caused her to sit in floods of tears for hours after they had gone; going to Groningen to buy the black garments she considered essential and relating, seemingly endlessly, her father's perfections to Mary Jane, while crying herself sick again.

Mary Jane found it all a little difficult to stomach— father and daughter had hardly had a happy relationship while he was alive, now that he was dead he had somehow become a kind of saint. But she liked Emma, although she found her histrionics a little trying, and she did what she could to keep her as calm as possible, addressed countless envelopes and kept out of Fabian's way as much as possible.

He came frequently, but her quick ears, tuned to the gentle hum of the Rolls-Royce or the exuberant roar of the Jaguar, gave her warning enough to slip away while he was in the house. But one evening she had made the mistake of supposing that he had left the house; it was almost dinner time and there was no sound of voices from either of the sitting rooms. He must have gone, she decided, while she had been up in the attic, packing away Jonkheer van der Blocq's clothes until such time as his daughter found herself capable of deciding what to do with them. The small sitting room was dimly lit by the firelight and one lamp, and Freule van der Blocq was lying asleep on the sofa. Fabian was on one of the easy chairs, his legs thrust out before him, contemplating the ceiling, but he got up as Mary Jane started to leave the room as silently and quickly as she had entered it. Outside in the hall he demanded: 'Where have you been?'

'Upstairs in the attics, sorting your uncle's clothes.'

'Have you, by God? Surely there's someone else to such work? And that was not what I meant. Where have you been? Whenever I come, I am conscious of your disappearing footsteps. Do you dislike me so much?'

She eyed him thoughtfully. 'I never think about it,' she said at length, not quite truthfully.

His expressive eyebrows rose. 'No? You thought I had gone?'

'Yes.'

He grinned. 'I'm staying to dinner, and now you're

here there's no point in retreating, is there? We'll have a glass of sherry.'

She accompanied him to the big sitting room and sat down composedly while he poured their drinks. When he had settled himself near her he asked, 'When do you want to go home?'

'I should like to go as soon as the funeral is over. I understand that Emma is going away the day after—I could leave at the same time.' She sipped her sherry. 'If you would be kind enough to let me have some more money, I can see about getting my ticket.'

'No need. I shall take you with the car.'

She kept her voice reasonable. 'I don't want to go in your car. I'm quite capable of looking after myself, you know. Besides, you have your work.' She looked at him, saw his smouldering gaze bent upon her and added hastily, 'I'm very grateful, but I can't let you waste any more time on me.'

'Have I ever complained that I was wasting my time on you?'

'No—but one senses these things.'

He gave a crack of laughter. 'One might be mistaken. Would you feel better about it if I told you that I have to go over to England anyway within the next few days—I'm only offering you a lift.'

She said doubtfully, 'Really? Well, that's different, I'll be glad to go with you.'

She missed the gleam in his eyes. 'Tuesday, then. Cousin Emma will be fetched by her friends after breakfast. I'll come for you about four o'clock. I've a ward round to do in the morning and a couple of patients to see after that. We'll go from Rotterdam, I think straight to Hull.' He thought for a minute. 'If we leave here after tea we shall have plenty of time to catch the ferry at Europort. If I'm not here by half past four, have tea and be ready to leave, will you?'

'Certainly.'

'You'll want to telephone Mrs Body.' He strolled across the room and picked up the receiver from the telephone on the delicate serpentine table between the windows. 'What is the number?'

It was nice to hear Mrs Body's motherly voice again. Mary Jane listened to her comfortable comments and felt a wave of homesickness sweep over her. It would be lovely to be home again. She told Mrs Body her news and heard that lady's voice asking if the dear doctor would be staying. Mary Jane hadn't thought about that. She repeated the enquiry and he turned to look at her. 'I began to think you weren't going to ask me,' he remarked mildly. 'A day or so, if I may.'

Mrs Body sighed in a satisfied manner when Mary Jane told her. 'That will be nice,' she said as she rang off, leaving Mary Jane wondering how much truth there was in that remark. Probably they would quarrel again before his visit was over, and there was nothing nice about that.

But at least they didn't quarrel that evening, tacit consent, they allied to keep Cousin Emma interested and amused, and succeeded so well that she didn't cry once and went to bed quite cheerful. Mary Jane, quite tired herself, went to bed early too and closed her eyes on the thought that when Fabian wished, he could be a most agreeable companion.

* * *

She saw little of him until Tuesday, when Cousin Emma, vowing eternal thanks, was packed off to stay with her friends and Mary Jane found herself alone in the house except for Jaap and the cook. The morning passed slowly enough because she had nothing much to do but go for a walk, but after her solitary lunch she settled down with a book until four o'clock, when she did her face and hair once more, got Jaap to bring down her case and went to the window to watch for the car. It didn't come; it hadn't come by half past four either. She had her tea, punctuated by frequent visits to the window, and when she had finished, put on her outdoor things, made sure that she had every thing with her, and sat down to wait. It was a quarter to six when the car's headlights lighted up the drive. She went into the hall to meet him, saying without any hint of the impatience she felt: 'You'd like a cup of tea, wouldn't you? I asked Jaap to be ready with one.'

'Good girl. I missed lunch—an emergency—I was called back to theatre.'

She was already on her way to the kitchen. 'I'll get some sandwiches.' She paused. 'I hope it was a success.'

'I think so—we shan't be certain for a couple of days.'

She nodded understandingly as she went, to return very soon with a tray of tea and buttered toast, sandwiches and cake. She poured the tea, gave him his toast and sat down again. Presently he said:

'You're very restful—not one reproach for being late, or missing the boat or where have I been.'

'Well, it wouldn't help much if I did, would it?' she wanted to know in a matter-of-fact voice. 'Besides, there's time enough, isn't there? The Rolls goes like a bomb, doesn't she, and the ferry doesn't leave until about midnight.'

'Sensible Miss Pettigrew! But I had planned a leisurely dinner on the way. Now it will have to be a hurried one.'

She smiled at him without malice. 'That won't matter much, will it? Now if I'd been the girl you were with the other night, that would be quite a different kettle of fish...'

He put down his cup slowly. 'You're a great one for the unvarnished truth, aren't you?'

She got up and went over to the big gilt-framed mirror at the opposite end of the room and twitched the beret to a more becoming angle.

'Seeing that we have to deal with each other until I'm thirty,' she said in a tranquil voice, 'we might as well be truthful with each other, even if nothing else.'

'Nothing else what?' He spoke sharply.

She went to pour him a second cup. 'Nothing,' she told him.

They set out shortly afterwards. It was a cold dark evening and the road was almost free of traffic and Fabian sent the car tearing along on the first stage of their journey. He showed no signs of tiredness but sat relaxed behind the wheel—it was a pity it wasn't light, he told her, for they were going to Rotterdam down the other side of the Ijsselmeer, and she would have been able to see a little more of Holland. Mary Jane agreed with him and they sat in silence as they ripped through the flat landscape. Only when they reached Alkmaar and slowed to go through its narrow streets did he say, 'I'm poor company. I'm sorry.'

'The case this afternoon?' she ventured, to be rewarded by his surprised, 'How did you guess? Would it bore you if I told you about it?'

She wasn't bored; she listened with interest and intelligence and asked the right questions in the right places. They were approaching Rotterdam when he said finally, 'Thank you for listening so well—I can't think of any other girl to whom I would have talked like that.'

She felt a little pang of pure pleasure and tried to think of something to say, but couldn't.

They had their dinner in haste at the Old Dutch restaurant, and Mary Jane, seeing how tired Fabian looked, did her utmost to keep the conversation of a nature which could provoke no difference of opinion between them, and succeeded so well that they boarded the ferry on the friendliest of terms.

The journey was uneventful but rough, but they were both too tired to bother about the weather. They met at breakfast and she was delighted to find that his humour was still a good one. Perhaps now that they wouldn't be seeing much of each other, he was prepared to unbend a little. She accompanied him down to the car deck, hoping that this pleasant state of affairs would last.

It didn't, at least only until they reached the Lakes to receive a rapturous welcome from Mrs Body and sit down to one of her excellent teas. They had barely begun the meal when Mary Jane stated, 'I intend to buy a horse tomorrow.'

'No, you won't.' Fabian spoke unhurriedly and with old finality.

She opened her eyes wide. 'Haven't I enough money?' she demanded.

'Don't make ridiculous statements like that—you have plenty of money. If you want a mount, I'll come with you, and you will allow me to choose the animal.'

'No, I won't! I can ride, you know I can.'

'Nevertheless, you will do as I ask, but before you start spending your money there are one or two details to attend to, I must ask you to come with me to the bank at Keswick, and Mr North will be coming here tomorrow morning. He will bring the last of the papers for you to sign, and as from then your income will be paid into your account each quarter. Should you need more money, you will have to advise me and I will advance it from the estate, should I consider it necessary.'

She boiled with rage. 'Consider it? It's ridiculous— it's like being a child, having to ask you for everything I want!'

He remained unmoved by her outburst. 'How inaccurate you are! You have more than sufficient to live on in comfort, and as long as you keep within your income, you will have no need to apply to me.'

She snorted, 'I should hope not—I'd rather be a pauper!'

'Even more inaccurate.'

There seemed no more to be said; she wasn't disposed to say that she was sorry and she could see that such an intention on his part hadn't even crossed his mind. He excused himself presently and she saw him cleaning the Rolls at the back of the house. From a distance he looked nice. He was a handsome man, she had to admit, and amusing when he wished to be, and kind; only, she told herself darkly, when one got to know him better did one discover what an ill-tempered, arrogant, unsympathetic… She ran out of adjectives.

He stayed two more days, coldly polite, unfailingly courteous and as withdrawn as though they were complete strangers forced to share a small slice of life together. She told herself that she was glad to see him go as the Rolls went through the gate and disappeared down the road to Keswick. He hadn't turned round to wave, either, and he must have known that she was standing in the porch. His goodbye had been casual in the extreme and he had made no mention of their future meeting. Mary Jane stormed back into the house, very put out and banged the door behind her, telling Major in a loud angry voice that life would be heaven without him.

Chapter 5

It was heaven for three or four days, during which Mary Jane explored the house from attic to cellar, examining with affection the small treasures her grandfather had possessed and which were now hers. She worked in the garden too, sweeping the leaves from the frosty ground, and went walking each day beside the lake with Major. It was cold now, and the snow had crept further down the mountains, but the sun still shone. She drove to Keswick, and to Carlisle to see Mr North, reflecting that it would have been marvelous weather for riding. But she had stubbornly refused to allow Fabian to choose a horse for her, and only after he had pressed the matter had she said that she wouldn't buy one at all if she couldn't have her own way; a decision she was regretting, for she had cut off her nose to spite her face, and a lot of good it had done her.

He hadn't even bothered to write to her—out of sight, out of mind, she muttered bitterly to herself, quite forgetting that she had hardly contributed to increase any desire on his part to have any more to do with her other than businesswise. It was that night, as she lay in bed very much awake, that she made the astonishing discovery that she actually missed him. She examined this from all angles and decided finally that it was because his extreme bossiness had imposed itself far too firmly upon her mind. Well, she was free of him now. She had a house of her own and what seemed to her to be quite a fortune—she could do exactly what she liked, whether he liked it or not—and she would too. She fell asleep making rather wild plans.

She found herself, as the days passed, filling them rather feverishly, quite often doing things which didn't need doing at all, taking walks which became increasingly longer, making excuses to get out the Mini and drive into Cockermouth or Keswick, and although she was happy she was lonely too, missing the rush and bustle of hospital life. In a few short weeks it would be Christmas and she wondered what to do about it. She hadn't a relation in the world whom she knew of and her friends were miles away in London, and what was more, they wouldn't be free over Christmas—nurses seldom were. She wondered what her grandfather and Mrs Body had done in previous years and went to ask that good lady, who chuckled gently and said:

'Well, Miss Mary Jane, not a great deal—your grandfather liked his turkey and his Christmas pudding, and his friends came in for a drink. When he was younger, he used to give a dinner party—even have a few of his closer friends to stay, but they've died or gone away. The last few years have been a bit quiet.' She looked a little wistful. 'I suppose you haven't any friends who could come—a few jolly young people?'

Mary Jane explained about nurses not getting holidays at Christmas and Mrs Body said: 'Well, there's Doctor Morris, and there's Commander Willis—he's a very old friend of your grandfather's, but Lily was telling me that he's not been so well lately...'

They stared at each other, empty of ideas and a little depressed. The sound of a car turning into the drive sent them both into the hall to peer out of the small window beside the front door. 'It'll be that nice Doctor van der Blocq,' breathed Mrs Body happily, 'Oh, how lovely if it is!'

Mary Jane was looking out of the window; if it was keen disappointment she felt when she saw that the car was an Alfa Romeo and the man getting out of it wasn't Fabian, she was quite unaware of it. The man was a stranger, young, fair and not very tall. He seemed to be in no hurry to ring the bell but stood staring at the house and then turned his attention to the garden. Only when he had looked his fill did he advance towards the door. As he rang the bell Mary Jane retreated to the sitting room, waving an urgent hand at Mrs Body. She just had time to sit down in her grandfather's chair and take up the morning paper before the housekeeper, after the shortest of colloquies, put her head round the door. She looked surprised and excited.

'A young gentleman to see you, Miss Mary Jane. Mr Pettigrew from Canada.'

Mary Jane cast down the paper and goggled at her. 'Mr Pettigrew?' Enlightenment struck her. 'Do you suppose he's the cousin—the Canadian cousin—did he say?'

Mrs Body shook her head. 'He wants to see you.'

Mary Jane went into the hall. The young man was standing by the wall table, one of the Georgian candlesticks which rested upon it in his hands, examining it carefully.

She frowned. Even if he were a relation, it was hardly good manners to examine the silver for hallmarks the moment he entered the house. She said coolly, a question in her voice: 'Good morning?'

He put the candlestick down without any trace of embarrassment and crossed the hall, smiling at her, and she found herself smiling back at him, although her first impression of him hadn't been a good one. When he spoke it was with a rich Canadian accent.

'You must think I've got an infernal cheek…' He paused and widened his smile, and Mary Jane, a little on her guard now, allowed her own to fade, but this didn't deter him from continuing: 'I'm a Pettigrew—Mervyn John Pettigrew. My grandfather was your grandfather's cousin—he talked a lot about him when he was alive.' He put a hand into his pocket and withdrew a passport. 'I don't expect you to take me on trust—take a look at this.' And as she stretched out a hand to take it, 'You're Mary Jane, aren't you? I know all about you too.'

She glanced at the passport and gave it back, studying his face. She could see no family likeness, but probably there wouldn't be any; his mother had been a Canadian; he might take after her side of the family. She said quietly, 'How do you do? Why are you here?'

'We get the English papers—I saw a notice of my great-uncle's death. I had a holiday owing to me, so I decided to fly over and look you up.' He smiled again—he smiled too much, she thought irritably. 'My old man's dead—died two years ago. Mother died when I was a boy, and I'm the only Pettigrew left at home, so I thought I'd look you up.' He gave her a searching glance. 'I don't blame you for not quite believing me, despite the passport. If you'd give me ten minutes, though, I could tell you enough about the family to convince you.'

He had light eyes, a little too close together, but his look was direct enough. Mary Jane said on an impulse. 'Come in—I was just going to have coffee. Will you have a cup with me?'

She was bound to admit, at the end of ten minutes, that he must be a genuine cousin. After all, her grandfather had told her often enough that the nephew in Canada had a son—this would be he; he knew too much about the family to be anything else. And when he produced some letters written by her grandfather to his own father, there could be no further doubt. True, he didn't give them to her to read, but he showed her the address and the signature at the end, explaining. 'Great-uncle was very fond of my grandfather, you know—he was always making plans to visit him. He never did, of course, but he had a real affection for him—Dad was always talking about him too. Have you still got Major?'

Her last misgivings left her. She said with cautious friendliness:

'Yes—he's eleven, though, and getting a bit slow. He's in the kitchen with Mrs Body. Would you like to stay to lunch? Are you passing through or staying somewhere here?'

He accepted the invitation with an open pleasure which won her over completely. 'I'm touring around, having a look at all the places the old man told me about. I'm staying at Keswick and very comfortable.'

'Did you bring your car?' She corrected herself. 'No, of course you couldn't if you flew.'

'I've rented one.' And when he added nothing further she suggested that they should walk down to the lake. Their stroll was an unqualified success, partly because Mary Jane, who wasn't used to men—younger men, at any rate—taking any notice of her, found that not only did her companion listen to her when she spoke, but implied in his replies that she was worth listening to as well, and the glances he gave her along with the replies gave her the pleasant feeling that perhaps she wasn't quite as plain a girl as she had believed. It was a pity, she reflected, while the young man waxed enthusiastic over the scenery, that Fabian wasn't with them so that he could see for himself that not everyone shared his opinion of her. The horrid word tiresome flashed through her mind; it was amazing how it still rankled. A vivid picture of his face—austere, faintly mocking and handsome—floated before her mind's eye. She dismissed it and turned to answer Mervyn Pettigrew's eager questions about the house and its history.

She told him all she knew, studying him anew as she did so. He had good looks, she conceded, spoiled a little by the eyes and a mouth too small—and perhaps his chin lacked determination, although, as she quickly reminded herself, after several weeks of Fabian's resolute features, she was probably unfairly influenced, but these were small faults in an otherwise pleasing countenance. She judged him to be twenty-five or six, thick-set for his height and age. His clothes were right—country tweeds and well-polished shoes. On the whole she was prepared to reverse her first hasty impression of him, and admit that he might be rather nice. It was certainly pleasant to have someone of her own age to talk to; over lunch he told her about his home in Canada, volunteering the information that he was an executive in a vast business complex somewhere near Winnipeg, that he was a bachelor and lived in the house where he had been born—an oldish, comfortable house, by all accounts, with plenty of ground around it. He rode each day, he told her, getting up early so that he could take some exercise before breakfast and going to the office. 'Do you ride?' he wanted to know.

Mary Jane frowned. 'Yes. I haven't a mount, though. I—I've a guardian who wouldn't allow me to choose a horse for myself, otherwise I would have had one days ago.'

Her cousin looked sympathetic. 'Don't think I'm interfering,' he begged her, 'but why not tell me about it? Perhaps there's some way…surely he can't stop you…' He waved a hand. 'This is all yours, isn't it? And I suppose Great-uncle left you enough to live on in plenty of comfort, and you're over twenty-one.' He added hastily, 'At least, I suppose you are.'

He was very well informed, she thought vaguely; he knew so much. 'I'm twenty-two.' She hesitated; the temptation to confide in someone was very great, and he was family. 'It's a little complicated,' she went on, and proceeded to tell him a little about Fabian and the conditions of her grandfather's will. She was strictly fair about Fabian. He was, she supposed, a good guardian and quite to be trusted with her money, she didn't want her companion to be in any doubt about that, and she was careful not to go into any details about her inheritance—indeed, when she had finished she wasn't sure if she should have mentioned it at all, but Mervyn had seemed very sympathetic and she was further reassured by his brief, vague reply before he changed the subject completely.

He left soon after that and when she asked him if he would like to come again, agreed that he would. 'But not for a few days,' he told her. 'I have some business to do, in Carlisle—friends I promised to look up for someone back home, but I'll call and see you again when I get back.'

She watched him go with some regret; he had helped to pass the day, it had been pleasant to talk to someone and have company for lunch. She went along to the kitchen where Mrs Body was sitting in the shabby, comfortable armchair she had used ever since Mary Jane could remember, and asked that lady what she thought of their visitor.

'He seems nice enough,' said Mrs Body, 'very friendly too. Is he coming again?'

'He said he would.' Mary Jane picked up one of the jam tarts the housekeeper had put to cool on the kitchen table and ate it.

'You'll get fat,' declared Mrs Body, 'picking and stealing between meals. Where's he from?'

Mary Jane ate another tart and told her.

'Why did he come?'

Mary Jane explained that too and then asked a little worriedly, 'Don't you like him, Mrs Body?'

'I've no reason to dislike him, but I don't know him, do I? I'm not quick to take a fancy to anyone.'

'You liked Mr van der Blocq…'

'That's different. Now if you take Major for a quick walk, I'll have tea ready by the time you get back.'

'Let's have it here,' begged Mary Jane, and went off obediently with the dog.

Mervyn didn't come for five days, during which time Mary Jane thought of him quite a lot while she busied herself about the house and the garden, writing letters to her friends at Pope's and answering a long dramatic letter from Cousin Emma, who, it seemed, had quite recovered from her father's death and was engaged in refurbishing her wardrobe—several pages were devoted to the outfits she had bought and intended to buy, to the exclusion of all other news. Fabian wasn't mentioned, nor had he written. That he was a busy man, Mary Jane was well aware, but he could surely have telephoned? But that took time, especially if he needed every free minute he had in order to take pretty girls out…she was aware that she was being unfair to him, but he could have taken some notice. When she wrote her Christmas cards, she sent him one too, and although sorely tempted to put a note in with it, she didn't do so.

She was in the kitchen helping Mrs Body and Lily with the Christmas puddings when Mervyn arrived. He apologised for disturbing her, offered her a box of chocolates with disarming diffidence and invited her out to lunch. 'There's a place in Cockermouth,' he told her, 'where we could eat, and I wondered if you would help me choose one or two things to take home with me—presents, you know.'

She felt faint dismay. 'You're not going back to Canada before Christmas?'

'I haven't any reason for staying longer.'

'What a pity! I was going to invite you to spend Christmas Day here.'

He didn't answer at once and he had turned his head away as he replied:

'That's a sufficiently good reason for me to cancel my flight, Mary Jane.' He turned and gave her a long, steady look. 'I've thought of you a good deal. When I came to England I decided to come and look you up, because you were family—but now I keep thinking of all kinds of excuses to keep me here.'

Mary Jane listened to him, enchanted. No one—no young man, that was—had ever talked like that to her before. All of a sudden she felt beautiful, sought after, and dripping with charm; it was a pleasant sensation. She smiled widely at him and said a little breathlessly, 'Well, don't go until after Christmas—it's only ten days.' They stared at each other in silence and then she said, 'I'll go and put on my coat—there's a fire in the sitting room, I won't be a minute.'

It was the first of several such expeditions. They would return after their shopping and have tea, and then, later, dinner, to return to the sitting room fire and talk until Mervyn got up to go about ten o'clock. He was an amusing talker, preferring to tell her about his own life than ask her questions about her own, although sometimes she would find that, almost without knowing it, she was answering questions she had hardly noticed about the house and its contents and whether she had enough to run it properly and if her capital was in safe hands. She told him about Mr North, assuring him that he had been the family solicitor for years and was very much to be depended upon.

'Oh, is that the North who lives in Keswick?' he asked carelessly.

'Is there one in Keswick? No, Carlisle—Lowther Street. The firm's been there for ever.'

He had made no comment and had gone on to talk about something else.

He got up to go soon after and she walked with him to the door. As he put on his coat he said, 'I've some business to see to in the morning—a call to Winnipeg. May I come after lunch and take you out to tea?'

She nodded happily and he kissed her lightly on the cheek as she opened the door. It took her a long while to go to sleep that night; it was a pity that her excited thoughts of Mervyn were interlarded with unsolicited ones of Fabian.

She felt a little shy when he arrived the next afternoon, but it seemed that he felt no such thing; he kissed her again, a good deal more thoroughly this time, and told her gaily to get her coat and drove her into Keswick, where they had tea, bought a few things Mrs Body had need of, and drove home again. It was dark already, although it was barely four o'clock, for the mountains had swallowed up what light there had been, only the water of the lake gave back a dim reflection. It would be cold later on, but they didn't care. They roasted chestnuts by a blazing fire and ate their dinner together, and after Mervyn had gone, with yet another kiss, Mary Jane had skipped into the kitchen, her plain face alight. Mrs Body looked up as she went in, asked Lily to take some more logs to the sitting room and when she had gone, observed, 'You're happy, Miss Mary Jane.' Her kind eyes were sharp. 'Has he proposed?'

Mary Jane flung her arms round Mrs Body's ample waist. 'Oh, Mrs Body, do you think he's going to? No one has ever proposed to me before.'

'Which is no good reason for accepting him,' counselled her companion shrewdly.

Mary Jane knitted her fine pale brows. Mrs Body's remark was a sensible one, but it didn't fit in with her own reckless mood. 'Oh, I know that,' she declared gaily, 'but we get on so well and he's such a dear— you know, thoughtful and interested in the house and careful of me—making sure that my future's secure and all the rest of it.' She laughed. 'He actually wanted me to take out an insurance policy!'

Mrs Body said quickly, 'You didn't take any notice of that?'

'Well, I couldn't even if I'd wanted to, Mr van der Blocq sees to all that, but I didn't bother to tell Mervyn... What shall I give him for Christmas?'

Mrs Body made one or two uninspired suggestions, adding, 'And that nice Doctor van der Blocq, what are you sending him?'

'Why, nothing,' said Mary Jane. 'He's got everything in the world, you know.' She danced off again to take Major for his bedtime trot around the garden.

It was several days later, when they were out walking on the hills, heavily wrapped against the cold, that Mervyn let fall that he had met someone who had a roan for sale, sixteen hands, with plenty of spirit but good-tempered with it. 'I know you promised this guardian of yours not to buy a horse, but if you gave me an open cheque, I could buy it for you. I'm not a bad judge and I dare say I could strike a good bargain.'

Mary Jane paused on the slope they were working their way down. 'Well, I'm not sure—I should love it, but Fabian did say that I wasn't to buy one...'

'Yes, but don't you think that he said that because he wasn't here to give you his advice? Probably he was afraid that you might be tricked out of your money— you know how unscrupulous some people are—but surely if I picked out a good mount for you, he wouldn't raise any objection?'

Put like that, it had a ring of reasonableness. Besides, Fabian probably wouldn't come again for months—she would never get a horse of her own. She said thoughtfully: 'All right, I'll give you a cheque. Will you see to it for me, please? I'm sure Fabian won't mind.'

The words sounded curiously false in her own ears, Fabian would mind. He would mind on principle, because he was her guardian and considered that she shouldn't do anything at all without first asking his permission. Indignation swelled her bosom and gave way to a feeling of sneaking relief because he wouldn't know anyway.

The horse arrived two days later, a nice beast who went to his stable quietly enough, although he had a rolling eye. Mervyn explained that the animal was a little nervous but would settle down in a day or so. He told her what he had paid for him too, a price which rather shocked her, but when she ventured: 'Isn't that rather a lot?' she was met with a chilly surprise.

'I had to haggle to get him at that price, but if you could have done better…' He left the rest of the sentence in mid-air, where it hung between them like a small, disturbing cloud. It evaporated during the day, but she made a mental note that Mervyn was touchy about money and she would have to remember that.

It was Christmas Eve the following day, and Mervyn had said that he wouldn't be out until the afternoon, but he had kissed her warmly as he had said it and she hadn't really minded because she had planned to go riding—just a short canter across the fields by the lake, to see how Prince went. The morning was bright and clear and still very cold as she saddled him and led him out of the stable. He was still nervous, dancing along beside her, shying at every stone, and although she wasn't nervous herself, she could see that she would have to go carefully; he was a great deal more spirited than Mervyn had led her to believe. Perhaps in Canada they were used to horses that bucked and shied at every blade of grass. She had him away from the house by now, walking him across the meadow towards the

water, she coaxed him to a standstill with some difficulty and was preparing to mount when Fabian spoke
very quietly somewhere behind her.

'Don't, Mary Jane, I beg of you.' He was beside her
now and had taken the reins into his own hands while
she stared up at him speechlessly, a little pale in the
face and with a most peculiar tumult of feeling inside
her. He was pale too, but all he said was: 'He's not the
horse for you—I told you to wait until I could find
you something suitable. You broke your promise…'

'I didn't,' she said quickly, 'Mervyn bought him.'

She missed the sudden fire in his dark eyes.
'Mervyn?' repeated Fabian softly. 'Let us go back to
the house and you shall tell me about—er—Mervyn!'

He began to lead Prince back to his stable and she
perforce, walked with him and waited while he saw to
the animal, and then accompanied him into the house
to find Mrs Body, beaming with delight, hurrying with
coffee and some of her mince pies.

'I knew you would come, Doctor dear,' she told him
happily, 'with Christmas tomorrow.' She put down the
tray and went to the door. 'I've the nicest piece of beef
in the oven ready for your lunch.'

She went out of the room and Mary Jane said with
polite haste, 'I hope you'll stay to lunch.' She busied
herself with pouring coffee and didn't look at him.
His clipped 'thank you' sounded coldly on her ears.

After a lengthening silence during which she sought
for and discarded a number of conversational openings,
Fabian said, 'And now if you would be good enough
to explain about this horse.' He spoke in tones which
brooked no hindrance; she explained at some length

and in a muddled fashion which in the end left her
with no alternative but to tell him about Mervyn too.
He heard her out, no expression upon his calm, handsome features, and saying nothing, so that when she
had finished she was forced to ask: 'Well?'

He raised his eyebrows. 'My dear Mary Jane, what
am I expected to say? I haven't met this cousin yet,
although I shall be delighted to do so, even if only to
point out to him that I find his taste in horseflesh a
little on the inexperienced side.'

Her gentle eyes flashed. 'Pooh! You only say that
because you didn't pick Prince yourself.'

He ignored this. 'And what did you pay for him?'

She was a truthful girl, so she told him, waiting for
his expected comment on the excessive price, but he
said nothing, staring at her with narrowed eyes. Presently he said, 'Not a local animal, I fancy.' He sounded
so casual that she let out a sigh of relief. 'No, Mervyn
told me he had heard of him from someone he knew
in Keswick.'

'Is that all you know?' She sensed the mockery in
his voice and bristled as he continued, 'Surely you
have the receipt and the bill of sale?'

'Mervyn will let me have them,' she protested,
feeling guilty because she hadn't given the matter a
thought. 'How is your cousin?'

If she had hoped to change the conversation she was
unlucky. 'Very well, thank you. And when is Mervyn
coming to see you again?'

She muttered, 'This afternoon,' and fidgeted under
his look.

'Excellent. I shall enjoy meeting him. Had you

planned anything? I shan't be inconveniencing you in any way?' His cold politeness chilled her. He got up. 'By the way, Prince has a slight limp in his left hind leg—you will agree with me that it should be attended to at once? I know it's Christmas Eve, but I'll see what I can do.'

He went out of the room, leaving Mary Jane with her mouth open in surprise. She hadn't noticed any limp, though now that she came to think about it, Prince had stumbled once or twice. She wouldn't be riding for a day or two; it might be a good idea to get it looked at.

Fabian came back presently and she asked, 'Did you find a vet?'

He strolled over to the window and stood half turned away from her, looking out on to the wintry morning. He said at length, 'Yes—he'll see what he can do some time today.'

'It's not serious?'

He turned to look at her across the pleasant room. 'No, but I don't think you should ride him, though. Now tell me, how are you managing? Have you sufficient money?'

They spent the remainder of the morning in a businesslike fashion, and over lunch they kept to commonplaces while she wondered silently why he was so abstracted in his manner. Once or twice she found him staring at her in an odd fashion, with an expression which she couldn't understand, and indeed, he was so unlike his usual cool, arrogant self that she began to feel quite uncomfortable. And asking questions hadn't helped either, for she had tried that with singularly little success, in fact he had remarked after one such probe into what he had been doing: 'I have never known you take such an interest in my life—should I feel flattered?'

She felt as uncomfortable as she knew she looked. 'No, of course not, but I haven't seen you for several weeks. I just wanted to—to hear what you've been doing.'

His eyes held a gleam in their depths. 'Then I am flattered. Tell me, what are your plans for Christmas?'

'Well, nothing much. Mervyn's coming for Christmas Day—after church, you know, and I expect he'll stay until after dinner, and on Boxing Day some of Grandfather's friends are coming for a drink. Mervyn will be coming to lunch again, but he says he can't stay to meet Doctor Morris, he's got some people to see. It's a pity, because Doctor Morris knew his father, I believe.'

Fabian leaned back in his chair. 'A great pity,' he commented in a dry voice. 'It sounds very pleasant.'

'And you?' she asked politely, and then struck by a sudden thought, added in tones of the utmost apprehension, 'You're not staying for Christmas, are you?'

Somehow the thought of Mervyn and Fabian together filled her with an uneasiness she knew was quite unjustified; she closed her eyes on the vivid picture her mind had conjured up of Fabian blighting Mervyn's cheerful talk with his damping politeness.

His companion's face remained unaltered in its blandness. 'I wasn't aware that I had been asked. Set your mind at ease, Mary Jane, I shall be leaving within an hour or so.'

'Oh well, that's all right,' she exclaimed, so relieved that she hardly realised what she had said. 'Do you mind sitting here while I see if lunch is ready? There's some sherry on the window table, do help yourself.'

She went out of the room, humming cheerfully. If Fabian was going so soon, he and Mervyn would only have to meet for a very short time, perhaps not at all.

Her optimism was ill-founded. They had barely finished Mrs Body's excellent lunch when Mervyn drove up, parked the car in front of the door, and walked in. To say that he was surprised was too mild a way of putting it—Fabian had put his car in the garage; there had been no hint of anyone else being in the house, so Mervyn came breezing into the sitting room, to stop short just inside the door, looking so disconcerted at the sight of Fabian lounging in a chair by the fire that he could say nothing. It was Mary Jane who plunged into speech.

'Mervyn—hullo. Fabian, this is Mervyn Pettigrew, my—my cousin from Winnipeg. Jonkheer van der Blocq, my guardian.'

Fabian had risen and advanced to meet Mervyn, saying in a suave voice which somehow disturbed Mary Jane: 'Ah, Mr Pettigrew, Mary Jane has been telling me about you. I'm glad to have this opportunity of meeting you.'

He smiled, but his eyes were cold, and before Mervyn could say anything he went on: 'You must tell me about your home—Canada is a place I have often wished to visit. Your home is in Winnipeg? In the city itself or outside?' He waved Mervyn to a chair. 'Sit down, my dear fellow, and tell me about it.'

The conversation was in his hands; Mary Jane sat helplessly listening to Mervyn answering her guardian's questions, and even when she made attempts to change the conversation, she was frustrated by Fabian's blandly polite pause while she did so, only to have him resume his remorseless cross-examination again. Quite fed up, she suggested an early cup of tea because then Fabian might remember that he was leaving shortly... She was half way to the door when she heard a car, voices and some sort of commotion; she got to the window in time to see a horse-box and a Land-Rover disappearing down the drive. Prince's head was just visible.

She cut ruthlessly into Mervyn's description of the grain harvest. 'They've taken Prince!' she uttered, and turned to look at Fabian, who returned her startled gaze with a placid unsurprised face. 'I mentioned it,' he reminded her mildly.

'Yes, I know—but I didn't know he was going. Where is he going to?'

'The vet has taken him into his stables. A very good man, I believe.'

'Prince? The horse I bought for Mary Jane?' Mervyn's voice sounded strained. 'What's wrong with him?'

'A limp—the near hind leg, my dear fellow. Nothing much, probably he did it after you saw him. A splendid animal, I must congratulate you on your choice. Which reminds me, Mary Jane couldn't remember from whom she had bought him—you have the papers on you, I daresay.'

Mervyn searched his pockets. His face was a little

pale, he looked harassed. 'I've left them at the hotel,' he muttered. 'I quite intended to bring them—I must remember tomorrow.'

'Of no consequence.' Fabian's voice had a silkiness which struck unpleasantly upon Mary Jane's ears as she came back into the room. 'What did you pay?'

Mervyn answered before she had a chance to remind Fabian that she had already told him, and rather to her surprise, Fabian merely nodded his head, remarked that the price of horseflesh had risen out of all bounds, and went on to say that doubtless such a splendid beast would be well known in the district. 'I must go along and see his owner,' he observed casually, 'and see if he has anything as good. Where did you say he lived?'

Mary Jane watched the hunted look on Mervyn's face and wondered about it, and when he said at length that he couldn't exactly remember, helpfully suggested the names of some of the local breeders, to all of which Mervyn answered rather shortly that none of them was correct. At last, goaded by her excessive helpfulness, he said, 'It wasn't a breeder—just someone selling privately.'

'Ah,' Fabian's voice was still hatefully silky. 'Doubtless one of the small estates around here—I should have no difficulty in finding him.'

There was no knowing what Mervyn would have replied to this if Mrs Body hadn't come in at that minute with the tea tray. Mary Jane poured tea and oil upon what she felt might be troubled waters if she allowed the two men to go on long enough, but she need not have bothered, for Fabian seemed to have lost interest in Prince and his former owner. He was talking, much more freely than he usually did, she thought, uneasily, about the house and it contents, which, he assured Mervyn in a manner quite unlike his own somewhat reserved one, were by no means without value and likely to become more so. 'A very nice little property,' he said as he got up to go, 'worth quite a considerable sum in the market today.'

He was about to shake hands with Mary Jane when Mervyn spoke.

'I may not see you again—I hadn't intended to say anything just yet, but as you are here… I want to marry Mary Jane—I understand from her that she needs permission from you before she can marry. Well, I should like it now.'

This speech, uttered in urgent tones, had the effect of silencing Mary Jane completely, although it had no such effect upon her guardian, who remarked airily, 'My dear chap, why didn't you mention this earlier? Now I am forced to leave on most urgent business, and you can quite understand that I'm not prepared to give my consent until we have had a little talk about your prospects and so on. But I imagine that you will be here for another week or so? I'll endeavour to come and see you at the earliest opportunity.'

He glanced at Mary Jane, his face empty of expression. 'I'm sure that you both have a great deal to talk about. Goodbye, Mary Jane. I have no need to wish you a happy Christmas, have I—but I do, just the same.'

He took her hand, and she stared up into his face, completely out of her depth, filled with the ridiculous wish that he wouldn't go away, but stay for Christmas.

She whispered some sort of reply and stayed in the middle of the room, watching him walk away.

Mervyn talked a lot after Fabian had gone. He talked about their future together and how he had been wanting to tell her that he loved her for several days. 'We'll get married after Christmas,' he urged her. 'There's no reason why we should wait, is there? I can move in here…'

She was surprised at that. 'But won't you have to go back to Winnipeg? What about your work? Do you want to give up your job there? And if you come here to live you'll have to get something else. Wouldn't it be better if I came to Winnipeg?'

He was adamant that that wouldn't do. 'You would be homesick,' he told her, 'and this will be a marvellous home for us both—we'll get another car, and a boat—something fast.'

She agreed happily, in a rose-coloured future, not quite real. She asked him, 'And your income? Is it enough for us to live on?'

'Oh, don't worry your little head about that,' he assured her, and kissed her. 'We'll go into all that when we're married.'

'But I don't suppose Fabian will let me get married until all that's sorted out. He takes his duties very seriously.'

Mervyn caught her hands in his. 'Look, darling, why do we wait for him? If we get married he can't do anything about it, can he? He's far too busy a man to get involved in our business—besides, he'll be glad to be rid of this guardianship—that is, unless he's feathering his own nest with your money.'

Mary Jane felt a sudden fierce rush of sheer rage. 'That's a beastly thing to say!' she said loudly. 'Fabian is the most honest man alive, he wouldn't touch a penny that wasn't his—besides, he's frightfully rich.'

Mervyn apologised at once, turning it into a joke, but the sour taste of it stayed with her for the rest of the evening, despite his gay talk, although she found it hard to resist his charm. He would be a delightful husband, she assured herself, and how lucky she was that he had appeared out of the blue to fall in love with her and want to marry her. She wished him a warm good night, all her small qualms forgotten, and went along to find Mrs Body making last-minute preparations for the following day while Lily stood at the sink cleaning the vegetables. Mary Jane drew up a chair to the table and began to blanch a bowl of almonds standing on it.

'He's gone,' said Mrs Body sadly.

'Just this minute, but he'll be back for lunch tomorrow.'

Mrs Body thumped the stuffing she was making with quite unnecessary vigour. 'Not him,' she sounded aggrieved, 'Doctor van der Blocq, and I'd like to know where he's going to spend his Christmas.'

Mary Jane, her mouth full of almonds, said indistinctly, 'Holland, I suppose.'

The housekeeper gave her an impatient look. 'Now, Miss Mary Jane, you know as well as I do that he can't get back all that way by tomorrow morning—not with the car, he can't. What are you about not to think of that? It fair bothered me to see him driving off alone this afternoon—didn't you give him a thought?'

'Yes—no—I had something else to think about. Mrs Body, darling Mrs Body, I'm going to be married!'

'To that Mr Pettigrew? Well, I suppose it was to be expected, though how he could allow you to ride that wild animal I can't think. I never was so pleased to see the animal go again—he should have known better. Good thing dear Doctor van der Blocq came along like he did.'

'Oh, Mrs Body, aren't you pleased?' Mary Jane sounded as forlorn as she suddenly felt. 'I thought you would be—I'm not going to be an old maid after all.'

Mrs Body rallied. 'Of course I'm pleased, my dear, there's nothing I'd like better than to see you wed. But Canada's a long way off.'

Mary Jane reached over the table and kissed her housekeeper and friend on the cheek. 'But I'm not going there—Mervyn suggested that he should move in here just as soon as we're married.'

'And Doctor van der Blocq—does he know?'

'Oh yes, Mervyn told him this afternoon, and Fabian said he'd come back very shortly and they'd have a talk—about money and things.' She got up. 'I'm going to get something to drink—we'll toast Christmas before we go to bed.'

She went to sleep almost at once, thinking about the perfect future she was going to have with Mervyn, but she didn't dream of him, she dreamed of Fabian, driving his car endlessly through a lonely Christmas. She remembered it when she wakened in the morning and it became real somehow when Mrs Body brought her early tea and laid a small package on the bed.

'A Happy Christmas, Miss Mary Jane,' she said,

'and the dear doctor asked me to be sure and give you this first thing in the morning.'

There was a velvet box inside the wrapping paper, and in the box was a brooch, a true lovers' knot in rose diamonds, exquisitely beautiful. Mary Jane stared at it for a long time because it somehow seemed to be part and parcel of her dreams, its sparkle, a little blurred because of the sudden tears in her eyes, tears because she hadn't given him anything at all—she hadn't even invited him for Christmas. She remembered with shame that she had let him see her relief when he had told her that he was going away again. He must have said that because he was too proud a man to say anything else. She wondered forlornly where he had gone.

Chapter 6

Downstairs, Mary Jane found a delicately painted porcelain bowl on the breakfast table, filled with a gorgeous medley of tulips, hyacinths and dwarf iris. She sniffed their perfume delightedly and looked for a card. They would be from Mervyn, of course. She wandered into the kitchen to wish the others the compliments of the season, exclaiming: 'Those heavenly flowers—I wonder where he got them this time of year?'

Mrs Body dished bacon and eggs before replying. 'Brought them all the way from Holland, he did—made me promise to look after them and put them on the table first thing in the morning. It's a lovely bowl—ever so old. He gave us presents too, but we haven't opened them yet.'

Mary Jane remembered her remorse before she had

gone to sleep, and it came crowding back into her head now—even if the flowers and the brooch had only been a gesture from a guardian to his ward, they had been gifts, and she had been horribly unkind. Once more she wondered where he had gone and if he had expected to stay. She pushed the thought away and with it the faint regret that the flowers hadn't been from Mervyn, even the brooch, although possibly he couldn't have afforded that. It struck her anew that he had never talked about money to her at all, only sketched in a vague background, leaving her to suppose that he was comfortably off. She sighed, for she was a romantic girl and had always cherished the idea that a man in love went to any lengths to please his girl-friend, and yet it had been Fabian, not Mervyn who was so in love with her, who had taken care that there would be presents waiting for her when she got up on Christmas morning. She ate her breakfast thoughtfully and then went, with Mrs Body and Lily, to church. Mrs Body and Lily wore the new leather gloves Fabian had given them, and Mary Jane wore the brooch.

They had a drink when they got back and then got the lunch ready together. Mrs Body and Lily had friends to share theirs, so Mary Jane laid the table in the dining room for herself and Mervyn. By the time he arrived she was feeling gay and lighthearted, having spent a good deal of the morning persuading herself that Fabian had only called in on his way to somewhere and wouldn't have stayed even if she had asked him.

She had bought Mervyn a picture, a landscape by a local artist of some repute. She gave it to him when he arrived and watched while he unwrapped it, admired it and then laid it on the table in the window. There was an awkward pause until he said, 'I had no idea what to get you—we'll go together and find something later on.'

She made excuses for him—perhaps in Canada they didn't set much store by Christmas—but surely he could have brought a few flowers? She wasn't a greedy girl, only hurt because she had expected that because he loved her, he would have wanted to express that love with some small gift. She stifled the hurt and smiled at him. 'That will be nice,' she agreed. 'And now what about a drink before lunch?'

The bowl of flowers was on the table; he couldn't help but see it. He commented idly upon it, remarking that it looked a valuable piece.

'I don't know about that,' she said uncertainly. 'Fabian sent it.'

He frowned. 'Now that we're going to be married,' he stated categorically, 'I'm not sure that I like you receiving valuable gifts from him, even if he is your guardian.'

She flushed a little and said with a spurt of temper, 'Why ever not? As you said, he is my guardian, and what harm is there in giving a girl flowers? We do it a lot in England—for birthdays and Christmas.'

It was his turn to get angry. 'I don't like it,' he reiterated stubbornly. 'Before you know where you are he'll be giving you something really valuable—jewellery— bought with your money, no doubt.'

'I hope you'll apologize for that.' Mary Jane's voice was quiet, but it shook a little. 'I thought I had made it plain to you that Fabian wouldn't touch a penny of my money—he's my guardian, not a thief,' she added defiantly. 'He gave me this brooch.'

Mervyn stared at it across the table. Presently he said sullenly:

'Oh, all right, I'm sorry I said it—I didn't mean it, you have to make allowances for a man being jealous when he's in love.' His eyes were still glued to the brooch. 'It looks very expensive—I thought it was something you had inherited from your grandfather.'

He smiled at her. 'I'm a brute behaving like this on Christmas Day, darling. I'm sorry—I suppose I'm a bit on edge. I want to marry you, you see, as soon as possible, and I can't think of anything else but that. I promise I'll make it up to you when we're married.'

He was charming for the rest of the day; she basked in his admiration and listened happily to the delightful things he said, knowing right at the back of her mind that most of them were grossly exaggerated if not completely untrue. No one had ever told her before that she was pretty, nor had they spared more than one glance upon her eyes, which Mervyn declared were quite remarkably lovely; her common sense, buried in a haze of wishful thinking, told her that. But no one had ever been in love with her before, she had no yardstick by which to measure him. She allowed herself to believe every word and squashed her common sense, almost squashing her resolve to wait for Fabian's permission before they married. It was tempting, especially when Mervyn showed her the special licence he had bought, sure that she would give in when she saw it. But she still refused and put his sulky silence down to disappointment on his part.

During the following few days he had become a little difficult, and once or twice, when she was alone and quiet, a small voice deep inside her wanted to know if she really loved him or was she just being swept off her feet because she had never been in love or loved before. She buried the thought under a host of more pleasant ones and scoffed at her doubts.

But they stayed; she asked Mrs Body about them, and that dear soul looked troubled even while she spoke reassuringly. 'And wait until the dear doctor comes,' she counselled. 'It can't be long now.'

It was Old Year's Day when Fabian came. Mary Jane had expected Mervyn to lunch; she had spent most of the morning helping Mrs Body in the kitchen because Lily had gone home for the day and now she sat at the desk in one of the sitting room windows, writing thank-you letters, and keeping an eye on the drive and the road beyond. It had turned cold once more, there were a few snowflakes falling and the frost had been heavy the night before. She had put on a new dress, a dark green pinafore with a matching crêpe blouse under it, and had pinned the diamond brooch into it. She had done her hair with more patience than usual too, but it was getting a little untidy again, for she had a habit of running her hand through it while she was writing and it was two hours since she had done it. She was shocked when she saw the time; it was past one o'clock—something must have delayed Mervyn, and she couldn't think what. She resolved to wait another half an hour and applied herself to her letters again, but only for a few minutes, for a car turned into the drive and she got to her feet and ran to the door without bothering to look out of the window.

It was the Rolls, and Fabian who got out of it. He came in slowly, looking tired, and the sight of his shadowed face stirred a desire deep inside her to help him. But Fabian wasn't a man to accept help or admit tiredness, so she said instead, 'Hullo, how nice to see you, and just in time for lunch—it's a bit late, because I'm expecting Mervyn. You'll be able to talk to him.'

'We have had our talk, and he won't be coming.'

He stood in the open doorway, towering over her, his face expressionless, staring down at her, making no effort to move or take off his coat.

Mary Jane gave him a puzzled look. 'Why isn't he coming? He particularly wanted to see you—he's got a special licence.' She bit her lip and went on in a cold little voice, 'Where did you see him?'

'In Keswick.' He paused. 'I have to talk to you, Mary Jane.'

'He's ill—hurt? Oh, Fabian, do tell me quickly!'

'It's neither. If we could go somewhere?'

'Yes, of course, and you must have something, you look tired to death.'

He smiled grimly. 'When I have finished what I have to say and you still want me to remain perhaps you will ask me then.' He sounded suddenly impatient. 'The sitting room?'

He didn't sit down, but walked over to the window and then turned to face her. 'Mervyn isn't coming. He won't be coming again. He has left Keswick and is already on his way to catch his plane, back to Canada.'

She felt the blood leave her cheeks. 'I don't believe you—he loves me.'

'I wouldn't lie to you, Mary Jane. He was no good, my dear girl—you are such an innocent.' He sighed. 'Oh, he was your cousin all right, always borrowing money from your grandfather, like his father before him, an undischarged bankrupt with not a penny to his name, who came to hear of your grandfather's death and saw a chance of easy money. And how much easier could it have been?' His voice took on a mocking, angry note. 'You, a little bored already, with a house of your own and money—quite a lot of money…'

She interrupted him, almost stammering. 'He had no idea—I never told him.'

'No? But he tricked old Mr North into telling him how much the estate was worth. I suppose you told him where North lived?' And when she nodded miserably: 'I thought so. And Prince—how could you have been so feather-witted, Mary Jane? Did you not wonder why he never showed you the papers connected with the sale, or the receipt? Why, I smelled a rat the moment you said—or were you so infatuated with him that you couldn't be sensible any more? Do you know what he paid for Prince? Exactly half the amount he told you. He had the rest; he hired a car in your name too—I paid the bill just now, and the hotel—he owed several weeks' bills and told them that you would pay.' He thrust an impatient hand into a pocket and tossed some papers at her. 'There, see for yourself.'

She left them to drift to the floor. 'How—how did you find out all this?' She tried to speak in a normal voice, but it came out in a miserable whisper.

'I asked around—it wasn't difficult—and then I flew to Winnipeg and made some enquiries.'

'You went to all that trouble?' She had her voice nicely under control now, but the effort to hold back the tears was getting beyond her. She said in a sudden burst: 'Did it matter? He's the only man who has ever asked me to marry him, do you know that? He said he loved me and now you've spoiled it all—I believe you want me to go on living here for ever and ever—I hate you, I hate you, I wish I'd never set eyes on you!' She hiccoughed and choked, then took a breath, for she had by no means finished. Her heart, she most truly believed at that moment, was broken, and nothing mattered any more. All she wanted to do was to hurt the man standing so silently before her; his very quiet made her feelings all the hotter. But the words tumbling off her tongue were stilled by the entrance of Mrs Body with a loaded tray, who after one sharp glance at Mary Jane addressed herself to Fabian.

'I saw the car, Doctor dear, and I said to myself, "He'll be cold and hungry, I'll be bound," so here's coffee and sandwiches, and a Happy New Year to you.' She poured the coffee. 'And where did you spend Christmas, if I might ask?'

'Oh, in Keswick, Mrs Body. I had business there.'

'But why didn't you stay here? If Miss Mary Jane had known…'

'That had been my hope.' He smiled at her with great charm, and Mrs Body, quite overcome, exclaimed, 'You mean to say you came for Christmas and we never even gave you a good Christmas dinner?'

'It didn't matter. As it turned out I had a good deal to do. Thank you for the coffee.'

'Well, you look as though you need it, and no mistake, Doctor dear—worn out, you are. Have you come from Holland?'

He shook his head. 'Canada.'

Mrs Body was no fool. She said, 'Lor' bless my soul! I always knew…' She shot another look at Mary Jane, standing like a statue, taking no part in the conversation, and went out of the room, shutting the door very gently.

Fabian had made no attempt to drink his coffee, and when Mary Jane turned her back upon him he watched her for a few moments and then said softly: 'Mary Jane,' and when she didn't answer: 'I'm sorry, but I had to do it. I couldn't see you throw yourself away on a wastrel and ruin your whole life.' He paused. 'Do you want me to stay?'

She didn't turn round, only shook her head. She heard him cross the room and then the hall, and presently the front door was opened and shut again, and the Rolls murmured its way down the drive. By straining her ears Mary Jane could hear it going down the road, back to Keswick and, she guessed miserably, Holland. He wouldn't come again. There was no need to hold the tears back any longer; she flopped into the nearest chair and cried her eyes out, and when Mrs Body came back, sobbed out the whole sorry story to her, to be comforted and scolded a little and comforted again. 'And that poor man,' said Mrs Body, 'gone again without a bite to eat inside him, and him such a great man.'

'He can starve!' said Mary Jane savagely into Mrs Body's ample bosom.

'Now, now, dearie, that's no way to talk. I never said so, but I didn't fancy you marrying that Mr Pettigrew— far too glib, I found him. I know your heart's broken, but it'll mend, my dear, and you'll think differently later on, and when Mr Right pops the question you'll have forgotten all this.'

'But there isn't a Mr Right!' wailed Mary Jane.

'I'm not so sure about that,' said Mrs Body bracingly, and smiled to herself over the tousled brown head on her shoulder.

But despite Mrs Body's comforting words, Mary Jane found the days which followed hard to live through; she walked herself into a state of exhaustion, going over and over in her mind all that had happened, forcing herself to face the truth—that Mervyn hadn't loved her at all, only her money and her home, seeing her as an easy way to live in comfort for the rest of his life. Just as Fabian had said. She told herself that she would get over it, just as Mrs Body had told her, but in the meantime she was utterly miserable, not least of all because Mervyn hadn't written. He could have at least wished her goodbye—but then she hadn't said goodbye to Fabian either, had she? She had let him walk out of the house, cold and tired and hungry; even if she hated him—and of course she did—she had been pretty mean herself.

By the end of the week she wasn't eating much, nor was she sleeping; her mood was ripe for the letter from Pope's which arrived after a particularly bad night. It was from Miss Shepherd, telling her that there was a severe 'flu epidemic in London, the hospital was half-staffed and overflowing with patients, and how did Mary Jane feel like helping out on a temporary basis for a week or so?

Mary Jane went straight to the telephone, packed a bag, hugged Mrs Body and Lily goodbye and got into the Mini. She would only be gone for a week or so, but the prospect of having some hard work before her was just what she needed. She drove down the motorway, still unhappy, it was true, but finding life bearable once more.

It was amazing to her that she could slip back into life at Pope's with such ease, and still more amazing that it should be Women's Surgical to which she was sent, because the regular staff nurse was herself down with 'flu. Mary Jane went on duty a few hours after her arrival to find Sister Thompson sitting in her office, drumming impatient fingers on the desk while she harangued a part-time staff nurse whom she obviously didn't like; she didn't like Mary Jane either, but at least they knew each other, a fact she pointed out somewhat acidly before giving her a dozen and one things to do. Mary Jane, impervious to her bad temper, and relieved to have so much on her hands that she had no time to think, went into the ward, to be greeted happily by several nurses she had known. The ward was heavy and full with beds down the centre and cases going to theatre, to return requiring expert care and nursing. Sister Thompson sailed up and down between the beds, giving orders to anyone who was within earshot, complaining bitterly that there were no good nurses any more, and what was the world coming to—a purely rhetorical question which none of her harassed staff had neither the time nor the inclination to answer, at least not out loud.

Mary Jane, worn out after her hard day, slept as she hadn't slept for nights, and what was more, ate her breakfast the next morning. Despite her hard work, a faint colour had crept into her white face and the hollows under her eyes, while still there, weren't quite so noticeable. She was off duty in the afternoon, the day was cold and grey and the staff nurses' sitting room in the Home looked bleak—there were several of her friends off duty too, so she rounded them up and they went in a cheerful bunch to Fortnum and Mason's where they had tea before embarking on a quick inspection of the January sales. She went back to the ward refreshed, and because Sister Thompson was off duty that evening, the work went better than it usually did. She went off duty that evening with the pleasant feeling that at least she had done a good day's work and slept soundly in consequence.

The days slid by, each one packed with work and the small petty annoyances which went with it. Mary Jane found little time to think of anything but drips, pre-meds, closed drainage and the preparation of emergency cases for theatre, and at night she fell into bed and was asleep before she had time to shed one single tear over her broken romance with Mervyn. Just once or twice, when she was in theatre with a patient, she was reminded of Fabian, because the operating theatre was his world; it surprised her that in place of the rage which had possessed her against him, there was now only a dull feeling, almost a numbness. Beneath the mass of bewildered thoughts and memories she had expected him to write to her despite the manner of his going, but nothing came, only letters from Mrs Body, detailing carefully the day-to-day life at home. She had hoped for a letter from Mervyn too, against all her better judgement, but as the days went by and she realised that he wasn't going to write, she knew that that was the best thing. He had never loved her, and she had been a fool to have imagined he did. He would never have left in that craven fashion if he had had even a spark of feeling for her, and certainly nothing Fabian could have said would have deterred him from at least explaining to her. She sighed; it was a pity she didn't like Fabian, for quite obviously he had done his best for her, though in an arrogant fashion and with a total disregard of her feelings for which she would never forgive him.

With each day she found that she was recovering slowly. It was no good moaning over the past, and she had much to be thankful for; a home, enough money, kind Mrs Body and the willing Lily. She would go back to them soon and pick up the threads of her life where Fabian had so ruthlessly broken them off. She would have to find something to do, of course; Red Cross, part-time nursing, something of that sort. And she could sail and ride—only she hadn't a horse, and unless Fabian came to see her again, she was unlikely to have one. Perhaps she would have to wait until she was thirty and free to do as she wished. Her thoughts were interrupted by Sister Thompson's sour voice, enquiring of her if she intended to be all day making up that operation bed and how about Mrs Daw's pre-med?

And Mary Jane, who had already given it, said 'Yes, Sister,' in a mechanical way and went to see how the last case back from theatre was doing.

Op days were always extra busy. Sister Thompson went off duty after lunch and the atmosphere of the ward brightened perceptively even though an emergency appendix was admitted, followed by a severely lacerated hand. Mary Jane slogged up and down the ward, a little untidy now but still cheerful though a thought tired. She was going out that evening with some of her friends; there was a film which was supposed to be marvellous, but the way she felt by teatime, she didn't really care if she saw it or not, though probably once she was there she would enjoy it, and anything was better than sitting and thinking.

She was almost through giving the report to Sister Thompson before she went off duty when she was interrupted by the telephone. Sister Thompson lifted a pompous hand for silence and addressed the instrument with her usual severity, although this softened slightly when she discovered that the speaker was Miss Shepherd. She put down the receiver with a strong air of disapproval, observed: 'Matron'—she still called Miss Shepherd Matron because she didn't agree with all the new-fangled titles everyone had been given by the Salmon Scheme—'Matron,' she repeated, 'wishes to see you in her office as soon as possible. First, however, you will finish the report.'

Mary Jane, luckily at the tail end of her recital, made short work of the rest of it, wished her superior good night, waved to such of the patients who were in a fit state to notice, and started off down the corridors and staircases which separated her from Miss Shepherd's office. The hospital was fairly quiet except for the distant clatter of dishes denoting the advent of patients' suppers. She met no one and paused only long enough to fling open the door of Men's Medical where one of her friends worked, acquaint that young lady with the tidings that she might be late and they had better go on without her, and then tear on once more. The office was at the end of a short passage. Mary Jane knocked on the door, watched the red light above it turn to green, and went in.

Miss Shepherd was sitting at her desk and Fabian was standing in the middle of the room with his hands in his pockets, contemplating a very bad portrait of the first governor of Pope's. He took his eyes from it, however, as Mary Jane entered and met her startled gaze. She went red and then white, opened her mouth to speak, clamped it shut and turned for the door, quite forgetful of Miss Shepherd. It was that lady's calm voice which recalled her to her senses.

'Ah, there you are, Staff Nurse. Your guardian is most anxious to speak to you,' she smiled across the room at him as she spoke. 'I'm sure you will want to hear what he has to say.'

'No,' said Mary Jane baldly, 'I wouldn't.' She looked at Fabian. 'Why should you want to see me? I can't imagine any good reason…' She stopped because he was looking at her so oddly, and Miss Shepherd said smoothly:

'All the same, I think you might like a little talk.' She got up and went to the door and Fabian opened it for her with a smile. 'I have a short round to make, ten minutes or so. I daresay that will be long enough.'

She had gone. Fabian leaned against the door, watching Mary Jane, who, very conscious of his gaze, stared in her turn at the portrait on the wall.

'I had no intention of seeing you for some time,' Fabian began coolly, 'this is purely to oblige Cousin Emma. I did a thyroidectomy on her a week ago—she is doing very well, but now she insists that she won't return home unless you are there to look after her. I telephoned you, of course, but Mrs Body, although she knew you were here, had no idea how long you would be staying. Miss Shepherd tells me that she can let you go immediately.'

'There are plenty of nurses in Holland,' said Mary Jane flatly, while she thought with sudden longing of the old house in Midwoude and even more longingly of Fabian's great house by the canal. 'I don't want to go,' she added for good measure.

He chose to ignore this. 'Emma likes you—more, she has an affection for you, she feels that she will never make a complete recovery unless you are there to help her. And it is important that she recovers completely, for Trouw has asked her to marry him and although she longs to do so, she says that she will refuse him unless she is quite well again. And I think that you are the one to convince her.'

Womanlike, Mary Jane had fastened on the piece of news which aroused her interest most. 'Married? How marvellous! Oh, I am glad, and of course she must marry Doctor Trouw. I always thought…she must be very happy.'

Her voice died away because she herself should have been feeling very happy too, married by now, surely—instead of which, she was standing here in Miss Shepherd's office listening to Fabian's calm demands on her time and energy. She said in a husky little voice, à propos of nothing at all:

'I haven't a horse—what happened to Prince?'

Fabian made a sudden movement and then was still again. 'I know. Prince is now owned by the vet. I believe he's very content and they suit each other very well.' He began to walk towards her. 'Mary Jane, I told you that I had no intention of coming to see you, for I am only too well aware of your feelings towards me—you made them abundantly clear—but I am fond of Cousin Emma and I want her to be happy; she has spent a great deal of her life looking after Uncle Georgius—very inadequately, I must admit, but she did her best. And now happiness is within her reach and unless we help her, her stubbornness is likely to ruin everything.' His voice roughened. 'And you need entertain no fears that I shall be under your feet. When I come to see Cousin Emma it will be as her surgeon, not as your guardian. In future any meetings we may have shall be strictly on a business footing, I promise you that.'

For some unaccountable reason her heart sank at his words, for despite his indifference towards her, she had come reluctantly to regard him as someone to whom she could turn. She knew now, standing so close to him in the austere little room, that she had always been aware of him somewhere in the background, ready to help her if she needed help, and despite their dislike of each other he never had and never would let her down.

She was horrified to find her eyes filling with tears. They spilled down her cheeks and she wiped them away quickly, miserably aware that she looked quite hideous when she wept. But she was too proud to turn her face away. 'I'll come because Cousin Emma wants me,' she told him, 'not because you asked me.'

'I hardly expected that.' His voice was remote, as was his expression. They stared at each other in silence for a few seconds and Mary Jane, watching his calm face felt a keen urge to talk to him, to tell him how she felt. She blew her nose and wiped away the last tear and would have embarked on heaven knew what kind of speech, only she was interrupted by the return of Miss Shepherd, who sat down at her desk and asked pleasantly, 'Well, all settled, I hope?'

'Indeed yes, Miss Shepherd. You did say that my ward could leave immediately?'

'Of course. We are very grateful to the girls who came back to help us, but we wouldn't dream of keeping them a moment longer than necessary—Staff Nurse Pettigrew would have been going in a day or two, in any case.'

'Splendid!' He turned to Mary Jane. 'I'll send your tickets to the front lodge, shall I? Could you be ready to leave tomorrow evening?'

She was surprised. She had taken it for granted that she would be with him; that he would take her back to Holland. She was on the point of saying so and prevented herself from doing so just in time, for of course he would have no wish for her company and she had

no wish for his. Her voice was as cool as his own had
been. 'Yes, I can.'

'You have enough money?'

'Yes.'

There was a little pause until Miss Shepherd said
briskly, 'Well, that seems to be settled, doesn't it? I
won't keep you, Staff Nurse—you are off duty, I believe.'

Mary Jane said that yes, she was. She thanked Miss
Shepherd, said goodbye in a cold voice to Fabian and
went through the door he was holding open for her. It
shut behind her, a fact which disappointed her; she had
half expected him to follow her out. She even loitered
down the corridor, so that, if he wished, he would have
ample time to catch her up. He did no such thing, so
rather put out, she went off to the Home.

Her friends had gone, leaving a note saying that
they would wait outside the cinema until seven o'clock
and after that it would be just too bad. Her watch said
twenty minutes to the hour; to bath, change, catch a
bus to Leicester Square and arrive at seven o'clock was
an impossibility. She would spend the evening writing
to Mrs Body and packing her few things. She tore off
her cap and flung it on the bed, flung off her apron
and belt too and was about to give her uniform dress
the same rough treatment when there was a knock on
the door.

'Oh, come in,' she called crossly, ripping pins out
of her hair, and turned to see Fabian standing in the
doorway. She forgot that they were barely on speaking terms, that she hated him, that he was arrogant
and always had his own way. 'For heaven's sake,'

she breathed, 'you can't be here! This is the Nurses' Home—it's private…' She waved an agitated hand at him. 'Men don't come upstairs—there's a little room by the front door…'

'For boy-friends?' he wanted to know. 'But I'm not a boy-friend, Mary Jane.' He sounded serious, but she could have sworn that he was laughing. 'There was no one downstairs, you see, so I looked in the Warder's office and found your room number.'

'You've got a nerve!' she told him fiercely, still whispering. 'Go away!'

'Of course, if you'll have dinner with me.'

She tossed a curtain of honey-brown hair over her shoulders. 'No, I won't,' she said tersely, then gasped as he came in. 'Supposing the Warden comes along?' she begged him. 'Do go—I'll get into trouble and—and you'll lose your reputation.'

She gave a small shriek at the great roar of laughter he gave. 'Oh, please, Fabian,' she said, quite humbly.

He went to the door at once. 'Half an hour,' he told her. 'I'll be in the—er—boy-friends' room, and don't try and give me the slip. Possibly you will find the situation easier if I assure you that I'm not asking you out for any other reason than that of expediency. I'm leaving England in a few hours and I should like to tell you about Emma before I go, it will be easier for you when you arrive.'

She joined him in half an hour exactly, wearing new clothes she had bought for herself because she had wanted to look nice for Mervyn—a burgundy red coat with its matching dress, a red velvet cap on her pale brown hair, expensive gloves and handbag and suede boots with leather cuffs. She was thankful that she had found time to pack them when she left home to go to Pope's, for she had nothing much else with her—a skirt, a handful of sweaters and her sheepskin jacket which she had flung into the back of the Mini.

They dined at a nearby restaurant, and it wasn't until he had ordered and they were sipping their drinks that he abandoned the polite, meaningless conversation with which he had engaged her during their drive from Pope's. She had answered him in monosyllables, fighting a feeling of security and content, induced, she had no doubt, by the comfort of the Rolls and the anticipation of a delicious meal.

'You are sure that you have enough money?' he wanted to know again.

She mentioned the amount she had and he raised his eyebrows in surprise. 'My dear girl, you will be with Emma for at least two weeks, that's barely enough to keep you in tights.'

'How do you know I wear tights?' she demanded.

His lips twitched. 'I don't live in a monastery. I'll see that there's some money with your ticket. You had better travel to the Hoek by the night boat from Harwich. Someone will meet you there and drive you up to Midwoude. Emma is still in hospital, I should like you to be there when she is fetched home—that will be arranged. You'll need some overalls or something similar for a few days. What size are you?'

'Twelve,' she told him. She had no idea that he was such a practical man.

He eyed her thoughtfully. 'Twelve what?' His voice was bland.

'Well, that's my size—the number of inches I am.'

'Vital statistics?' and she saw the twinkle in his eyes and said severely: 'Yes.'

He made a note. 'Must I guess?' he asked mildly. 'Thirty-four, twenty-two, thirty-five or six—inches, of course. Is that near enough?' and when she nodded, speechless, he went on pleasantly: 'Now, as to Emma—I did a sub-total on her. She has needed it for a year or more, but she always refused—you know how thyroidtoxicosis cases refuse treatment. Besides, I think she felt that she would be letting Uncle Georgius down in some way, but now the way seemed clear for an operation; it was Trouw who persuaded her. It is all very successful, but she doesn't believe it yet—I think you will be of great help in convincing her. Besides, you can encourage her to make plans for her wedding.' He stopped, staring at her, his eyes hooded and she felt her cheeks go white.

'That was unpardonable of me, Mary Jane, I'm sorry.' He looked away from her strained face and continued in an impersonal voice, 'She has made a satisfactory recovery—a sore throat and hoarseness, of course. She's on digitalin and Lugol's iodine, and there are several more days to go with her antibiotic.' He added, 'She's a terrible patient. If you decide to change your mind, I shall quite understand.'

'I haven't changed my mind.'

'I didn't think you would.' He smiled at her and beckoned the waiter. 'The chocolate gateau is delicious here, would you care to try it?'

They were halfway through it before he spoke again. 'Mary Jane, you shall have your horse. I'll go over to the Lakes as soon as I can spare the time and find a good mount for you.' He shot her a lightning glance. 'You need not worry, I won't expect an invitation to stay.'

She didn't look at him. 'That sounds like a bribe.'

She wished she hadn't said it, for he at once became remote and haughty and faintly impatient. 'Don't talk nonsense,' he told her sharply. 'And now if you will listen carefully, I will finish telling you about Emma's treatment.'

The rest of the evening was businesslike in the extreme, for the talk was of such a professional nature that they might have been on a ward round at Pope's. He took her back without loss of time after dinner and wished her goodbye at the hospital gate with the air of a man who had concluded a satisfactory deal and now wanted to forget about it for pleasanter things.

'He's so unpredictable,' said Mary Jane, talking to herself as she went through the hospital to the Home, and a harassed night nurse hurrying in the opposite direction flung over her shoulder, 'They all are, ducky.'

Mary Jane left the following evening, her ticket and more money than she could possibly spend safely in her handbag, what clothes she had stowed in her case. She had wished Sister Thompson goodbye and had been told, to her surprise, that she was no worse than all the other girls who thought they were staff nurses, and if she chose to return at any future date, she, Sister Thompson, would personally ask Miss Shepherd if she could be posted to Women's Surgical ward. Mary Jane, overwhelmed by this treat for the future, thanked her nicely, took a brief farewell of such of her friends as were about and climbed into her taxi, reflecting that even if life wasn't treating her as kindly as it might, at least she had no time to sit and repine. When the friendly taxi-driver asked her if she was going on holiday she told him, 'Work,' adding to puzzle him, 'Work is the great cure of all the maladies and miseries that ever beset mankind.'

He grinned at her. 'Have it your own way, miss.'

Chapter 7

It was Doctor Trouw who met the boat at the Hoek van Holland, and Mary Jane, a little wan after a rough crossing, was delighted to see him, although the delight was tinged with disappointment—probably she told herself bracingly as she responded to the doctor's friendly greeting, because she was tired and for some reason, lonely. She would feel better when she reached Midwoude, where she had no doubt her days would be filled.

Doctor Trouw had a Citroën, large and beautifully kept. She sat beside him responding suitably to his pleased speculation upon his hoped-for marriage to Cousin Emma. 'We have always been fond of each other,' he told her gruffly, 'and now that my wife is dead…' He paused. 'I feel that life still has much to offer.' He coughed. 'Of course, we are neither of us in the first flush of youth.'

'I don't see that that matters at all,' said Mary Jane with sincerity. 'There's not much point in getting married unless you're sure that you're going to be happy, and that could happen at any age. I'd rather wait for years and be certain.'

Her companion looked pleased and plunged into plans for the future; she suspected that he was really thinking aloud for the pure pleasure of it—which left her free to consider what she had just said. If she had married Mervyn would he have been the right man? Unbidden, the thought that she hadn't liked him when she had first seen him crossed her mind, to be instantly dismissed—he might have treated her badly, but that was no reason for her feelings to change, or was it? If she had loved him, surely her feelings wouldn't have changed. What did she feel for him now, anyway? Dislike—indifference? She wasn't sure any more, she wasn't even sure now that she had ever loved him. It was all very bewildering and a relief when Doctor Trouw stopped for coffee.

They reached Midwoude just before noon, to be welcomed by Jaap, and Doctor Trouw didn't wait—he had some cases to see, he explained, but he would be back at two o'clock, if she could manage in the meantime.

She and Jaap managed very well, each speaking their own language and understanding the other very well in spite of it. She had the same room as she had had previously and he took her case up for her, telling her that lunch would be in half an hour and leaving her to unpack, do her face and tidy her hair. She did this slowly, savouring the peace and quiet and comfort around her. After that afternoon, when Cousin Emma was home again, she wouldn't be quite so free, so she might as well make the most of her leisure now.

The hospital at Groningen was large and imposing with a medical school attached. Doctor Trouw skirted the main building, and halfway down a side turning ran the car under a stone archway and into an inner courtyard, where he parked the car. Mary Jane, getting out, guessed it to be the sanctum of the senior staff of the hospital and knew she was right when she saw the Rolls in a far corner. They entered the hospital through a small door which led to a short dark passage which spilled into a wide corridor with splendid doors lining its walls, and scented with the faint unmistakable smell of hospital cleanliness. It was also very quiet. The consultants would gather someone behind these richly sombre walls, as would the hospital board, and VIPs visiting the hospital would, no doubt drink their coffee, cocooned in its hushed affluence. All hospitals are alike, Mary Jane decided, treading carefully in Doctor Trouw's wake.

He opened a door almost at the end of the corridor and gave her a kindly prod. The room was large, its centre taken up by an oblong table hedged in by a symposium of straight-backed chairs. There were other chairs in the room, easy ones, grouped round small tables, and the air was thick with cigar smoke. It seemed to her that the room was full of men—large, well-groomed men, every single one of whom turned to look at her. In actual fact there were a bare dozen, senior members of the hospital medical staff who had just risen after a meeting.

'Over in the far corner,' said Doctor Trouw in her ear, and began to steer her to where Fabian was standing. He had his back to them, talking to two other men, but he turned and saw them and came to meet them. He looked, thought Mary Jane a trifle wildly, exactly what he was; a highly successful surgeon with plenty of money, plenty of brains and so much self-confidence that he could afford to look as though he had neither. She felt depressed and a little shy of him, for he seemed a stranger, and her reply to his pleasant 'Hullo, Mary Jane' was stiff and brief. But he seemed not to notice that; enquiring after her journey, whether she had slept and if she felt herself capable of undertaking the care of Emma within the hour. She told him yes, checking an impulse to address him as sir, and with a perception which took her by surprise he remarked:

'We all look rather—er—stuffy, I suspect. Whatever you do, don't address me as sir.'

She smiled at that. 'Not stuffy,' she assured him. 'It's just that you all look so exactly like consultants, and so many of you together is a bit overpowering.'

The two men laughed as they ushered her to the door again, pausing on the way to introduce her to various gentlemen who would have gone on talking for some time if Fabian hadn't reminded them that they were expected elsewhere. They traversed the corridor once more, this time to a lift. It was a small lift, and with Doctor Trouw's bulk beside her and Fabian taking up what space there remained, she felt somewhat crowded, and more so, for the two men carried on a conversation above her head, only ceasing as the lift purred to a halt, to smile down at her for all the world as though they had just remembered that she was there.

They stepped out into another wide corridor, this time lighted from the windows running its whole length and lined on one side by doors, each numbered, each with its red warning light above the glass peephole in its centre. They entered the first of these to find Cousin Emma sitting in a chair, dressed and waiting, and if Mary Jane had been in any doubt as to Fabian's sincerity when he had told her how much his cousin needed her, it could now be squashed. Cousin Emma uttered a welcoming cry, enfolded her against a fur-clad, scented bosom and began a eulogy upon Mary Jane's virtues which caused her face to go very red indeed.

'I knew you would come!' breathed Emma. 'I said to Fabian, "If Mary Jane doesn't come, I shall make no effort to recover from this dreadful operation."' She paused, allowed Mary Jane to assume the upright and swept aside her mink coat.

'The scar,' she invited dramatically. 'Look at the scar—is it not dreadful? How can a maimed woman accept an offer of marriage with such a blemish?'

Mary Jane considered the hair-fine red line drawn so exactly across the base of her patient's throat. 'You won't be able to see it in three months' time,' she pronounced. 'Even now it's hard to see unless one stares—and who's going to stare? All you need to do is to get a handful of necklaces which will fit over it exactly—we'll do that, one for each outfit.'

She smiled at Cousin Emma, her eyes kind, unheedful of the two men standing close by.

'I feel better already,' declaimed Emma, and smiled with all the graciousness of some famous film star. 'I'm ready.'

Fabian drove her back in the Rolls and Mary Jane followed behind with Doctor Trouw in the Citroën, giving all the right answers to her companion's happy soliloquising. He would be, she considered, exactly right for Cousin Emma, for he obviously worshipped the ground she trod upon, while being under no illusion regarding her tendency to dramatise every situation. She asked: 'When do you hope to get married, Doctor Trouw?'

'Well, there is no reason why we shouldn't marry within a week or so. All the preliminaries are attended to—I persuaded her to become *ondertrouwt* before she went into hospital. Perhaps you could persuade her?' He looked at her hopefully. 'She is a sensitive woman,' he explained, just as though Mary Jane wasn't already aware of it, 'and prone to a good deal of dejection. Once we are married, I believed that can be cured.'

He turned the car in through the open gates and pulled up beside the Rolls. 'Willem is home,' he told Mary Jane as they got out. 'I daresay he will be over one day to see you.'

'How nice,' said Mary Jane, not meaning it—she foresaw a busy time ahead, acting as confidante to father and son while each confided their romantic problems to her. She sighed soundlessly and followed him into the house.

She had said almost nothing to Fabian, nor he to

her, nor did he attempt to speak to her before he left
very shortly afterwards. He had told her, she recalled,
that he would be his cousin's surgeon when he called
and not her guardian, now it seemed he had every intention of keeping his word. She answered his brief
nod as he went with something of a pang and went to
make Cousin Emma comfortable.

It proved an easier task than she had supposed. For
one thing the operation had been a success; in place
of the emotional, overwrought woman she had been,
Cousin Emma had become quieter; her feverish gaiety
and sudden outbursts of tears had been most effectively
banished. She was still rather tearful, but that was post-
operative weakness and would disappear with time.
In the meanwhile, Mary Jane kept her company, saw
to her pills and tablets, cared for her tenderly, talked
clothes, reassured her at least twice a day that the scar
was almost invisible, and coaxed her to eat her meals.
And when Fabian came, as he did each day, she met
him with a politely friendly face, answered his questions with the right amount of professional exactitude,
commented upon the weather, which was bitterly cold
once more, listened carefully to any instructions he
chose to give her, and then retired to a corner of the
room, to resume her knitting. Only when he got up to
go did she put it down—thankfully, as it happened,
because she wasn't all that good at it, and walk to the
door with him and see him out of the house. It was on
the fifth day after her arrival that he paused on the
steps and turned round to face her.

'Have you recovered?' he wanted to know coolly.

'Though perhaps I'm foolish to ask such a question, for you're not likely to tell me, are you?'

'No, I'm not,' she replied in an outraged voice, her eyes no higher than his waistcoat. She spoilt this by adding: 'It's not your business, anyway.'

He grinned. 'Who said it was? Willem Trouw was asking about you yesterday. He doesn't know about your broken romance and he's having difficulties with his own love life. I believe you might console each other.'

Mary Jane was furious, so furious that for a moment the words she wanted to say couldn't be said. At last: 'You're abominable—how dare you say such things? You're cruel and heartless!' She tried to shut the door in his face, but he took it from her and held it open.

'Probably I am,' he agreed, 'but only when I consider it necessary.' He bent suddenly and before she could turn her head, kissed her mouth. Then he shut the door gently in her surprised face.

Willem came over that very afternoon, and remembering Fabian's words, she was hard put to it to be civil to him; supposing Fabian had said the same sort of thing to Willem? Perhaps men didn't confide in each other, but to be on the safe side she refused Willem's invitation to go out with him that evening, doing it so nicely that he could always ask again if he wanted to.

She had been there more than a week when Fabian, on one of his daily visits, mentioned casually that the continuous frost had made it possible to skate on the lake. 'Do you skate?' he wanted to know.

They were in the little sitting room, Cousin Emma in an easy chair, leafing through a pile of fashion mag-

azines, Mary Jane determinedly knitting. She bent her
head over it now, rather crossly picking up the stitches
she had dropped, and became even crosser when Fabian remarked:

'I think you are not a good knitter, for you are always unpicking or dropping stitches or tangling your
wool.'

He was right, of course; she had been working away
at the same few inches for days, for the pattern always
came wrong. Probably she would tear it off the nee-
dles and jump on it one day. Now she left the dropped
stitches and knitted the rest of the row, briskly and
quite wrongly, just to let him see how mistaken he
was. It was a pity that he laughed.

'There are skates in the attic,' Cousin Emma informed anyone who cared to listen. 'I shall not skate,
naturally, but you, Mary Jane, must do so if you wish.
It is a splendid exercise and Willem could come over
and teach you if you aren't good at it.' She added com-
placently, 'I'm very good, myself.' She glanced at her
cousin. 'What do you think, Fabian?'

Mary Jane wasn't sure how it happened. All she
knew was that within minutes she had agreed—or
had she?—to spend the following afternoon skating
with Willem. It would be so convenient, said Emma,
because Doctor Trouw was coming over to discuss
wedding plans with her, and Willem could come with
him. They would stay to tea, of course, and Mary Jane
might like to make that delicious cake they had had a
few days ago—Cook wouldn't mind.

Mary Jane replied suitably, doggedly knitting. But
in the hall she said to Fabian: 'I don't particularly wish

to skate with Willem, and I should be much obliged if you would mind your own business when it comes to my free time…'

He put on his car coat and caught up his gloves. 'My dear girl, have I annoyed you?' His voice was bland, he was smiling a little. 'Perhaps you have other plans—other young men you prefer to skate with?'

He was still smiling, but his eyes were curiously intent.

'Don't be ridiculous, you know I haven't.' She went on gruffly: 'When can I go home? Emma is almost well.'

He was pulling on his gloves and didn't look at her. 'No one would wish to keep you here against your will, Mary Jane, but I think that Emma would be broken-hearted if you should wish to go home before her wedding.'

'Will they marry soon?'

'I imagine so. Are you homesick?'

She raised puzzled eyes to his. 'No—at least, I don't think so. I—I don't know. I feel unsettled.'

He put a compelling finger under her chin. 'Unhappy?' His voice was gentle. And when she shook her head, 'The truth is that you are still in a mist of dreams, are you not? But they will go, and you will find that reality is a great deal better.'

He went away and she stood in the lobby watching the Rolls being expertly driven down the frozen drive and away down the road. Sometimes he was so nice, she thought wistfully, wondering what exactly he had meant.

She went skating with Willem when he came because there was nothing she could do about it—he arrived with his father, his plans laid for an afternoon on the ice with her. He had even borrowed some skates, and despite everything, she enjoyed herself. The lake was crowded, the bright colours of the children's anoraks lent the scene colour under the grey sky, their shrill, excited voices sounding clearly on the thin winter air. Willem was a good skater, if unspectacular. They went up and down sedately while he told her about the girl he wanted to marry and who didn't seem to want to marry him. 'I can't think why,' he told her unhappily. 'We're such good friends.'

'Sweep her off her feet,' advised Mary Jane. 'I don't know much about it, but I think girls like that. You could try—you know what I mean, be a bit bossy.'

'But I couldn't—she's so sure of what she wants, at least she seems to be.'

Mary Jane executed a rather clumsy turn. 'There, you see? Probably she doesn't know her own mind. Where is she now?'

They were going down the length of the lake again. 'As a matter of fact she's in Groningen.'

'Today? This afternoon?' Mary Jane came to such an abrupt halt that she almost lost her balance. 'What could be better? Go and fetch her here, make her put on skates and rush up and down with her until she's worn out—show her who's master.' She gave him a push. 'Go on, Willem—she'll be thrilled!'

'You think so?' He sounded undecided and she reiterated: 'Oh, go on, do!'

'But what about you?'

'I'm all right here. If I'm not back by dark you can come and fetch me.'

'Really? You don't think I'm being—being not friendly towards you, Mary Jane?'

'No, Willem. It's because we're friends that we can make this plan.' She started off, waving gaily. 'Have fun!'

She didn't look round, but when she turned and came back, he had gone.

The afternoon darkened early and became colder, but she, skating with more enthusiasm than skill, glowed with warmth; she had on her sheepskin jacket and a scarf tied tightly over her bun of hair, and she had stuffed her slacks into a pair of Cousin Emma's boots—they were too big, but they did well enough, as did the thick knitted mitts Jaap had found for her. Her ordinary little face was pink with pleasure and exercise, her eyes sparkled; that she was alone didn't matter at all, because there were so many people around her, enjoying themselves too. She skated to the end of the lake and then, the wind behind her, came belting back. There were fewer people now; the children were leaving, and there was more room. She was almost at the end when she saw Fabian some way ahead, right in her path. Even in the gathering dusk there was no mistaking his tall, solid figure. She began to slow down, for, most annoyingly, he hadn't moved. She was still going quite fast when she reached him, but he stayed where he was, putting out a large arm to bring her to a standstill.

'Whoops!' said Mary Jane, breathless. 'I thought

I was going to knock you over—you should have moved.'

He was still holding her. 'No need. I weigh fifteen stone or thereabouts, and I doubt if you're much more than eight.' He laughed down at her. 'You show a fine turn of speed, though I don't think much of your style.'

'Oh, style—I enjoy myself.'

He had turned her round and they were skating, hands linked, back down the lake. Presently he asked, 'Where is Willem?'

'He's gone to Groningen to meet his girl-friend.'

'I thought he was spending the afternoon with you?'

'Oh, we started off together, then he started telling me about her and really, he was so fainthearted, I thought I'd better encourage him to go after her.'

'So you gave him some advice?'

'That's right. Have you the afternoon off?'

'More or less, but I must go home shortly. Will you come and have tea with me? Willem is presumably occupied with his girl, and Cousin Emma and Trouw will be engrossed with each other. That leaves us.'

She considered. 'Well, tea would be nice—but won't they wonder where I am?'

'I'll let them know. Shall we race to the end—you can have twenty yards' start.'

She did her best, but he overtook her halfway there, and then dropped back to skate beside her until they reached the bank, where they took off their skates and walked through the bare trees to where he had parked the car.

His house was warm and inviting, just as she had remembered it. They had tea in a small, cosily furnished room with a bright fire burning and lamps casting a soft glow over the well-polished tables which held them. And the tea was delicious—anchovy toast, sandwiches and miniature cream puffs. Mary Jane, with a healthy appetite from her skating, ate with the pleasure of a hungry child. She was halfway through the sandwiches when she exclaimed, 'We haven't telephoned Midwoude—do you think we should?'

Fabian got up at once. 'I suppose I can't persuade you to stay to dinner?'

She refused at once very nicely and was at once sorry that she had done so, because she would very much have liked to spend the evening with him. She told herself urgently that it was foolish to be charmed by him just because he was being such good company—besides, there was Mervyn. She pulled herself up with the reflection that there wasn't Mervyn; she owed nothing to him, neither loyalty to his memory or anything else; not, said her heart, even love, for it hadn't been love, only a plain girl's reaction to being admired...

'You're looking very thoughtful,' remarked Fabian and sat down again. 'You said you wanted to go home—will you agree to stay until Emma is married as I asked you? I think the wedding will be very soon, probably we shall hear something when we go back presently.'

She spoke at random to fill the silence between them: 'This is a lovely house.'

'You like it? It needs a family—children—in it. You like children, Mary Jane?'

'Yes.' She was unconsciously wistful as they lapsed into silence once more. She had abandoned her con-

fused thinking, and it seemed a good thing; she needed
peace and quiet to sort herself out, and Fabian's pres-
ence had the effect of confusing her still further. She
wasn't even sure what she wanted any more—only one
thing was clear, he didn't mind if she returned home;
she had watched his face when she had told him that
she wanted to go and its expression hadn't changed
at all. Not meaning to say it, she asked: 'When I go
home, will you need to visit me again?'

His casual, 'Oh, I think not; everything is arranged
very satisfactorily. If you should need my services you
can always write or telephone,' daunted her, but she
tried again.

'But what about the horse?'

'I asked the vet to keep an eye open—he'll let me
know when he finds something worth while.'

She said, 'Oh, how nice,' in a small forlorn voice,
aware that she had been using the horse as a line of
communication, as it were, and Fabian had cut the
line. She got to her feet. 'I think I should be getting
back,' and when he got to his feet with unflattering
speed, 'You said we wouldn't meet—that you would
only be Emma's surgeon—I forgot that this afternoon.
Did you?'

His dark eyes rested briefly on hers. 'No, I hadn't
forgotten, Mary Jane, but there is such a thing as a
truce, is there not?'

He fetched her outdoor things and they went out to
the car. A good thing, she thought savagely as she got
in, that she hadn't accepted his invitation to dinner—
uttered out of politeness, no doubt, for he was obviously
longing to be rid of her. Telling herself that it didn't

matter in the least, she kept up a steady flow of chat as he drove her back to Midwoude, her voice a little high and brittle.

But he seemed in no hurry to be rid of her company or anyone else's when they reached the house. Cousin Emma and Doctor Trouw were in the sitting room, the tea things still spread around them, deep in wedding plans. They would be married, declared Emma, with a suitable touch of the dramatic, in four days' time—the *burgermeester* of Midwoude had promised to perform the ceremony in the early afternoon at the Gemeente-huis, and afterwards they would cross the street for a short ceremony in church. 'And you will come, Mary Jane, because you have been so kind and good…' the ready tears sprang to her eyes, 'and when you marry I shall come to your wedding.'

'How nice,' said Mary Jane briefly. 'Tell me, what will you wear?'

Her companion was instantly diverted and the two ladies became absorbed in the bridal outfit. They were still engrossed in this interesting topic when the gentlemen wandered off to the other side of the room to have a drink, and when after a few minutes Fabian said that he must go, he did no more than pass a careless remark about their pleasant afternoon before he took himself off.

There was no time for anything but the wedding preparations during the next day or so. Cousin Emma, fully recovered from her operation, plunged into a maelstrom of activity with Mary Jane doing her best to hold her back a little. Recovered she might be and in the happy position of having others to attend to her every want, she still needed to rest. Mary Jane gently bullied her on to the chaise-longue in her bedroom each afternoon and by dint of guile and cunning, kept her there until Doctor Trouw called at tea-time. Fabian came too, but only for a few minutes, to check his cousin's progress, although on the day previous to the wedding he remained long enough to tell Mary Jane that should she wish, he would arrange for her to travel home on the day after the wedding. 'But time enough to let me know,' he assured her carelessly. 'There are few people travelling at this time of year, it will only be a question of a few telephone calls.' He had nodded cheerfully at her and added, 'I shall see you at the wedding, no doubt.'

Getting Cousin Emma to the Gemeentehuis proved a nerve-shattering business. Not only was she excited and happy, she was tearful too, and when almost dressed declared that she looked a complete guy, that her shoes pinched and that her scar was so conspicuous that she really hadn't the courage to go through with the ceremony. It was fortunate that her bridegroom—come, as Dutch custom dictated, to fetch his bride to their wedding—had brought with him his wedding gift, a string of pearls which exactly covered the offending blemish. Mary Jane, rather pink and excited herself, left them thankfully together and hurried to the front door. Jaap was to drive her to the village and she was already a little late. He wasn't there, but Fabian was, strolling up and down the hall in morning clothes whose elegance quite dazzled her.

'There you are,' he remarked. 'I sent Jaap on, you're

coming with me.' He stood looking at her. 'Now that is a new hat,' he decided, 'and a very pretty one.'

Mary Jane gave him a doubtful look. The hat had taken a good deal of thought and she hadn't had all that time to escape from Cousin Emma. It matched her coat exactly, a melusine with a sideways-tilted brim ending in a frou-frou of chiffon. Not at all her sort of hat, but after all, it was a wedding and one was allowed some licence. It added elegance to her ordinary face too and gave it a glow which almost amounted to prettiness.

'Someone told you,' she accused him.

'No, indeed not,' he laughed at her, 'and it really is pretty.'

She wished that he would say that she was pretty too, although that would be nonsense, but he didn't say anything else, but tucked her into the Rolls beside him and drove off to the Gemeentehuis, a small, very old building, ringed around now with a number of cars and little groups of people from the village. Inside, Fabian found her a seat at the back before he went to take his place with his family in the front row. The ceremony was short and quite incomprehensible to her, but the service in the church was more to her taste, for she was able to follow it easily. And when it was over she watched the bride and groom and their families, correctly paired, walk down the aisle to the door of the church. She knew none of them, save for Fabian and Willem. They looked, she considered, a little haughty, very well dressed and faintly awe-inspiring, although the younger members of the party were gay and smiling and enjoying themselves. Willem, she was glad to see, had his girl with him—at least, she hoped it was his girl. He certainly looked happy enough, and Fabian—Fabian was escorting a truly formidable lady of advanced years, just behind the bridal pair.

She waited until almost everyone had gone and made her way to the door, looking for Jaap. He was nowhere to be seen. There were still several groups of people lingering around the porch, but they were all strangers to her. She supposed she would have to walk. She frowned—how like Fabian to forget all about her; she wished she hadn't come, he was horrible, thoughtless, thoroughly beastly… He touched her arm, smiling at her, so that she felt guilty, and felt even more so when he said, 'I knew you would have the sense to wait until I came for you—Great-aunt Corina isn't to be hurried. Come on.'

She travelled back sitting with the old lady, who wasn't haughty at all, while a large young man, whom Fabian introduced as Dirk—a cousin—squeezed in beside them. Fabian introduced the girl sitting beside him too—a blue-eyed creature wrapped in furs. Her name was Monique, and even though he said she was a cousin, Mary Jane didn't take to her. She was still pondering the strength of her feelings about this when they arrived at the house.

The vast drawing room had been got ready for the reception, with a long table and a number of smaller ones grouped around it. Mary Jane, seated between Dirk and an elderly uncle of the bride, found that she was expected to make a good meal. She went from champagne cocktails to lobster meuniere, from venison steaks to chocolate profiteroles, each with its accompanying wine. It was a relief to hear from Dirk that a wedding cake wasn't customary, for what with the wine and champagne and the warmth of the room, she began to feel a little lightheaded. Even the haughty members of the family didn't seem haughty any more, indeed, those she had spoken to had been charming to her. She glanced round her. Everyone looked very happy, but then marriages were happy occasions, although if she married she would want a quiet one with just a few friends. The corners of her gentle mouth turned down; the sooner she stopped thinking that romantic nonsense, the better. She turned to Dirk, who was quite amusing although a little young, she considered, and when he asked her if he might take her out to supper that evening, she refused with a charm which drew from him a regretful smile and a promise to ask her again the very next time they met. It seemed pointless to tell him that she was going back to England the next day, she laughingly agreed and listened with all her attention while he told her about his ambition to be as good a surgeon as his cousin Fabian.

The guests began to leave as soon as the bridal pair had gone; car after car slid away into the winter darkness until there were only a very few left, their owners delaying their departure for a last-minute chat or waiting for each other. Mary Jane felt rather lost; the drawing room was in the hands of the caterers, under the sharp eye of Jaap, being returned to its usual stately perfection. Sientje was in the kitchen, the daily maid had gone long ago. Mary Jane stood in the hall, remembering how cheerfully Fabian had asked 'Tomorrow?' when she had asked him on the way to the wedding if he would arrange for her to travel home.

'I'll send the tickets here to you,' he had told her casually, 'in plenty of time for you to catch the boat train from Groningen. Jaap will drive you to the station.'

Now she wondered if that was to be his goodbye. She had helped him when he had asked her to; her own affairs were in order, there was nothing more for him to do; did he intend to drop their uneasy acquaintance completely? Just as well, perhaps, she mused, they had never got on well. She wandered into the empty sitting room and sat down by the window, staring out into the dark evening, her mind full of useless regrets, her fingers playing with the diamond brooch Fabian had given her and which she had pinned to her coat. She had written and thanked him for it. It had been a long letter and she had tried very hard to show her gratitude, but he had never answered it, or mentioned it—she wasn't sure if he had even noticed that she was wearing it today. She got up and strolled back into the hall, empty now. Not quite empty, though, for Fabian was there, sitting in the padded porter's chair by the door. He walked over to meet her and said easily, 'Hullo—I'm just off. You're fixed up for the evening, I hear. Dirk told me earlier that he intended taking you out to supper.' He smiled. 'He's good company, you'll enjoy yourself.'

'Oh, indeed I shall,' she assured him, her voice bright. How pleased he must feel, thinking that she was settled for the evening and that he need not bother... 'I hope you have a pleasant evening too,' she assured him untruthfully, 'and thank you for seeing about the tickets. I'll say goodbye.'

She held out her hand and had it engulfed in his,

and it became for an amazing few seconds of time the only tangible thing there; the hall was whirling around her head, her heart was beating itself into a frenzy because she had at that moment become aware of something—she didn't want to say goodbye to Fabian, she didn't want him to go, never again. She wanted him to stay for ever, because she was in love with him— she always had been. But why had she only just discovered it? And what was the use of knowing it now? For even as the knowledge hit her he had dropped her hand and was at the door. He went through it without looking back.

Chapter 8

Mary Jane stood staring at the door for a few seconds, hoping that he might come back; that he had forgotten something; that he would ask her to go out with him that evening, Dirk or no Dirk. Anything, she cried soundlessly; a violent snowstorm which would make it impossible for him to drive away, something wrong with the Rolls, an urgent message so that she could run after him with good reason... Nothing happened, the hall was empty and silent, there was a murmur of voices from the drawing room where there was still a good deal of activity, and from outside the crunch of the Rolls' wheels on the frozen ground. They sounded remote and final; she waited until she couldn't hear them any more and then went in search of Jaap.

If the old man was surprised at her decision to go to bed immediately, he didn't show it. They had become used to each other by now, so it wasn't too difficult to let him suppose that she had a headache and wanted nothing for the night. He wished her good night and went back to the caterers.

She slept badly and got up early, which she realized later had been a silly thing to do, for the morning stretched endlessly before her. She wouldn't be leaving until the late afternoon, and somehow the time had to be helped along. She spent some of it with Jaap and Sientje, but conversation was difficult anyway, and they had their work to do—they were to go on a short holiday and return to make the house ready for Cousin Emma and her husband, who had agreed to the happy arrangement of leaving his own house for his son's use and carrying on his practice from Midwoude. Mary Jane, sensing that much as Jaap and Sientje liked her, they wanted to get on with their chores, offered to clear away the silver and glass which had been got out for the wedding, and then went around freshening up the floral arrangements; probably Jaap would throw them out before he closed the house, but it gave her something to do. But even these self-imposed tasks came to an end, and she ate her lonely lunch as slowly as possible, hoping that Fabian would telephone; surely he would say goodbye? But as the minutes ticked by she was forced to the conclusion that he had no intention of doing so. Perhaps he would be at the station—if she could see him just once more before she went away… She told herself it was foolish to build her hopes on flimsy wishes, a good walk would do her good and she had plenty of time. She went and got her coat, tied a scarf over her head, snatched up her gloves, and went in search of Jaap. He seemed a little uncertain about her desire to go out, but she could understand but little of what he said and she wasn't listening very hard; she wanted to get out and walk—as fast as possible, so that she might be too tired to think about Fabian. She made the old man understand that she would be back in good time for him to drive her to the station, and fled from the house before he could detain her longer.

The afternoon was bleak and frozen into stillness; the ground was of iron and she quickly discovered that it was slippery as well. She walked fast into an icy wind, down to the village, and when she looked at her watch and saw that she still had time to kill, she walked on, towards the path which led eventually to the lake. Here the bare trees gave some pretence of shelter even though the ground under her feet was rough and treacherously slithery, something she hardly noticed, trying as she was to outstrip her unhappiness, forcing herself to think only of her future in the house her grandfather had left her. She came in sight of the frozen water presently and paused to look at her watch again. She would have to return quite soon and she decided not to go any further.

There were people skating on the lake, turning the greyness of its surroundings into a gay carnival of sound and colour. Mary Jane drew a sighing breath, the memory of her afternoon with Fabian very vivid, then turned on her heel and started to retrace her steps along the path, and after a short distance, lured by the cheerful sight of a robin sitting in a thicket, turned off it and wandered a little way, absurdly anxious to get a

closer view of the bird. But he flew just ahead of her so
that when she finally retraced her steps the path was
hidden. She hurried a little, anxious to find it again
because it would never do to lose the boat train. She
didn't notice the upended root under her foot—she
tripped, lost her balance on the smooth ice, and fell,
aware of the searing pain in the back of her head as it
struck a nearby tree.

It was like coming up through layers of grey smoke;
she was almost through them when she heard Fabian's
voice saying 'God almighty!' and it sounded like a
prayer. With a tremendous effort she opened her eyes
and focused them upon him. He looked strange, for
he was in his theatre gown and cap and a mask, pulled
down under his chin.

'You sound as though you're praying,' she mumbled at him.

'I am,' and before she could say more: 'Don't talk.'
His voice was kind and firm, she obeyed it instantly
and closed her tired eyes, listening to him talking to
someone close by. He had taken her hand in his and
the firm, cool grip was very reassuring; she allowed
the soft grey smoke to envelop her once more.

When she wakened for the second time, the room
was dimly lit by a shaded lamp in whose glow a nurse
was sitting, her head bowed over a book. But when
Mary Jane whispered, 'Hullo there,' she came over
to the bed and said in English, 'You are awake, that
is good.'

Mary Jane suffered her pulse to be taken, and in a
voice which wasn't as strong as she could have wished

said, 'I'll get up,' and was instantly hushed by the nurse's horrified face.

'No—it is four o'clock in the morning,' she remonstrated, 'and I must immediately call the Professor— he wishes to know when you wake, you understand? Therefore you will lie still, yes?'

Mary Jane started to sit up, thought better of it because of the pain at the back of her head and said weakly, 'Yes—but no one is to get up out of his bed just to come and look at me. I'm quite all right.'

'But the Professor is not in his bed,' explained the nurse gently. 'He is here, Miss Pettigrew, in the hospital, waiting for you to wake.'

She went to the telephone as she spoke and said something quietly into it, then came back to the bed. 'He comes,' she volunteered, 'and you will please lie still.'

He was there within a few minutes, this time in slacks and a sweater. To Mary Jane's still confused eyes he looked vast and forbidding and singularly remote, and the fact disappointed her so that when she spoke it was in a somewhat pettish voice. 'You stayed up all night—there was no need. I'm perfectly all right.' She frowned because her headache was quite bad. 'It was quite unnecessary.'

He said tolerantly, 'It's of no matter,' and took her wrist between his finger and thumb, taking her pulse. 'You feel better? Well enough to talk a little and tell me what happened?'

She blinked up at him. His face looked drawn and haggard in the dim light and she felt tender pity welling up inside her so that she could hardly speak. 'I'm sorry,' she managed, 'I mean I'm sorry you've had all this trouble.'

'I said it didn't matter. What happened?' His voice was quiet, impassive and very professional. He would expect sensible answers; she frowned in her efforts to be coherent and not waste his time.

'I went for a walk,' she explained at last. 'You see, I hadn't anything to do until it was time to leave. I went to the village and there was still lots of time—I went down the path between the trees to the lake. There was a robin, I went to look at him and I slipped and hit my head—I can remember the pain.' She stopped, thankful to have got it all out properly for him. 'I don't know how long I was there. Did I dream that I saw Jaap and it was very cold?'

Fabian had pulled up a chair to the side of the bed. 'No—you were cold, and it was Jaap who found you when he went to look for you because you hadn't gone back to the house and he was worried, only he didn't find you straight away because you were a little way from the path. You have a slight concussion—nothing serious, but you will stay here, lying quietly in bed, until I say otherwise. And you will do nothing, you understand?'

She muttered 'Um' because she was drowsy again, but she remembered to ask, 'Where's here?'

'The hospital in Groningen.' And she muttered again, 'Thank you very much,' because she was grateful to be there and wanted him to know it, but somehow her thoughts weren't easy to put into the right words. Forgetting that she had already said it once, she thanked him again. 'I'm such a nuisance and I am sorry.' A thought streaked through the fog of sleep which was engulfing her. 'I'm going home today,' she offered in a groggy voice.

'Yesterday—no, Mary Jane, you are not going home, not just yet. You will stay here until your head-ache has gone.'

She managed to open her heavy lids once more. 'I don't want...' she began, and met his dark eyes.

'You'll stay here,' he repeated quietly. 'Nurse will give you a drink and make you comfortable and you will go to sleep again.'

She was in no state to argue; she closed her eyes and listened to his voice as he spoke to the nurse, but he hadn't finished what he was saying before she was asleep again.

It was afternoon when next she woke, feeling almost herself, and this time there was a different nurse, a big, plump girl with a jolly face, whose English, while adequate, was peppered with peculiar grammar. She turned Mary Jane's pillow, gave her a drink of tea and went to the telephone.

Fabian was in his theatre gown again. He nodded briefly with a faint smile, took her pulse and, satis-fied, said: 'Hullo, you're better. How about something to eat?'

She didn't answer him. 'You're busy in theatre,' she observed in a voice which still wasn't quite hers. 'What's the time?'

'Three o'clock in the afternoon.'

'Have you a long list?' She hadn't meant to ask, but she had to say something just to keep him there a little longer.

'Yes, but we're nearly through. How about tea and toast?'

She nodded and started to thank him, but sneezed instead. 'I've a cold,' she discovered.

'That's to be expected. The temperature was well below zero and you were half frozen. I'll see that you get something for it.'

She sneezed again and winced at the pain in her head. 'That's very kind of you,' she said meekly. 'I'm quite well excepting for a bit of a headache.'

He gave her a smile which he might have given to a child. 'I know. All the same, you will stay where you are until I say that you may get up.'

Mary Jane nodded and closed her eyes, not because she was sleepy any more, but because to look at him when she loved him so much was more than she could bear. When she opened them he had gone and the large cheerful nurse was standing by the bed with tea and toast on a tray.

It took two more days for her headache to go, and even though she felt better, the cold dragged on. Two days in which Fabian came and went, his visits brief and impersonal and kindly, during which he conferred with the nurse, made polite conversation with herself, read her notes and went away again. On the morning of the third day he was accompanied by a young man whom he introduced as his registrar, a good-looking, merry-faced young man, trying his hardest to copy his chief's every mannerism; something which might have amused Mary Jane ordinarily, but which struck her now as rather touching. He listened attentively while Fabian explained what had happened to her and agreed immediately when Fabian suggested that she might be ready to leave hospital. He stayed a little longer, talking to Mary Jane, and then at a word from Fabian, took himself off.

She had got up and dressed that morning and had been sitting by the window watching the busy court-yard below, but she turned round now to face Fabian. She had had a few minutes to pull herself together; she said in a matter-of-fact voice, 'I should like to go home tomorrow if you will allow it and it isn't too much trouble to arrange. I'm perfectly well again. Thank you for looking after me so well...'

He made a small, impatient sound. 'You will do nothing of the kind, that would be foolish, at least for the next few days. As soon as I consider you fit for travelling I will arrange your journey. In the meantime you will come to my house—my housekeeper will look after you.'

She sat up very straight in her chair, which caused her to cough, sneeze and give herself a headache all at the same moment. Her voice was still a little thick with her cold when she spoke. 'I don't think I want to do that—it's very kind of you, but...'

'Why not?' he sounded amused.

'I've been quite enough trouble to you as it is.'

His ready agreement disconcerted her. 'Oh, indeed you have—you will be even more trouble if you don't do as I ask now. I shall be in Utrecht, and Mevrouw Hol will be delighted to have someone to fuss over while I am away. You shall go back to England when I return.'

Her reply was polite and wooden. If ever she had

needed to convince herself of his indifference to her, she had the answer now. His obvious anxiety to get her off his hands even while he was treating her with such care and courtesy and arranging for her comfort, told her that, and he didn't care a rap for her...

'What are you thinking?' he demanded.

'Oh, nothing, just—just that it will be nice to be home again. Are you going to Utrecht straight away?'

He was leaning against the wall, staring at her. 'To-night. You will be taken to my house tomorrow morning, Mevrouw Hol is expecting you. Her English is as fragmental as your Dutch; it will be good for both of you. She is a very kind woman, you will be happy with her. She has the same good qualities as your Mrs Body—to whom, by the way, I have written.'

Mary Jane was startled to think that she had quite forgotten to do that.

'Oh, I forgot—how stupid of me, I'm sorry.'

'You have had concussion,' he reminded her, and added with a little smile, 'And you have no reason to be apologetic about everything.'

She coloured painfully and just stopped herself in time from saying that she was sorry for that too. Instead she wished him a pleasant time in Utrecht, her quiet voice giving no clue to her imagination, already vividly at work on beautiful girls, dinners for two... perhaps he had another house there. He strolled to the door, his eyes on her still.

'But of course I shall,' he told her. 'I always do.' He opened the door and turned round to say, 'We shall see each other before you go, I have no doubt.' With a careless nod he was gone, and presently, by craning

her neck, she was able to see him crossing the courtyard below, Klaus Vliet, his registrar, beside him. She
couldn't see them very clearly because she was crying.

She left the hospital the following day, just before
noon, and was driven to Fabian's house by Klaus, who
called to fetch her from her room in the private wing of
the hospital, explaining that his chief had told him to
do so—furthermore, he was to see her safely installed
with Mevrouw Hol and call daily until such time as
her guardian told him not to. Mary Jane, now she was
up and about, was disappointed to find that she still
had a headache, it made her irritable and she would
have liked to have disputed this high-handed measure
on Fabian's part, but she couldn't be bothered. She accepted the news without comment and closed her eyes
against the dullness of the city streets.

But inside Fabian's house it wasn't dull at all, but
gay with flowers and warm and welcoming. Mevrouw
Hol was a dear; round and cosy and middle-aged with
kind blue eyes and a motherly face. Mary Jane, whose
headache had reached splitting point, took one look at
her and burst into tears, to be instantly comforted, led
to a chair by the fire in the sitting room where she had
tea with Fabian, divested of her outdoor things, told
not to worry, and given coffee while Klaus tactfully
left them to fetch her case and carry it upstairs. He
joined her for coffee presently, ignoring her blotched
face, and when they had finished it, ordered her to lie
down the minute she had eaten the lunch Mevrouw Hol
was even then bringing to her on a tray. He gave her
some tablets too, with strict instructions to take them
as directed. 'And mind you do,' he warned her kindly,

'or the chief will have my head.' He got up. 'I'm going now, but I shall be here tomorrow morning to see how you are. Mevrouw has instructions to telephone if you feel at all under the weather.'

Mary Jane smiled shakily at him. 'You make me feel as though I were gold bullion at the very least!'

'Better than that,' he grinned, 'above rubies.' He lifted a hand. 'Be seeing you!'

She ate her lunch under Mevrouw Hol's watchful eye and went upstairs to lie down. Her room was at the back of the house, overlooking a very small paved courtyard, set around with tubs full of Algerian irises and wintersweet. The room was delightful, not very large and most daintily furnished in the Chippendale style with *Toile de Jouy* curtains in pink and a thick white carpet underfoot. She looked round her with some interest, for it didn't seem at all the kind of room Fabian would wish for in his home. She had always imagined that above stairs, the rooms would be furnished with spartan simplicity. She didn't know why she had thought that, perhaps because he was a bachelor, but of course, the house would have been furnished years ago, for everything was old and beautiful. As she closed her eyes she thought how nice it would be to live in the old house, nicer than her grandfather's even.

She felt much better the following morning. She had done nothing for the rest of the previous day, only rested and eaten her supper under Mevrouw Hol's kindly eye and gone to bed again, and now after a long night's rest she felt quite herself again, even her headache had gone.

Perhaps it was her peaceful surroundings, she

thought, as she accompanied the housekeeper on a gentle tour of the kitchen regions, for it was peaceful back in the hall. She stood still, listening to the rich ticktock of the elaborate wall clock before wandering into the sitting room to sit, quite content, in one of the comfortable chairs, doing nothing. The sound of the great knocker on the front door roused her though and she got up to greet Klaus, who, after carrying out a conscientious questioning as to her state of health, joined her for coffee. He stayed for half an hour, talking gently about nothing in particular, and when he got up to go, promised to return the next day. When she assured him that this was quite unnecessary, he looked shocked and told her that he had been asked to do so by the chief and would on no account go against his wishes. Nor would he allow her to go out, not that day, at any rate.

'Well,' said Mary Jane, a little pettish, 'anyone would think that I had a subdural or a CVA or something equally horrid. I only bumped my head...'

'And caught a cold,' he told her, laughing.

Two more days passed and she felt quite well again. Even her cold had cleared up and Klaus, looking her over carefully each morning, had to admit at last that he could find nothing wrong with her, a remark which caused her to ask: 'Well, when's Professor van der Blocq coming back?'

Klaus put down his coffee cup and looked at her in bewilderment. 'Coming back? But he has never been away.' His pleasant face cleared. 'Ah, you mean when does he come back to his house? Very soon, I should suppose, for I am able to give him a good account of you today, so surely he will not allow you to return to your home.' He grinned at her disarmingly. 'He is not of our generation, the chief—he holds old-fashioned views about things which we younger men think nothing of.'

She went a bright, angry pink. 'Don't talk as though he were an old man!' she said sharply. 'And I share his views.'

Klaus smiled ruefully. 'I see that I must beg your pardon, and I do so most sincerely. You must not think that I mock at the chief—he is a mighty man in surgery and a good man in his life and much liked and respected—I myself would wish to be like him.' He looked at her with curiosity. 'You knew, then, that he was living in the hospital until you are well enough to leave his house?'

'Of course.' Her voice, even to her own ears, sounded satisfyingly convincing. 'I am his ward, you know. It's like having a father...'

The absurdity of the remark struck her even as she made it. Fabian was no more like a father than the young man sitting opposite her. 'Well, not quite,' she conceded, 'but you know what I mean.'

He agreed politely, although she could see that he had little idea of what she meant; she wasn't certain herself. He got up to go presently, wishing her goodbye because he didn't expect to see her again, 'Although I daresay that you will visit your guardian from time to time,' he hazarded, 'and I expect to be here for some years.'

She gave him a smiling reply, longing for him to go so that she could have time to herself to think. To learn that Fabian had been in Groningen all the time she had been at his house, and had made no effort to come and see her, had been a shock she was just beginning to realize. Maybe he was old-fashioned in his views, she was herself, and she could respect him for them, but not even the most strait-laced member of the community could have seen any objection to him going to see her in his own house—or telephoning, for that matter—and surely he could have said something to her? There was only one possible explanation, he was quite indifferent to her; considered her a nuisance he felt obliged to suffer until she was fit to return home. It would have been nice to have confronted him with this, but then he might ask her how it was that she knew he had been in Groningen, and unless she could think of some brilliant lie, poor Klaus would get the blame for speaking out of turn. She allowed several possibilities, most of them highly impractical, to flit through her head before deciding regretfully that she was a poor liar in any case, and she would not have the nerve, not with Fabian's dark, penetrating gaze bent upon her, so she discarded them all to explore other possibilities.

She could run away—a phrase she hastily changed to beating a retreat—if she did that, it would save Fabian the necessity of arranging her journey and at the same time save her pride and allow him to see that she was quite able to look after herself. She didn't need his help, she told herself firmly, in future she would have nothing to do with him. Doubtless he would be delighted—had he not told her that she was tiresome to him? Mary Jane paced up and down the comfortable room, in a splendid rage which was almost, but not quite, strong enough to conceal her love for him. But for the time being, it served its purpose—she would write him a letter, thanking him for all he had done… She began to plot, sitting before the fire in the pleasant room.

By lunch-time she had it all worked out, she would leave that very afternoon. She wouldn't be able to take her case with her, but Klaus had said that she might go for a short walk if she had a mind to. He had told Mevrouw Hol this—it made it all very easy; she had her passport and plenty of money still, she could buy what she needed as she went, and this time she would fly—it would be quicker and she supposed that there would be several flights to London once she got to Schiphol. She ate her lunch on a wave of false excitement and over her coffee began the letter to Fabian.

Her pen was poised over the paper while she composed a few dignified sentences in her head when the door opened and he walked in. If he saw her startled jump and the guilty way she tried to hide her writing pad and pen, he said nothing.

'Young Vliet tells me you're quite recovered,' he began without preamble. 'I've arranged for you to travel home this evening.'

She gazed at him speechlessly, feeling dreadfully deflated after all her careful planning, and when she didn't speak, he went on, 'I expected you to express instant delight, instead of which you look flabbergasted and dreadfully guilty. What have you been doing?'

'Nothing—nothing at all.' Her voice came out in a protesting, earnest squeak. 'I'm surprised, that's all.

I—I was—that is...' She remembered something. 'Did you have a nice time in Utrecht?'

'Yes. I see you're writing letters—leave them here and I'll see that they're posted.'

She was breathless. 'No—that is, they're not important—there's no need...' She tore the sheet across and crumpled it up very small and threw it on the fire. She had only got as far as 'Dear Fabian,' but she didn't want him to see even that. She sighed loudly without knowing it and said with a brightness born of relief, 'There, I can write all the letters I want to when I get home.'

Fabian had seated himself opposite her and was pouring himself the coffee which Mevrouw Hol had just brought in. 'Not to Mervyn, I hope?'

'Mervyn?' She stared at him, her mouth a little open. She had forgotten about Mervyn because there wasn't anyone else in the world while Fabian was there. 'Oh, Mervyn,' she said at last, 'no, of course not. I don't know where he is.' She stared at the hands in her lap. 'I don't want to know, either.'

'The temptation to say "I told you so" is very great, but I won't do that.' He put down his cup. 'The train leaves here about six o'clock—do you need anything or wish to go anywhere before you leave?'

He wanted her out of the way. She got to her feet and said coldly, 'No, thank you—I'll go and put a few things together...'

'Five minutes' work,' he was gently mocking, 'but it's as good an excuse as any, I imagine.' He went to the door and opened it for her. 'I shall be in the study if you should want anything,' he told her.

She made no attempt to pack her case when she reached her room; he was right, five minutes was more than enough time in which to cast her few things in and slam the lid. She sat down in the little bucket chair by the window and stared down into the little courtyard, not seeing it at all. It was a very good thing that she was going away, although perhaps not quite as she had planned. She should never have come in the first place, only Fabian had been so insistent. She allowed her thoughts to dwell briefly on Cousin Emma and Doctor Trouw and wondered if she would ever see them again—perhaps they would come and stay with her later on, then she would get news of Fabian. Although wasn't a clean break better? He had told her that her affairs were now in good order, anything which needed seeing to could be done by letter or through Mr North.

She got up and prowled round the room, touching its small treasures with a gentle finger—glass and porcelain and silver—Fabian had a lovely home and she would never forget it. Presently she sat down again and dozed off.

Mevrouw Hol wakened her for tea, bustling into the room, wanting to know if she felt well and was she cold, or would she like her tea in her room. Mary Jane shook her head to each question and went downstairs. There was no sign of Fabian; she ate her tea as she had always done, from a tray on the small table by the fire. He must have gone back to the hospital. She poured a second cup, wondering if he had left instructions as to how she was to get to the station.

She finished her tea and went back upstairs to ram her things into her case in a most untidy, uncaring fashion, not in the least like her usual neat ways, and, that done, went back downstairs and out to the kitchen where Mevrouw Hol was preparing dinner. Mary Jane watched her for a moment and asked in her frightful Dutch: 'People for dinner?' and when Mevrouw Hol nodded, felt a pang of pure envy and curiosity shoot through her. 'How many?' she wanted to know.

The housekeeper shot her a thoughtful glance. 'Three,' she said, 'two ladies and a gentleman.'

'Married?' asked Mary Jane before she could stop herself.

Mevrouw Hol nodded, and Mary Jane, her imagination at work again, had a vivid mental picture of some distinguished couple, and—the crux of the whole matter—a beautiful girl—blonde, and wearing couture clothes, she decided, her imagination working overtime. She would have a disdainful look and Fabian would adore her. She got down from the edge of the table where she had perched herself. 'I'll get ready,' she said in her terrible Dutch.

She went downstairs at twenty to six, because Fabian had said that the train went at six o'clock, and perhaps she should get a taxi. She was hatted and coated and ready to leave and there was no sign of anyone. Fabian came out of his study as she reached the hall. He said briefly: 'I'll get your case,' and when he came downstairs again she ventured, 'Should I call a taxi—there's not much time.' She searched his tranquil face. 'I didn't know you'd come back,' she explained.

'I've been here all the afternoon—I had some work to do. If you're ready we'll go.'

'Oh—are you taking me to the station? I thought...'

'Never mind what you thought. Don't you agree that as your guardian the least I can do is to see you safely on the way to England?'

She had no answer to that but went in search of Mevrouw Hol, who shook her by the hand and wished her *'Tot ziens,'* adding a great deal in her own language which Mary Jane couldn't understand in the least.

The journey to the station was short, a matter of a few minutes, during which Mary Jane sought vainly for something to say. She couldn't believe that she was actually going—that perhaps she might not see Fabian again for a long time, perhaps never, for he had no reason to see her again.

She looked sideways at his calm profile and then at his gloved hands resting on the wheel. She loved him very much; she had no idea that loving someone could hurt so fiercely. She went with him silently into the station and on to the platform and found the train already there. She watched while Fabian spoke to the guard, took the tickets which he handed to her and thanked him in a small voice.

'There's a seat in the dining car reserved for you,' he told her. 'Someone will fetch you. The guard will see about a porter for you when you reach the Hoek. Just go on board, everything is arranged. There's a seat booked on the breakfast car from Harwich. Have you your headache tablets with you?'

'Yes, thank you, and thank you for taking so much trouble, Fabian.'

'You had better get in,' he advised her, and disappeared, to reappear within a few minutes with a bundle of magazines. 'Don't read too much,' he told her.

She lingered on the steps. 'I must owe you quite a bit—for the journey—shall I send it to you?'

'Don't bother. Mr North will settle with me.' He put out a hand. 'Goodbye, Mary Jane, have a good trip.'

She shook hands and answered him in a steady voice—how useful pride could be on occasion! She even added a few meaningless phrases, the sort of thing one says when one is bidding someone goodbye at a railway station. He dismissed them with a half smile and got out of the train. She watched him getting smaller and smaller as the train gathered speed and finally went round a curve, and then he was gone.

The journey was smooth and so well organised that she had no worries at all; it was as though an unseen Fabian was there, smoothing her path. She wondered to what trouble he had gone to have made everything so easy for her. It was a pity that his thoughtfulness was partly wasted, for she spent a wretched night and no amount of make-up could help the pallor of her face or the tell-tale puffiness of her eyelids. She arrived, thoroughly dispirited, at Liverpool Street station in the cold rain of the January morning, and the first person she saw was Mrs Body.

Chapter 9

Later, looking back on that morning, Mary Jane knew that she had reached the end of her tether by the time she had reached London, although she hadn't known it then, only felt an upsurge of relief and delight at the sight of Mrs Body in her sensible tweeds and best hat. She had almost fallen out of the train in her eagerness to get to her and fling herself at the older woman, and Mrs Body, standing foursquare amidst the hurrying passengers, had given her a motherly hug and sensibly made no remark about her miserable face, but had said merely that the dear doctor had been quite right to ask her to come to London, much though she disliked the place, for by all accounts Mary Jane had had a nasty bang on the head. She then hurried her into a taxi and on to the next train for home, and Mary Jane, exhausted by her feelings more than the rigours of the journey, slept most of the way.

She had been home for almost a week now, a week during which she had filled her days with chores around the house and long walks with a delighted Major trailing at her heels. Her evenings she spent chatting with Mrs Body, talking about the village and what had happened in it while she had been away, various household matters, and the state of the garden. Of Holland she spoke not at all, excepting to touch lightly upon the wedding and her fall, and to her relief neither Mrs Body nor Lily had displayed any curiosity as to what she had done while she was there, nor, after that one remark Mrs Body had made on Liverpool Street station, had Fabian been mentioned. It should have made it all the easier to erase him from her mind, but it did no such thing; she found herself thinking of him constantly, his face, with its remote expression and the little smile which so disconcerted her, floated before her eyes last thing at night, and was there waiting for her when she wakened in the morning; it was really very vexing.

She tried inviting a few of her grandfather's old friends in for drinks one evening and realised too late that they were deeply interested in her visits to Holland, and wanted to know all about that country, and what was more, about her guardian too. They discussed him at some length—very much to his advantage, she was quick to note—and old Mr North, when asked to add his opinion to those of the other elderly gentlemen present, observed that, in his judgement, Jonkheer van der Blocq was a man of integrity, very much to be trusted and the right man to solve any problem. 'That episode with Mr Mervyn Pettigrew, for example,' he began, and then coughed dryly. 'I beg your pardon, Mary Jane, I should not have mentioned him; doubtless your feelings on the matter are still painful.'

He smiled kindly at her, as did his companions, and she smiled gently back, happily conscious that her feelings weren't painful at all, at least not about Mervyn. 'It doesn't matter,' she assured them, 'I got over that some time ago.' She realised as she said it that it was only a few weeks since her heart had been broken and had mended itself so quickly. 'I made a mistake,' she said calmly. 'Luckily it was discovered in time.'

'Indeed yes, and solely due to your guardian's efforts. To travel to Canada when everyone was enjoying their Christmas showed great determination on his part. I feel that your future is in safe hands, my dear.'

The other gentlemen murmured agreement, and Mary Jane, busy playing hostess, wished with all her heart that what Mr North had said was true; there was nothing she would have liked better than to have had a safe future with Fabian, not quite such a one as her companions envisaged perhaps, but infinitely more interesting.

The next morning, urged on by a desire to do something, no matter what, she took the Mini to Carlisle and bought clothes. She really didn't need them; she had plenty of sensible tweeds and jersey dresses and several evening outfits which, as far as she could see, she couldn't hope to wear out, let alone wear. She had bought them when Mervyn had come to visit her. Now, speeding towards the shops, she decided that

she loathed the sight of them; she would give them all
away and buy something new.

Once having made this resolve, she found that nothing could stop her; several dresses she bought for the
very good reason that they were pretty and she looked
nice in them, even though she could think of no occasion when she might wear them. She balanced this
foolishness by purchasing a couple of outfits which
she could wear each day, and, her conscience salved,
bought several pairs of shoes, expensive ones, quite
unsuitable for the life she led, and undies, all colours
of the rainbow.

She bought a red dressing gown for Mrs Body too,
and more glamorous undies for Lily, who was going
steady with the postman and was making vague plans
for a wedding in the distant future.

She and Mrs Body and Lily spent an absorbing evening, inspecting her purchases, but later, when she
was alone in her room, she hung the gay dresses away,
wondering wistfully if she would ever wear them. It
seemed unlikely, but it wasn't much good brooding
over it. She closed the closet door upon them and got
into bed, where she lay, composing a letter to Fabian,
reminding him that she still hadn't got a horse to ride.
The exercise kept her mind occupied for some time and
although she knew that she would never write it, and
certainly not send it, it gave her a kind of satisfaction.
She should have said something about it in the short,
stiff letter she had written to him when she arrived
home, a conventional enough missive, thanking him
for his thoughtful arrangement of her journey and his
care of her while she had been in hospital. It had taken

her a long time to write and she had wasted several sheets of notepaper before the composition had satisfied her. He hadn't answered it.

The weather, which had been almost springlike for a few days, worsened the next morning, with cold grey clouds covering the sky, a harsh wind whistling through the bare trees and a light powdering of snow covering the ground. A beastly day, thought Mary Jane, looking out of the window while she pulled on her slacks and two sweaters. She had promised Mrs Body and Lily most of the day off too, to attend a wedding in the village, and heaven knew what time they would get back; weddings were something of an event in their quiet community and the occasion of lengthy hospitality. With an eye to the worsening weather, Mary Jane saw them off after an early lunch and went back to the kitchen to wash up and set the tea tray. This done, she wandered into the sitting room. It looked inviting with a bright fire burning and Major snoozing before it, but there was a lot of the day to get through still; she decided on a walk, a long one down to the lake and along its shore for a few miles and then back over the hills, and if the weather got too bad she could always take to the road. It would get rid of the restlessness she felt, she told herself firmly, and went to put on an old mackintosh and gumboots.

They set off, she and Major, ten minutes later—it was no day for a walk, but she was content to plod along in the teeth of the wind, thinking about Fabian, and Major was content to plod with her.

They got back home at the end of a prematurely darkened afternoon—the snow had settled a little, de-

spite the wind, and the daylight had almost gone. The
cold had become pitiless. Mary Jane and Major, tired
and longing for tea and the fire, turned in at the gate
and hurried up the short drive. The house looked as
cold as its surroundings; she wished she had left a
lamp burning as a welcome, then she remembered as
she reached the door that she hadn't locked it behind
her—not that that mattered, she had Major with her.
But Major had other ideas; he had left her to go round
the side of the house to the back door; years of training having fixed in his doggy mind that on wet days
he had to go in through the garden porch.

She went in alone, pulling off her outdoor things as
she went and casting them down anyhow. The hall was
almost in darkness and she shivered, not from cold but
because she was lonely and unhappy. She said quite
loudly in a miserable voice: 'Oh, Fabian!' and came
to a sudden shocked halt when he said from the dim-
ness, 'Hullo, Mary Jane.'

She turned to stare at him dimly outlined against
the sitting room door and heard his voice, very matter-
of-fact, again. 'You left the door open.'

She nodded into the gloom, temporarily speechless, but presently she managed, 'Have you come about
my horse?'

'No.'

She waited, but that seemed to be all that he was
going to say, and suddenly unable to bear it any longer, she said in a voice a little too loud: 'Please will
you go?'

'If you will give me a good reason—yes.'

She didn't feel quite herself. She supposed it was

the shock of finding him there, but she seemed to have lost all control over her tongue.

'I've been very silly,' her voice was still too loud, but she didn't care. 'It's you I love. I think I've always loved you, but I didn't know—Mervyn was you, if you see what I mean.' She added, quite distraught: 'So please will you go away—now.' Her voice shook a little, her mouth felt dry. She urged: 'Please, Fabian.'

He made no movement. 'What a girl you are for missing the obvious,' he observed pleasantly. 'Why do you suppose I've come?'

She wasn't really listening, being completely taken up with the appalling realisation of her foolish and impetuous speech, but she supposed he expected an answer so she said, 'Oh, the horse—no, you said it wasn't, didn't you. Have I spent too much money? You could have written about that, there was no need for you to have come...'

He crossed the hall and took her in his arms. 'You're a silly girl,' he told her, and his voice was very tender. 'Of course there is a need. Only perhaps I have been silly too—you see, my darling, you are so young and I—I am forty.'

'Oh, what has that got to do with it?' she demanded quite crossly. 'You could be twenty or ninety; you'd still be Fabian, can't you see that?'

His arms tightened around her. 'I'll remember that,' he told her softly, 'my adorable Miss Pettigrew,' and when she would have spoken he drew her a little closer. 'Hush, my love—my darling love. I'm not sure when I fell in love with you, perhaps when we first met, although I wasn't aware of it—that came later, the night

Uncle Georgius died and I opened the sitting-room door and you were on the stairs looking lost and unhappy. But after that you were never there, always disappearing when I came. I waited and waited, hoping that you would love me too, and then Mervyn turned up. I have never been so worried...'

'You didn't look worried,' Mary Jane pointed out.

'Perhaps I'm not very good at showing my feelings,' he told her, 'but I'll try now.' She was wrapped in his arms as though he would never let her go again—a state, she thought dreamily, to which she was happily resigned, and when he kissed her she had no more thoughts at all.

Presently she said into his shoulder, 'I was going to run away, but you came back. I thought you didn't like me being in your house—that you wanted me to come back here.'

He loosed his hold a little so that he could see her face. 'My dearest darling, there was nothing I wanted more than to have you in my home, but you were my ward...'

'You let me go.' She frowned a little, staring up into his dark eyes. 'You arranged for me to go.'

'Because I knew that you would run away if I didn't—you see, my love, I know you better than you know yourself.' He pulled her quite roughly to him and kissed her thoroughly. 'I haven't been the best of guardians, but I shall be a very good husband,' he promised her, and kissed her again, very gently this time.

It was quite dark in the hall by now, and Major, fed up with waiting at the back door, pattered in and came to sit down beside them, thumping his tail on the floor. 'He wants his supper,' said Mary Jane in a dreamy voice.

'So do I, my darling girl.'

She wasn't dreamy any more. 'Oh, my darling Fabian, you're hungry! I'll cook something.' But when she would have slipped from his arms he held her fast. 'Not just yet…'

'We can't stay here all night—Mrs Body and Lily won't be back for ages—they've gone to a wedding.' She smiled up at him, quite content to stay where she was for ever.

'They shall come to ours, my darling.'

'Oh, Fabian!' She could hardly see his face although it was so close to her own, but that didn't matter, nothing mattered any more. Life had become blissfully perfect, stretching out before them for ever. She clasped her hands behind his neck and because she couldn't put her happiness into words, she said again, 'Oh, Fabian!' and kissed him.

* * * * *

A MATTER OF CHANCE

Chapter 1

Cressida Bingley stood at the corner of narrow, dingy street in the heart of Amsterdam and knew that she was lost—temporarily at least. She peered at the map she was holding without much success; the October afternoon was darkening, so that to study it was fruitless. She tried to remember in which direction she had walked from the Dam Square, but the city was built like a spider's web with canals for its threads, and she had wandered aimlessly, looking around her without noting her whereabouts. She bent her head and peered down once more, but the long, foreign names, only half seen in the gathering dusk, eluded her; she was frowning over them when someone spoke behind her and she almost dropped the map. Presumably she had been addressed in Dutch, for she hadn't understood a word. She sighed, for this was the third time that afternoon that a man had stopped and spoken to her; she had been polite with the first one, a little impatient with the second, but now she was vexed. She turned sharply and said in a cold voice, 'I can't understand you, so do go away!'

Her voice died as she saw him; he towered over her own five feet eight inches by at least another eight inches. But it wasn't only his height, he was large, too, blocking her way, and even in the poor light she could see that he was handsome, with a nose which dominated his face, its flared nostrils giving it an air of arrogance. She couldn't see the colour of his eyes, but the brows above them were winged and as pale as his hair. He wasn't quite smiling, his mouth had a mocking quirk, that was all.

'English,' he observed, 'and telling me to go away when you're lost.' His deep voice mocked her, just as his smile did, and it annoyed her.

'I am not lost,' she protested untruthfully. 'I stopped to look at the map…there is no need for you…'

A large, gloved hand took the map from her grasp and turned it right side up. 'Try it that way,' he suggested, 'and unless you are quite sure where you are, even in the dark, I suggest you put your pride in your pocket and let me show you the way—it will be night in another ten minutes, and,' he added blandly, 'this isn't a part of Amsterdam which tourists frequent—certainly not young women such as yourself, at any rate.'

She could hear the amusement behind the blandness and her annoyance sharpened even while she had to admit that she was lost. The street was empty too, and even if someone came along they might not understand her; she would be at a disadvantage. She said stiffly: 'If you would direct me to the Rembrandt Plein—I can find my way from there.'

He looked down at her, smiling quite openly now. 'Very well. Go to the end of this street on your left, turn right and take the second turning on the right— there's a narrow lane half way down which will bring you out into a small square which has five streets leading from it—take the one with the tobacconist's shop on the corner; you'll find the Rembrandt Plein at the end of it.'

Cressida shot him a cold look. 'I think I'll do better if I find my own way, thank you, though I'm sure you mean to be kind…'

He shook his head. 'I'm seldom that,' he assured her placidly, 'but I intend to take you as far as the Rembrandt Plein—it isn't far and I know all the short cuts.' He added silkily: 'You can always scream.'

The thought had crossed her mind too, so that she said very emphatically: 'I have no intention of doing any such thing; I'm very well able to look after myself.'

He smiled again and began to walk briskly down the street he had pointed out to her, and after a moment or so, made a few desultory remarks about Amsterdam and the weather, adding the kind of questions usually asked of tourists: had she seen the Dam Palace, Rembrandt's House, the Rijksmuseum… She answered briefly, intent on keeping pace with his long stride, managing to steal a glance or two at him as they went. He was older than she had first supposed, well into his thirties, she would imagine, and dressed with a quiet elegance which, for some reason, reassured her. If they hadn't started off on the wrong foot, she thought belatedly, she could have asked him where he lived—what he did...'Am I taking you out of your way?' she asked suddenly.

She got an uncompromising 'Yes,' and he added, 'but it's of no importance,' and at that moment they turned a corner and she saw the Rembrandt Plein not many yards away. 'I'm sorry,' she said stiffly. 'I must have taken up your time—I know where I am now.' She came to a halt. 'Good night, and thank you.'

'Don't be silly,' he spoke with amused impatience. 'Where is your hotel?'

Rather to her own surprise, she told him quite meekly, and fell into step beside him again while he crossed the square, its cafés and clubs still half empty before the evening crowds arrived, and took another narrow street on its opposite side.

'This isn't the way,' said Cressida, and stopped again.

'A short cut. My dear good girl, when will you realise that I am merely seeing you to your hotel as quickly as possible, and am not bent on getting to know you—picking you up is the expression, I believe.'

If she had known where to go, she would have left him then and there, but she didn't. She walked beside him, too furious to speak, until the street turned at right angles and opened into the broad street running beside a canal where her hotel was. At its door she wished him a chilly good night, offered even chillier thanks, and whisked herself in through its narrow door. The chilliness was wasted on him, though, for he laughed softly and didn't say a word. He was detestable, she told herself, as she ran up the precipitous stairs to the top floor.

The hotel was small and narrow, supported on either side by equally small and narrow houses—hotels too—a dozen of them in a neat row, with immaculate curtains at their shining windows and semi-basement dining rooms where their guests breakfasted, and where they could, if they wished, have a snack in the evening. Cressida reached the top floor and went down the passage with its rows of doors. Her room was at the end, small, spotlessly clean and pleasantly warm. It was almost six o'clock. In half an hour she would go all the way downstairs again and have coffee and a *broodje* and then come back and pack her bag, but now she sat on the bed, still in her coat, suddenly doubtful about everything. If someone had told her two weeks ago that she would be staying in an Amsterdam hotel, en route for a job in Friesland, she would have laughed at the very idea, yet here she was—and looking back, she wondered at the quirk of fate which had hurried her along towards it, making everything so easy and giving her no time to think until she was here…she took off her coat and started to unpin her hair and then sat brushing it, while she brooded about her future.

Her hair was fine and silky and very dark, hanging down to her waist. Her brows were dark too, thick and well shaped above large brown eyes, generously lashed. Her nose was small and straight and her mouth curved delightfully—a beautiful face, and she had a figure to match it. But although she was staring at her reflection in the small wall mirror, she didn't really see it. 'I must be mad,' she said out loud, and quite forgetful of her hair, put down the brush and did nothing at all while she looked back over the last week or so. Not too far back; she still couldn't think of her father's death and then her mother's so soon after without a deep grief which threatened to engulf her. Her father had been ill for only a few days; visiting a parishioner with 'flu, he had fallen a victim to it himself, and while the parishioner recovered, her father had died, and then, within a week, her mother, leaving her alone and desolate but with little time for grief, for the rectory had to be vacated, the furniture sold and a few modest debts paid, and when that was done, there was very little money over.

It had been a wrench to leave the village in Dorset where she had spent her childhood and all her holidays since she had taken up nursing; she had gathered together a few of her parents' most loved bits and pieces, packed her clothes, and gone to stay with her mother's elder sister, a small, bustling woman who lived alone in a minuscule thatched cottage on the edge of a village in the same county. It was while she was there that she decided to give up her job at the big London hospital where she was Sister of a medical ward, and until she could make up her mind about her future, take private cases. And Aunt Emily had agreed; change, she had observed wisely, was absolutely essential when one had been dealt such a severe blow—and time, time to think about the future and come to terms with it. She thought privately that Cressida would certainly marry later on, once the icy grief which held her fast had thawed a little and she could laugh again and enjoy meeting people. But that was something she couldn't tell her niece; all she could do was to tell her to regard the overcrowded little cottage as her home and know that she was welcome there.

A couple of weeks' peace and quiet had helped Cressida a great deal. Armed with excellent references and a resolve to make a new life for herself, she went up to London and presented herself at an agency highly recommended by her hospital. The temptation to take the first job offered to her was great, but she still had a little money, enough to stay in a rather seedy hotel for a week, until a case turned up which would appeal to her, so she rejected the first few offered to her; a child film star with tonsillitis, a young drug addict, a wealthy widow who really wanted a slave, not a nurse. After the third day she wondered if she was being unduly fussy; some of the girls she met there came in, accepted a case, and were away again in five minutes. But there was another girl who was choosy too—Molly, a small, fair creature with a sweet, rather weak face, who confided to Cressida that she was waiting for a job as far away as possible because she had quarrelled with her fiancé and never wanted to see him again. It was towards the end of the week when she told Cressida that she had got a job, and not through the agency. 'My uncle got it for me; at least, this doctor asked him to find a nurse who could type, and I can. You see, he's writing a book and he needs an English girl—a nurse who'll understand the medical terms—so that she can help him with the English and type it too—and he lives in Holland, so I can get away from Jim.'

She skipped away in great good spirits, leaving

Cressida to make the difficult choice between a case of delirium tremens and an elderly lady who wanted someone to see her through the brief trials of having all her teeth out. Cressida decided against them both, was treated to a brief homily by the agency clerk on being too fussy, and left in her turn, to walk in St James's Park and wish that the months could roll back and she could be on her way home for her holidays. She walked on steadily; she wasn't going to cry, she told herself firmly, not in the middle of a public park, at any rate. She had sat down on a bench and made a great business of feeding the birds with the sandwiches she had brought with her for lunch and didn't want.

She hadn't seen Molly on the following morning and hadn't expected to; probably she was on her way to Holland already. Waiting her turn, she promised herself that she would take the first case she was offered, but when she got into the office the clerk said briskly: 'Sorry, there's nothing today—if you'd been here half an hour earlier I could have fixed you up... Better luck tomorrow.'

She smiled her bright, meaningless smile and Cressida smiled back, not sure if she was relieved or not. She was standing in the agency entrance, trying to make up her mind what to do with her empty day, when Molly came dashing towards her.

'I hoped I'd find you,' she cried breathlessly. 'I've a whole lot to tell you and it'll take a minute or two. There's a café down the street, come and have some coffee.'

'You've made it up with your Jim,' declared Cressida.

Molly caught her by the arm. 'Yes, I have, isn't it super? But that isn't all.'

She had dragged Cressida down the street towards the café. 'That job—the one I said I'd take in Holland—well, I can't go now, can I? I mean, Jim wants us to get married straight away—so I thought of you...' She had paused maddeningly as they entered the café, found a table and ordered coffee. 'You can type, you told me so—and the job is about the alimentary system and its disorders, and you've had a medical ward...don't you see? It's just made for you.'

'But I can't,' said Cressida. 'I don't know this doctor and he doesn't know me.'

Molly opened her handbag and dragged out a small pile of letters. 'Here are all the letters so's you can see that it really is a job—and my uncle says if you could go and see him—he lives in Hampstead, he's got a practice there—this afternoon after surgery...' She had sugared her coffee and continued: 'Oh, you must! You wanted something interesting and different, didn't you? Uncle says it would take about six or seven weeks, and the pay's good. At least go and see my uncle.'

And Cressida had said yes quickly before she could change her mind.

Molly's uncle had been nice; elderly and a little slow, and although he had asked her a great many questions, he had been so nice about it that she hadn't minded answering them. 'It seems to me,' he told her finally, 'that this job is just what you need. I appreciate your need to get away, Miss Bingley, and Doctor van Blom is most anxious to find someone who can type adequately as well as give him occasional help with the turn of a phrase and so on.' He smiled kindly. 'May I take it that you will help him out?'

Cressida had said that yes, she would like to very much, but she would have to get her passport renewed and pack a few things. He had nodded and said, 'Quite—could you be ready in four or five days' time?'

They had made their arrangements there and then, but it was Cressida who had decided to leave two days earlier and spend them in Amsterdam. One of her friends at the hospital gave her the name of the hotel and she had had no difficulty in getting a room.

She had spent her two days exploring the city, spending hours in the museums, walking endlessly beside the canals, looking at the old houses which lined their banks, eating frugally at lunch bars, and window-shopping. And now, in the morning, she would catch a train to Leeuwarden where she would be met.

She glanced at the clock and began to coil her hair rapidly; the dining room was only open for a short time each evening; the hotel guests were expected to dine out, the snacks were for those who had just arrived, or who, for some reason or other, were going to spend their evening in their rooms.

There was a very small room by the entrance where one could get a drink or coffee, but Cressida had never seen anyone in it. She did her face and washed her hands and went down the staircase once more, to the basement, where she sat down at a table for one, drank the coffee she ordered and ate two ham rolls. They were excellent, but she had very little appetite. Indeed, she had grown thin during the last few weeks; meals, like so many other things, had become just something to get through as best she might. She supposed that in time everything would be normal again, as the incoming rector had assured her when he had called to make himself known to her and arrange to move into the rectory. Time he had said, healed everything, and she hadn't disputed that fact; only time, when it lay heavy, took a long time to pass.

She went back to her room presently and packed her case, had a shower in the cramped cabinet down the passage, and got into bed. She wasn't sleepy, but bed gave an illusion of cosiness. She had a sudden, vivid memory of the sitting room in her old home, with a log fire blazing in the hearth and the shabby armchairs pulled close to it, and for a moment she couldn't see the map she was studying for the tears in her eyes, but she brushed them away resolutely and applied herself once more to its perusal. Molly's uncle had told her that Doctor van Blom lived in a village between Groningen and Leeuwarden, he had told her the name too, but the two cities were thirty miles apart and from the numerous villages between, not one of their peculiar-looking names rang a bell of recognition. She would have to wait and see.

The tram Cressida took to the station in the morning was packed with early morning workers, but the train, when she eventually found the right platform and caught it by the skin of her teeth, was almost empty. She sat in her corner seat, watching the small flat fields give way to the woods and heaths of the Veluwe and then fields again, but now they had become wide and rolling and the towns less frequent. She had chosen to

go via Groningen, and that city, when the train reached
it, looked invitingly picturesque as well as large and
bustling. As the train pulled away from the station she
craned her neck to see the last of its spires and towers
and then turned to look at the countryside with some
eagerness. Somewhere close by was the village where
she was to spend the next few weeks. She stared at the
strange names on the station boards as they passed,
but both Dutch and Friesian names were quite incomprehensible to her. However, she had been told not to
worry about the language; Doctor van Blom spoke excellent English and the people she would meet would
have a sufficient knowledge of it to make her lack of
Dutch no problem at all.

She got out at Leeuwarden station with much the
same feeling as she experienced when she entered a
dentist's surgery; her future employer might be bad-
tempered, impatient, a slave-driver... She stood under
the clock on the platform as she had been told to do,
and looked around her, and a great many people looked
back at her, for she was quite eye-catching, her beautiful face pale with excitement and apprehension, her
nicely cut tweed coat showing off her slenderness to
perfection, the brown fur hat perched on top of her
shining bun of hair highlighting its vivid darkness.

She didn't have to wait long; from the people around
her there emerged a short, stout man in his late middle
years. He came straight at her, beaming all over his
nice round face, beginning to talk to her long before he
reached her. 'Miss Bingley—Miss Cressida Bingley—
what a charming name! I am delighted to welcome you;
you see that I knew you at once.' He was pumping her

arm up and down as he spoke. 'My old friend Doctor Mills described you so well...you have luggage with you? This case only? Then we will go to the car at once and return to my home as quickly as possible. We will drink coffee together and talk of my book which I am so anxious to complete.'

He walked as he talked, his hand on her arm, edging her towards the station entrance where a splendidly kept dark blue Chevrolet stood. He ushered her into the front seat, put her luggage in the boot and got into the driving seat. 'Fifteen of your English miles,' he observed, 'we shall be there very shortly.'

But not as shortly as all that, Cressida discovered. They drove very slowly through the city, a busy, bustling place she wanted to explore, and she wondered if there was something about Dutch motoring laws she didn't know—a twenty-mile speed limit in towns, for instance, and yet everyone else was travelling twice as fast. Perhaps her new employer was just a very cautious driver. On the outskirts of Leeuwarden he achieved a steady thirty, while cars flashed past at thrice that speed and Cressida, who in happier times had driven her father's car rather well, longed to stretch out a neatly booted foot and slam it down on the accelerator, for it seemed to her a crying shame to own such a powerful car and not make use of it. She kept her itching foot still and watched the slowly passing scenery while she answered her companion's stream of questions. Even if he was a shocking driver, he was rather an old dear.

They turned off the main road presently and trickled cautiously down a narrow lane. 'Eestrum,' the doctor informed her as they approached and passed through a smallish village. 'We go to Augustinusga, that is where I live, so well placed between Leeuwarden and Groningen. It is convenient for me—and my partners—to travel to either place.'

'Partners?' asked Cressida. No one had mentioned them.

'Doctor Herrima—we share a house and a housekeeper—and Doctor van der Teile, who is the senior partner and does not live in the village. We consult him, you understand; all the more difficult cases, but for the most of the time he is either at Leeuwarden or Groningen, for he has beds in both hospitals as well as consulting rooms. He is a distinguished physician and travels a good deal.'

Cressida murmured politely; he would be a very elderly man, she imagined, for Doctor van Blom was certainly in his sixties and this other partner was the senior...the third partner would be the youngest and the junior. The three bears; she suppressed a giggle.

Her companion had dropped the car's speed to a smart walking pace and began pointing out local landmarks. A windmill, standing lonely in the wintry fields by a canal, a little wood on the other side of the water, bare and dull in the morning's grey bleakness, but, she was assured, a charming place in the spring. An austere red brick church with plain glass windows came into view and a cosy little house beside it. 'The *dominee* and his wife live there,' explained Doctor van Blom. 'A good friend of ours, and here, at the beginning of the village, is an excellent example of our Friesian farms.'

Cressida was still craning her neck to see the last of it as they entered the village itself, circled the square lined with houses and stopped cautiously outside one of them, a red brick house with its door exactly in the centre and its windows arranged across its face in mathematical rows. She hoped it wasn't as plain inside as it was out, and had her hope realised; the front door opened on to a long, narrow hall, lofty-ceilinged and a little dark and from which numerous doors opened. Doctor van Blom threw open the first of these and ushered her in, at the same time raising his voice in a mild bellow. This was instantly answered in person by his housekeeper, a tall, thin woman, no longer young but with such a forceful air about her that one could have imagined her barely in her prime. She smiled at the doctor, smiled at Cressida, shook her hand and followed them into what was obviously the sitting-room, comfortably furnished, the leather chairs a little shabby perhaps, but there was some beautiful china and silver lying around on shelves and tables, rather as though someone had just been admiring the objects and set them down haphazardly. There were shelves of books, too, and an old-fashioned stove giving off a most welcome heat.

Cressida took the chair she was offered and sur-rendered her coat to the housekeeper, her unhappy heart much cheered by her kindly reception, and when Juffrouw Naald went away and came back a moment later with a tray laden with coffee-cups and biscuits, she partook of these refreshments with more pleasure than she had felt for some time.

They had been sitting for perhaps ten minutes when

the door opened and a tall, thin man, about the same age as Doctor van Blom, came in. 'My partner, Doctor Herrima,' her employer told her, and after introductions had been made, Cressida found herself sitting between the two of them, filling their coffee-cups and answering their gentle questions.

'A pretty girl,' observed Doctor Herrima to no one in particular, 'a very pretty girl.' He looked keenly at her. 'And you can type, I understand?'

She assured him that she could.

'You are also a nurse?'

'Oh, yes,' she told him, 'I've been trained for more than four years.'

He looked across at his partner. 'A splendid choice.' And when his partner nodded happily, 'What do you think of our country, Miss Bingley?'

Cressida put down her cup. 'Well, I haven't seen a great deal of it. Two days in Amsterdam and then coming here by train...'

'You must see Leeuwarden and Groningen—now there are two magnificent centuries-old cities. Do you drive?' It was Doctor van Blom who spoke.

'Yes—we had a rather elderly Morris.'

'Ah.' He pondered this for a minute. 'My car is a powerful one, as you may have noticed, and Doctor Herrima runs a BMW. I do not know if you feel competent to drive either of them?' He sounded doubtful.

Cressida thought of the snail-like pace at which they had driven from Leeuwarden and replied soberly that she thought she would be capable of driving either of the cars. Indeed, the idea of driving the Chev on one of the excellent motorways appealed to her very much:

to drive and drive and drive, away from her grief and loneliness.

She shut her mind to the idea and made a suitably admiring remark about the car, to which Doctor van Blom responded with instant eagerness. They were two dears, she decided; unworldly and content in their rather cluttered, pleasant sitting-room.

She asked diffidently about their practice and was told at some length and sometimes twice over that it was a large one, covering a great number of outlying villages and farms; that they had a baby clinic once a week, a small surgery for emergencies, and dealt with a wide variety of patients.

'There are quite a number of accidents,' explained Doctor van Blom, 'farms, you know—they have these modern machines, some of them are complicated and if a farm worker doesn't understand what he is doing...' He gave a little shrug. 'And then of course there are those who live some way away, and they tend to delay sending for us or coming to the surgery, and some-times the injury or illness is made much worse in con-sequence. We have splendid hospitals, of course, and our senior partner is always available for consultation.' He wagged his balding head. 'A very clever man,' he stated, 'as well as our great friend. He had an English godfather, and you will find his English excellent.'

Cressida dismissed this paragon with a nice smile and asked about the book. 'When would you like me to start?' she wanted to know.

'You feel that you could start today? Splendid, Miss Bingley—perhaps after lunch?'

'That would be fine, and please will you call me Cressida?'

They both beamed at her. 'With pleasure. And now you would like to go to your room and unpack. We have lunch at noon—is that time enough for you to settle in?'

They escorted her to the door, cried in unison for Juffrouw Naald, and stood watching her as she trod up the steep, uncarpeted stairs to the floor above, with the housekeeper leading the way.

Her room was in the front of the house, a corner room with big windows so that she had a wide view of the square below and the houses around it. It was nicely furnished if a trifle heavily, with Second Empire mahogany bed, matching chest of drawers, a ponderous dressing table and an enormous clothes closet. There was a small easy chair by the window and a writing table and a little shelf of books. Leading from it was a well-appointed bathroom; after the tiny room in Aunt Emily's cottage, it seemed like luxury to Cressida. Someone had put chrysanthemums in a vase by the bed too; she smiled and touched them and looked at Juffrouw Naald who smiled and nodded and said something Cressida couldn't understand, but it sounded friendly.

When the housekeeper had gone, Cressida unpacked quickly, tidied her hair and did her face and repaired downstairs, to find both doctors waiting for her.

'We drink Jenever, but for you we have sherry—shall we take a glass now before lunch? You are hungry?'

They both stood looking at her with eager kindness

and she hastened to assure them that she was—a pleasant sensation after weeks of not bothering what she ate. She accompanied them into the dining-room, a lofty apartment, furnished with mahogany as solid as her bedroom was and with a crimson carpet underfoot and crimson curtains at its windows, a suitable background for the snow-white tablecloth and shining silver. The meal was a simple one; the doctors, they assured her, liked their dinner in the evening after surgery, but she found the soup, dish of cold meats and the basket of various breads more than sufficient. There was no surgery that afternoon, she was told, so that there was no need for them to hurry over their meal, and after it she and Doctor van Blom could retire to his study while Doctor Herrima did the afternoon round. If he explained his work, suggested the doctor, perhaps she might make a start on sorting out the manuscript and preparing it for typing? She could have the evening too, while he took surgery. He passed his cup for more coffee and while she was pouring it, the door opened and in walked the man who had taken her back to her hotel in Amsterdam the day before. Cressida put down the coffee-pot carefully, and with the cup and saucer still in her hand, sat staring at him, her pretty mouth very slightly open.

'Giles,' boomed Doctor van Blom, 'what good fortune—now you can meet the young lady who is to help me with my book—Miss Cressida Bingley.' He waved a hand. 'Cressida, this is our senior partner, Doctor van der Teile.'

He closed the door after him and crossed over to her chair. 'You look surprised,' he observed blandly.

'Well, I am... I didn't expect...'

'No? But my dear girl, it was inevitable.' He took the cup and saucer from her, handed it across the table to his partner and pulled out a chair for himself. 'Cressida and I have already met,' he told his partners, and when the fresh coffee came, accepted a cup before asking her, in the politest manner possible, if she would forgive him if he discussed a case with his partners.

And if that isn't a hint to make myself scarce, I don't know what is, thought Cressida. She gave him a haughty look and got up at once. 'I have my unpacking to finish,' she assured him, and sailed to the door, only to find him there to open it for her.

'I'll be gone very shortly,' he murmured as she went past him. 'You can safely come down again in half an hour.'

Chapter 2

Doctor Van Der Teile had gone by the time Cressida, rather uncertain as to what was expected of her, went downstairs again, but Doctor van Blom put his head round a door as she reached the hall, obviously on the lookout for her, and invited her to enter his study.

'No time like the present,' he assured her with the air of a man who had just thought up a clever remark, and ushered her in. Compared with the sitting-room it was quite small, furnished with a large desk with a leather chair behind it, a pair of similar chairs on either side of the stove, and a smaller desk against one wall with a typewriter on it. The walls were lined with vast quantities of books; Cressida, who liked reading, promised herself a good browse through them when the opportunity occurred, but now she sat down in the chair opposite the doctor's and gave him her full attention.

Would she mind working early in the morning? he wanted to know anxiously—before surgery started at eight o'clock. He himself was an early riser and had formed the habit of putting in an hour's work before breakfast, which was at half past seven each day except Sunday.

Cressida paled a little at the prospect of rising at six o'clock each morning; she had no objection to getting up early and it was a job, after all, which she was being paid for, but surely the hour was a bit much? She caught her companion's eye fixed pleadingly on her, and heard herself say cheerfully that she didn't mind in the least, wondering at the same time how long her working day was to be.

She was enlightened almost at once. 'If you could work on your own during surgery,' went on the doctor. 'We have coffee about ten o'clock, before we do our rounds; if you would like to take an hour's break then and afterwards continue working until we have our lunch? The afternoon surgery is at half past one— if you would work until we go on our afternoon visits. You could be free then until we have a cup of tea on our return—about half past four. We might do another hour's work together until evening surgery starts. We dine at half past seven...' He cast her a look which she rightly interpreted.

'After dinner?' she prompted, and he brightened visibly.

'I am not a slave-driver? Just a short spell perhaps—

not every evening, of course. I am so anxious to get the book finished.'

'Well, of course you are,' agreed Cressida bracingly, 'and I can see no reason why we shouldn't go ahead like wildfire. You have the manuscript here? Have the publishers given you a date?'

The doctor settled back in his chair. 'The manuscript is almost finished—just the final chapter and of course the whole thing to be given a final correction. It's in longhand, I'm afraid, and my writing...'

Cressida nodded. Doctors were notoriously bad writers; she had become adept at deciphering their almost unreadable scrawls. 'And the date for the publisher?' she reminded him.

He shuffled the pile of papers before him into thorough disorder until he unearthed a letter. 'Let me see, today is October the twenty-sixth and they ask for the completed typescript by December the twelfth.'

'Is it a long book?' asked Cressida faintly, with visions of getting to bed at three o'clock in the morning and getting up again at six. She was a good typist, but rusty, and she had only two hands—besides, he had hinted himself that his writing was awful.

'Oh, no—eight chapters, about nine thousand words in each, and I believe you will be able to reduce those, for I tend to write with too much elaboration, especially in English.'

'You would like me to check that? But I don't know anything about...'

He lifted a podgy hand. 'My dear young lady, I am sure that I can rely on your judgment—it is merely a question of simplifying my English where it is necessary.'

I shall have to take the wretched manuscript to bed, thought Cressida gloomily, and check every word of it. Well, she had wanted something different; it looked as though she had got it, and yet she had the feeling that she had found exactly what she needed; a job which would keep her on her toes and help her to forget the last sad weeks. And when it was finished and she returned to England, perhaps she would be able to settle down to another job in hospital—another ward to run, surgery this time, perhaps. She sighed without knowing it and Doctor van Blom said quickly: 'You are tired—I have no right to expect you to start work so soon after your arrival.'

It took her a minute or two to assure him that she wasn't tired at all and only too willing to start then and there.

They worked together for the rest of the afternoon, and Cressida, glad to have something to occupy her mind, sorted pages, skimmed through the first chapters and then arranged her desk to her satisfaction before typing the first few pages. She had learned to type years ago, before she had trained as a nurse, and she had kept her hand in ever since, typing her father's sermons, the parish magazine and quite a number of his letters when she had been home for holidays or days off; she was pleased and surprised to find that she hadn't lost her skill, and moreover, Doctor van Blom's book was going to be interesting, although she could see that his English was indeed on the elaborate side. She made one or two tentative suggestions which he accepted immediately, saying happily: 'This is just what I needed—someone to check my errors. You will prove yourself to be of the greatest help, Cressida.' He beamed at her. 'You are the answer to a prayer, my dear young lady.'

She hadn't been called anyone's young lady for quite some time, although her father's friends had frequently addressed her as such—elderly gentlemen who had known her since she was a little girl—but now she was very nearly twenty-seven. Doctor van der Teile had called her young woman, which hadn't sounded nice at all—perhaps it was the way he had said it. It was strange that they should have met again and still more strange that he should have made that remark about their meeting being inevitable... She frowned and her companion said instantly: 'You have difficulty? My writing, perhaps?'

She hastened to reassure him; she mustn't allow her thoughts to wander; a month was hardly time enough to get the book ready for the publisher and certainly didn't allow for any other thoughts than those concerned with it.

The day passed pleasantly; her elderly companions absorbed her into their household with kindly speed, so that she felt at once at ease with them—indeed, they kept her talking so long after dinner that Juffrouw Naald came in, addressed them in severe tones and bore her off to her room, where she pointed to the bed, turned on the bath and produced a glass of hot milk for Cressida to drink—not that she needed any inducement to sleep; her head had no sooner touched the pillow than she was in deep slumber.

It was after breakfast on the third morning, while she was typing out a chapter which Doctor van Blom had decided was now complete, that Doctor van der Teile came in. Cressida, her fingers arrested above the keys, wished him a cool good morning and wondered why she should feel so pleased to see him. After all, he hadn't shown any particular liking for her; indeed, he appeared to dismiss her as a necessary nuisance in his partners' household. Perhaps it was only because she had been wondering about him—his work, where he lived... She sat with her hands folded quietly in her lap, waiting for him to speak.

'Nose to the grindstone, I see,' he observed without bothering to return her good morning or ask her how she fared. Instead he turned back to open the door for Juffrouw Naald, who steamed in with a coffee tray, set it on the desk, glanced at them in turn with coy speculation, and went away again.

There were two cups on the tray, and: 'You pour,' said Doctor van der Teile.

'I have my coffee at ten o'clock with the doctors, thank you,' Cressida told him a little crossly; he was interrupting her work and disturbing her mind too, and why shouldn't he pour his own coffee?

'It's only nine o'clock, and I missed my breakfast,' and he managed, despite his size and obvious splendid health, to look and sound wistful and half starved. 'Go on,' he urged her, 'be a dear kind girl.' He lifted the lid of the dish on the tray. 'Buttered toast—bless old Naaldtje!'

Cressida picked up the coffee-pot, a handsome silver one of a size made for giants. 'She is extremely kind,' she observed primly.

He took his cup from her, sat down behind his partner's desk and began on the toast. 'She is also very romantic; she has been trying to find me a suitable wife for the last ten years. She contrives to bring to my notice every likely female she happens to approve of and offer them for my inspection. I rather fancy that you are the latest.'

Cressida choked into her coffee. 'What utter rubbish! I have no intention—it's too silly...'

'Well, there's no need to get worked up about it. She means well, bless her, and it isn't as though I've shown any interest in you.'

His voice was bland, and so reasonable that she had to swallow the furious retort she longed to utter, although she did allow herself the comfort of an indignant snort. He took no notice of this but went on: 'In any case, she's wasting her time—I've found the girl for myself and I intend to marry her.'

Cressida nibbled at a biscuit and wondered at the disappointment she was feeling; only a few minutes ago she had wished him married; he needed a wife, for he had by far too big an opinion of himself.

'If she'll have you,' she observed severely.

'Ah, yes. A moot point, although I'm not sure what moot means—we can always deal with that when the time comes.' He passed his cup. 'And how is the book going? Not too much for you, I hope?'

There was silky amusement in his voice and she pinkened. 'The book goes very well, and as I am here

merely to type it and make a few small adjustments, I
believe that it won't be too much for me.'

'You're a touchy young woman, aren't you? Ready
to swallow me alive, given half a chance.' He passed
his cup yet again. 'Any plans to marry?'

Really, the cheek of the man! She said haughtily:
'No.'

The haughtiness went unnoticed or he had a thick
skin. 'Boy friend?'

'Certainly not!'

'Ah—I apologise, I shouldn't have asked such a
silly question.'

Cressida fired up immediately. 'And why not, pray?'

'Because you are as good as you are beautiful, Cressida.' He smiled at her across the desk, his eyes very
bright. 'You are also sad. Why is that?'

She made a great business of putting the cups and
saucers back on the tray. The unexpected urge to tell
him took her by surprise so that she had to keep a tight
hold on her tongue. He didn't even like her, and she
was almost sure that she didn't like him, with his easy
self-assurance. She shook her head and said nothing
at all, and after a moment he said quietly: 'Ah, well,
you shall tell me some time—it's good to talk about
one's sorrow. It eases it—you must know that from
your patients.'

'Yes, oh yes—but listening isn't the same as telling someone…'

He got up and wandered to the door. 'We all do it at
some time,' he pointed out. 'Any messages?'

'Who for?' Her lovely eyes opened in surprise.

'I'm on my way to London, I shall be at the Royal General tomorrow.'

Cressida stared at him; he would ask anyone there and they would tell him why she had left; that her parents had died; that she had had to get away. She said: 'No, thanks,' in a doubtful voice, and he said at once: 'Don't worry, I shan't try to find out anything about you—you'll tell me yourself sooner or later.'

He left her sitting there, staring down at the sheet of typewriting in front of her, the only thought in her head that he would keep his word.

He was back in two days and this time she saw him arrive, for she had been for a brisk walk after lunch, well wrapped up in her good tweed coat against the cold and damp. The sky had been sullen all day and now it was rapidly darkening, the little village looked sombre and bleak and there were already lights in some of the small houses. An afternoon for tea round the fire... She sighed involuntarily and quickened her step. The book was going very well, but she would have to keep at it. The next day was Sunday and she would be free, but she already had plans to work for a large part of the day. She had nowhere to go and nothing much to do. She would go to church in the morning and then browse through the bookshelves until she found something to her liking. She had her knitting, and any number of letters to write too, but still she felt sure that there would be time and to spare for her typing.

She started round the square towards the doctor's house and then turned her head at the sound of the car coming from the other end—a Bentley, silver grey and sleek, whispering powerfully to a halt. She stood and watched while Doctor van der Teile got out and took the shallow steps two at a time to the front door of her employer's home. Even at that distance she could see that he was elegantly turned out, his car coat making him appear even larger than he was. When the door opened and he had gone inside, she walked on, but instead of using the great brass knocker on the front door, she went past it to the surgery entrance and so to Doctor van Blom's study, where she took off her outdoor things, warmed her chilly hands by the stove and then sat down at her desk. It wasn't time for tea yet, she might as well get another page done.

She had typed just three lines when the door opened and Doctor van der Teile came in. Cressida jumped a little at the suddenness of his appearance and made a muddle of the work she was typing—he was a disquieting person. She erased the mistake, said 'Good afternoon, Doctor,' and gave him an inquiring look.

'Hullo.' He sounded friendly. 'You weren't here just now. Do you use a secret passage or something?'

'I came in through the surgery.'

His eyes rested briefly on her coat. 'Ah—you didn't want to be seen, was that it? Probably you saw me arrive... All right, you don't have to say anything; your face is an open book. What are you doing tomorrow?'

Really it was no business of his, and yet she found herself giving him a brief resumé of her plans.

'I'll be here at nine o'clock,' he told her. 'Where would you like to go?'

'Go?' repeated Cressida.

'Come, come, girl, you must have some preference. Leeuwarden? Groningen? the Afsluitdijk? Amsterdam?'

'Are you asking me out?' And before he could reply: 'I was going to church.'

'We will go to Groningen, there is a very beautiful church there, then we might go back to Leeuwarden and then Alkmaar.'

She said stiffly: 'You've very kind, but I can't impose on your free time.'

'You won't be; I have to see a friend of mine who lives close to Leeuwarden. He has an English wife who asked me for lunch, and when I told her about you being here she asked me to bring you.' He paused and went on persuasively: 'They have a baby and two toddlers and three dogs.'

Cressida had to laugh. 'Are those an inducement?'

'Yes. I think you like babies and children and dogs. Am I right?'

'How on earth...'

'Did I not tell you that your face was easy to read? Will you come?'

'Thank you, I should like to—you're sure your friends won't mind?'

'No, they'll be delighted.' He straightened up from leaning against the door and opened it. 'Shall we have tea?'

'I was going to type...'

'After tea.' He waited while she joined him. 'Doctor van Blom is delighted with your work; he's a clever man and this book has been his pleasure and study for some time. I fancy it will be well received when it is published.'

Surgery was over for the afternoon and both doctors were back from their rounds. They all had tea together, talking about nothing in particular, and presently Cressida excused herself and went back to her desk. She worked hard until bedtime, spurred on by the thought of her day out on the morrow. She hadn't seen Doctor van der Teile again, although she had heard the Bentley's quiet engine as he drove away later in the afternoon. It struck her that she still had no idea where he lived; it couldn't be far away if he worked in both Leeuwarden and Groningen, and besides, Doctor van Blom had told her that as a general rule he took a surgery with them at least twice a week, but of course he had been in England...

It would be super to have a day out, seeing something of Holland. She frowned; it would be vexing if they annoyed each other, though. She would have to be careful and frightfully polite whatever he said. After all, he would be giving up quite a lot of his day too, even though they were going to visit his friends. The happy thought that she might be able to glean some information about him from his friend's wife popped into her head as she got into bed and turned out the light. It would be interesting to know—she wasn't being curious, or was she? She fell asleep wondering.

The sky was still sullen when she woke up the next morning and there was more than a hint of rain in the air; she put on a dark green woollen dress she had been saving for some special occasion and brushed her hair into shining smoothness before going down to breakfast. The two doctors were already at table, deeply immersed in some medical argument which Cressida begged them to continue while she drank her coffee and gobbled her roll and cheese. She was put-

ting on her coat when she heard the car draw up in the
square below, and pausing just long enough to tug on
her round fur hat, snatch up her handbag and gloves
and take one last look at herself in the looking glass,
she hurried downstairs. At least she hurried until the
thought struck her that Doctor van der Teile might be
amused to see her rushing to meet him like an enthusiastic schoolgirl. She slowed her impatient feet to a
dignified walk, greeted him with pleasant coolness,
accepted with a charming smile the two older doctors'
good wishes for an enjoyable day, and allowed herself
to be ushered out of the house and into the cold morning outside. But the car was warm, deliciously so, with
a faint smell of leather. Cressida wrinkled her lovely
nose with pleasure at it.

'If you're not warm enough there's a rug in the
back,' her companion said laconically as he got in beside her. 'A pity it isn't a better day.'

She murmured something about it being November, feeling suddenly shy; she didn't know this man
beside her at all, and on the occasions when they had
met they had hardly been on the best of terms. Now
the whole day stretched before them. In all likelihood
they would fall out within the first hour of it. But
long before the hour was up she knew that she had
been wrong about that; he had no intention of giving
her cause to dislike him, even argue with him. His
conversation was confined to the countryside around
them until they reached Groningen, and after that they
were in St Martin's Church, a splendid edifice about
which he seemed to know a great deal. During the service he confined himself to whispered directions as to

what came next, finding the hymns for her, and even though she couldn't understand a word of it, opening the prayer book at all the right places.

They lingered on after the service was over, so that she might take a closer look at the dim, lofty interior, and then went outside, where she craned her neck to see the five-storied spire. When she had had her fill, they didn't go back to the car right away, but walked across the vast square and into a wide main street, to drink coffee in one of the cafés there. He was a nice companion, Cressida decided, restful and gently amusing and always ready to answer her questions. The day was going to be fun after all and she started to relax, so that by the time they were in the car once more, speeding towards Leeuwarden, she had lost her shyness and was talking away as though she had known him for years.

The people they were to lunch with lived in a small village west of Leeuwarden and close to Franeker, so that her view of Leeuwarden was confined to a drive round its streets, with the doctor pointing out everything of interest before they drove on, to reach the village, turn in through a great pair of wrought iron gates, and stop finally before a pleasant old house, square and solid and peaceful. But only for a moment; its doors was flung wide and a large, comfortably plump woman stood waiting for them to enter.

'Anna, the housekeeper,' said Doctor van der Teile, and paused on the step while everyone shook hands. 'Ah, here is Harriet.'

His hostess was a year or so older than Cressida, small and dainty and pretty. She came dancing down the staircase to meet them and flung herself at the doctor. He gave her a kiss and a hug and said: 'Harry, this is Cressida, working for Doctor van Blom as I told you.' He left the two girls together and went on into the hall. 'Friso, how's life?'

Friso was large too, and very dark and good-looking. He shook Cressida's hand and exclaimed cheerfully, 'Hullo, how nice to meet you. Giles, this house is filled with women and children—Harry may be only one woman, but she seems like half a dozen— which is delightful, mind you, and the children get into and on to everything.' He smiled at Cressida. 'I hope you like children?'

She said that she did and was borne away to remove her outdoor things and take a quick peep at the baby. 'Ducky, isn't she?' asked Harriet, looking down at her very small daughter in her cot. 'Little Friso is four and Toby's two and she's almost three months. We're so pleased to have a girl.'

She led the way downstairs again and into the sitting-room, a large, comfortable well-lived-in apartment with easy chairs grouped around a great fire. The two men were standing before it with the three dogs. J. B., a bull-dog, Flotsam, a dog of no known make with an enormous tail and an engaging expression, and a great black shaggy dog with yellow eyes and a great deal of tongue hanging out of its enormous jaws—Moses. They came to meet the two girls, were patted and made much of and rearranged themselves before the fire once more, taking up a lot of room. They all got up again when the door was opened to admit Friso and Toby, who, having been introduced, got on to their father's knee, where they sat staring at Cressida unwinkingly until it was time to go in to lunch.

It was a delicious meal; onion soup to keep out the cold, as Harriet explained, chicken à la king and a magnificent trifle, which she disclosed with some pride she had made herself. 'It's about all I'm any good at,' she explained to her guests, but Friso interrupted from his end of the table with: 'You make an excellent stew, my love,' and smiled at her in such a way that a pang smote Cressida's heart. It would be wonderful to be loved like that...

'The first meal Harry ever cooked for me was a stew,' Friso told her. 'We ate it in a flooded house under the dyke while the tide came in; it had everything in it and it smelled like heaven.' He put a spoon into Toby's small fist and smiled again at his wife before he went on to talk of something else.

They didn't stay long after lunch, which was a pity because Cressida, robbed of a cosy chat with Harriet, hadn't been able to discover anything about Doctor van der Teile. True, there had been frequent references to mutual friends, but she was still in the dark as to where he lived and what exactly he did. A consultant—well, she knew that, but in which branch of the profession? and had he a practice beside the one he shared—if you could call it sharing—with his partners? And what was his home like and where was it? She wondered if the girl he was going to marry approved of it. She made her farewells with real regret and got into the Bentley.

'Nice people,' commented the doctor as he took the road to the Afsluitdijk and Alkmaar. 'I've known Friso for years, of course—Harry came to Franeker to spend a holiday with a friend and they met there and married in no time.'

They were on the Afsluitdijk now, tearing along its length in the gloom of the afternoon, but Cressida didn't notice the gloom; just for a little while she felt happy and blissfully content; somehow her companion had, in a few hours, lightened her grief. Probably when they next met they would fall out, but for the moment they were enjoying each other's company.

She found Alkmaar enchanting. They parked the car and walked through its narrow streets, looking at the cheese market and the Weigh House, and waiting for the figures on the topmost gable to ride out and encircle the clock when it struck the hour. If it hadn't been so cold, Cressida would have gone back and had another look, but a mean little rain was falling now and the suggestion of tea was welcome. They went to a small tea-room in the main street, almost empty of customers but cosily warm and pretty, with its pink lampshades and small tables. A tiny jug of milk was brought with their miniature teapots, and Cressida, just beginning to get used to the weak, milkless tea the doctors drank, was delighted. Nor did the cake trolley fail in its delights. She chose an elaborate confection of nuts and chocolate and whipped cream and ate it with the gusto of a schoolgirl on a half-term treat, something which caused her companion a good deal of hidden amusement.

It was getting dark as they went into the street again and walked back to the car, and it was as they started back in the direction of Groningen that Cressida inquired artlessly: 'Do you have far to go after you drop me off?'

'No great distance.' And that was all he said, and that in a cool voice which didn't invite any more questions. Probably he thought that she was being curious, but he need not have sounded so snubbing. In a polite, wooden voice she remarked: 'What a pity it is dark so quickly, but I have enjoyed my day—it was so kind…'

'It's not over yet, and I'm not kind. I felt like company.'

Her pleasure in the day evaporated and gave way to temper, so that she said tartly: 'How convenient for you that I accepted your invitation, although now that I come to think about it, you didn't invite me—you took it for granted that I'd come.' She added sweetly, 'Pray don't expect that a second time.'

'Who said anything about a second time?' he wanted to know silkily, and put his foot down hard, so that the Bentley shot forward at a pace to make her catch her breath. Nothing would have made her ask him to drive more slowly, so she sat as still as a mouse and as stiff as a poker until he remarked carelessly: 'It's all right, you don't need to be frightened.'

If it had been physically possible, she would have liked to box his ears for him.

They left Afsluitdijk behind them and he slowed the car through Franeker and Leeuwarden and slowed it still more as they neared the village. Cressida, mindful of her manners, had sustained a conversation throughout the latter part of their journey; she would dearly have loved to sulk, but that would have been childish and got her nowhere; dignity was the thing. It made her sit up very straight beside him and talk nothings in a high voice, hurrying from one harmless topic to the next, giving him no time to do more than answer briefly to each well-tried platitude which passed her lips. Dignity, too, helped her to mount the steps to the front door beside him, still talking, to pause at the door and plunge into stilted thanks which he ruthlessly interrupted.

'I'm not coming in,' he told her. 'I had thought that we might have dined together, but at the rate you are going, you would have had no social conversation left, and by the time we had finished the soup you would have been hoarse.'

Cressida's mouth was open to speak her mind, but she didn't get the chance. 'My fault,' he said, and didn't tell her why, and when Juffrouw Naald opened the door he turned without a word and went back to the car. Cressida went indoors feeling as though she had been dropped from a great height and had the breath knocked out of her. It wasn't a nice sensation and she didn't go too deeply into it. She had her supper with the two doctors and went to bed early, expecting to lie awake with her disturbing thoughts, but surprisingly she didn't; she was conscious of only one vivid memory; Doctor van der Teile's lonely back as he had walked away from her on the doorstep.

Chapter 3

The first thing she thought of when she woke up the next morning was Doctor van der Teile, and the second that he had made no mention of the Royal General, nor asked her a single question about herself. She got up and dressed rapidly, telling herself rather peevishly that quite likely he wasn't in the least interested in her—and why should she mind that? She wasn't interested in him. She scowled horribly at her lovely reflection and went downstairs to thump her typewriter with such speed and energy that Doctor van Blom, when he joined her presently, begged her not to tire herself out so early in the day.

They made good progress during the next few days; the book was taking shape, and Doctor van Blom, now that there was someone to sort out his muddle of notes and reduce his flowery prose to matter-of-fact

English, was happier than ever. He worked too hard, of course; he and Doctor Herrima had scant leisure and quite often not enough sleep, and Cressida found herself wondering if their senior partner realised just how busy they were. And he? Most likely leading the well-ordered life of a top consultant, with only urgent cases disturbing his nights; junior doctors to do the spadework for him in hospital and almost certainly a nurse and secretary to help him in his consulting rooms. She worried away about it while it nagged the back of her mind, and when one morning, just as she was putting the finishing touches to a chapter before her coffee break, she heard the Bentley slide to a standstill outside the house, she got to her feet with the half-formed resolve to speak to him about it eddying around her head.

But half way to the door she paused. Mingled with the doctor's deep voice, addressing Juffrouw Naald at the door, was a woman's voice, light and laughing, saying something which made the doctor laugh in his turn. Cressida went back to her desk and put a clean sheet of paper in her machine and began on the next chapter. She would give coffee a miss; she had plenty of work to get on with and it would be a frightful waste of time to go to the sitting-room…the door opened and Doctor van Blom put his elderly head round it. 'Cressida, coffee is ready—why do you not come?'

'Well, I thought I'd get on with the next chapter—it's going so well…'

'All the more reason for you to take a little break.' He smiled and held the door wide so that she had no choice but to go with him.

The moment she entered the sitting-room she wished that she hadn't come; the woman sitting by the stove was everything that she had always wanted to be; her pretty face exquisitely made up, a fur coat tossed carelessly over a chair, a velvet trifle arranged just so on her fair hair, the hands she held out to the warmth white and narrow with pink nails. Cressida was all at once conscious of her hastily powdered face, and hair put up with more speed than style, and her tweed skirt, well cut though it was and its matching angora jumper, were no match for the visitor's cashmere two-piece.

She was led to the stove and introduced. 'Monique de Vries,' said Doctor van Blom, 'a great friend of us all and especially of Giles,' and Cressida shook hands and listened to the artless voice speaking in a charmingly broken English, making all the right remarks, smiling across at Doctor van der Teile as she did so as though she shared some delightful secret with him. Perhaps she did, thought Cressida sourly, and good luck to her.

She made suitable replies to the visitor's conversation as she took stock of her; not young, well into her thirties, but so skilfully made up that no one—no man, at least—would know that. She was aware that Doctor van der Teile was watching her, and she looked at him just long enough to wish him good morning. There was a thoughtful look on his face and he didn't smile; he didn't greet her either, only grunted in what she considered to be a very rude manner. She turned a shoulder to him, accepted coffee from Doctor Herrima and embarked on somewhat wishy-washy chat about the weather while she drank it, and then excused herself gracefully and went back to the study.

There would be no chance of talking to Doctor van der Teile now; he obviously had a day off from his work, for his appearance was that of a man of leisure who had nothing much to do, who slept soundly each night without the telephone to drag him awake and who had the time to take his meals at his leisure too—he wouldn't be interested. It was really most unfair.

The door opened and he came in, shutting it behind him. 'What have I done?' he asked mildly.

'Done?'

'Or said—or not done and not said.'

It was a splendid opportunity to speak her mind, but now that she had the chance, she found it surprisingly difficult to start. He sat down in one of the chairs by the stove and looked at her without speaking, so that presently she said in a voice a little louder than usual: 'They're overworked. I've been here just over a week and they're on the go all the time and they're not young any more; out at night, at everyone's beck and call.'

His voice was still mild, dangerously so, she thought. 'And I should do something about it?'

She had the bit nicely between her strong white teeth now. 'Yes—you're still young, and—and probably you have more leisure...'

'Ah, yes. Naturally.' His face was bland but there was a nasty little smile twisting his mouth. 'A consultant has any amount of time on his hands, underlings to do the chores for him, someone to write his letters; such a life of leisure tends to make him selfish.'

Cressida didn't like the smile at all, nor the glint in his

eyes, but she said gamely: 'It's none of my business...' and was brought to a halt by his silky: 'You're quite right, it is none of your business. If I were you, I should confine myself to the work I am being paid for and try to keep my nose out of other people's affairs.' He got to his feet, looming very large, and strolled to the door. 'I'm glad to hear that you consider me still young,' he observed reflectively.

Cressida thumped her desk with a furious fist. 'You are extremely rude—you could at least treat me with common courtesy!'

He paused to look at her, his head a little on one side. 'No, I don't think I could do that.' He left the room without another word, leaving her to sit and worry. He had been quite insufferable, but she supposed she had deserved it, and he had been quite right; she had no business to poke her nose into other people's lives, she was a stranger in the house and she had only got what she had asked for. All the same, she remembered Doctor Herrima's tired face at breakfast that morning because he had been out most of the night—interfering or not, she was glad that she had spoken as she had. Perhaps Doctor van der Teile would think it over and do something about it.

She typed half a page and then paused to think again. There had been a receptionist before she came—an older woman who had retired and left the village, and no one had come to replace her. It was difficult, Doctor van Blom had explained, to get a young woman to take a job in the country, and the hours were awkward. Cressida typed the rest of the page and before she started on the next one, paused to think again. The book was taking all her time, but when it was done, perhaps she could stay on. She would have to learn to speak and understand Dutch pretty quickly, but surely to begin with she could get by with the basics of that language? The idea was worth thinking about later on. She began to type again and kept on steadily until it was time for lunch.

There was a letter from her aunt in the morning, enclosing a newspaper cutting; there was a 'flu epidemic imminent in the western world, it stated, a virulent type, too, equally bad for young and old. Aunt Emily added a postscript of her own, telling her to take care of herself. Cressida showed it to Doctor Blom later in the morning and he startled her by nodding agreement with it. 'This is quite true, there are already a number of cases—Giles warned us.'

She had a vivid little picture of him, sitting at an imposing desk, telling his secretary to be sure to warn his partners. 'I wonder what he specialises in?' she said out aloud.

Her companion answered her with ready enthusiasm. 'Chests. Bronchial conditions, asthma, CA of lung, emphysema…he's one of the best men we've got at the moment. Brilliant, quite brilliant; never spares himself, either.'

Cressida couldn't agree with this; Doctor van der Teile had been sparing himself on the previous day, and in good company too. She asked quickly before she could think better of doing so, 'Mevrouw de Vries— you said she was a great friend.'

Doctor van Blom cast a lightning glance over the tops of his old-fashioned gold-rimmed spectacles. 'And so she is—her late husband was Giles' best friend. A charming lady, is she not?' He smiled guilelessly. 'She amuses him, for she is always lively. They have known each other for many years.'

'She looks so young,' observed Cressida innocently, and felt mean because he said at once, 'She is a very pretty woman still, but she must be nearing forty. Her husband—Wim—died, let me see, it must be four years ago. He left her comfortably off and they had no children, so she is able to live as she likes.' He gave her another look. 'You are interested in her, Cressida?'

She had been on the point of asking where the lady lived, and then, given the chance, leading the conversation round to Doctor van der Teile to find out where he lived, too, but she saw that that wouldn't do. She said instead: 'People are always interested in pretty women, you know. Would you like to read this paragraph before you go? I've turned some of it round the other way, but I'd like you to approve it before I get it typed.'

'Of course. We really are getting on with the book now, aren't we? I seemed in such a muddle before you came, but now you have tidied it all up so nicely.'

'Well, it's so much easier for a strange eye. With luck it will be ready before the publisher has asked for it.' They exchanged the pleased smiles of two people who had worked hard and were reaping their reward, before they settled down to work again.

There was a case of 'flu the next morning—an elderly man in one of the outlying farms; he had been poorly for several days, but he had been tough all his life; there was no need to call the doctor, he had told his wife, and by the time she had made up her mind to disobey him, it was too late—he died very shortly after Doctor van Blom got to him. There were two more cases the next day, and then two more, and on the third day it was in the village itself. Cressida, who relied on her skeleton news each morning from whichever doctor had the time or inclination to translate it for her, asked anxiously if the epidemic was spreading.

'I fear so,' said Doctor van Blom, 'and all over Europe. It is bad in England, especially in the eastern counties, and it is most serious in Germany and France, also Belgium, and here in Holland it is bad too. The hospitals are already full. We are asked whenever possible to treat the patients at home unless life is in danger. Fortunately, if we can get at it in its early stages, antibiotics will help, although it is a pity that this particular virus has not yet been identified. You are not nervous, Cressida?'

'Me? Heavens, no. I was wondering if I might help a little. I could cut down on the book for a few days and give you a hand in the surgery. I know I shan't be of much use because I can't speak Dutch, but I can understand just a little, and I could give injections, and take blood pressures and put on bandages, things like that. It might give you more time for the important cases.'

She looked at her elderly companions; they were both tired, she thought worriedly, and no wonder. They had had no time to themselves for several days now and there had been no sign of Doctor van der Teile. Surely he was supposed to take the surgery twice a week? She was on the point of mentioning this when Doctor Herrima coughed and said in his nice, slow voice, 'That is very kind of you, Cressida. I think we shall be very pleased to accept your offer. As you suggest, there are a great many small tasks which you might undertake, and just at present we are busy.'

'Good. I'll start right away, shall I? I suppose there isn't an overall I could borrow?'

The garment was found and Juffrouw Naald pinned her into it, and rather nervous now that the actual moment had arrived to start work, Cressida went into the waiting room.

It was packed out with a cross-section from the village inhabitants and the neighbouring hamlets and farms; small boys with arm plasters, crying babies, elderly gentlemen with thunderous coughs, small, sniffing, tearful children and their mothers. Just one with 'flu, thought Cressida gloomily, and everyone will get it. But she didn't allow the gloom to show. She smiled at them all, wished them good day in her bad Dutch and went to tap on Doctor Herrima's door.

'Could you let me have a list of patients?' she asked him. 'I'll send them in and that will save you getting out of your chair each time. Is there a bell?'

There was. One ring for the next patient, two rings if she was wanted. She crossed the room to Doctor van Blom's door and repeated the exercise and then, armed with her lists, went back to the waiting room and called the first name, 'Juffrouw Aapinga', who proved to be a very old lady indeed who needed help to walk to Doctor Herrima's surgery before she was free to inquire from the faces round her which of them was Aerde Welmer. He turned out to be a small boy with an arm plaster and a scowl, accompanied by an elder sister. Cressida ushered the pair of them into Doctor van Blom's surgery and went back to the old lady; Doctor Herrima would want her coat off…

They were drinking their coffee two hours later when Cressida asked: 'Where do they all come from? I mean, the surgery was packed, and such a variety of complaints.'

'The time of year—and probably this afternoon there will be no one at all.'

He was wrong, of course. True, there were only five patients in the waiting room when Cressida went in. Two of them wanted their ears syringed, the other three had 'flu.

The next day the surgery was almost empty, but the telephone rang all round the clock. Juffrouw Naald, a tower of strength in any emergency, provided hot food at all hours and appeared with piping hot coffee just when it was most needed, and for the unfortunate who was called out during the night, there was a thermos jug of hot chocolate standing on the hall table. Cressida, although she didn't need to get up at night, lay awake in her pleasant room, listening to the doctors' quiet footfall and the tinkle of the telephone, and after two such nights, she suggested to her tired companions at breakfast that perhaps it might be a good idea if she were to forsake her typing altogether for the moment and give a hand in some other way. 'I could drive you on your rounds,' she suggested diffidently, 'then you could at least rest between visits. I'm quite a good driver and I've got my licence with me.'

'My Chevrolet?' asked Doctor Blom doubtfully. 'Is that not too powerful a car for a girl to drive, my dear?'

'Well, no, I don't think so. Could I not try it? And if you don't like the idea I won't go on with it.' She studied their middle-aged faces. What they both needed was a night's uninterrupted sleep. Surely Doctor van der Teile could take over for a couple of nights so that his partners could have a much-needed rest? It was unlikely that he would go out much at night and she could see no reason why he shouldn't take his share in the circumstances. If she had known his telephone number, or even where he lived or worked, she would have got up from the table then and there and telephoned him, whether it was her business or not, but she didn't know, and when she suggested tactfully that they should get in touch with him and ask him to lend a hand, she was gently but firmly discouraged from continuing the conversation.

Her days were full now; despite her lack of Dutch, she managed in the surgery well enough, and after an initial nervousness, she managed the Chev and Doctor Herrima's BMW as well, so that once they had allayed their fears about her inability to drive, they were able to sit beside her, relaxing or even, at times, dropping off into a light doze.

She was driving Doctor van Blom back from his afternoon calls when she happened to glance at him and saw how ill he looked. Her heart sank; it wasn't exhaustion which made him look so ghastly, she had seen enough 'flu victims by now to know that, and not only did he look awful; his breathing was laboured and his eyes were closed. She broke his rigid rule about the Chev's speed and sent the needle up between ninety and a hundred and prayed that Doctor Herrima would be home.

He was; they got Doctor van Blom up to his bed and into it, and he raised no objection at all, but lay very quiet, not even bothering to open his eyes, and when Doctor Herrima plunged the antibiotic into him he didn't seem to notice that either. Doctor Herrima was called out a few minutes later, leaving Cressida to look after his partner, and Juffrouw Naald to answer the door bell and the telephone and provide, as it were, a supporting line.

It was some two hours later that the housekeeper came silently into the room to tell Cressida, in one-syllable Dutch and a good deal of sign language, that Doctor Herrima was delayed; might not even be back until midnight or later—a baby, said Juffrouw Naald.

Cressida went to look at her patient again; his pulse was rising, so was his temperature, and his breathing was getting more difficult, but Doctor Herrima had left instructions that the next dose of antibiotic wasn't to be given before midnight. It seemed to her that that particular antibiotic wasn't doing its work—something else should be tried without delay. Juffrouw Naald had gone downstairs again, leaving her a heartening cup of coffee, and now she took the cup in her hand and prowled round the room. She was looking for Doctor van Blom's little notebook in which he kept telephone numbers; she had seen it a dozen times, for he had a habit of leaving it around in the oddest places. It had struck her suddenly that possibly Doctor van der Teile's number would be in it. If she could find the book and it was, she was going to telephone him.

She found the book under a chair, and his number was in it, or at least, there were three numbers, two in Groningen and one in Leeuwarden. She dialled the first number and a man's voice answered and she asked to speak to the doctor urgently. The voice told her to hold the line in quite tolerable English, and after a few minutes which seemed like hours to her, she heard the doctor's 'Hullo, Cressida.' He sounded in a hurry and there was a faint question in his voice.

She didn't waste time but plunged at once: 'Doctor van Blom has 'flu and he's ill. He's in bed and Doctor Herrima gave him a shot of antibiotic more than two hours ago, but he's not responding and Doctor Herrima is out on a baby case and doesn't expect to be back until midnight at the earliest. You've got to do something…' She had started off calmly, but now, to her vexation, she heard her voice spiralling higher and higher.

The doctor heard it too. 'Don't panic,' his voice was quiet in her ear. 'I can't come immediately, but I'll be with you in, let me see…' he paused, presumably to look at his watch, and she heard him speak to someone and a woman's voice reply. 'An hour, perhaps—it may be longer. Keep a sharp eye on him.' He rang off without saying goodbye.

It was almost two hours before her anxious ears heard the Bentley coming round the square. Doctor Herrima was still out and Juffrouw Naald, who had refused to go to bed, had appeared silently with coffee and a reassuring air which had changed to satisfaction when Cressida had told her what she had done. She listened now to the opening of the house door and the murmur of voices, and a moment later Doctor van der Teile was in the room, dwarfing everything there with his size. He nodded at her without speaking and went to bend over his partner. Presently he straightened up and said across the bed: 'Tell me about it.'

She told him, in a concise, unhurried manner, not forgetting anything and not exaggerating either, and when she had finished he opened his bag and took out a syringe and phial. 'I'm going to try this—we've been having some success with it—it must be repeated in three hours, and keep on with the hourly TPR. Get him to drink if you can, if not I'll have to get a drip up.'

Cressida moved round beside him to hold a lamp so that he could see what he was doing, and for the first time in the dimly lit room, saw his face clearly. 'My goodness, you're tired!' she jerked out in surprise, seeing the deep lines etched between nose and mouth and his weary eyes.

He flicked her a mocking glance. 'You see what a life of ease and idleness does to a man,' he observed blandly. 'Where's Doctor Herrima?'

'At Tjalkes Farm—Mevrouw Tjalkes went into labour late this afternoon—it's a first baby. Doctor Herrima thought it would be a long case.'

'It's close on midnight. Were there any other urgent calls?'

She was arranging the bedclothes carefully. 'Yes, two. Old Mevrouw Jagersma across the square complaining of her chest, and Mijnheer Kulk with a pain in his leg.'

'Your Dutch has improved enormously since I last saw you.'

He was laughing at her, but she answered seriously, 'No. Juffrouw Naald takes the messages and we manage to understand each other very well. I asked her to tell them that there wasn't a doctor available but he'd come as soon as he could.'

He nodded. 'Stay here, I'll be back.' He had gone. Cressida heard his almost silent step on the stair, Juffrouw Naald's fierce whisper, the clink of cup on saucer and then the closing of the front door. His steps sounded louder in the square outside as he walked the few yards to Mevrouw Jagersma's little house.

He was back quite soon, beside her, looking over her shoulder at her neatly kept chart.

'Mevrouw Jagersma?' she asked in a whisper.

'A mild coronary. There'll be an ambulance very soon—her daughter's with her. I'm going to Mijnheer Kulk and then on to the Tjalkes'.'

He had gone again, leaving the room full of vitality and confidence.

Cressida managed to keep awake somehow, walking about the room in her stockinged feet, drinking cup after cup of strong coffee. She had persuaded Juffrouw Naald to go to bed and made her understand that she would be of far more use in the morning, when everyone else would be dead on their feet. The house was quiet save for the doctor's troubled breathing, and that, she fancied, was a trifle easier; his pulse was slower too. She gave him his second injection on time, and resumed her prowling. The ambulance had come and gone again, the square outside was pitch dark and still. She shivered with tiredness and the cold that comes from lack of sleep, and then went back to the window;

a long way off still she could hear a car engine—two, and a few seconds later she could see their lights across the flat country. Juffrouw Naald had left coffee on the stove in the kitchen and a tray of sandwiches besides. Cressida looked at her sleeping patient and decided that the men could help themselves; she would stay where she was until they had taken a look at their partner.

The cars stopped with only a whisper of sound before the house, and she had to strain her ears to hear the doctors come in. They entered the room together and went straight to the bed, to bend over it and mutter together. Presently Doctor van der Teile straightened himself and came over to where she was standing. 'He's no worse,' he told her. 'You'll have seen that for yourself.' He looked down at her weary face. 'Is Naaldtje in bed?'

'Yes, about two hours ago, although she didn't want to go.'

'Unnatural woman! And you? You look as though you could do with some sleep.'

'Doctor van Blom can't be left. I'll go to bed when Juffrouw Naald is up and about again.'

'You'll go now, Cressida. We shall want you wide awake enough to drive one or other of us on our rounds later. We'll manage morning surgery between us.'

She eyed Doctor Herrima across the room and Doctor van der Teile said quietly, 'He's going to bed now.'

'What about you?' she wanted to know, and regretted the question the moment she had uttered it, for he smiled quite nastily.

'Should I be flattered by your concern? Surely I'm only getting what I deserve?'

He had strolled away to speak to his partner before she could think of a reply to that, and when the older man told her kindly to go to bed, she went without another word.

She was awakened by Joukje, the young girl who came in to help Juffrouw Naald, bearing a tray with coffee and rolls, and Cressida, rubbing the sleep from her eyes, saw with horror that it was almost ten o'clock. It was of no use engaging the girl in conversation, so she took the tray with a smile of thanks and the moment Joukje had gone, jumped out of bed. She bathed and dressed in slacks and a sweater, breakfasting as she did so, feeling horribly guilty, and then went along to see how Doctor van Blom was. He was asleep, so she lost no time in going downstairs where she found the doctors having their coffee, making up their morning rounds. Doctor Herrima looked every day of his sixty years despite his brief sleep, but Doctor van der Teile, with his back to the dull morning light, appeared at first glance to be his usual immaculate self. Only as Cressida crossed the room did she see that the lines were still there and a little deeper, and his eyes were heavy-lidded although alert still.

They had both got to their feet as she went in, although she begged them not to. Doctor Herrima sank back into his chair, but his younger partner stayed on his feet, saying in a matter-of-fact voice: 'Hullo— we've been planning the work load. Doctor Herrima is going to bed now—luckily there is no afternoon surgery. Naaldtje will keep an eye on Doctor van Blom, who is holding his own quite nicely, and you are to drive me on the morning round. With luck we should get an hour's rest before the afternoon visits. Doctor Herrima will take the evening surgery while you and I take to our beds—I'll take any night calls and can keep a watchful eye on Doctor van Blom for the second half of the night. It's a poor plan at its best, but it will have to do. There's no help to be got—nurses and doctors are in short supply and we must manage as best we can.'

Cressida considered carefully and then remarked kindly: 'I think that's quite well arranged. I can see one or two holes in it, but I expect you saw them too and there's nothing much to be done about them, is there? I'm sure we can manage. Is there anything you want me to do for Doctor van Blom before we go?'

Doctor Herrima had nodded off. 'No. Naaldtje and I dealt with the necessities. If you are ready shall we get started?'

She went back upstairs and got into her coat and a warm headscarf; it was raw outside and she still felt cold. She wondered which car she was to drive, and when she got downstairs she discovered that it was to be the Bentley.

She paused at the front door to say: 'Do you mean to say that you trust me to drive your car?'

He glanced down at her and then back at the gloves he was putting on. 'My dear girl, what has that to do with it? I badly need to sleep, even if in short snatches, and I can see no other way of doing it.'

'Well!' said Cressida on an indignant breath, and swept down the steps. Indignation got her into the driving seat and stiffened her spine so that she drove

off with something of a flourish and quite forgot to be
nervous because she was driving a Bentley.

'The Tjalkes first. Across the square and follow the
road on the left for five kilometres. There's a turning
on the right, and you can see the farm from the road.
Wake me up when we're there.'

She cast him an indignant glance and saw that his
eyes were already shut.

They were back by one o'clock and they could have
got back sooner than that, but she had taken pity on
him and slowed down between the less urgent cases so
that he might doze for a few precious minutes.

She hadn't expected to feel hungry, but Juffrouw
Naald was waiting for them with a tureen of *erwten*
soup, hot and savoury and satisfying. She ate with appetite and went upstairs to attend to Doctor van Blom's
small wants. He was feeling a little better and being, on
the whole, a good patient, although his chest was proving troublesome. She gave him an inhalation, tucked
him up again for the afternoon with strict instructions
to drink all the lemonade she had put on his bedside
table, and went to her own room. It was too late to have
a rest; the afternoon rounds were almost due, so she
did her face again and her hair, changed her sweater
and slacks for a jersey dress, put on her coat once more
and went downstairs to the hall. Doctor van der Teile
was already there, sitting in a leather armchair in one
corner, fast asleep. She stood for a moment looking at
him while she admitted that he was proving a tower of
strength, although she couldn't understand why he had
waited until she had telephoned before coming to his
partners' aid. He must have known that they were hard

pressed, and besides, even then, he hadn't come at once and he had sounded annoyed—no, not annoyed, but there had been something… She stretched out a hand and touched him gently. 'Doctor van der Teile, should we be going?' Her voice was as gentle as her touch.

His eyes opened immediately, their gaze clear and steady, and although he didn't speak Cressida found herself flushing under his look and when he smiled she looked away; she hadn't seen him smile like that before, it made her heart jump in a ridiculous fashion and upset her breathing. She must have been more tired than she realised, she told herself, and asked briskly which patient he intended visiting first.

The round was finished more quickly than that of the morning; this time she didn't slow down the Bentley's pace at all, but spurred on by the prospect of bed, she drove fast. It meant that her companion had very little time to doze, but he would be in his bed all the sooner.

There was a meal waiting for them when they got in, but she went first of all to see how Doctor van Blom was faring, and Doctor van der Teile went with her. Only when he was quite satisfied as to his colleague's condition did he go away again, leaving her to freshen up the bed, get her patient a drink and take his temperature, and by the time she had done this she was too tired to go downstairs again.

She undressed in a haphazard way, let her hair fall from its pins, got into her nightdress and climbed into bed. Her lovely, untidy head had barely touched the pillow when there was a knock on the door and Doctor van der Teile came in carrying a tray upon which reposed a cup and saucer and a steaming bowl. 'I advise you to have this,' he observed in a kindly impersonal doctor's voice, 'or you will be awake in a couple of hours, dying of hunger.'

He gave her the tray and sat down in a chair by the window. 'And do hurry up,' he begged her, 'otherwise I shall go to sleep too, and that would never do.'

She was too tired to say anything, although she knew that he was right. She ate the soup in the bowl and then drank her tea, her eyes owl-like in her pale face. When she had finished he took the tray from her and tucked her up as though she had been a little girl. She was almost asleep by then, so that it might have been the edge of a dream when she felt his kiss on her cheek.

Chapter 4

Juffrouw Naald, bearing a tray of tea and sandwiches, wakened Cressida before midnight, her tall spare frame wrapped cosily in a woolly dressing gown of a thickness to defy the coldest night. She set the tray down, nodded and smiled and pointed to the clock, patted Cressida on the shoulder and said '*Arme kind*,' and Cressida smiled sleepily back. It was comforting to be called a poor child in that motherly voice—indeed, she wished very much that she could cast herself upon the dear soul and have a good weep. Instead she sat up in bed with what she hoped was alert wakefulness while the housekeeper conveyed the news that Doctor van Blom was holding his own still, that there were three more cases of 'flu in the village, and that she herself was about to retire for the night. She then wished Cressida a good night and departed, whereupon Cressida tossed back the bedclothes and between bites and gulps contrived to shower, get into slacks and sweater, tie her hair back without much regard to style, and with no make-up on her pretty, still sleepy face, made her way to her patient's room.

He was awake and greeted her with a weak smile, unlike Doctor van der Teile, standing by the bed, who had frowned across the room at her as though she was the very last person he wanted to see.

'Oh,' said Cressida, taken aback by the fierceness of the frown, 'I didn't know... I just popped along to see... I'll come back.' She smiled at Doctor van Blom, cast a cold look at his partner, who was still frowning, and slid away to the kitchen.

She was setting the place to rights when he joined her. He was wearing slacks and a vast sweater and somehow managed to look wide awake, well rested and faultlessly turned out at the same time. He wasted no time on pleasantries. 'I'm not too happy about Doctor van Blom's chest,' he observed, and from his manner he might have been in the middle of a consultant's round with a bevy of students, nurses, physiotherapists and the like, hanging upon his every word. 'I should like him well sat up throughout the night, inhalations three-hourly, pulse hourly, and he must be encouraged to cough. He must also drink all the fluids you can get into him. His antibiotic is due in two hours' time and again at six o'clock. He has refused his sleeping tablets. Doctor Herrima is in bed; he'll take morning surgery and the morning visits. Naaldtje will be down at seven o'clock. Have your breakfast before then if you can and then go to bed; I shall need you to help with the afternoon surgery and the visits afterwards.'

She listened to this string of instructions, said 'OK,' rather pertly and asked: 'And you? What are you going to do?'

She watched his eyebrows climb in surprise. 'Is it necessary for you to know? I'm not in the habit…'

'Oh, stuff,' said Cressida roundly, 'you're not in your consulting rooms now, you know. Supposing I should want you in a hurry, where will you be? Bed?'

His smile was nasty, but she deserved it, she supposed. 'You're a cheeky young woman. I shall be in the surgery writing up notes and filling in forms. Should I have to go out I will either let you know or leave a note by the telephone.'

He had gone before she could answer him.

She heard the telephone shortly after she had gone back upstairs to settle Doctor van Blom down for a nap, and very soon after that the Bentley's gentle purr, and when her patient slept she padded downstairs to have a look by the telephone. Sure enough, there was a message. He had been called out to Wolkertsje Willemse, a five-year-old girl Cressida had seen in the surgery not many days since. He had added the telephone number, and as she was reading it, the telephone rang. She answered it in some trepidation; she had had to take messages once or twice already and hadn't enjoyed it at all, but this time it was a young farmer whose wife had been at the surgery only the day before and who was expecting a baby in a few weeks' time. Cressida warned him in her careful Dutch: 'Speak slowly,' and then listened carefully to his excited voice:

the baby—several weeks early, and could the doctor go at once?

Cressida reassured him in her peculiar mixture of English and Dutch, heavily interlarded with OKs, remembered to take his telephone number and then dialled the Willemses' house. She had to wait for the doctor and when he did get to the telephone, all he said in a terse voice was: 'Well?'

She explained. 'And here's the number. I don't know how long she's been in labour. Is there anything I can do?'

'No. This child's ill, she'll have to go to hospital. I'll telephone about the baby and go there as soon as the ambulance gets here. Are you managing?'

She said yes, stoutly. 'And if I can't understand, I'll give them the number where you're most likely to be.'

There were two more calls after that, both, as far as she could understand, urgent. She tracked down the doctor and passed on the names and addresses and what she hoped was the right information and went back to Doctor van Blom, who dozed and woke and became fretful towards morning. But his temperature was down and it seemed to her that his breathing was a good deal easier. There was no sign of Doctor van der Teile by five o'clock; she washed and tidied her restless patient, gave him a cup of tea and had the satisfaction of seeing him sink at last into a refreshing sleep. She was in the kitchen, cutting slices off the loaf while the kettle boiled, when she heard the front door click shut, and Doctor van der Teile came in. He looked dog-tired now, his face drawn and haggard—moreover, he was in need of a shave. He put down his bag on the kitchen table and asked without preamble, 'Doctor van Blom?'

'He seems better, his respirations are down, so is his temperature. He's slept for short periods and since I settled him an hour ago, he's sleeping peacefully.'

She made the tea and put the bread in the toaster, then got another cup and saucer and plate from the dresser. 'You've had a busy night.'

She thought he was going to laugh, but all he said was: 'So-so. Is there any marmalade?'

She fetched the Dundee marmalade the doctors liked with their breakfast and poured the tea. 'Was the baby all right?'

He nodded. 'A boy—he'll do. They're a sensible couple and her mother's on the way there—there isn't a nurse to be had.'

She took the toast from the toaster and put in two more slices. 'Is the epidemic at its height?'

'Just about. It's been hectic…' She waited to hear what he was about to say, but he changed his mind and passed his cup for more tea. 'You feel able to manage the day's work ahead?'

'Yes, thanks. I'm used to long hours,' she paused, 'or at least I was until I left hospital.'

He buttered toast and piled on the marmalade. Without looking at her: 'Why?'

At any other time she might have declined to answer him, but she was bone-weary, and in that half world of tiredness nothing seemed quite real. 'My father was ill. He died, and my mother died a few days after him.'

Strangely she felt better now she had told him, but

it wouldn't do to bore him with details, so she asked him in a bright voice if he would like some more toast.

He was staring at her across the table. 'No doubt you will be furious with yourself for telling me,' his voice was kind and gentle, 'but don't be that—I'm a doctor, you know, and one can tell doctors things one would never dream of mentioning to anyone else. And it's not right to lock one's grief away as though it were something to be ashamed of. Sorrow is for sharing, and so is love. And it has nothing to do with whether we like each other or not; you told your confidence to a doctor, not to a man you aren't quite sure you like.' He grinned tiredly. 'You are at perfect liberty to go on disliking me if you wish, and you may disagree with me as much as you like.'

'I've never said…'

'Er—no, not in so many words, but I am a lazy, thoughtless man who has to be reminded of his duty to his partners and has far too easy a life; rich patients filling the consulting rooms, eight hours' sleep every night, leisure to spend the day driving my girl-friends round the country…'

'I never…' began Cressida once more, bristling with indignation even while she had to admit that was exactly what she had thought of him—but not any more. She looked him in the eye and said soberly: 'You're quite right, I did think something like that, but I don't now; you've been super, working round the clock and never complaining. I daresay it only needed someone to remind you…'

He let out a tired roar of laughter and she asked snappily: 'Now what have I said?'

'Oh, my dear girl, you're a dozen women rolled into one! Go to bed, do, before I say something I shouldn't.'

She had got to her feet, but now she paused. 'What?'

'Never mind what—disregard anything I've said, I'm tired. Disregard this too.' He had come round the table and caught her close. Even with a bristly chin his kiss was something to remember.

After six hours' sleep Cressida felt marvellous; she consumed the meal Juffrouw Naald had brought to her room, then dressed in a skirt and jumper and put her hair up, for if she was to help in the surgery she would have to look tidy. As she dressed she was aware that she would have liked to pause and think over her conversation with Doctor van der Teile. For someone she wasn't quite sure she liked, he was beginning to make quite an impression on her. But there was really no time now. She skipped along to see her patient and found him propped up in bed, the shadow of his former chubby self but feeling decidedly better. She spent a little time with him, washing his hands and face, making his bed and brushing his fringe of hair before taking his temperature and pulse. They were both returning to normal and she saw with satisfaction that his breathing was greatly improved. She stood over him while he drank the glass of lemonade and ate the milk pudding she had fetched for him and then went downstairs, taking the tray with her. Juffrouw Naald was in the kitchen, putting the finishing touches to the nourishing stew she was preparing for their evening meal. She had wisely given up the more elaborate dishes she took such pride in serving, and now produced food which could be eaten quickly and whenever anyone wanted it. She set the saucepan on the stove and smiled at Cressida, looking at the clock. There was almost ten minutes before the afternoon surgery was due to start; without a word she reached for a teapot and made tea, and Cressida, sitting down at the kitchen table to drink it, exclaimed: 'What a dear you are!' and the housekeeper smiled again, understanding what her words implied.

The hot tea topped up her returning energy very nicely. Cressida hurried down the passage and into the hall, ready for work once more. She was half way to the surgery door when the front door was opened and Doctor van der Teile walked in. He was still in his sweater and slacks and a car coat, and although he had shaved, he looked even more tired than he had done at five o'clock that morning.

'You've not been to bed,' she accused him, 'you can't possibly take surgery—what you need is ten hours' sleep...' Her voice sharpened. 'Where have you been? Surely not another case?'

He blinked at her as he took off his coat and handed her his bag. 'Put that in the surgery for me, will you? I'll be with you in ten minutes.' He paused at the foot of the staircase. 'No case, Miss Busybody; I had a date with a lady. I couldn't disappoint her even though I knew I ran the risk of being met at the door by a harridan firing questions at me like bullets from a gun.'

He went upstairs two at a time, leaving her gaping openmouthed after him.

He reappeared in exactly nine minutes, to sit behind Doctor van Blom's desk in his surgery. He was wearing a suit now, a beautifully cut one, Cressida noted as she ushered in the first patient. She liked his tie too; he looked just what he was, a successful consultant, self-assured, impersonal, kind…and desperately weary. She wondered uneasily if he had had any sleep at all.

Two hours later, driving the Bentley once more through the grey afternoon, she was sure he hadn't, for almost before they had left the house he was asleep. The first visit was some kilometres away so that he had ten minutes before, reluctantly, she woke him up. He slept on and off between each patient and she marvelled how he was able to be instantly alert as she drew up at each house. The list was finished at last and she drove quickly back to the house; they had hardly spoken to each other in the surgery or on the round, and that was hardly to be wondered at, she supposed. Harridan indeed…! She ground the gears as they rounded the square and sensed him wincing.

In the hall she said coldly, 'It's none of my business, but I think that you should go to bed, Doctor van der Teile!'

'For once we can agree about something, Cressida. Doctor Herrima will take the evening surgery and be on call until midnight. I suggest that you give him a hand and then get to bed yourself. Could you find time to see to Doctor van Blom first?'

He had spoken quite pleasantly; now he turned away and went towards the kitchen, leaving her to go upstairs and start on the task of getting her patient comfortable and ready for the light supper he was allowed.

The evening surgery wasn't too crowded and there were no calls. Cressida and Doctor Herrima ate their meal in peace before she went upstairs again to per-

suade Doctor van Blom to settle down for the night.
To her surprise he needed little persuasion and within
half an hour she was able to leave him with a promise
of a further visit before she went to bed herself. There
had been no further telephone calls, so she went along
to the sitting-room to spend half an hour with Doctor Herrima. She found him sitting in his chair and
one brief glance at his face told her that here was the
next victim of the 'flu. She didn't waste time brooding
over the complications his illness would cause to the
household. 'You're going to bed,' she told him firmly.
'I'm going to help you this very minute. There aren't
any calls and surgery is finished—if anything turns
up I'll warn Doctor van der Teile. Besides, Juffrouw
Naald is here, and she's a wonderful help.'

He didn't need much persuasion. She could see that
he felt ill; past caring about anything much. She helped
him upstairs, left him to get into bed and ran downstairs to get a tray of lemonade and a hot drink. She
would have to get Doctor van der Teile out of his bed
shortly, so that he could write up the antibiotic and
confirm that it really was 'flu.

She glanced at the clock. It was four hours since
Doctor van der Teile had gone to bed; he hadn't had
nearly enough sleep, but there was nothing else she
could do. The kitchen door stood open, so she went
in, sorting out her small store of Dutch words in order
to acquaint Juffrouw Naald of this latest disaster, and
then forgot all about them. The housekeeper was sitting at the table, her head in her hands, her eyes closed.
She was a nasty colour too, Cressida noted that with a
professional eye while she swallowed despair. Some-

how she would have to get her up the stairs and into her bed.

Juffrouw Naald opened her eyes and looked at her blankly, muttered something in Dutch and closed them again.

'Bed,' said Cressida brightly, thankful that the word was the same in both languages, and heaved on the housekeeper's arm. Juffrouw Naald was game; somehow she struggled to her feet and tottered out of the kitchen, leaning heavily on Cressida's arm. The pair of them wove their way across the hall like a couple of inebriates and began their difficult climb up the stairs. Cressida, feeling her companion's weight becoming heavier and heavier, despaired of ever reaching the top, but they did, to sink down helplessly on the top step. They would have to get up again, she knew, but for the moment, rest was essential.

Doctor van der Teile's quiet: 'Good God, what in heaven's name are you doing there?' roused her. He was standing outside his room, clad in a magnificent dressing gown, and she said apologetically: 'Did we wake you? I'm so sorry, we tried to be quiet. Juffrouw Naald has the 'flu—I'm just getting her to bed.'

'But she's twice your size.' He had come over to look at the housekeeper she was supporting. 'You silly girl, why didn't you get Doctor Herrima to help you?' He frowned. 'He's still up?'

'No, he's not.' Her voice was tart; silly girl, indeed!—'He's got the 'flu as well.'

The arm he had flung round her shoulders tightened. 'My dear valiant Miss Bingley, why didn't you wake me?' He bent to move the housekeeper to one side and Cressida felt herself whisked to her feet. She stood for a moment, his arm still solidly comfortable round her shoulders. She looked at him and away again. 'You called me a harridan,' she said, as though that explained everything. She felt his arm grip her and then fall away. 'I'll go and turn down her bed.'

She had the covers off by the time he reached the room, carrying Juffrouw Naald. 'Get her to bed, will you?' he asked her. 'I'll go along to Doctor Herrima.'

'Temperature a hundred and three, pulse a hundred and twenty, breathing rapid but not laboured. He's been in bed less than half an hour. I was getting him a drink when I found Juffrouw Naald.'

The doctor nodded. 'I'll take a look at his chest and give him a shot. By that time you'll be ready.'

The housekeeper wasn't all that easy to undress, although she tried very hard to help, but at length she was in bed, sitting up nicely against her pillows. Doctor van der Teile, when he returned, examined her carefully, gave her an injection too, pronounced himself satisfied that she wasn't too bad, urged her not to worry about anything and went away to dress, leaving Cressida to settle her new patients with drinks and any small comforts they might require. She was coming out of Doctor Herrima's room, having settled them both to her satisfaction, when she met Doctor van der Teile, dressed now and very wide awake.

'Doctor van Blom's asleep. Are there any calls?'

'No, none at all.'

'Good. We'll have some coffee and work out some sort of routine to cover the next twenty-four hours.'

It wasn't easy. Whichever way they looked at it,

they were going to be hopelessly short-handed. 'I'll get Joukje to sleep in,' the doctor decided. 'She can get the meals and answer the telephone if we're busy or not here—you'll have to look after the three of them, I'm afraid, and give a hand in the surgery if you have the chance. I'll do the visits and we had better split the night half and half. Which half do you prefer?'

'I don't mind.'

'We'll decide later, shall we?' He smiled suddenly. 'Cressida, did I call you a harridan? I don't know why I said that—I suppose I was tired and worried. I'm sorry. We shall have to work very closely together for the next day or two. Will you mind very much? Working with someone one doesn't like is most unsatisfactory.'

She would have liked to explain to him that she had changed her mind about that; that she liked him after all, indeed, she was beginning to wonder why she had disliked him in the first place. True, he vexed her frequently and their relationship was hardly a smooth one and she still wanted to know why he had waited until she had telephoned him before finding out if his partners needed help... She said sedately: 'I don't mind at all; you're a doctor and I'm a nurse; I don't see that personal feelings enter into it.'

He stared at her rather hard, but she was pouring the coffee and the telephone rang and he went to answer it. 'Old Mijnheer Kulk,' he told her, coming back into the kitchen. 'He's worse and his wife's worried. I'll go now. The number's in the book if you should want me.'

He was businesslike and faintly aloof as he gave her a few directions regarding the patients. Cressida took careful note of them and followed him into the hall, but he went out of the door without saying anything else and the house was suddenly very quiet.

Surprisingly, all three of her patients were sleeping. She tidied the surgery and waiting room with an eye to the morning, laid the table in the kitchen for breakfast and set three trays. It was, surprisingly, not yet midnight and she thought of her bed with longing, wondering how the night could be arranged; if the doctor had to go out on another case, she would have to stay up. She yawned and then became suddenly alert as she heard the car stop before the house. She had been in the sitting-room with the carpet sweeper and a duster; Joukje would have little time for housework if she was to cook the meals, see to the kitchen and do the shopping; besides, having something to do kept her awake. She was on the point of leaving the room when the doctor came in.

'Good lord, haven't you enough to do?' he greeted her. 'Go to bed; I'll keep an eye on things and if there's a call that I think will keep me away for any length of time, I'll call you. You won't need to get up, just stay awake in case the telephone rings. If all's quiet I'll get you up at four o'clock and go to bed myself. Joukje will be here at half past seven, and if she sleeps here it will be of great help.' He yawned hugely and shrugged off his coat. 'Is there any coffee?'

'In the kitchen. I'll get it...'

'No need. When pushed, I can do quite a lot for myself. Good night, Cressida.'

She went upstairs with mixed feelings, resentful that he was so impatient of her company. True, he had apologised for calling her a harridan, and he had, although she didn't choose to think about it, kissed her—although he had probably been so tired that he didn't know what he was doing—probably he had mistaken her for Mevrouw de Vries. Cressida giggled weakly at that, put her tousled head on the pillow and went fast asleep.

She was awakened at half past three by the doctor, bearing a cup of tea in his hand. 'There's a child in the next village—I shouldn't be long. No need to dress, but do stay awake if you can—you can have another nap when I get back.'

She was still collecting her sleepy thoughts when he went away.

She got up and dressed; whatever he might say, it would be near enough to four o'clock by the time he got back, and time for him to go to bed. She did a quick round of her patients and found Juffrouw Naald awake and worrying about who was to run the house and do the cooking. Cressida had no difficulty in understanding her while she shook up the pillows, took her temperature and gave her a cooling drink and reassured her as best she could in her peculiar Dutch. The news about Joukje seemed to cheer up the housekeeper and when Cressida told her to go to sleep again, she did so almost at once, leaving Cressida free to go downstairs and make a pot of tea against the doctor's return.

He came straight to the kitchen; somehow they had taken it for granted that it should be the focal point of their activities until things got back to normal. 'I told you not to get up?' His voice was impatient and questioning.

'Well, it's almost four o'clock,' she pointed out in a

reasonable voice. 'They're all OK upstairs; Juffrouw Naald was awake, but she's sleeping now. Is there anything I can do while you're in bed?'

He took the tea she offered him. 'No—you'd better call me if there's anything urgent, though.' He thought for a moment. 'Try and get a couple of hours' sleep after lunch, will you, while I take surgery. If I go to bed now I'll get some sleep before the morning surgery and I may have the chance of a nap during the day.'

She nodded. Neither of them had mentioned the obvious hazard of an emergency call.

They got through the day somehow, and the night too, and the following day was a pattern of the first. On the third morning Doctor Herrima felt so much better that he had to be restrained from getting up and sitting behind his desk to take his surgery. Juffrouw Naald was better too, only Doctor van Blom was having a fight for it. Cressida, getting up and going to bed when she was told to, no longer cared what time of day it was. She had given up doing anything to her face and although she brushed her hair after a fashion, she tied it back with anything that came handy and let it hang down her back.

The epidemic was on the wane, Doctor van der Teile told her during one of their brief spells of conversation. The hospitals were almost fully staffed again, although there was still no one to spare and no hope of getting help. He spent a good deal of time on the telephone and although she was really too tired to mind, she supposed his calls were to Mevrouw de Vries. Not that she cared, she assured herself in a woolly fashion—it was a pity he wasn't able to go back to wherever he had come from in the first place, for he was poor company. But then so was she; with conversation limited to the state of the patients, the calls to be made and whose turn it was to sleep, it would have been difficult to be anything else. She was a poor substitute indeed for the charming Monique de Vries.

It was that evening, after surgery and the few evening visits that had had to be made, that he told her brusquely that he was going to Groningen. 'Doctor Herrima has a telephone by his bed, he'll deal with anything urgent until I get back. If it's absolutely necessary, you'll have to drive him to the patient—I shall be gone for several hours.'

Cressida stared at him in horror. She had taken a call from Mevrouw de Vries only an hour earlier and fetched him to answer it, and here he was, tearing off to see her, leaving her to hold the fort. And what about Doctor Herrima? He was very much better, but only that morning she had heard Doctor van der Teile tell his partner that the next day was the very earliest that he would allow him to do even an hour's work. 'You can't,' she said loudly, 'you simply can't—can't you make her understand? Doesn't she know...'

'She?' His voice was icy, but she went on, not really listening. 'Mevrouw de Vries. You forget that I took the call—she's always telephoning you—but must you go? If Doctor Herrima has to go out and gets a chill... you're being selfish. Besides, you haven't been to bed, you'll go to sleep at the wheel and have an accident and then where shall we be?'

'Far better off without me, I should imagine, judging from your remarks.' His voice was cold and expressionless. 'I'll see you later.'

She went upstairs to Doctor Herrima and told him firmly that on no account was he to get out of his bed unless she said so, then she went downstairs again to see if there was anything she could do to help Joukje, but everything was under control, and Cressida, feeling strangely restless, wandered round the house, doing quite unnecessary jobs, all the while thinking about Doctor van der Teile. He must be quite hopelessly in love with the glamorous widow—and she *was* glamorous and her clothes had been lovely... Her head began to ache and she sat down in the great chair in the hall, still thinking about him. He was a selfish man, she had told him so once and she would tell him again. Granted he had worked for three during the last few days, but after the well-organised life he doubtless led, that would do him no harm.

She glanced across at the clock; he had only been gone an hour, but it seemed much longer than that and her headache was getting worse. She had had no fear of getting the 'flu, for she was a healthy girl and sensible; it didn't enter her head now that she might have fallen a victim herself, only as her head got steadily worse and her shivers and aches made themselves felt, she kept her eyes on the clock, wanting Doctor van der Teile to come back, however selfish he was. The clock danced up and down now, but she went on looking at it, as if it were a kind of talisman, determined to keep awake at all costs; there were three people upstairs left in her charge and if Doctor Herrima was called out she had been told to drive him.

'I think I feel very ill,' she said out loud, and took fresh courage as the clock struck the hour; Doctor van der Teile had been gone for almost three hours, he couldn't be much longer now.

Chapter 5

Cressida wasn't aware that she had closed her eyes, but somehow the clock face had become that of Doctor van der Teile bending over her. He was very close and she noticed in a detached way that his eyes were very blue and bright. She said weakly: 'I'm so sorry, I don't feel very well. I thought I'd wait here for you—you've been gone for such a long time.' She made an enormous effort to be coherent. 'Of course I quite understand why...'

'Oh, you do, do you? My poor little Cressy.' She had never heard him speak like that before, in such a tender, gentle voice; his arms were gentle too as he picked her up and carried her up to her room.

'Get out of those clothes and into bed, I'll be back in a few minutes.' He sat her on the side of the bed and took off her shoes and untied her hair ribbon before going away. Getting undressed was very tiresome, she discovered, and quite exhausting, but she struggled out of her clothes at last and into a nightdress and crept into bed, shivering and aching and miserable. She hardly noticed when the doctor came back, gave her an injection, took her temperature, felt her pulse and sat her up against her pillows. Joukje came in too with a jug of lemonade and she was made to drink some of it very much against her inclination before she was urged, quite unnecessarily, to go to sleep.

She wakened several times during the night and each time the doctor was there, but towards morning she slipped into a deep slumber and woke from it, hours later, feeling much better. But this time he wasn't there; Monique de Vries was. Cressida, although she still felt awful, was surprised at the surge of ill-feeling she had at the sight of her. 'You shouldn't be here,' she mumbled, ''flu…'

'I've had it,' the face smiled at her in a most friendly fashion before fading away out of focus. Cressida frowned in her effort to think straight. That was why Doctor van der Teile had rushed off to Groningen and why he had telephoned so often. Just to make sure she asked: 'Do you live in Groningen?'

The pretty face came back and smiled at her. 'Yes, my dear. Do you feel well enough to take your temperature and pulse? Giles told me to ask you to do it if you felt you were able to. I have no idea how to do it—and then you are to have a drink.'

Her temperature was still high, so was her pulse. She watched Monique write them down on a piece of paper, drank the lemonade she was offered and went to sleep again. The doctor's voice roused her. She had no idea how long she had slept and she said hullo without bothering to open her eyes.

'There's a jab coming,' he warned her, and when it was done: 'Headache better? Aches and pains? No pain in your chest?'

She shook her head and opened her eyes reluctantly. 'The others?'

'Doing nicely. Doctor Herrima will be back in a day or so now, and so will Naaldtje. Doctor van Blom is on the mend too, I'm glad to say.'

'You're tired.' Her head still ached and for the moment she had quite forgotten where she was. 'But you've got Mevrouw de Vries now—I daresay you were very worried about her and you had to come here. No wonder you were so…you don't even like me…'

He muttered something in his own language and then said matter-of-factly: 'We none of us could have managed without you, Cressida.'

She pushed the hair away from her face with an impatient hand and looked up at the impassive face above her. 'You called me Cressy.'

His bland expression didn't change. 'Dear me, did I? I shall have to be more careful, shan't I?' A remark which made no sense at all. 'Go to sleep now, there's a good girl, you're going to feel a lot better when you wake up.'

And she did. Her head was clear and she hardly ached at all. It was bliss to feel normal again—well, nearly normal. She stretched luxuriously, turned over and went to sleep again.

When she woke it was to waning daylight with a

brisk wind howling round the square and she lay for a
moment, astonished to think that she had slept for so
long; she was still a little hazy, but she must have been
lying there for almost forty-eight hours. And now she
felt clear-headed again and very hungry. She got out
of bed, disregarding the jelly-like feeling in her legs,
put on her dressing gown and slippers and went out of
her room, intent on finding food. The house was quiet
although she could hear voices somewhere, and from
the top of the staircase she could see that the big clock
in the hall showed the hour of half past three. Holding to the banisters because her legs weren't quite her
own yet, she had to pass the sitting-room door to do
this and as it was half open she peered in.

Doctor van der Teile was there, standing by the window, and Monique de Vries was with him. Neither of
them saw her, which was a good thing, because Monique had her head on his shoulder and his arm was
round her. Cressida backed away; one didn't encroach
on such scenes, it was like reading someone else's letters. She went slowly back to her room again, quite
forgetful of her hunger, and the tears streamed down
her face although she had no idea why she was crying. She got back into bed and mopped her face and
tried to go to sleep again, quite unsuccessfully, and
presently they both came in quietly, and although she
had her eyes shut it was no use, for he said at once:
'You're not asleep—and you've been crying. Why?'

She said the first thing which came into her head,
'I'm hungry,' and wondered uneasily if he would notice that her dressing gown, which had been hanging
behind the door, was now thrown down anyhow on a

chair. Apparently he hadn't, for he smiled a little as he took her pulse and asked his companion to see that Joukje got a tray ready. 'Something light—soup, thin bread and butter—there are some grapes too—oh, and a pot of tea.'

Monique went away and he sat down beside the bed. 'Now tell me why you've been crying,' he invited her gently.

'I don't know,' and she didn't. 'I just felt miserable, but I really don't know why.'

He went to stand by the window, his hands in his pockets, jingling his loose change. He wasn't looking at her, but at the grey day outside. 'You must stay in bed for another two days,' he told her. 'You are making a good recovery, but you were tired out and we'll not take any chances.'

'I feel perfectly able to get up.'

'Yes? I see that you have already done so. Very foolish of you, Cressida.'

So he had noticed. She asked quickly: 'How are the doctors and Juffrouw Naald?'

'Naaldtje is better, she threw it off very well, Doctor Herrima is just about ready to get into harness again, but Doctor van Blom will have to take things easy for another few days—his chest hasn't quite cleared.'

'Will you stay here until he is better?'

'No, I can't do that. As soon as Doctor Herrima is able to carry on I must return.'

Cressida sat up a little higher in bed. 'Is—is Mevrouw de Vries staying here?'

'Yes, but I shall take her back with me when I go.'

He turned round and came back to stand by the

bed. He looked very tired and she wondered how much sleep he had been getting; it wouldn't be enough. 'You must be longing to get back,' she said flatly.

He smiled down at her. 'Yes, I am most anxious to return.'

'All your private patients,' she muttered peevishly.

He appeared not to notice her peevishness, for he agreed placidly, 'As you say, all my private patients.' He looked over his shoulder as the door was opened and Mevrouw de Vries came in with a tray. 'And here is your tray—I'll look in later.' With a careless nod he had gone.

Cressida recovered quickly; she was a strong girl, not given to illness, and by the end of the next two days she was sitting out of bed, and when no one was about, pottering downstairs to visit Juffrouw Naald in her kitchen, for although that lady was by no means quite well again, nothing would prevent her from over-seeing Joukje's efforts. And Doctor Herrima had taken his afternoon surgery that afternoon and had signi-fied his intention of resuming his work in the morn-ing. His partner was convalescing but improving so rapidly now that things would be back to normal in a few days. Their senior partner, Doctor van Blom had told her, would be able to return to his own home on the following day. 'We shall miss him,' he declared. 'What a task he took upon himself, and at the expense of his own patients too, not to mention his own peace of mind.'

Cressida had wondered what his peace of mind could have to do with it, but she didn't like to ask, and the doctor went on: 'We shall miss Monique too—hard work is hardly her *forte*, so it is all the more appreciated. And you, my dear Cressida, we shall never be able to thank you enough,' he beamed at her. 'I do not know what we should have done without you. However, now you will be able to return to your typewriter.'

She was sitting with Doctor van Blom the following afternoon, reading over some of his manuscript to refresh his memory about several alterations, when Doctor van der Teile came in. He was dressed for the road, and Cressida, who hadn't seen him all day, presumed that he was back from the afternoon round. She was quite right, he was; he was also on the point of departure.

He talked with his partner for a few minutes, uttered a few commonplace remarks to her, wished her goodbye with casual politeness, and went. She hadn't said a word and her goodbye, muttered in surprise, was lost to him, for he was already half way down the stairs by the time she had her mouth open to speak.

'Go and wave from the window,' suggested her patient. 'Monique came to see me while you were in the study; she had been looking for you so that she might say goodbye. She left a number of kind messages for you and hopes to meet you again soon.'

'I bet she does,' thought Cressida vulgarly, and went obediently to look out into the square below. Mevrouw de Vries was already in the Bentley and she looked up and waved and blew a kiss when she saw Cressida and then spoke to someone standing, presumably, in the doorway. Doctor van der Teile came into view seconds later and looked up too. But he neither waved nor smiled and he certainly didn't blow a kiss, only stared up at her, looking vaguely irritable as though he hadn't wanted to do it.

Cressida stared back at him; he was going away and she didn't want him to; she wanted him to stay for ever; better still, she would have liked to turn the elegant Monique out of the Bentley and take her place. It was, she told herself gloomily, the silliest time in which to discover that she loved him.

She turned away from the window abruptly, unable to watch him get into his car and drive away. And it's not just away from here, she thought sadly, it's away from me, even if I see him again—and he had said goodbye as though he was pleased to say it.

'Giles has gone?' asked Doctor van Blom from his chair.

'Yes, he's gone.' Her voice, regrettably, shook just a little.

Another few days and they were back—almost— in their usual way of life once more. True, Joukje still did the lion's share of the work while Juffrouw Naald confined her activities to cooking and the supervision of the house cleaning, made easier by Joukje's younger sister, Trusje, who came in to help each day. And Doctor Herrima took his surgery and did the visits with Cressida driving him, and after a few days, Doctor van Blom got into his clothes and insisted on doing at least one surgery a day.

In between these activities, Cressida started her typing once more, working until quite late at night and taking the manuscript to bed with her and working on that too, until she couldn't keep her eyes open any longer. It stopped her from thinking, something which she wished to avoid for the next week or so. 'Out of sight, out of mind,' she consoled herself, knowing that there wasn't a word of truth in it. But she did try very hard, taking herself for a long walk each day, sandwiched in between the surgery and the rounds; it was astonishing what a great deal of ground one could cover in an hour, and if one walked fast enough one had little time to think…all the same, she wakened each morning to her unhappy thoughts and went down to the study with such a pale face that Doctor van Blom wondered aloud if he was asking too much of her. 'This wretched 'flu,' he exclaimed, 'you haven't recovered from it, Cressida, and I'm working you too hard—I'm working myself too hard too; it will do me good to have a day free from the book, and you must have a day to yourself.'

It was the last thing she wanted, for what would she do? Go to Groningen, she suspected, and walk the streets, hoping that she would come face to face with Giles van der Teile. She refused politely and applied herself even more zealously to her typing, pointing out that they had lost precious time and she would need every minute she could spare in order to have the book ready by the date the publishers had set.

It was the following afternoon that Doctor van der Teile came. Doctor Herrima had finished surgery and refused her offer to drive him on his rounds, now considerably lighter. Doctor van Blom was happily engaged on the final polishing of the last chapter and she was back at her typewriter. But she had barely started when the front door was opened and shut with something of a thud, and Doctor van der Teile came into the room, bringing with him the cold air from outside and a feeling of strong purpose.

Cressida hadn't expected to see him, but she had been thinking of him constantly, so that she went quite pale and then flushed a little, making her lovely face even lovelier. He gave her a casual 'Hullo,' and an equally casual glance before addressing himself to his colleagues in his own language, and she bent over her typewriter again and missed his intent gaze upon her even though he was engaged in conversation with Doctor van Blom.

He stared at her in the manner of a man who couldn't see enough of her and spoke abruptly in English. 'Doctor van Blom thinks that you should have a break from work. You have been doing too much and you're barely out of bed.'

These words caused her to stop in the middle of a sentence and look at him. 'Me? Working too hard? I'm not!'

'Probably you're unaware of it,' he said smoothly. 'Why not come back with me to Groningen and have dinner there?' He smiled suddenly. 'There is someone who would like to meet you.'

'Meet me?' asked Cressida. She felt that her conversation hardly sparkled, but she couldn't help that; she was still wondering why on earth he should bother himself to ask her out—and who would want to meet her?

'A splendid idea.' Doctor van Blom for once spoke firmly. 'There is no typing for you to do until I have re-read this chapter. Run along now, Cressida, and put on your coat and go with Giles.'

He gave her a fatherly nod, his cheerful face full of benevolence, pleased to be the instrument, in part, of an evening out for her, so that to disappoint him would have been out of the question—or so she told herself as she did her hair and her face, and then, warmly wrapped against the cold dusk, went downstairs to join Doctor van der Teile.

They occupied the journey to Groningen with polite conversation, casual on the doctor's part, and rather stiff on her own; she was so afraid that he would discover how she felt about him that she leaned over backwards to appear cool and casual and utterly impervious to his charm, but all she succeeded in doing was to utter a series of commonplace remarks hardly remarkable for their interest. But her companion, beyond a faint twitch of the lip, seemed unaware of this, blandly matching her efforts with even more commonplace replies, so that by the time they reached the city she was quite illogically put out with him. He could at least talk about something interesting. She asked a thought snappishly: 'Where are we going?'

For answer he swung the car between open iron gates and drew up before what was obviously a hospital entrance. 'In here,' he told her briefly, and before she could question him further, he had guided her inside, into a lift and out of it again, down a long quiet corridor lined with doors, and finally, through the last door at its end.

The room was small but pleasant, with pretty curtains, a comfortable chair and a polished wood floor, and there were flowers everywhere; they formed a frame for the occupant of the bed, a middle-aged lady with handsome features and a commanding appearance despite the fact that she had been, and still was, Cressida could see, quite ill. She was carefully made up and her hair was done in what Cressida called to herself a continental knot. She wore a high-necked long-sleeved nightdress of some fine silk in a pretty shade of blue, exquisitely embroidered and trimmed with lace—the blue matched her eyes exactly, eyes as astonishingly blue as her son's.

'Dear Giles,' she greeted him, 'how nice to see you—and you have brought Miss Bingley to visit me.' She offered a cheek for his kiss and held out a beautifully manicured hand to Cressida, who shook it gently with a polite murmur.

'Of course Giles would not have told you that he was bringing you to see me,' went on his mother in effortless English. 'His mind is almost wholly occupied with other people's chests, you know, and he has no time for the niceties—only I very much wanted to meet you, my dear—you see I heard all about the magnificent way in which you coped with this wretched 'flu. Giles thought of a dozen reasons why you wouldn't want to come, but I think that you would not mind satisfying the whim of an old lady?'

This description of herself made Cressida smile; anyone less elderly, even when recovering from whatever it was that had laid her low, would be hard to find; she fancied that the lady lying in bed would probably ignore illness and even when she had succumbed to it, had made up her mind to get better, whatever anyone else thought.

'I don't mind in the least,' she told her. 'In fact, it's

very nice to meet someone who speaks English—the doctors do, of course, but not Juffrouw Naald—oh, and of course Doctor van der Teile...'

The blue eyes twinkled. 'I expect you both had far too much to do to have the time to get to know each other,' suggested Mevrouw van der Teile. 'Giles, go and look at some X-rays or something while I talk to Cressida—I may call you that?' She smiled at her son. 'Come back in half an hour—no, don't frown, I know I'm not allowed to have visitors for more than fifteen minutes.'

'Knowing you, Mama,' he observed smilingly, 'I imagine you entertain whoever you wish for as long as you wish.' He walked to the door. 'Fifteen minutes, then.' He gave Cressida a cool nod and went out, shutting the door gently behind him.

'The dear boy,' remarked his mother fondly, and glanced at Cressida. 'Always so busy, you know. His practice—a very large one—and the hospital here and beds at Leeuwarden too, and then his partnership with Doctor Herrima and Doctor van Blom—not a real partnership, but during the Occupation they tried to help his father and when Giles heard of it he swore that he would help them in his turn. He is what you call a sleeping partner.' She paused. 'And now of course his clinic is running successfully...' She paused again, invitingly, and Cressida asked, inevitably. 'What clinic?'

'Oh, hasn't he told you about it?' Mevrouw van der Teile gave her an innocent look. 'Perhaps I should not do so, but you are a nurse, are you not, and I am sure that you would be interested to hear about it. He started it four years ago, for he felt that the chest cases which he saw in hospital needed more specialised care when they returned home; despite health visitors and reminders from the hospital, so many of them didn't bother to return for check-ups, which meant that their stay in hospital was so often useless, often they didn't bother to see their own doctor either. But strangely, the clinic is a great success, possibly because it is in a part of the city where living conditions are not ideal even though modern flats are being built—it is, as it were, just round the corner, if you see what I mean. A man with bronchitis or asthma might not bother himself to come across the city to visit the hospital, but he would slip round to the clinic one evening—and now the local doctors with patients unwilling to go to hospital for an examination have taken to sending them in for Giles to see. He does it in his spare time, of course...' She paused to get her breath and Cressida said gently: 'Should you be talking so much, Mevrouw?'

'No, my dear, but I wanted you to know. I'm surprised that Giles hasn't said anything to you about it—but then, very few people know about it, he prefers it that way.'

'Well, he doesn't know me very well,' said Cressida. 'There's no reason why he should tell me anything about himself.'

'I don't suppose he told you that I became tiresomely ill on the very day you telephoned him for help?'

'Oh, dear,' said Cressida, and remembered all the awful things she had said to him about being a well-heeled consultant and not pulling his weight. 'No, he didn't—I had no idea...that's why he went to Groningen when he should have gone to bed. He didn't say a word...' She coloured faintly. 'Well, as a matter of fact, he did say that he had to keep a date with a lady...'

His mother laughed. 'I despair of him,' she declared, not sounding in the least despairing. 'And now tell me, do you like working for Doctor van Blom?'

'Very much. It's a change from nursing and he is very kind, so is Doctor Herrima—and Doctor van der Teile,' Cressida added hastily, and caught his parent's eye. 'I—that is, we...' She stopped and tried again. 'He doesn't like me, I think, although he's always very... very...'

Mevrouw van der Teile was examining the pink nails of one hand and interrupted her without looking up. 'And you, my dear—you dislike him?'

'No.' Cressida struggled to think of something suitable to say and could think of nothing, so she filled the silence with: 'I don't suppose I shall be here much longer, the book is going very well and it's almost finished...' She paused and let out a small thankful sigh as the door opened and Giles came in and his mother said at once: 'We have had a most delightful talk—I have been telling Cressida about your clinic and I daresay you will be very annoyed at that, but I quite thought that you would have told her already. Are you very vexed?'

Cressida took a quick peep; he wasn't vexed, he was in a cold rage about it. 'Not in the least,' he assured his mother with untruthful, icy politeness, 'although I cannot conceive of what interest it may be to Cressida.'

His mother ignored this. 'Well, why don't you take her to see it?'

He frowned. 'Perhaps—at some future date.'

'This evening, Giles—why not?' Her eyes held his own frosty ones. 'So nice to share your interests with someone who understands them,' she remarked in dulcet tones.

Cressida, watching him, gave way to a desire to stoke his rage a little. How tiresome he was, and how she loved him. 'I'll not tell anyone,' she assured him in kindly tones, and was rewarded by a glacial look and: 'I shall be delighted to take you—we can perhaps arrange a date later on.'

After she was back in England. 'Why not this evening, Giles?' His mother's voice, still dulcet, was persistent too. Only good manners, Cressida decided, prevented him from grinding his splendid teeth.

'Oh, yes, please,' she chimed in, and added a sweet smile, flicking her long lashes down on to her cheeks and then opening her eyes wide at him. She was pleased to see that he showed unwilling interest even though he was still in a rage.

The polite chill of his voice froze her bones. 'Very well, but I doubt if you will find it interesting. Shall we have dinner first?' His tone implied that dining with her would be a duty.

'If you like.' If he wasn't going to ask her nicely then she wasn't going to answer nicely either. She went on: 'I'm sure I shall find this clinic very interesting, although you don't seem to think so. I'm very surprised, I thought you were just a consultant.'

He was arrogant now as well as angry, looking down his nose at her. Cressida wondered why she was being so beastly when what she really wanted to do was throw her arms round his neck and tell him he was everything she had ever hoped for in a man. His mother broke the small silence. 'Run along, then, my dears,' she commanded, and offered her cheek for her son's kiss and then took Cressida's hand, smiling at her. She was weary now, but she was a woman who had no intention of giving way to anything as unimportant as weariness. 'We shall see each other again.'

The doctor opened the door with exaggerated politeness and with a final nod to his mother followed Cressida into the corridor. They didn't speak in the corridor or in the lift. It wasn't until they were sitting side by side in the Bentley that he remarked bitingly, 'You are a scheming minx, Cressida, and clever with it. I don't know how you managed to worm so much out of my mother, but you succeeded very well. It was— unworthy of you.'

He started the car and drove to the hospital gates where he was forced to pull up until he could slide into the traffic of the main road. It gave Cressida the chance to get her door open; she had one leg out before he leaned across, swept her back in with one arm, fastened her safety belt and closed the door.

'Of all the rude, self-opinionated, unpleasant men...! I will not have dinner with you!'

'No? Perhaps that wouldn't be such a bad idea in the circumstances. We will go straight to the clinic.'

'I do not want...' she began, and was interrupted by his smooth: 'You're going, whether you want to or not,' and when she stole a glance at his profile she was surprised to see that he looked amused.

He swung the car into the traffic and was fully

occupied in driving it through a chain of side streets which seemed to go on for ever, until he finally stopped in a narrow, shabby square. Without a word he opened her door, ushered her out of the car and across the pavement, through a door and into a long whitewashed passage from which led a great many doors. Cressida could hear voices from behind them and one was opened and a man in a white coat came out, walking towards them. When he caught sight of them he hurried to meet them and spoke to the doctor with some surprise. After a few moments' talk, Doctor van der Teile said briefly: 'This is Jan Vinke—he works here.'

He waited while she shook hands and then marched her on. 'What does he do?' she asked him, refusing to be crushed by his manner.

'He is one of the nurses.'

'How many work here?'

'Four.'

'Is it a large clinic?'

'You shall see for yourself.' He opened a door and urged her in so smartly that she paused to eye him severely. 'You're in a very nasty temper,' she told him, 'and I refuse to be bullied around after the quite beastly things you said to me just now. In any case, your high-handed ways cut no ice with me.' She turned her back on him then, because when one loved someone it was really very difficult to be angry with them for more than a few minutes at a time.

He took no notice of her at all; the door shut behind them and she found herself in a large room crowded with people sitting on benches. She was led between them, the doctor nodding here and there as they went until they reached a door at the further end which he opened. There was another man here, sitting behind a desk, writing furiously, but he jumped up as they went in and broke into speech.

He looked rather nice, youngish and thickset and very fair. He seemed pleased to see the doctor, although a little in awe of him. Cressida, watching them talk, saw the icy blandness go from his face and sighed to see it reappear as he introduced his colleague.

'Cressida, this is Doctor Felix de Boer.'

The younger man shook hands with every appearance of friendliness and said in excellent English: 'I am enchanted; we do not often have visits from young ladies of such beauty. You are interested in the clinic?'

'Yes, I am, but I know almost nothing about it.'

'I cannot suppose that it can interest you in the least,' interrupted Doctor van der Teile, faintly bored.

'Oh, come now, Doctor,' said the other man, 'you're saying that because you dislike people knowing of your work here. Miss Bingley, I could tell you...'

'Oh, do,' urged Cressida, and smiled sweetly at Giles' handsome face and got no response at all. She didn't give up easily, but addressed him directly: 'How many patients do you have, and do you work here every evening?'

He spoke repressively. 'We have about ninety patients each week and we open three evenings in the week. None of us works full time. And now that you have had your wish and have seen all that you came to see, I think we might go.'

'You're very impatient,' she smiled again at him

and he looked annoyed. 'I haven't seen anything at all, really. Do you share the work?' she asked Doctor de Boer.

'There is another doctor—we each do an evening, but there are often extra clinics.'

She turned to Doctor van der Teile again. 'It must give you a very long working day,' she said, and he nodded curtly without speaking. It was like getting blood from a stone, and suddenly she felt beaten. She said on a sigh: 'I'm wasting your time—your whole evening, in fact. I'm sorry.' She held out a hand to Doctor de Boer. 'I mustn't keep you from your patients. I have enjoyed meeting you. Thank you.'

She went through the door, not looking to see if Giles was behind her. He was. He opened the car door for her without speaking and she asked in a sober little voice: 'Will you please take me home?' and choked back sudden anger at his bland: 'With pleasure, Cressida.'

He had nothing more to say until he drew up before his partners' house and, rather to her surprise, went inside with her. In the hall he remarked pleasantly, 'I hope you don't mind going to bed supperless, Cressida.'

It was more than enough. 'I'm famished!' she told him in a shrill voice which threatened to become a wail. 'And I think you're quite—quite...'

'Beastly?'

She flew upstairs and banged her door behind her, then tore off her clothes and had a bath, crying all the time. Then she brushed her hair, secured her dressing gown firmly round her person and went stealthily out of her room again, into the silent house and down the stairs. Everyone would be sleeping—they still kept early hours after the last exhausting fortnight. She padded to the kitchen, poured herself a mug of milk, cut herself a massive slice of bread, buttered it, laid cheese thickly upon it, and bore her supper back to her room. She paused at the foot of the stairs to take a bite, for her hunger had got the better of her. She was savouring it blissfully when a faint sound made her look round. Doctor van der Teile was standing across the hall, watching her. Before she could speak, he had reached her and taken the milk and bread from her, setting them carefully on the stairs. 'I cannot think of anything to say,' he muttered. 'This will have to do instead.'

She felt his arms around her as he bent to kiss her, then picked up her supper and put it back into her hands. Cressida could think of nothing to say, for she could hardly tell him that his kiss had been quite out of the ordinary and that she had enjoyed it very much, and to wish him a prosaic good night didn't seem to fit the occasion. She went back upstairs without looking at him, shut the door, softly this time, and got into bed to enjoy the remains of her supper and ponder the doctor's behaviour. She had, until now, almost given up hope of his liking her, but now she wasn't sure and hope surged higher within her with every minute, only to be quenched by the thought that he couldn't really like her; hadn't he refused to give her the dinner he had invited her to share with him—not invited, either—insisted, now she came to think of it.

She put down her mug, disposed of the last morsel

of bread and lay down. She was still worrying away at the puzzle like a dog with a bone, when she heard the Bentley slide past under her window and gather speed as it tore into the night.

Chapter 6

Cressida spent most of the next day wondering how she should behave towards Giles van der Teile when she saw him next, but she need not have worried; there was no sign of him, nor on the following day either. He was due to see some patients on the day after that; Doctor Herrima had mentioned it at breakfast, a statement which had caused her to make a great many mistakes in her typing that morning, and sent her upstairs before lunch to redo her face and pile her shining hair even more neatly than it was already, and this was a waste too, for at lunch she was told—by Doctor van Blom this time—that their partner had been called away to Utrecht and wouldn't be back in time to see any of his patients that afternoon.

Cressida swallowed disappointment with her soup and spent the whole afternoon working with a ferocity which was quite remarkable. At this rate, Doctor van Blom told her happily, the book would be ready in plenty of time to meet the publisher's date, and he added: 'But I shall be sorry too, my dear, for we have enjoyed having you here with us, and you have been invaluable, for you are such a sensible young woman and seem able to turn your hand to anything.'

She thanked him for the compliment and wished for the hundredth time that her command of the Dutch language was sufficient for her to suggest that she might remain with them as a surgery nurse and secretary, for they certainly needed someone…she had done her best to pick up a few basic sentences, and with Juffrouw Naald's help and the aid of a dictionary, she hadn't done so badly, but she doubted if she knew enough to cope with the daily demands of a busy surgery.

She had managed well enough during the brief period when they had all had 'flu, but that had been rather a different matter. It just wouldn't work, she admitted regretfully, and turned back resolutely to her desk, where she stayed, pausing only for a cup of tea. By dinner time she was quite worn out, which was a good thing, for she slept the moment her head touched the pillow. But her waking thought was of Giles; it was stupid, she told herself crossly, that she was unable to clear her head of the man; it was a complete waste of time thinking about him. He was rude and arrogant and she suspected that she amused him, although she wasn't sure why—and yet he was the only man in her life and she knew that there would never be another. He could be as cross as two sticks and look down his nose at her and not care if she went supperless to bed; it made no difference.

She dressed and went down to the study, where she attacked the last chapter with Doctor van Blom, and became so immersed in it that they were late for breakfast, and because there were a great many patients in the surgery that morning, she helped there before going back to the study.

They were all a little tired by lunchtime, but there was no surgery that afternoon, so that the two doctors could have an hour or two's leisure. Cressida covered her typewriter and decided reluctantly that she would go for a walk. It was a cheerless sort of day, but the fresh air would do her good. She put the study to rights, then went without haste into the hall and came face to face with Doctor van der Teile.

He had just arrived, for he was still wearing his car coat and was in the act of stripping off his gloves. He said pleasantly, 'Hullo—I thought we might go out for lunch.'

She wished with all her heart that she had on something more glamorous than the thick brown tweed skirt and its toning jumper. She hadn't done her face for ages, either. 'Why?' she asked.

He laughed. 'Let us say an impulse, Cressida, even a wish to make amends for your lack of supper the other evening.'

'How kind,' her voice was a little too loud, 'but I don't think I can manage it.'

He raised his brows. 'And what exactly does that mean?'

She stood in front of him, stubbornly refusing to

give in to a weak desire to say yes. 'It's a polite way of saying I don't want to have lunch with you.'

This time his laugh was a great bellow. 'Don't be mulish, Cressida—and you're not usually so polite…'

'I should have to change.'

His surprise was genuine. 'Why? You look quite all right to me. You'll need a coat, though.'

Men! thought Cressida peevishly, and wondered if he was as uncritical of Monique de Vries, and doubted it. She was on the point of saying firmly that she wouldn't go when she caught his eye.

'Run along, there's a dear girl. I'll give you five minutes—ten if you insist on changing everything.' He grinned suddenly. 'And don't tell me that that won't be long enough; looks like yours don't need fussing over.'

Her instant pleasure at this remark was cut to the ground by his: 'Monique considers you to be one of the prettiest girls she has ever seen.'

So it hadn't been his own opinion, but something Monique had said. Cressida looked away so that he shouldn't see her face. 'I'll be less than five minutes,' she told him quietly, and sped up to her room. There was no point in spending more time than that on her person; he wasn't going to look at her, not really look— she didn't think that he ever had, or he might have thought up a compliment for himself instead of relying on his Monique… She tugged on her coat, rammed the fur cap on to her head and snatched up her handbag and gloves, all the while fighting a strong impulse to wear her elderly mac and a headscarf—she didn't even bother to powder her nose.

On her way downstairs she wondered what was his

real reason for inviting her out to lunch, and she was
to discover that soon enough. They were in the car,
speeding towards Groningen, when Doctor van der
Teile remarked casually, 'My mother would like you to
visit her again—I thought perhaps after lunch? I have
a couple of patients to see in the hospital; I could leave
you with her and pick you up afterwards—you're not
committed to anything this afternoon?'

'Only my typing,' she told him dryly.

'Ah—yes, I hadn't forgotten, but Doctor van Blom
tells me that you haven't been taking nearly enough
time off for the last few days and that you're well ahead
with the book.'

He was cutting the ground from beneath her feet,
inch by inch. 'I shall be delighted to visit your mother,
Doctor van der Teile.'

'Giles.'

'Giles, then.'

They were in the city by now and he drew up presently in an old narrow street leading off one of the
main squares, in front of a gabled house so discreetly
converted into a restaurant that it was difficult to see,
at first glance, that it was just that.

Inside it was warm and gently lighted against the
winter's day outside, and they were shown at once to
a snugly placed table by one of the windows in the
oak-panelled room. Cressida, as she sat down, noted
with some chagrin that the women at the tables around
them were smartly dressed, most of them with fur
coats thrown back over their chairs. She allowed the
waiter to take the tweed and threw a reproachful look

at her companion, who said at once: 'You don't have to look like that.'

'Like what?'

'As though you are wearing all the wrong clothes. Believe me, when a girl is as pretty as you are, you could get away with wearing the tablecloth.'

She wondered if Monique de Vries had said that too. 'Two compliments within the hour,' she observed. 'Thank you.'

He only smiled a little. 'What would you like to drink?' he asked. 'There's a rather nice dry sherry…'

She agreed to that, not knowing much about drinks, and fell to studying the menu card. It was written in French, which was a good thing, because if it had been in Dutch he would have had to translate it to her. She was searching for something not too wildly expensive when the matter was taken out of her hands, her companion suggesting that she might like the *Truite Saumonée au Champagne*, with the *Pâté Maison* to precede it. 'Unless you care to join me in an underdone steak?' he added, and when she wrinkled her nose: 'I thought not, but I can recommend the trout.'

Cressida thought privately that at that price anyone would be safe to recommend it, and when the *pâté* came, polished it off delicately with a splendid appetite before tackling the trout. Giles had done right to order it for her, for it was delicious; she ate every morsel and enjoyed it while they talked of nothing in particular. Her companion appeared to be on his best behaviour, too, for he said nothing to annoy her to which she could take exception. Indeed, he put himself out to entertain her and it was impossible to discover if he was enjoying her company or not. Certainly if he disliked her, he was concealing it very well; on the other hand he showed no partiality for her either.

She accepted his suggestion to try the chocolate soufflé, and allowed her glass to be refilled with the Sauterne he had chosen, for after all, she would probably not eat another meal like the present one for some time—perhaps never.

The early afternoon was already darkening as they left the restaurant, but she hardly noticed; she was enjoying herself—she wouldn't see very much more of Giles after this outing together; she was going to extract every scrap of pleasure she could from it. Never mind what he thought of her, just being with him was a happiness she had never expected or imagined. Probably because of the Sauterne, her face was a little flushed and her eyes sparkled, so that when they entered his mother's room that lady greeted them with: 'I can see that you have been enjoying yourselves, my dear. Cressida, come and sit down and talk to me while Giles sees those patients of his.'

So Cressida sat, answering the questions put to her by the formidable lady in the bed; for she was formidable and accustomed to getting her own way without doubt, taking it for granted that when she wanted something done, it would be attended to immediately and without question, and yet she was charming too and, Cressida suspected, very lovable. She wondered how mother and son got on, for they both had strong personalities, and as though the invalid had been reading her thoughts, she remarked in her commanding voice: 'Giles and I are devoted to one another, you know. His father died some years ago—he was in a concentration camp during World War Two, and although he survived it, it killed him eventually. He was a doctor too, and a brilliant one; he was also a man of iron will with a fierce temper.' Her face softened. 'We were ideally happy, which is strange, because I am strong-willed too. Giles is mostly his father, I think,' she smiled, 'especially the fierce temper, although he seldom allows it to show, but he can be—difficult at times.' She added innocently: 'I expect he has annoyed you?'

'Yes,' said Cressida.

Her companion nodded. 'I know—he can be so vexing that one could shake him. Monique has said it of him many times.'

'They're old friends?' It hurt to keep her voice casual, but she managed it.

'Oh, very old. She is in Paris for a week or two buying clothes. She is the kind of woman who has to go to Paris for them.' There was a slight edge to Mevrouw van der Teile's voice.

So that was why he had asked her out to lunch, thought Cressida painfully; he had been at a loose end. She wondered when he was going to marry Monique and longed to ask, but pride tied her tongue. She observed brightly: 'It must be fun to buy things in Paris, but I've seen some lovely clothes here—in Amsterdam and Groningen.'

'Den Haag,' stated the older lady categorically, 'that is the place to go for clothes. If ever you should wish to shop there, let me know, Cressida, and I will tell you the names of the best places.'

'Thank you, Mevrouw,' said Cressida composedly, 'but I don't expect to buy clothes of that kind.'

'One never knows,' stated Mevrouw van der Teile, and she uttered the trite phrase with pleased emphasis, just as though she had invented it for herself. 'You dress well, child.'

'Thank you, Mevrouw.' The conversation, Cressida discovered uneasily, was centred upon herself. In a moment her companion would be starting on her round of questions again. She said hastily: 'I expect you are looking forward to leaving here—have you any idea when you are to go home?'

'I spoke to the doctors this morning,' observed Mevrouw van der Teile, and Cressida was quite sure that was exactly what she had done, flattening out the poor men before they could get behind their professional faces. 'I wished to know exactly what they thought, and provided they have told me the truth, I expect to leave here within the week. One must naturally allow for unexpected events.'

Like collapsed lungs, heart failure, pneumonia again, bronchitis…all nasty complications which could follow a severe chest infection and all presumably lumped together in the lady's mind as events. Cressida had a sudden ridiculous urge to take the formidable lady in her arms and give her a hug. 'I'm sure that D… Giles will see that you get home just as soon as possible,' she said soothingly. 'I know you aren't his patient, but he has probably been consulted about you.'

His mother nodded regally. 'Indeed, yes. Any other man than Giles would have had a swelled head and an exaggerated opinion of himself by now—he has many faults, but thank heaven conceit is not one of them.' She coughed. 'Do you like my son, Cressida?'

Cressida choked, went pink and opened and closed her mouth like a beautiful fish suddenly finding itself without water. 'I... I...' she began, knowing that she would have to say something under those compelling eyes, and then let out a long soundless sigh as the door opened and the object of their conversation walked in.

He sat down at once and engaged them in a conversation which allowed of no personalities at all, and presently, when Cressida suggested that she should perhaps be going, he acquiesced with a readiness which quite shook her. But he was still the pleasant, perfectly mannered host, waiting while she bade his mother goodbye and then ushering her out to the car without hurrying her. It seemed to take no time at all to reach the village, but as he had the habit of driving fast, she could hardly attribute his speed to a wish to be rid of her company as soon as possible. Besides, he maintained a steady flow of small talk all the way, which gave her no clue as to his real feelings. He went into the house with her, cut short the polite speech of thanks she was on the point of making, and swept her rather impatiently into Doctor van Blom's empty study.

'What have I done?' he wanted to know, and when she didn't answer from sheer surprise: 'Or what haven't I done? Or what have I said—or perhaps my mama has said?'

'Nothing.'

He addressed the room at large. 'Why does a woman always say "nothing" to a man while all the time she is only waiting for the right moment to pour the vials of her rage upon his unfortunate head?'

'You seem to know a lot about it.' Cressida had taken off her cap and was standing half turned away from him.

'Of course I do. I have a mother, have I not? And over the years I have had a number of girl-friends, you know.'

'And one in particular,' snapped Cressida, quite unable to hold her tongue.

He gave her a long, thoughtful look. 'As you say, one girl in particular.'

She went to her desk and uncovered her typewriter; it gave her something to do. 'Thank you for my delightful lunch, and I enjoyed meeting your mother again.'

It was disobliging of him not to answer her. In the silence which followed she sought desperately for a graceful phrase with which to fill it. Her head filled immediately with snatches of song, the first lines of a dozen hymns, even a half forgotten recipe for bread, but not a single graceful phrase. She gave him a look of deep exasperation and he said, half smiling, 'You're not going to tell me, are you, Cressida? Not now, at any rate.'

'Not ever,' she assured him.

'That sounds like a very long time. No matter. I am, when it suits me, a very patient man.'

He wasn't smiling any more, he looked to be on the point of saying something else, but the door opened at that moment and Doctor van Blom came in. Cressida slipped away to her room and stayed there prudently until, peeping from her window, she saw the Bentley slide away from the front door.

For the rest of the day she worked for two; if she kept on at the rate she was going, the book would be finished well in advance of the publisher's date, and that might be a good thing, for then she could go back to England and forget all about Giles; it didn't seem likely that she would, but she would have to try, and pride might help her. Her heart told her that she had no pride where Giles was concerned, but common sense got the better of her feelings; she would finish the book as quickly as she could and leave. She spent the next two days typing assiduously, but on the third morning Doctor van Blom, supported by his partner, decreed that she was to have a day off; to sit at a desk all day was not good for her, they pronounced. The book was almost done now, there was no longer any need for her to work so hard—besides, the weather had turned cold and frosty, ideal for a day out. Doctor Herrima mentioned that he was going to Leeuwarden and wouldn't it be a good idea if she were to telephone Harriet and invite herself to lunch?

Cressida hesitated, and Doctor van Blom said slyly: 'As a matter of fact, Giles was there yesterday and she asked particularly after you and asked if you couldn't spend a day there, and he suggested that you might like to lunch with them today—Doctor Herrima will drop you off...'

'Well,' said Cressida on an indignant breath, 'of all the...!' She didn't finish the sentence, because her two kindly companions were looking at her expectantly, delighted with their little plot, waiting to be praised and thanked.

She did both, generously, and watched their smiles. They really were two of the nicest, kindest men she had ever met. She left them to fetch her outdoor things; Doctor van Blom reaching for the telephone to tell Harriet that she was on her way, and Doctor Herrima making for his car.

'You're sure you can manage?' she asked Doctor van Blom anxiously as she arrived in the hall again, dressed for outdoors.

'Of course, my dear—there is only the morning surgery today, as you know, and Doctor Herrima will be back here for lunch. Have a good time—Friso will drive you back this evening.'

He went with her to the door, settled her into the car beside his partner and stood waving goodbye until they were out of sight.

She sat quietly beside Doctor Herrima while he eulogized about the Dutch countryside in his pedantic, precise English, and indeed it looked delightful under the light blue sky, even though the sunshine was pale and without warmth.

Friso's house, when they reached it, looked superb against its calm background, and her welcome was everything that could have been desired. Cressida bade Doctor Herrima goodbye and went indoors with Harriet to drink coffee and play with the babies until Friso came home for lunch, a delightful domestic meal which left her full of vague feelings of loneliness and longing for a home and a family of her own. Perhaps, she thought forlornly, they were made worse because she loved Giles. She shook the thought from her, for little Friso was demanding her attention.

It was impossible to feel unhappy for long in that happy household, though; and although she hadn't told Harriet about her parents' deaths she seemed to know all about it and what was more, talked about them in a perfectly natural way, asking Cressida about her home, giving her a chance to talk about them, something she knew now she had been longing to do for weeks. By tea-time she was laughing and talking as though she hadn't a care in the world, and as she helped put the babies to bed she said rather shyly, 'I feel quite different, Harry—talking about Mother and Father... I suppose I've had it all bottled up inside me. And being here with you—you're so happy.'

Her youthful hostess gave her a shrewd look. 'Yes, we are,' she said simply. 'I never knew that I could be so happy.' She smiled to herself. 'Friso and I—when we first met, you know—we weren't friends at first— at least I wasn't, and I thought he was going to marry someone else. He's like a rock, Cressida. You'll meet someone like him one day.'

It would have been lovely to confide to Harry that she already knew her particular rock and a lot of good it had done her. She managed some laughing reply and went with her hostess to tidy herself for dinner. Told to make her own way down to the drawing-room when she was ready, she made leisurely repairs to her face and hair, and went back downstairs.

The drawing-room appeared empty as she entered it; she was making her way down to the welcome warmth of the great fire at the opposite end of the room when Giles got out of a great winged chair turned a little away from her and she stopped short, said 'Oh…' and waited for her breath to come back.

'Now that is the kind of enthusiastic welcome I like,' he observed blandly.

'You surprised me.'

'Oh, dear—like meeting a bull in a field or finding a spider in the bed?'

Cressida chuckled despite herself. 'Don't be absurd— I just didn't expect to see you.'

He had drawn up a small crinoline chair to the fire for her and then sat down opposite her. 'I've been invited to dinner,' he told her, 'so I'll drive you back.'

'Well—thank you; Friso was going to…'

'Friso has a wife and three children he adores and never sees enough of; if you could steel yourself to endure my company instead of his, I fancy he will be secretly delighted; he treasures his evenings at home with Harry.'

Cressida said 'Oh,' again, and Giles laughed and got up as Harriet and Friso came in. The talk became general at once and stayed that way while they had their drinks and went in to dinner, and afterwards they sat round the fire, drinking their coffee; the two girls together talking about clothes and babies, and the two men, wreathed in cigar smoke, discussing some knotty medical problem in their own tongue.

'I suppose you speak perfect Dutch,' observed Cressida enviously.

Harriet laughed. 'Me? Heavens, no—Friso and I always speak English when we're together. I speak Dutch to Anna and Hans and our Dutch friends, of course, and I get along well enough in the shops. I had lessons for a year, but I'm by no means perfect.' She smiled. 'I don't suppose you've needed to speak Dutch, have you, though it must have been awkward when you all had the 'flu.'

'It was, but Juffrouw Naald and I have invented our own way of talking to each other; it works very well.' Cressida paused as the dainty little Sèvres clock on the table beside them chimed the hour. 'It's nine o'clock— shouldn't we be going? I've been here almost all day.'

Harriet laughed. 'And very nice too—you simply must come again before you go back to England. Giles comes quite often, you could come with him.' Something in Cressida's face made her add: 'Or Friso could pick you up when he goes to Groningen—he has some beds at the hospital there.'

They left half an hour later, and Cressida, looking back as they went down the short drive, saw that the great front door was still open and Friso and Harriet were standing just inside, arm-in-arm with the dogs sitting in a tight bunch beside them. She spoke her thoughts aloud. 'They're very happy, aren't they?'

Giles turned the car into the narrow road. 'Very. Wasn't it your Jane Austen who wrote "Happiness in marriage is entirely a matter of chance"? I don't agree with her—do you, Cressida?'

'I don't know,' she said soberly. 'I've not been married, so how would I be able to tell?'

It was a dark night now with a fitful moon fighting to escape the clouds which threatened to engulf it; it was cold too, she could see the frost sparkling in the fields and the thin ice already covering the canals.

They were almost at their journey's end, driving along a dyke with a canal on either side, when the Bentley's powerful headlamps pinpointed a car ahead of them. It was being driven slowly, weaving from one side of the road to the other, and Cressida could see frightened faces looking at them from the rear window.

The doctor had slowed down. 'Steering gone?' he wondered out loud. 'A drunk? A coronary perhaps—he'll be in the canal if he doesn't watch out.'

He was proved right almost immediately—the car in front of them slewed across the road and toppled quite slowly into the canal. Giles slammed on the brakes and was out of the car almost before the other vehicle had hit the water.

Cressida gave a gasp of horror and got out too. She had no idea how one set about getting out the occupants of a drowning car, especially on a dark, bitter cold night. A torch, she thought wildly as she scrambled on to the slippery grass, but the doctor already had one in his hand; he thrust it at her and peeled off his coat, elegant jacket and waist-coat and dumped them on the grass.

'There were children, I think—I'll get them first,' he told her with a calmness she envied. 'You may have to take them from me—better get your coat off, no point in getting it wet.'

He took the torch from her and set it on the ground where its beam would give them some light, then slid into the black, icy water. Cressida watched him disappear with even greater horror and then floundered down the bank herself, clutching frantically at the rough, slippery grass as she tried to find a firm foothold; she was petrified by now, but the occupants of the car would be even more so; besides, Giles was there... She dipped a cautious booted foot into the water, and then another, and discovered, a little late in the day, that the bank was sheer, there was no ground under her feet... She was still clinging to the grass with both hands, her legs getting more and more numb with every second, when there was an oily splash close to her and the doctor's powerful frame, covered in mud and weed, appeared. He had a small child across his shoulder; he thrust him at her without a word and disappeared into the murky depths again.

Cressida had had to let go of her grass; now she bobbed up and down with the limp little creature held awkwardly to her, but a mouthful of muddy water galvanised her into action; somehow she scrambled up the bank and laid the child down. There was no time to examine him; she rolled him on to his stomach, turned the wet head carefully to one side and slid, very reluctantly, back into the canal.

Just in time; the doctor surfaced almost beside her, pushed a slightly older child towards her, said: 'There's a woman—the man's dead,' and slid silently back. Cressida was getting over her fright now; the child was a good deal heavier than the first one, but what could be done once would be done again. She clawed her precarious way on to the bank once more, half drowning both herself and the child, and laid it beside the other little form. She was numb with cold by now and her boots—the only good boots she had, too—were filled with water and like lead on her feet, and her clothes clung wetly, turned icy in the wind.

The only thing which wasn't quite ruined was her fur cap, and if the doctor expected her to haul a grown woman on to the bank, that would be a ruin too.

But he didn't; he heaved a young, stoutly built woman out of the water himself, and when she made feeble attempts to help herself, told Cressida to get her higher up the bank before he ducked back into the water again.

It was a struggle, for Cressida didn't know enough Dutch to encourage her half-drowned companion, or tell her what to do; she caught a handful of coat across the woman's back and heaved and tugged and then pushed from behind, until the pair of them were lying by the children.

'Shan't be a minute,' Cressida told the woman, quite uselessly, and went slithering down the bank for the last time.

Giles was having no easy task; the man was short but heavily built and a dead weight. He pushed him out of the water and told Cressida to hang on to his shoulders while he got himself out. But he wouldn't let her help after that, but hauled the man up the bank to where the others lay. Cressida, eager to join him, got to her feet, forgetting that they were numbed to deadness by now. Her first step sent her slithering down the bank and into the water once again, a good deal faster this time, so that she went under and came up with a terrified yelp which brought the doctor into the canal beside her.

'Good God girl,' he snapped, 'did you have to fall in too? And it's only a couple of feet from the bank.'

In the torch's light, she could see how white and haggard his face was, and he was in a rage with her, too.

She steadied her chattering teeth to tell him, 'I can't swim.'

Chapter 7

If Cressida hadn't been soaking wet and almost dead with cold and fright, the consternation on Giles' face might have given her enormous pleasure. As it was, she clutched his shirt sleeves with terrified fingers and kept her eyes shut. And when he spoke, it was in his own language; it sounded very forceful, and probably he was as angry as he looked. She opened one eye to see, and he looked so ferocious that she shut it again as she was tossed, without much respect for her person, on to the bank. 'Get into the car,' he ordered her in a no-nonsense voice, 'the front seat. You can take the smallest child on your lap, the others can go in the back.'

She stumbled painfully up the bank and he put out an arm and hauled her along beside him. 'But the man,' she protested weakly, 'he's…'

'Yes, he is, but we must still get to hospital with all despatch. Luckily, the others are in no fit state to realise…'

The child he put into her lap was breathing, and despite the cold and wet, a little colour was creeping into his cheeks; Cressida had barely made sure of that before the doctor had got the other three into the back of the car and had climbed in beside her, throwing her coat and his behind him.

'Thank heaven they didn't have time to drown— they're shocked and they've taken in a lot of water, but bar accidents, they should be all right, excepting for the man, of course—poor fellow.' He started the car, dripping muddy water over everything, and said with deliberate cheerfulness. 'Lord, how we do smell!'

His remark recalled her to her own slimy, weedy condition. Perhaps, when the poor souls with them had been taken care of, she might be allowed to take a bath and borrow some dry clothes at the hospital, but there was no point in worrying about that at the moment; she began to rub the small icy hands and feet as best she might, for the doctor was driving at speed.

'Which hospital?' she asked.

'Groningen. We're on a country road which will bring us out at Kollum. I had intended to go across country from there, but now we can take the other fork and join the motorway—it's only another few minutes now.' He added, 'I can get along faster.'

Cressida received this information with no enthusiasm at all; true, the sooner they got to the hospital, the better, but she was in no state to travel at a hundred miles an hour or more; they were already doing eighty on a road intended for sedate local traffic. She forced her eyes from the speedometer and bent her attention on to the child. When she looked up presently she saw the flashing blue lamp ahead of them and gasped: 'A police car, and heaven knows what speed you're doing...'

'A hundred and ten miles an hour,' stated the doctor placidly, 'and they're just the people we want.' He sent the Bentley roaring ahead, to draw up alongside the police car, open his window and shout across to its driver. Both cars pulled up then and one of the policemen got out, took a look in the car, listened to what the doctor had to say, nodded, got back into his own car and rocketed ahead, siren blaring, blue light flashing, the Bentley hard on his bumper.

It was like being in a particularly nasty dream, thought Cressida muzzily. She was feeling sick now and very worried about the child on her lap; his breathing had become loud and rasping and his pulse was rising.

'Is it far?' she asked.

'Child not too good? At this rate, less than five minutes. Do you want me to stop?'

'No—there's nothing much we can do, is there, and the others need attention as quickly as possible.'

The car's blessed warmth was beginning to creep into her bones. Her teeth had stopped chattering too, although water was trickling down her back, accumulating in icy patches here and there. She sighed with relief when the first houses of Groningen closed in around them. They hardly slackened their pace going through the city: the police car, still ahead, carved a way for them through the scanty traffic and pulled up at last in the hospital's forecourt.

The police must have radioed ahead, for there was another police car waiting and a group of doctors, nurses and porters poised ready with their trolleys. Giles got out of the car, said: 'Stay there,' to Cressida and went to give brief instructions to those waiting. She watched the brisk transport of the unfortunate occupants of the car, sitting in her sopping, ruined clothes—at least the mother and two children were alive; the children crying thinly, the mother tearful too and not yet completely conscious. Giles had his head through the police car window now, talking to its occupants, and then he was beside her again, and the car purred into life. She thought he said: 'Poor little Cressida,' but she was so weary and bemused that she decided that she had fancied it. She was too tired even to ask where they were going.

Not very far, it seemed—across the city and into a tree-lined street with a canal running down its centre. The houses on either side were mostly in darkness, but she caught glimpses of them in the car's headlamps; great gabled mansions standing shoulder to shoulder, their fronts richly decorated with carved wreaths of flowers, their splendid windows guarded by shutters. The doctor stopped the car in front of one of these and got out, to carry her across the narrow brick pavement and up double steps to a massive carved door which someone was holding open. She heard a man's voice answering the doctor when he spoke, and the sound of a dog's heavy breathing as she was borne rapidly along a narrow hallway into an inner hall and then up a staircase set at right angles to it. There was someone else with them now, hurrying just in front, making soothing sounds, and at the top of the staircase, crossing the gallery to open a door for them. She felt herself laid down on a bed and for a moment Giles' face was bent over hers. He still looked very white and angry. Cressida closed her eyes and sighed. His anger was something she couldn't cope with just then, all she wanted to do was to be allowed to sleep; she was long past caring about her wet, cold clothes and her numb feet.

'No, you don't,' said the doctor, 'not yet. Ineke here will help you undress and into a hot bath, then you are to have a warm drink and be allowed to sleep for as long as you like.'

'Doctor van Blom...?' she asked sleepily.

'I'll telephone him now.'

'You'll catch your death of cold,' she told him owlishly, and heard him laugh.

'Here's Ineke,' he said, and went away.

Ineke was plump and middle-aged, with a kind, plain face and small, twinkling boot-button eyes. She clucked and soothed as she peeled off Cressida's wet things, wrapped her in an enormous bath towel and led her to the bathroom adjoining, where she soaked in the fragrant hot water while Ineke washed her filthy hair. She would have stayed to fall asleep if she hadn't been firmly helped out, dried, put into a voluminous, long-sleeved, high-necked nightgown of finest silk and put back to bed where her kindly helper dried her hair, saw that she drank the milk which had been set ready by her bed, and finally, with another flow of clucks and tuts, allowed her to lie down and close her eyes. Cressida was aware that she was being tucked in before she slept.

She awoke to a fairytale room. She sat up in bed, feeling little the worse for her ducking, and looked around her. It was a pretty apartment, the furniture of satinwood polished to glowing brilliance, the curtains and bedspread and chair covers in pale chintzes of pinks and blues. The bed was elaborately carved at head and foot and covered with a thick pink eiderdown, and the sheets, she noticed with some awe, were very fine linen, embroidered and edged with lace. She sat up a little higher in bed as she counted the hours rung out by the various churches in the neighbourhood—ten o'clock; she would have to get up, but a glance round the room revealed the fact that none of her clothes were visible. She would have to find someone…

She had one foot out of bed when there was a knock on the door and she put it back in again and called 'Come in'. Giles entered, looking immaculate, well rested and not in the least like a man who had spent quite a few minutes in an icy canal only a few hours earlier. There was a dog with him, an Irish wolfhound, looking at her with a benevolent, whiskered face. His hullo was casual and followed by his amused: 'Good lord, you're lost in that thing, aren't you?'

Cressida regarded the generous folds of silk with pleasure. 'It's pure silk,' she told him with satisfaction, 'and the lace is handmade, I think—quite beautiful.'

He smiled and came to sit on the edge of the bed. 'Feeling better?'

'Yes, thank you. I had a lovely sleep. Do you feel all right?'

His careless 'Of course,' made her feel foolish for asking, so that her next question was abrupt. 'Where am I?'

'Ah, the classic remark of all heroines. You're in my house.'

'Oh, and don't call me a heroine—I let you down dreadfully.'

He got up from the bed and went to look out of the window. 'You were a very brave girl—it needed courage to do what you did.'

Before she could stop herself, she said: 'But you were there...' He gave her a long, thoughtful look and she added hastily: 'What I mean is—well...' It was impossible to say what she meant; that because he had been there, she had felt quite sure that he would save her if she needed saving; that her trust had been greater than her fear. She stared at him silently and then when he smiled slowly, looked away and said in a high voice: 'What a gorgeous dog,' and then: 'It's very late. I hope I haven't disorganised your household. If I could have my clothes I'll dress, then I could perhaps telephone Doctor van Blom.'

'I have already done so; I told him that I would bring you back after lunch. Ineke is seeing to your clothes, I believe, and she will be here with your breakfast in a few minutes. I'm on my way to my consulting rooms and I'll be back to pick you up just after one o'clock. Ineke will see about your lunch.' As he spoke the housekeeper came in with a tray. 'I'll leave you to enjoy your breakfast.'

He was as good as his word. It had barely chimed the hour when he entered the house once more, and Cressida, once more in her own clothes, neatly cleaned and pressed but ruined for all that, was drinking her second cup of coffee after her lunch. She had spent an interesting morning, going downstairs rather hesitantly after she had bathed and dressed, to find a rotund little man with a merry face hovering in the hall. His 'Good morning, Miss Bingley,' took her by surprise, but she wished him a good morning too and gave him an inquiring look.

'I am Doctor van der Teile's houseman, Beeker, miss,' he informed her in heavily accented English. 'I opened the door to you last night, but you were too tired to notice anyone.' He waved a hand across the hall. 'If you would like to sit in this room? We call it the small parlour; the doctor spends a good deal of his time here—and in his study, of course. The other reception rooms are rather large and used only for company.'

He opened a double door and ushered her into a fair-sized room, most comfortably furnished with a well-balanced arrangement of beautiful old furniture and easy chairs. There were two velvet-covered sofas, one each side of the fireplace, and a smaller chair had been drawn up to the bright fire burning in it. 'I think you will find this a comfortable seat,' said Beeker in a kindly voice. 'You will find the English papers on a small table beside you. Ineke will be in at once with your coffee, miss.'

He beamed at her and trotted away and the house-keeper swept in with the coffee tray and the dog at her heels. She fussed gently around in a fashion which Cressida found quite delightful and presently went away, leaving her to read the papers and drink her coffee, while Barker, the dog, stretched himself before the fire and kept her company. Beeker had come back several times during the morning, to make up the fire in the marble hearth, to inquire if she would like more coffee; at what time she would like lunch; if she had sufficient to read…she had thought that in this day and age, there were no longer people like Beeker and Ineke, lapping one around with every comfort and seeming to enjoy it.

At lunch-time, when Beeker came to fetch her, explaining that they had laid the table in the small dining-room for her—'the large dining-room seats sixteen persons,' he explained further—she ventured to ask him how long he had been with the doctor.

'Oh, before he was born, miss—I came as a house-boy to the doctor's father. Ineke has been here almost as long. Of course there are two young girls who help in the house.'

He ushered her into a room across the hall, a small, panelled apartment with a rich, many-coloured carpet and sapphire blue brocade curtains at its tall, narrow windows. The dining table was circular, of inlaid walnut, as were the four chairs placed round it. Cressida ran her fingers lovingly over the marquetry as she sat down, and looked appreciatively at the fine napery and silver before her; Giles lived in some style, he must have an enormous and very lucrative practice. She frowned faintly; it would have been nice to have known all about him, but pointless, too.

Beeker stayed in the room while she ate: soup, a little vol-au-vent as light as air, filled with prawns, cold meat, a delicious salad and a variety of breads and excellent coffee with it. It was he who mentioned their watery adventure of the previous evening. 'Very brave of you, Miss Bingley, if I may say so. Ineke thinks so too. Our canals can be very unpleasant even for those who can swim. We are sorry that your clothes are spoiled, although we have done our best.'

'You've both been super,' declared Cressida. 'I thought they were a write-off—er—useless, but at least I can wear them back. I'm sorry you've had so much extra work because of me.'

Beeker smiled all over his face. 'A pleasure, miss. I think the doctor has just entered the house.'

Giles came in a moment later and Cressida made haste to say: 'I'm sorry I forgot to ask after those poor people—are they all right?'

'They are doing very well. The little boy may have to stay in for a time, but his mother and the other child will go home in a day or so.'

He had thrown off his coat and was rubbing Barker's ears, and as Beeker came back with a tray of coffee, he sat himself down in a winged armchair by the fire.

'And your mother? I did mean to ask after her too...'

'She is doing very well—I've just been with her. She sends her love to you.'

Cressida digested this in silence; perhaps he was just being kind, for somehow his forthright parent didn't seem the kind of person to send her love indiscriminately.

'No, I didn't make that up,' said the doctor quickly. 'She likes you.'

She went a little pink. 'I like her too.'

'Good, you cannot imagine what a relief that is to me.' He was laughing at her and she had no idea why, so she asked, to be told: 'Oh, we'll go into that some other time. If you're ready, we'll go—I've one or two patients to see and I want to have a look at Doctor van Blom at the same time.'

Cressida went straight back to her typing as soon as they arrived, despite Doctor van Blom's protests. 'I only got wet,' she told him, 'and honestly, I feel fine.'

So she retired to the study and got out the manuscript and went to work on it at once—she was almost at the end now; another few days—a week perhaps, and she would be finished and getting ready to go back home to Aunt Emily and the tiresome job of looking for a new post. She paused in her work to think about it and became so gloomy that she gave it up presently and went back to her typing.

Juffrouw Naald brought her her tea. The doctors, she made Cressida understand, were in consultation and did not wish to be disturbed, and towards the end of the afternoon she heard the front door close and the Bentley's gentle, almost soundless engine start up. Giles had gone; he could at least have put his head round the door and wished her goodbye. What a waste of time it was, she thought crossly, loving someone who treated her in such an offhand fashion—although he had no reason to do otherwise, especially when he was about to marry Monique de Vries. Cressida took out her ill feeling on the typewriter so that it jammed and she was forced to spend the rest of the evening getting it to go again.

It was the next morning, as she settled down to work after breakfast, that Giles walked in. She wished him good morning in a surprised voice and asked: 'Shall I fetch Doctor van Blom, or was it Doctor Herrima you wanted?'

'Neither. I came to see you, Cressida.'

'Me? Whatever for?'

He sat down in his partner's chair behind the desk. 'Will you marry me?'

The sheet of paper she was holding fluttered to the ground. When she found her voice she repeated 'Marry you?' in an unbelieving kind of way, and then: 'But you're going to marry Mevrouw de Vries.'

If he was surprised he didn't show it but replied blandly: 'Am I? Whoever told you that? I'm not, you know. She's in Paris now and is getting married there today.'

Something in his voice made her ask: 'Didn't you know that she was going to marry?'

'Not until this morning.'

Cressida's hands were clenched tightly in her lap, rage bubbled up so fiercely inside her that she could barely utter. 'And so you came straight here and asked me to marry you!' Her voice was a trifle loud, and despite her efforts, shook a little. 'Charming—on the rebound, I presume.'

There was no expression on his face, only his eyes had become so cold that she shivered. 'Is that what you think? That I wanted Monique and because I couldn't have her, I decided to ask the first girl I saw to marry me in her place?' His voice was unhurried and silky and although he was smiling now, she wished he wouldn't.

She looked at her tightly entwined hands. 'What else am I to think? I can hardly suppose that you love me—I may be a fool, but not such a fool as all that! Why, you don't even like me, you get furious with me for no reason at all…the other night, in that beastly canal—you—you shouted at me because I fell in, and you didn't mind at all when I didn't get any supper, and when you were here it was: "Cressida, get up, Cressida, go to bed, Cressida, help in the surgery, Cressida, drive the Bentley"…and now here you are…' her voice rose with the strength of her feelings, 'asking me to marry you!'

The doctor had been watching her closely during her tirade. Now when he spoke his voice was quite different; kind and gentle and understanding. 'I've taken you by surprise, and you are quite right, I have never given you any reason to believe that I loved you and now I have been clumsy—I'll say none of the things I intended to say, for I don't think it would help at all, but I had thought—I had hoped…' he paused to smile at her. 'Go back to England and think about it and make up your mind there, and in the meantime, don't stop me from seeing as much of you as I possibly can.'

He came round the desk and pulled her to her feet. 'I think we might be very happy together,' he said, and kissed her—a very gentle kiss. Illogically, she would have liked to have been swept off her feet and kissed breathless, whether he meant it or not…

'I'm free until this evening.' He spoke casually,

as though none of their astonishing conversation had taken place. 'Shall we go somewhere for lunch? Hilversum, perhaps? I feel like a long drive. I promise you I won't talk about us at all, not unless you want it.'

'But haven't you any patients?' she asked doubtfully.

'Not today.' He smiled at her, crossed the room and covered her typewriter. 'You look pale, dear girl, you need a change of scene.'

She needed more than that; she needed several hours alone somewhere, so that she could think, but she could see that she wasn't going to get them at present. Besides, she knew that she would go with him; he was restless and probably dreadfully unhappy, for he hadn't denied that he loved Monique. Her marriage must have come as a dreadful shock to him. Cressida remembered how close they had been standing that time she had gone down for something to eat; he must have felt quite sure of her then, and now the bottom had tumbled out of his world. It seemed likely that he hadn't meant a word of his amazing proposal; shock did strange things to people, but loving him as she did, she could help him in the only way possible; spending the next few hours with him, helping him to pass the time until his first shock and anger were spent.

She said quietly: 'I'll get my coat, I'd like a long drive too.' She paused at the door. 'I'll tell Doctor van Blom—you don't think he'll mind?'

'No, for I've already asked him. He's been worrying about you working too hard, but he's in his surgery if you want him.'

She peered round the door on her way upstairs and

his round, cheerful face lit up when he saw her. 'Now I am content,' he declared. 'You will have a day's holiday and be happy—and make Giles happy too.'

So he too knew about Monique. Cressida said soberly, 'I'll try.'

And she did; keeping up a cheerful flow of chat throughout their long drive, although her companion contributed very little in reply, only brief answers or an occasional grunt, but she persevered, ignoring his preoccupied manner and stern profile.

She kept it up throughout their lunch in the splendid hotel in Hilversum to which he took her, pretending a great interest in the food and trying not to notice his own lack of appetite, and after their meal, when he took her walking in the town, she offered intelligent comments and asked questions which he was forced to exert himself to answer. She had a headache by this time, and heartache too; perhaps it had been a mistake to go with him, perhaps he would have been better off with his own thoughts, however bitter. But apparently not; they were almost back at Augustinusga when he said warmly: 'Thank you, Cressida—you've helped me through the day and you haven't asked a single question—not even looked curious. I only wish we could spend the evening together, but it's my night for the clinic.'

'I'll come with you,' she said instantly, 'if you'll have me. There must be something I can do there, and as you'll have to drive me back afterwards you'll be so tired, you'll sleep.' She added carefully: 'But only if you like the idea.'

'I would like it, very much. The clinic finishes about

nine o'clock, we'll go somewhere and have a meal before I drive you back,' and when she objected: 'That will tire me out even better.'

Someone found her an overall at the clinic and she was given the task of helping the elderly patients off with their coats and scarves and woollies and then getting them back into them again when the doctor had finished with them. It was a pleasant surprise to discover that she needed no knowledge of Dutch for this simple task; nods and smiles and encouraging murmurs were quite sufficient to promote understanding. True, several of the smaller patients burst into tears for one reason or another, but she discovered that as long as she spoke to them soothingly it really didn't seem to matter that they couldn't understand a word of what she was saying. The evening passed quickly, even with the two nurses on duty; they all had their work cut out, what with ushering patients back and forth, collecting notes, finding X-rays, sending the patients on their way again and tidying up when there was a moment to spare.

Cressida saw very little of the doctor; a brief glimpse of him sitting at his desk as she admitted or removed a patient; withdrawn, totally engrossed in his work, quite remote from the man who had asked her, so surprisingly, to marry him. It might be a good thing to forget that, she decided, as she swathed a dear old man in a succession of winter garments. She had had several proposals in the last few years, but never one quite as strange as this one, and all the more strange because he didn't strike her as an impulsive man at all. But it must have been impulse which had caused him to speak as he had.

She saw the last patient off the premises and went to help the nurses with the clearing up; at least the day was almost over; she wasn't certain about his invitation to supper and perhaps it would be as well not to mention it. But he did, coming out of his surgery as she was washing down the tables and rearranging the magazines.

'*Erwten* soup,' he observed, 'with french bread and lots of butter and cups of coffee—there's a small snack bar near here, will that suit you?'

It suited her very well; they walked the short distance together talking about the clinic, Giles going over some cases in his deliberate way, weighing the pros and cons, assessing their chances of improvement, mulling over the cases which might need surgery later on. Cressida listened carefully, encouraging him to talk, treasuring the thought that he confided in her, just as though she were an old trusted friend or someone close—his wife. She wondered if he had talked to Monique in this fashion and thought it unlikely, but there was no way of finding out. However, he hadn't mentioned her again and she felt sure that he wasn't going to.

They reached the snack bar and took a small table in its window, where they had their pea soup and drank several cups of coffee, talking now of his mother, his partners' practice, the 'flu epidemic, which had, mercifully lost its grip, and the chances of a cold winter ahead. The kind of talk between friends, she was beginning to hope.

They drove back in silence, but it was a friendly silence, and when they reached his partners' house, Giles went with her to the door and unlocked it with his key and went into the hall with her, where they met Juffrouw Naald, who smiled with pleasure at the sight of them and went at once to fetch coffee. They had it in the sitting-room, which was warm and smelled of cigars. Cressida, worn out with the effort she had been making all day, felt comfortably drowsy.

'You're tired, aren't you?' asked Giles. 'Go to bed, I'll see myself out.'

'Well, I'll pour some more coffee first,' said Cressida, anxious to spin out the time spent in his company as long as possible. 'I enjoyed the day very much—Hilversum was very interesting, I had no idea...' She caught his eye and stopped because he was smiling.

'It's all right,' he told her, 'my rage has blown itself out, you don't have to distract my thoughts any more.' He took the cup she was offering him. 'Mama is coming out of hospital tomorrow. Will you come with me to fetch her home?'

'I'd like to, if Doctor van Blom doesn't mind.'

'It won't be until after six o'clock—I've too much to do. She will be staying with me for a week or two, just until she is quite fit.'

'Oh, I thought she lived with you.'

'She has a house just outside Groningen—a small villa my father bought for her a long time ago. She lives there most of the time, although she spends the odd week or so with me.' He got to his feet and crossed the room to pull her gently from her chair.

'How much more work have you to do on that book?' he wanted to know quietly.

'I'm on the last chapter—I've done most of the cross-references as I went along, so I only have the final correcting to do then. About three days.'

If she had hoped that he would refer to the future, she was to be disappointed. He merely reiterated: 'Go to bed, Cressida,' and walked her to the door. He made no attempt to kiss her goodnight; she went quickly upstairs, torn between regret that he hadn't and peevishness that he had, apparently, not wanted to.

She worked hard throughout the next day, with a half-formed idea at the back of her mind that it would serve him right if she finished her job earlier than she had told him, and then slipped away without saying anything to him—it wasn't what she wanted to do, of course; it would be a mean trick to play, but on the other hand there was absolutely no reason why she shouldn't do what she pleased—Giles had taken her a little for granted, she told herself indignantly.

She became increasingly peevish as the day wore on, so that by the time he arrived that evening her greeting was cold and very offhand, and when he inquired after her progress, answered him so evasively that he lifted an eyebrow at her and asked her affably enough if she was feeling quite well.

'I have never felt better,' she assured him snappily, and went to get her coat.

It seemed he hadn't noticed her ill-humour, for he kept up a cheerful flow of remarks as they drove to Groningen. But when they were on their way to his mother's room and she stole a look at him, she saw that something was worrying him still; there was a faint frown between his thick brows and his mouth was grim. But when they reached the invalid's room, there was neither frown nor grimness. He supervised his parent's departure with good-humoured patience, helped her carefully into the Bentley, invited Cressida to sit in the back of the car, and drove to his home.

Beeker was hovering, ready to open the door when they arrived, and Ineke was there too, so were the two girls who helped in the house; Mevrouw van der Teile was welcomed like royalty, and responded with all the graciousness of such. Cressida, bearing a variety of rugs, shawls, and flowers which at the last moment the patient felt she could not leave behind, was a little amused by it all, but she was touched, too, that Giles' mother should be greeted with such pleasure and affection, despite her imperious manner. She was borne upstairs, with Cressida still trailing behind, while the doctor went to his study to attend to some urgent telephone message. She was got to bed, the flowers arranged exactly as she wished, the bedjacket she fancied found and put on, her hair rearranged, and finally, a dainty tray with a light supper brought in.

Cressida, with nothing to do for the moment, leaned over the end of the wide canopied bed and surveyed its occupant, who was nibbling at the creamed chicken Ineke had prepared for her.

'I am a tiresome old lady, am I not?' asked Mevrouw van der Teile suddenly, and bit with appetite into a finger of toast.

'No,' said Cressida, 'for you're not old and you're not tiresome. I was just thinking, how delightful to be held in such affection—not just by Giles, but by everyone here.'

'Yes, it is, isn't it?' agreed her companion with some complacency, then said so sharply that Cressida jumped, 'Giles is upset and very angry. You know why?'

'Yes.'

'I expected better of Monique de Vries; the least that can be said is that it was unkind and wrong not to tell him.' She gave a dignified snort. 'Going to Paris to buy clothes—she told us all—and then breaking her word to him!'

Cressida wandered away to a corner of the room where the light was dim. 'I expect he'll get over it,' she suggested, and made great work of studying a charming little flower painting on the wall.

'Oh, yes, of course he will—but men remember that sort of thing. I've said nothing, of course. When he wants to, he'll no doubt tell me everything there is to know.'

Cressida murmured something and wished very much for the conversation to end. She had her wish, for the doctor came in at that moment, spent a few minutes talking to his mother and then announced that dinner was awaiting them downstairs.

Cressida hadn't expected that; she had thrown off her coat when she had come into the house, and flung the no longer new fur cap after it, and she wasn't as tidy as usual. 'My hair—' she began, and was interrupted by his impatient: 'It looks perfectly all right to me, but if it's going to spoil your dinner, Ineke shall take you somewhere and you can do whatever it is needs doing.'

'Of course Cressida wishes to freshen up,' declared his mother severely. 'Ring the bell for Ineke, Giles, and you may stay with me for a few moments while she is doing it.'

Cressida was taken to the room she had occupied previously, and presently, very neat once more, went down to the sitting-room where Giles was waiting to give her a drink before ushering her into the dining-room. There Beeker, looking jollier than ever, served them with iced melon, lobster Thermidor, and a straw-berry shortcake, made, she discovered, with fresh strawberries. She turned surprised eyes upon her host, who smiled blandly across the table at her and said:

'Shocked, Cressida? Appalled at the wicked extrav-agance of fresh strawberries in December? Perhaps you will enjoy them better if I tell you that they're grown at a small farm I own in Limburg—it has some rather fine hothouses there and a very old gardener who can grow anything. You shall meet him one day.'

It seemed prudent to let that pass; she made some trivial remark about Limburg, and he followed her lead, his eyes twinkling.

Cressida went to say goodnight to Mevrouw van der Teile after they had had their coffee in the sitting-room, and not much later, Giles drove her back to Augustinusga. When they arrived he got out of the car and opened the house door for her, but he didn't come in. But this time he did kiss her with fierce urgency, and then without a word pushed her gently through the door and closed it between them, leaving her to stand in the dim hall, wondering how anyone with a heart as broken as his could kiss like that. Probably, she thought wistfully, he had been pretending that she was Monique.

Chapter 8

Two days later Cressida had the manuscript finished, corrected and on Doctor van Blom's desk for his scrutiny. She had seen nothing of Giles and when she had asked Doctor Herrima at dinner that evening, in a studiedly nonchalant voice, if his partner had gone away, he had looked at her in some surprise and said no, he had been on the telephone not an hour since, and then he had been at his consulting rooms.

Cressida had at once plunged into conversation about something quite different and they had all had a second glass of the champagne Doctor van Blom had produced in honour of the completion of his book. Giles wasn't mentioned again, and she went to bed in quite a nasty temper, although she concealed that fact from her elderly companions.

The next morning, after a wakeful night, she

broached the subject of her leaving. They were sitting at breakfast, and two pairs of eyes regarded her with consternation. 'My dear Cressida,' said Doctor van Blom, 'you surely can't mean to leave us so suddenly? I know that my book is finished, but could you not stay for a day or so longer? You have no job waiting for you?'

She had to admit that she hadn't, and she was mustering several good reasons why she should return to England as soon as possible when the reason for her desire to be gone entered the room, closely followed by Juffrouw Naald, bearing fresh coffee.

'Cressida feels that she should leave us at once,' stated Doctor van Blom instantly.

Giles seated himself at the table and stared across it at her as she poured his coffee. 'Does she indeed? Now, I wonder why.'

'I have to get another job,' she told him, a little too quickly.

He brushed that aside. 'Have you made your decision?' he asked, and smiled a little although his eyes were intent on her, and she met them unflinchingly although she had gone pink.

'No,' she said, 'I haven't.'

He nodded. 'So you wish to go back to England—you want time.'

It was silly to say that; she didn't want time; here she was, ready and waiting to fling herself into his arms, only how could she with Monique's lovely shadow between them? She said: 'Yes, I do. I think we both do.'

He smiled a little. 'I can't agree with you there, but I'll not hurry you—I've already told you that.'

She said slowly, 'Yes, I know.' She had quite forgotten their two companions, sitting like two elderly mice, drinking in every word. 'You see, Giles, I have to be sure.' She didn't explain that it was of him she had to be sure. If he had said, just once, that he loved her, she wouldn't have hesitated, but he hadn't—probably by now he was regretting his impulsiveness; she would have to give him the opportunity of backing out, and that could be done more easily once she was miles away from him.

'When do you want to go?' he asked casually.

'Well, soon. It's too late to go tomorrow, isn't it, but the day after that?' She remembered the two silent doctors then. 'You wouldn't mind? I've loved being here with you, but I think it would be best if I went home as quickly as possible.'

'I've asked Cressida to marry me,' Giles spoke quietly, 'and for some reason she doesn't take me seriously.' He grinned suddenly at her across the table and went on with uncanny insight: 'She thinks that if she is in England and I'm here, we can jilt each other more easily.'

It was disconcerting to have her thoughts read so accurately. She felt the colour come into her face and was furious with herself for it, especially as all three men were looking at her. It was Doctor Herrima who said: 'How refreshing to see a girl blush—they never do these days. Do please take Giles seriously, Cressida, it would make us both very happy.' He chuckled. 'Besides, it would keep you in the practice, wouldn't it?'

He laughed comfortably at his little joke and his partner with him. Giles laughed too, only there was

mockery in it, as though he knew exactly what she was
thinking. She hoped he didn't, and said rather coldly,
because the smile had annoyed her: 'I could take your
manuscript with me, Doctor van Blom—it's expected
on the twelfth, isn't it? If I travel the day after tomorrow, I could take it to the publishers, it's quicker and
safer than the post.'

'Going home to Aunt Emily?' asked Giles carelessly.

She had told him about her aunt, she had even described exactly where she lived. 'Yes,' and then she
added hastily: 'I shall probably get another job right
away, though—I might just as well call in at the agency
while I'm in London.'

'A splendid idea,' observed Giles genially. 'Well,
we shall all be sorry to see you go, Cressida. I'm going
back to Groningen very shortly. How about coming
back with me and saying goodbye to Mama? And
surely you want to do some shopping...'

True, she did, and she couldn't go without saying
goodbye to Mevrouw van der Teile. She agreed a little
ungraciously, because he had trapped her into it, excused herself with the plea that she had the typewriter
to clean, and left the three men still sitting round the
breakfast table, although they wouldn't be there long;
surgery was almost due to start.

She went into the study and sat down at the desk;
she would clean the typewriter another time, she decided; she could better employ her time in making up
her mind as to her future. She supposed that if she
hadn't loved Giles so very much, she might have accepted him; but to marry him now, feeling as she did

about him, would spell disaster; she would never know how much he loved Monique, or what his real feelings for herself were; a man could marry for a variety of reasons, not necessarily love. It wouldn't work out, she told herself soberly. She would go home just as quickly as she could, and after a suitable interval, write to him.

The subject of her thoughts opened the door at that moment, gave her a shrewd glance and said carelessly: 'That's right, leave that thing—go and get your coat, there's a good girl—I've only one patient to see and I shan't be more than ten minutes.' He went away again without waiting for her to answer him.

She was a little longer than that, though, because she met Juffrouw Naald on the stairs, and that good lady, apprised of the news of her departure, wanted to talk about it. Cressida didn't understand every word which was said, but she did gather that she would be missed, and that the housekeeper hoped that she would be back before very long. She ended by saying something which Cressida could understand very well. 'Poor Doctor van der Teile!'

So his Naaldtje knew about Monique too; Cressida made a sympathetic murmur and added in her fragmental Dutch: 'I have to hurry—the doctor is waiting for me.' She smiled at the older woman. 'I shall miss you too,' she managed, and then flew up the rest of the stairs because if she had stayed one minute longer she would have burst into tears and cast herself on Juffrouw Naald's comfortable bosom.

But she was careful not to let any of her feelings show as they drove to Groningen. Indeed, she matched her companion's friendly manner, discussing the prospect of Doctor van Blom's book being a success, the chance of snow for Christmas, the possibility of her getting a Ward Sister's post at the Royal General...she wasn't sure how the conversation had got around to that, but somehow it had, and Giles was pinning her down to answers she didn't want to give, and bewildering her too, for hadn't he, only a short time ago, asked her to marry him? Now he was suggesting that she should carve herself a career...

'Of course, if you should decide to marry me, you wouldn't work,' said Giles, uncannily answering her unspoken questions for her. 'I've more than enough money to indulge your every whim and bring up a family besides.' He uttered this information in such a matter-of-fact voice that she found herself asking: 'Oh, do you like children? So do I—I think a large family would be super, provided one could educate them and clothe them decently and give them a start in life.'

The doctor thought fleetingly of his considerable wealth and smiled. 'Oh, I think that could be managed.' He was still very casual. 'I have some money of my own as well as what I earn, you know, and my home is big enough to house a dozen. Besides, I have a charming house in the country, as well as the farm—so convenient for holidays; children hate hotels.'

'Oh, yes, I remember...' Cressida stopped; the conversation was getting out of hand and was, in fact, quite absurd. They were talking about holidays with the children, just as though they were already married and with a family to plan for. She asked hurriedly: 'Where exactly is your other house?'

He gave no sign that he had noticed her effort to

change the subject. 'Close to the river Vecht. The garden runs down to the water and there's a small landing stage. When I was a small boy Beeker took me fishing—that was after the war had ended, of course—our houses were confiscated during the occupation and we had to share a flat with my grandmother.'

'You were a very little boy—did you realize what was going on?'

'Lord, yes. I was four or five when my father was arrested—I remember that he left me in charge until his return.'

Cressida sat silent, getting rid of the lump in her throat. 'He must have been a rather splendid man,' she said at last.

'He was—he was a fine doctor, too.'

'Did you never wish to be anything else but a doctor?'

He looked surprised. 'No—what else could I be? There have been doctors in the family for generations, it was in my blood, I suppose.'

He slowed the car as they reached the outskirts of the city. 'Would you like to do your shopping first? I've a couple of patients to see. Oh—I'll get my secretary to book you in on a flight tomorrow. Morning or afternoon?'

Cressida considered. 'Well, I'll have to spend the night in London if I'm going to the publisher's and the agency. Could I go in the morning, but not at crack of dawn? I've a friend at the Royal General who'll put me up—I can go on to Aunt Emily's some time during the next day.'

'Just as you like.' His voice was placid, even a little

uninterested, she considered peevishly. If he intended
to propose again, he would have to be very earnest
about it...but of course, he wouldn't; the sooner she
went the better, especially as he had shown very little interest in her departure. Her thoughts were broken as he turned into a quiet side street and stopped,
leaned across to open her door and said: 'Can you be
at the hospital in a couple of hours? Ask for me at the
porter's lodge.'

She nodded and got out and the Bentley slid away
at once. Probably he was late.

Cressida had spent very little of her earnings; she
thought with satisfaction of the guldens in her purse
and made a beeline for the shops. Something for Aunt
Emily, something for Helen, the girl she would be staying the night with; a gift for old Mrs Oakes at the Post
Office in the village, because she had always longed
to go abroad and never had, and some small keepsake
for herself.

She found a charming little silver dish for her aunt
as well as some thick, highly coloured knitted gloves,
chocolates for Helen, and a Delft blue candlestick and
its matching candle for Mrs Oakes and for herself an
exquisite little flower miniature. For the doctors she
bought ballpoints in vivid colours, for it was a standing joke with the three of them that neither of them
could ever find a pen and they always needed to borrow hers. And when her purchases were made there
was still time to look around the dress shops and admire their contents. Expensive, Cressida thought, but
just the kind of things she would have liked to buy
for herself. However, she had spent a good deal more

money than she had anticipated, and she might be out of a job for a week or more when she got back; there was very little in her account in England and she would have to be careful, for although Doctor van Blom had paid her return fare she still had the train journey to Dorset to pay for. She turned her back on the pretty clothes and prudently confined her shopping to an elegant headscarf, then made her way to the hospital before she should be further tempted.

Perhaps the porter had been warned of her coming, for he came to meet her as she went in, called to one of her underlings, and waved her on to follow the man with a friendly smile. They went along a great many passages and up and down several small staircases before her guide stopped before a big double door and opened it for her to go through. She found herself in a wide corridor with a number of doors on either side of it and glass doors at its end through which she could see a ward. She turned round to ask the porter if he had made a mistake in bringing her there, but he had gone, and she stood uncertainly, wondering what she should do.

But not for long; a tall, well-built girl in nurse's uniform shot out of a nearby door and advanced to meet her. 'Miss Bingley? We are warned that you come— come with me, if you please.'

Cressida went, thankful that someone knew where she was. The girl threw open another door and invited her in with a wave of her hand, then shut it behind her. Giles was sitting at the desk under the window, and he got up as she came to a halt.

'Hullo—I've been held up, I'm afraid; I asked them to send you up here while I get finished.'

He pushed the one other chair in the room forward and motioned her to sit down and then spoke into the intercom.

'I've arranged for Zuster Metz to show you round, if you would like that. I'll be through very shortly.'

Zuster Metz was small and round and bustling. She took charge of Cressida, speaking in a mixture of Dutch and bad English and making up for it by the warmth of her manner. 'Women's Medical,' she explained, as she led her from the room. 'Thirty beds and they are always filled. Doctor van der Teile has ten of them—chests.'

She raced into the ward, still talking, finding time to address the patients as they went round and at the same time giving Cressida a précis of their conditions, the number of beds in the hospital, the hours of duty, the number of nurses she had working on the ward, the food served in the hospital canteen, and lastly, the doctor's manifold perfections.

Cressida, her ears ringing, assimilated this information as best she might, thankful that it was only necessary to nod and smile and say yes and no and really every now and then to satisfy the dear soul. She arrived back at the office feeling slightly bewildered, and met Giles' amused look as he got to his feet. 'I'm sure you found that most interesting,' he observed smoothly, and thanked Zuster Metz. 'Shall we go?'

Cressida added her thanks to his and Zuster Metz bubbled her pleasure at meeting her, her hopes to see her again and best wishes for her journey to England into a rigmarole of Dutch and English, as she trotted to the door with them.

'A chatterbox,' commented Giles, as they went down the stairs, 'but one of the best nurses I have had the pleasure of working with.'

Cressida nodded. 'Oh, I know just what you mean,' she agreed seriously. 'She would talk you back to health and strength whether you wanted it or not.' She smiled at him. 'I liked her—and thank you for letting me see the ward.'

He stopped in the middle of the staircase the better to address her. 'I find myself anxious to show you every aspect of my life,' he told her, a remark which took her so much by surprise that she said 'Oh!' in a startled voice and tripped up on a step. He put out a hand and caught her tidily and set her on her feet again, and then didn't take the hand away. His arm felt very pleasant across her shoulder; she stifled an urge to tell him that she loved him as they walked side by side out to the Bentley.

Beeker opened the door as they arrived at his house and Cressida exclaimed: 'However does he know? He always seems to open the door at exactly the right moment.'

'It's an instinct—he prides himself on it; if I sneak in by the side door I am subjected to reproachful looks for the rest of the day.' He opened the car door and helped her out. 'Come inside and say goodbye to Mama.'

He was being far too cheerful about it, thought Cressida crossly, as they went into the lovely old house; almost as though he were glad she was going. She said austerely: 'You haven't told me if you were able to get me a seat on the plane.'

Giles had thrown off his car coat and given his bag to Beeker, who was holding it as though it contained the Crown Jewels. 'Didn't I? There's a seat for you on the midday plane—you'll be in London in plenty of time to reach your friend during the afternoon.' He took her coat and flung it on top of his own, and started across the hall with a hand under her elbow. 'Doctor van Blom is driving you to the airport.'

Her disappointment was so great that she couldn't speak for a moment, then she managed: 'How kind, but there's really no need... I could...'

'Walk? Take a bus? Hire a taxi? Don't be silly, Cressy.' He had opened a door at the back of the hall as he was speaking and stood aside for her to go into the room beyond. She hadn't been there before. It was smaller than the sitting-room but extremely elegantly furnished, with a bright fire burning in the steel fireplace, and rose-coloured curtains to shut out the winter nights. But now the sun was shining in a watery kind of way, highlighting the pastel colours of the carpet, giving a gloss to the rosewood tables and davenport against one wall, and depth to the blues and greens and pinks of the chair covers. A pretty room and, surprisingly, an excellent background for Mevrouw van der Teile, sitting in one of the more substantial chairs, gowned in sapphire blue velvet, her hair beautifully dressed, her commanding features skilfully made up. She looked up from her embroidery as they went in and said in vibrant tones: 'How nice, my dears—I do so appreciate young people sparing their time to talk to an old woman.'

Her son gave a shout of laughter, kissed her fondly and begged her not to talk rubbish. 'I've brought Cressida to wish you goodbye.'

His mother, just for a moment, looked very like her son at his most bland. 'So soon? My dear child, I had hoped that I would have had many more visits from you before you returned home. However, I daresay that you wish to go back to England—you have plans, perhaps?' She snipped a strand of silk with deliberation. 'You intend to marry?'

Cressida was shocked into a startled: 'Me? Marry? Oh, no! I'm going to get another job.' She avoided the doctor's eye.

'You have never had a proposal of marriage?' asked Mevrouw van der Teile with ruthless charm. 'You surprise me, you are such a very pretty girl.'

'Thank you.' Cressida, whose manners were nice even when harassed, managed to keep her voice matter-of-fact. 'I have had the chance of getting married a few times, only I didn't want to.'

'You are not against marriage?' inquired her interrogator relentlessly. She added in vibrant tones: 'Family life—children...'

'No, of course not, Mevrouw, only it wouldn't do with the wrong man, would it?'

Mevrouw van der Teile's voice rang out with the clarity and resonance of Big Ben; for someone as ill as she had been, she had made a remarkable recovery. 'But perhaps you have found the right man?'

Cressida, sitting in a little button-back chair,

looked at her hands lying so quietly in her lap and tried to decide what to say. She could bring the conversation to a speedy conclusion by saying that yes, she had; he was sitting there, in the wing-backed chair next to his mother. On the other hand she could tell the lady to mind her own business. There must be a safe, middle-of-the-road answer, if only she could think of it. Giles thought of it for her: 'I'll wager the Bentley against one of your hairpins that you never breathed a word to a soul once you had set your sights on Father.'

She chuckled richly. 'Indeed, I did not. Cressida, you must forgive me for being a rude old woman.'

'Oh, but you're not, indeed you're not. It's kind of you to take an interest...' She caught the doctor's eye and saw that he was smiling faintly and because of that she added briskly: 'I'm quite looking forward to getting a Ward Sister's post.'

'What a terrible waste!' declared her hostess, and before she could enlarge on that, Giles remarked carelessly: 'Oh, but she will make a splendid Sister, especially when she has had a few years' experience.'

His voice sounded so silky that Cressida knew that he didn't mean a word of it. All the same it annoyed her so much that she suggested gracefully that she should be going. 'Packing and so on,' she explained, and was surprised that when she took her leave, the elder lady kissed her with warm affection. Beeker slid into the hall too, and wished her, rather gloomily, a pleasant journey, and Barker licked her hand, his whiskered face the picture of doggy gloom. Only the doctor seemed unaffected by her departure. Indeed, in the car, driving fast back to his partners' house, he remarked cheerfully:

'Well, now you have the whole afternoon in which to pack, for from the tone of your voice just now, I can only conclude that you have a mountain of luggage, and I have no doubt that the so on, whatever that may be, will take time, too.' He added in the mildest of voices: 'If you hadn't sounded so urgent, I would have invited you to lunch.'

She glanced suspiciously at him, but his profile was as calm as usual. All the same, she suspected that he was laughing at her. 'It isn't the amount of packing there is to be done, there are—there are other things...'

'Yes, you said so, dear girl. "And so on". I wouldn't presume to argue.'

They were rounding the square by now; in another few minutes Cressida would have to say goodbye. She watched him get out of the car and come round and open her door. He had never looked more placid and, annoyingly, amused. She bounced out of the Bentley and up to the front door, and had her hand on the knob when it was opened from the other side by Juffrouw Naald, who broke into instant, urgent speech the moment she saw the doctor. They were all inside, with the door shut against the cold, before he explained.

'There is a patient Doctor Herrima wants me to see immediately, Cressida. I'm going at once—tell Doctor van Blom I'll be telephoning him, will you?'

He patted her rather absent-mindedly on the shoulder, kissed Juffrouw Naald on her cheek and went out again, leaving Cressida to take off her hat and coat and presently go to the dining-room and lunch with Doctor van Blom.

She didn't want anything to eat; food choked her, but the kind man sitting opposite her would only get anxious if she didn't pretend to eat. She swallowed whatever it was on her plate and tried not to think that she wasn't going to see Giles again, for of course he didn't really want to marry her—it had been his first reaction against Monique; perhaps he had been looking for an opportunity to tell her that, and now Providence had stepped in and he had been able to go away without any of the embarrassments of saying goodbye.

She packed her things after lunch, tied the typescript up securely and then went for a walk before driving Doctor van Blom on his afternoon round. There had been no sign of Doctor Herrima and certainly none of Giles, and by evening she was so depressed that nothing would have been nicer than to go to bed and have a good cry, but Doctor Herrima came in a few minutes before dinner and revealed that they had laid on a special feast as it was her last night with them, with the pick of Juffrouw Naald's special dishes and more champagne. So Cressida ate and drank and laughed, greatly helped by the champagne, and went to bed a good deal later than usual, determined to sleep, but despite her best efforts, she lay awake for most of the remaining night.

They left in plenty of time in the morning, which was a good thing, for Doctor van Blom drove no more than a steady thirty miles an hour all the way to Groningen, and once in the city, slowed to a walking pace.

Cressida was so engrossed in observing her companion's funereal driving that it wasn't until they were at the hospital and trundling sedately across its forecourt that she cried: 'Doctor van Blom, we've gone the wrong way—it's the airport...'

'Hours to spare,' grunted her companion. 'In a car of this power, we can reach the airport in minutes. Got someone to see.'

She followed him inside because he asked her to, although she hadn't the faintest idea why. It wasn't until they were in the lift, on their way to the fifth floor, that she turned to look at her companion with some suspicion. 'Isn't the fifth Medical?' she wanted to know. 'That's where G—Doctor van der Teile has his beds.'

The lift stopped and she was bustled out. 'Quite right, my dear,' agreed her companion as he hurried her down the corridor and in through the door at the end.

Giles was at the desk once more, looking remote, composed, and exactly as an eminent physician should look. He put down his pen and got up as they went in, and stopped looking like a physician, eminent or otherwise. 'Ah,' he said with satisfaction, 'sooner than I expected—you must have driven fast, Karel.' There was no trace of sarcasm in his voice.

His partner looked suitably modest. 'Fast enough, Giles, fast enough. Well, I'll go and see that patient of ours—be back in a few minutes—mustn't miss that flight.'

After he had gone Giles came round the desk and took Cressida's hand in his. 'I couldn't let you go without saying *tot ziens*,' he told her. 'Did you get all that packing done?'

It really wasn't fair; seeing him again was like re-opening an old wound; she had steeled herself to go, and now here he was, stirring everything up again. 'Yes, thank you.'

'Your friend will meet you?'

She was surprised. 'No. I'll get a bus from the Air Terminal.'

He nodded, frowning faintly. 'You have money enough?'

'Yes, thank you.'

He stopped frowning and smiled. 'We're not making much headway, are we? Will you tell me something, Cressy?'

She stared at his tie, his waistcoat, up as far as his chin. 'What do you want to know?' she asked.

'Why are you going back to England? Oh, not all the sound reasons you have given us—the real reason.'

She might just as well tell him, she decided tiredly—indeed, it might snap off the thread of their uneasy relationship. She made herself look at him and said in a clear voice: 'I love you, Giles, but you don't love me. That's why I'm going.'

His hand gripped hers so hard that she winced with the pain, then the door opened and Zuster Metz and Doctor van Blom came in together.

'Miss Bingley,' she exclaimed happily, 'how nice that you come again. I have asked Doctor van Blom to stay for coffee, but he says that he has no time at all—and now I hope that you will excuse me if I speak to

Doctor van der Teile on an urgent matter—a patient, you understand.'

It must have been urgent, Giles listened to what she had to say, and without a word or a look, followed her out.

Cressida had no idea how she got to the airport. Presumably she had answered any remarks Doctor van Blom had made on the way, for he hadn't asked if anything was wrong, and as she hadn't seen her poor white face, she was unaware that he, after one glance at her, had concluded that there was nothing that he could say, anyway. Only when her flight was called and she put out a hand to shake his did he suddenly lean forward and kiss her gently on the cheek.

She didn't allow herself to think of anything at all on the flight, and London was busy and bustling enough to keep her thoughts busy too until she arrived at her friend's flat. Somehow the evening passed and strangely enough she slept, to wake the next morning, feeling as though her inside had frozen and would never be warm again, but the day had to be got through; she helped tidy the flat, said goodbye to her friend, went to the publishers and then caught the first train she could to Weymouth.

She hadn't told her aunt at what time she would arrive and took an extravagant taxi out to the village, to find that lady in the little kitchen, potting mincemeat. The homely sight was too much for Cressida. She dropped her case, flung herself at her aunt and burst into tears. Presently she sniffed and said: 'Oh, Aunt Emily, it's so nice to be home!'

Her aunt smiled at her. She knew that that wasn't

what Cressida meant to say, but it would do for the present. Later on, perhaps, she would be told what had happened to make her niece's face so white and pinched.

Chapter 9

Being back in Aunt Emily's little house should have helped Cressida, but it didn't. Giles' face slid between everything she looked at and when she closed her eyes, there he was, beneath the lids. Besides, his voice was always in her ears, so that her aunt was forced to repeat herself on several occasions and then inquire anxiously if her niece was getting deaf. Cressida, denying this for the tenth time at least, very nearly a week after she had returned, offered to do the shopping by way of placating her aunt and went off briskly to the village stores. The little shop was nicely full and Mr Dent, the owner, was looking a little harassed, but her entry proved to be just what he needed, for two or three of his more impatient customers were pleasantly diverted at the sight of her, and engaged her in conversation until it was their turn to be served. Which left Cressida alone, finally, reading from her aunt's list, and having a chat with Mr Dent at the same time.

'I can't say as foreign parts suits 'ee, Miss Bingley,' he observed in his soft Dorset voice. 'It'll 'eve to be corned beef, I'm right out of cooked 'am—as I were saying, pale 'ee be, 'ee was pale a while back when the Reverend and your mother died, but that were natural— I mean to say... Didn't 'ee like it in Holland?'

'Oh, yes,' said Cressida brightly; after a few days in the village she knew exactly the questions to expect. 'Amsterdam was lovely, though I worked in the north of Holland—for a doctor, you know.'

Of course he knew. In a village so small, everyone knew everything, not because they were curious, but because they were a close-knit community, sincerely interested in each other. Mr Dent looked knowing. 'Any 'andsome young men over there?' he asked, and added: 'It'll 'eve to be Rich Tea biscuits...'

'Oh, yes, there were,' said Cressida chattily, 'but the doctor I worked for was quite elderly.' She paused. 'He had two partners, though.' Giles' face was so clear before her eyes as she spoke that she looked round, half expecting to see him in the shop too.

She took her groceries and walked back up the high-banked lane to the cottage, Giles' massive shade stalking beside her. She would have to stop being such a fool, she told herself sternly. Tomorrow she would go to London and take the first job the agency offered, and start looking around for a hospital job. In fact, she could go to the Royal General too and see if there was anything...

She went in through the back door, took off her anorak, hung it behind the door and went into the kitchen, where she unpacked her basket, called up the stairs to her aunt that she was back and would start getting their midday meal ready, and went to the sink.

The postman had been, but there were no letters for her; apart from a brief line from Doctor van Blom, which had contained no word of Giles, she had had no news. 'Out of sight, out of mind,' she said bitterly. 'If only I had held my tongue—what a fool I was to tell him that I loved him…like a silly lovesick girl.' She picked up a potato and began to peel it with ferocity. 'I hate him,' she said loudly. 'I hate him—I never want to see him again!'

'Try telling him that to his face,' said the doctor from the door behind her, and she whizzed round, dropped the knife with a clatter and let the potato roll across the floor between them.

'How long have you been there?' she demanded, joy at seeing him quite swamped by the fear that he must have heard what she had been saying.

'You didn't want to see me again,' he told her. 'Why? Have I missed any more observations?'

She ignored that. 'I've been here a week, I thought…'

He smiled at her and her heart turned over. 'That I should have written. My dear girl, a letter wouldn't have done at all; there are some questions… You told me that you loved me and in the same breath you declared that I didn't love you and that was why you were returning here, and all this at a time when it was impossible for me to answer you or even discover exactly what it was you meant.'

Cressida eyed him across the little room. His face

wore its usual bland expression, but she had the feeling that he wasn't bland at all. Perhaps he had come to tell her that she had done the right thing, that he hadn't been serious about wanting to marry her, perhaps he was going to tell her that he was interested in her after all, that he might manage to dismiss Monique from his mind...

She drew a deep breath. 'Monique—' she began, and saw his frown. 'You were in love with her, weren't you—still are, for all I know. It must have been ghastly for you when you discovered that she had married someone else. I suppose that's why you asked me to marry you—you had to rush off and ask the first girl you met to pay her out...' She sighed. 'I expect that's a natural reaction...' She looked at him and although there was no change in his expression, she took a step backwards.

'You really think that?' His voice was very quiet, but he spoke bitingly. 'You thought that of me—you didn't tell me.' His eyes were very cold.

Despite her efforts to stay calm and matter-of-fact, two tears welled up and trickled slowly down her cheeks. 'I thought it was true,' she mumbled, 'and— and you never said that you loved me—you haven't said it now...'

His icy stare sent her two shades paler even though he remained silent. 'Your attitude towards me was hardly encouraging,' he pointed out, 'and when, just once or twice, it was, you were in the throes of 'flu or I was ringed round with my work.'

She showed sudden temper. 'Oh, indeed—and what was I supposed to do? Do you imagine...' She choked, blew her nose defiantly, and began again. 'I thought you loved Monique—I saw you together one day at Doctor van Blom's. You were in the sitting-room together—you had your arms round her...'

He said with a studied patience which set her teeth on edge: 'Monique was married to a lifelong friend. We went to school together, he and I, and then to medical school, and eventually he held a consultant's post in Groningen. He died of CA three years ago, and I promised him that I would keep an eye on Monique, and she promised him that if ever she should remarry, she would first of all tell me; you see, Wim wanted it to be the right man; Monique is impetuous and she has a good deal of money. He hoped that she would seek my advice. And as for seeing us together'—he stopped to think, 'ah, yes, that day we came up to your room and you had been crying. Peeping, were you, Cressida? Not like you, I should have said... Monique was unhappy, I thought she was still grieving for Wim and I was comforting her as I would have comforted anyone, man, woman or child. And why I should be forced to make this lengthy explanation I cannot imagine.' He went on curtly, 'The trouble with you is that you allow your imagination to run away with you.'

He still hadn't said that he loved her, and somehow that mattered far more than knowing that he didn't love Monique. She was prompted to say with a fine disregard for the truth, 'Perhaps I do, but not any more I won't—you've made it plain that I imagined that I loved you, haven't you? And I'm sorry you found it necessary to explain so much of your private life to me—and don't dare answer that, for I can see that you're in a towering temper. Well, so am I, and I hope that I may never have to set eyes on you again!'

She heard herself utter the words with something like horror, and regretted them the moment they were out of her mouth, but it was too late. The eyes that she had found so cold were blazing now. He had turned and gone through the door, closing it quietly behind him, and her breathless, squeaky 'Giles,' was uttered to an empty room.

She should have run after him, but her legs refused to move at first; by the time she had wrenched the door open, darted down the passage and reached the front of the cottage, the Bentley's elegant tail was disappearing round a bend in the lane. It was silly to stand there calling his name; even if he had heard it, he wasn't going to come back.

Cressida went back indoors, and Aunt Emily, coming downstairs, paused to ask her if she felt all right. 'You're as white as a sheet, child,' she observed. 'Have you had a tiff with that nice-looking man who just plunged out of the front door?'

Cressida let out a wail and rushed into the kitchen and shut the door, and her aunt, being a sensible woman, went into the sitting-room and picked up her knitting. It was high time that lunch was prepared, but it was only too obvious to her that her niece, at the moment, had no interest in food. She rummaged round in her workbag and found a half-eaten block of chocolate and nibbled at it philosophically while she waited for Cressida to reappear.

Which she did after some twenty minutes, pale and red-eyed and subdued. She helped get their meal, laid the table, fed the cats and then sat pecking at her lunch, making bright remarks about nothing in particular, until Aunt Emily put down her knife and fork and said firmly: 'You had better tell me about it, Cressy. Who knows, I might be able to help you.'

'No one can help,' Cressida said a little wildly. 'I'll never see him again. You see, there was a muddle—a misunderstanding—I thought he was going to marry someone else and he wasn't...'

'He wanted to marry you?'

'He said so, and he came this morning—and I don't really know why we had to quarrel. It was me, I suppose.' She sniffed. 'He got very angry and I told him I never wanted to see him again, and he went...'

'A very natural reaction,' said her aunt comfortably. 'Men, especially men in love, are sometimes most unreasonable. What do you intend doing?'

'Well, I'll have to go after him, won't I? He's very pig-headed.'

'But you love him, Cressy.' Aunt Emily pushed back her chair. 'He looked rather super,' she remarked surprisingly. 'I had a good look from my bedroom window. Now there's a timetable somewhere—the one you had...it's too late to go today, but if you left in the morning you should get there by the evening.' She had found the timetable and was leafing through it. 'Yes, here we are: train to London and then down to Heathrow—let me see, a couple of hours for the flight—there's one to Groningen in the early afternoon—will that do? Wait a minute while I write the times down, then you'd better go to the Post Office and telephone.'

There was a seat on an afternoon flight. Cressida

booked it with much the same sensation as she always felt when she booked a dental appointment; something which had to be done and which she didn't look forward to. Giles would be angry, with that nasty cold rage which froze her very bones, but at least she could say she was sorry and if she felt brave enough, she could ask him if he loved her... Carried away on a flood of high resolve, she hurried back to the cottage to fling a change of clothes into a case and count her money.

It was snowing when Cressida arrived in Groningen and she had to wait a little while for a taxi. She was by now tired, hungry and filled with such impatience to get to Giles as quickly as possible that the hunger and tiredness didn't matter. When at length she got her taxi, she sat on the edge of the seat, quivering with excitement. In a very short time now she would see him, and despite the various speeches she had rehearsed during her journey, she still had no idea what she was going to say to him—perhaps she would know when she saw him.

The house looked welcoming as she got out of the taxi, the big windows lighted against the dark outside, the chandelier shining through the elaborate transom over the great door. She reached for the knocker and gave it a determined thump.

Beeker opened the door, beamed a surprised welcome and stood aside to allow her to enter. He picked up her overnight bag and set it down on one of the hall tables with the air of someone who expected her to stay, and the small gesture gave her courage to ask. 'The doctor? Could I see him, Beeker?'

He gave her a look of regret. 'The doctor is at the hospital, giving the last of a series of lectures to the post-graduates. He will not return for some time, miss—indeed, there was some talk of him spending the remainder of the evening with the Dean. I had orders not to wait up.' He looked at her more closely. 'You're tired, Miss Bingley. Allow me to get you a light meal and in the meantime Ineke will get a room ready for you.'

Cressida gave him a distracted look. A fine thing it would be if Giles refused to see her and she expected to spend the night at his home. 'I haven't time,' she told him urgently. 'I'm going down to the hospital—I know where it is. If you would please take care of my bag until I get back? I—I don't expect to stay here, but I've nowhere to put it for the moment.'

Beeker received this news with an impassive face. 'We shall hope to see you shortly, miss,' he assured her, and opened the door to show her out. 'Let me call a taxi for you, miss.'

Cressida paused. 'It's only a few minutes if I go down that funny little passage on the other side of the canal, isn't it? I'll walk, I'm sure I can remember the way.' She remembered to smile at him. 'Thank you, Beeker.'

She almost ran, despite common sense telling her that to arrive all breathless and worked up wasn't going to help her at all. On the other hand, suppose the lecture was finished and Giles had already gone? What was she to do? Follow him to the Dean's house? Go back to his home and accept his unoffered hospitality? Both were unthinkable. She flung common sense to the winds, and ran through the narrow passage between the houses which would bring her within a stone's throw of the hospital.

She hadn't stopped to think what she would do when she got there; it was surprisingly easy, as a matter of fact, for when she asked the porter on duty: 'Doctor van der Teile?' he called at once to a younger man, and put her in his charge. Cressida hurried along several passages and up and down a stair or two before he opened a quite small door rather cautiously and with finger to lip, motioned her to enter.

The lecture hall was filled to overflowing with medical students, post-graduates, house doctors and a sprinkling of well-dressed gentlemen in the front rows—fellow consultants, probably. She took a providential empty seat just by the door, high up at the top of the hall, and fastened her eyes on the platform. Giles was there, in the middle, standing behind a desk. There was a pile of notes before him, but he didn't seem to be using them. He was looking around his audience as he spoke, and she was thankful that the lighting was on the dim side. Besides, she was a long way from him.

She sat listening to his deep voice, not understanding more than a word here and there, but that didn't matter, just to be near him was enough for the moment. She became aware that she was very tired and a little woolly in the head; she should really use this time to make a few sensible plans, but none came, so she just sat, listening to his incomprehensible words and enjoying them. They lulled her to a tranquillity she hadn't enjoyed for some time now, so that she was quite surprised when his voice ceased and there was an outburst of applause. Should she whip through the door and wait for him in the entrance hall—and perhaps miss him? Or should she wait for the audience to go and make her way to the platform? She dithered too long and the people around started to move away, so that the platform was obscured for a moment. Cressida got up slowly, still undecided, and saw the platform was empty. 'Fool!' she admonished herself fiercely, and two young women doctors paused to stare at her on their way out.

The door beside her opened and Giles whisked her through it without a word; they had negotiated the various passages and steps, crossed the entrance hall and were actually by the Bentley before she had found her voice. 'You couldn't have seen me.'

'Of course I saw you—the only fur hat in the place, and coming in late, too. Get in.'

His manner was non-committal, but she did as she was told, wondering if she had made—and was about to make—a terrific fool of herself. The awkwardness of her situation struck her forcibly and gave her something to worry about as he drove back to his house without saying another word. Only as Beeker opened the door to them did he have something to say, and that was to his houseman and in his own language.

Cressida found herself swept into the sitting-room and offered a small armchair by the fire, and: 'Take off your coat,' invited Giles in the polite voice of a careful host, 'Beeker will be bringing coffee in a moment.' He cast her a lightning glance. 'When did you last have something to eat?'

She looked at him vacantly, trying to remember. 'I had coffee and a roll before I got on the plane.'

He crossed the splendid Aubusson carpet and tugged the bell-rope by the hearth and waited until Beeker came. 'Miss Bingley hasn't eaten for hours,' he told him. 'Will you ask Ineke to send something along? Soup and an omelette, perhaps.' He looked across at Cressida. 'Did you bring any luggage with you?'

'I—I asked Beeker to mind it for me, I hope you don't mind—just while I went to the hospital.'

'See that Miss Bingley's things go up to the room she had previously, will you, Beeker?'

It was disconcerting and annoying too that Giles had taken over the situation. 'No,' she said suddenly, 'I don't want to stay here.' She added belatedly: 'Thank you. You weren't pleased to see me—there's no reason why you should be, I suppose. I couldn't possibly stay.'

The doctor lifted an eyebrow at Beeker, who slid from the room with a blank face which became wreathed in satisfied smiles the moment he had shut the door behind him.

'Explain?' suggested Giles, his voice very gentle.

She got up and walked to the window and looked out into the quiet dark street; it would be so much easier to talk if she didn't look at him. 'I had to see you,' she began, 'to tell you that I was sorry. I don't deserve to be forgiven, but it was all lies, of course. I love you, I told you that, and it was very silly of me, too, but—well, it's made my love seem a very poor thing, hasn't it—not worth bothering about.' She swung round and made herself look at him. 'I won't stay here—I can't!'

Giles was standing with his back to the fire, his hands in his pockets. 'You will and you can,' he assured her affably. 'My poor darling, muddle-headed goose, do you really suppose that I could stop loving you just because you flew into a rage? I believe I know you better than you know yourself, Cressy. Do you think that I would have walked away and left you if I hadn't been sure that you would come to me? But I had to leave you, my darling, to make up your own mind once you discovered that you trusted me as well as loved me. And that I loved you.'

Cressida sniffed. 'You didn't speak... I'd thought of all the things I was going to say and when you didn't even say hullo, I couldn't remember one of them.'

He had left the fireplace and was standing close to her. 'If I say hullo now would that help you to remember them?'

A tear sparkled on her lashes and she wiped it away impatiently with the back of her hand. 'Only that I'm sorry.'

She was unprepared for his sudden swoop and the long lingering kiss he gave her. 'That will do for a start,' he told her, and sat her down again as Beeker came in with a tray, which he arranged carefully on a little papier-mâché table, painted and inlaid with mother-of-pearl, beside her chair. There was a coffee pot and cups, delicate little sandwiches, a covered cup of soup, strips of buttered toast and a garnished omelette on a silver dish. Cressida eyed it with pleasure, although it seemed quite wrong for a girl to want her supper just as her most romantic dreams seemed about to come true. Giles poured coffee for them both and said: 'Drink your soup, my darling girl, and polish off those odds and ends—I don't want you fainting on my hands.'

She smiled a little shyly at him then and fell to, while he sat in his great chair watching her. She was finishing the last morsel of toast when he said, half laughing, 'And now, if you have finished your supper...' and got out of his chair and plucked her out of hers to hold her close.

'The days have been very long,' he told her, 'and I wanted to come to you, and then suddenly there you were, staring at me over all those heads. It's a wonder that I finished my lecture, for I wanted to leap off that platform and pick you up in my arms...' He pulled her a little closer. 'I could think of nothing to say when I opened that door and you were still standing there—I was so afraid that you would be gone.' He kissed her slowly. 'But perhaps there is no need to say anything, just I love you, Cressy, and will you marry me as soon as possible.'

She looked up into his face. 'You're quite sure? You're not saying it just because I came running after you...' If she had had more to say, she would have had no opportunity to say it, and presently, getting her breath again, she could see that there was no point in saying any more, anyway. She kissed him quickly and observed, 'I may not be very suitable, Giles...'

She felt him shake with laughter. 'My love, you seemed entirely suitable the moment I set eyes on you, being so dignified about getting lost in Amsterdam, and I've never changed my opinion.'

'Why didn't you tell me that you didn't love Monique?' she asked him.

'You didn't ask me, dearest, and it never entered my head to tell you—why should it?'

'Oh,' said Cressida blankly, and then, remembering: 'But you were always so cross—when we went to the clinic you didn't want me to go with you.'

He kissed the top of her head. 'Darling, you must understand that it is a little difficult for a man to be with the girl he loves and not tell her so.'

'Then why didn't you?'

He smiled: 'I had the feeling that you didn't altogether approve of me.'

She smiled back at him. 'Oh, but I do, darling Giles; you could tell me now, if you like.'

Beeker, coming in to remove the tray, slid out again, a smile of intense satisfaction on his chubby face. At last the old house would have a mistress, there would be entertaining, children… He trotted off kitchen-wards, intent on passing on the good news to Ineke.

* * * * *

"You kissed me," he reminded her.

"The first time," she acknowledged.

"You kissed me back the second time."

"Has any woman ever not kissed you back?" she wondered.

"I'm not interested in any other woman right now," he told her. "I'm only interested in you."

The intensity of his gaze made her belly flutter. "I've got three kids," she reminded him.

"That's not what's been holding me back."

"What's holding you back?"

"I'm trying to respect our working relationship."

"Yeah, that complicates things," she agreed. Then she finished the wine in her glass and pushed away from the table. "Will you excuse me for a minute? I just want to give my mom a call to check on the kids."

"Of course," he agreed. "But I can't promise the rest of that tart will be there when you get back."

She gave one last, lingering glance at the pastry before she said, "You can finish the tart."

He was tempted by the dessert, but he managed to resist. He didn't know how much longer he could hold out against his attraction to Macy—or if she wanted him to.

Had he crossed a line by flirting with her? She hadn't reacted in a way that suggested she was upset or offended, but she hadn't exactly flirted back, either.

"Is everything okay?" he asked when she returned to the table several minutes later.

She nodded. "I got caught in the middle of an argument."

"With your mom?"

"With myself."

His brows lifted. "Did you win?"

"I hope so," she said.

Then she set an antique key on the table and slid it toward him.

Don't miss
Claiming the Cowboy's Heart *by Brenda Harlen,*
available February 2019 wherever
Harlequin® Special Edition books and ebooks are sold.

www.Harlequin.com

Looking for more satisfying love stories
with community and family at their core?

Check out **Harlequin® Special Edition**
and **Love Inspired®** books!

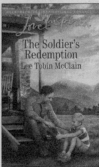

New books available every month!

CONNECT WITH US AT:

Facebook.com/groups/HarlequinConnection

 Facebook.com/HarlequinBooks

 Twitter.com/HarlequinBooks

 Instagram.com/HarlequinBooks

 Pinterest.com/HarlequinBooks

ReaderService.com

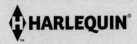

**ROMANCE WHEN
YOU NEED IT**

HFGENRE2018